WITH
GRIMM
RESOLVE

JEFFERY H. HASKELL

aethonbooks.com

WITH GRIMM RESOLVE
©2022 JEFFERY H. HASKELL

Aethon Books
www.aethonbooks.com

Print and eBook formatting by Steve Beaulieu. Artwork provided by Vivid Covers.

Published by Aethon Books LLC.

Aethon Books is not responsible for websites (or their content) that are not owned by the publisher.

This book is a work of fiction. Names, characters, places, and incidents are the product of the author's imagination or are used fictitiously. Any resemblance to actual events, locales, or persons, living or dead is coincidental.

ALSO IN SERIES

AGAINST ALL ODDS
WITH GRIMM RESOLVE
ONE DECISIVE VICTORY

CHAPTER ONE

M r. Albatross stepped off the shuttle, wrapping his hi-tech scarf around his nose as the sour smell of sulfur hit him like a slap in the face. The bitter cold clawed at his fingers as he pulled on his gloves. He hated Zuckabar Central, and he cursed the VP who sent him to deal with the Guild's terraforming operation.

The landing pad was little more than four lights anchored to a concrete slab next to the spaceport. No shelter, no covered walkway—it was like landing back in time.

A young man with dark skin and the uniform of an Alliance Marine waved to get his attention. "Mr. Albatross?"

Before responding, he scanned the area and picked up his anachronistic leather satchel with gold clasps.

"Yes?"

"Lance Corporal Samuel Torres, sir. I'm here to escort you to the governor's office."

Mr. Albatross looked the marine up and down. He prided himself as an excellent judge of character. It took him all of half a second to place Corporal Torres in the "unimportant" category.

"Where's the aircar?" he asked.

"This way, sir," Torres said with a gesture.

He led the way toward the farthest terminal, staying silent as they walked. Albatross noticed that the marine wore a sidearm, which seemed utterly ridiculous on a civilized planet inside the Alliance. A nearby shuttle fired up its air-breathing plasma engines, sending a blast of heat and noise across the field as it lifted off. Torres held his hand up to ward off the extra wind.

Once inside the terminal, his marine escort led him down the long passage to the exit leading to the parking garage. Albatross noted the changes from the last time he had visited. There were plenty of new constructions happening—the Alliance wasted no time in "fixing up" their acquisition. Clearly, they had money to spare, which worked in his favor. They had failed to pay the monthly fees to the Terraforming Guild since they had annexed the system. If they had the money to build, they had money to pay. He grinned beneath his filtered scarf. He always enjoyed outsmarting his clients.

Torres led him to the side garage where the transport vehicles were parked. Albatross stopped, snarling silently as the six-wheeled military vehicle came into view. Torres didn't hesitate to open the scissor-like door and climb into the large, ugly vehicle.

Albatross noted the calculated insult. First, sending a military driver, and second, transporting him like some kind of common soldier. He made a mental note to increase their rate by a quarter percent for such an inconvenience.

"I take it the military is running the system?" he asked as he circled the front.

The passenger door automatically opened, and Albatross placed his bag carefully on the deck before climbing up and latching himself in.

"Aye, sir, the Navy runs the station. We have the planet—not that it's much to have," Torres said.

The marine's idiotic grin annoyed Albatross further. Torres drove out of the garage, only pausing for a moment to make sure the way was clear before turning onto the main street. The large military vehicle—a "Mudcat," based on the metal identification plate on the center console—was nimbler than Albatross thought, based on its size.

"It's ten minutes to HQ, sir," Torres said.

Albatross ignored him. Instead, he was running the numbers. The nanite network installed in his brain gave him access to all the Guild's data on any planet.

The networks were exorbitantly expensive and far beyond the reach of any one civilian. Yet not beyond the Guild's reach. Besides data and authorizing his identity, this tech gave him instant access to a supercomputer and the ability to "remember" everything it held. There were downsides, of course. There always were. Heat was a problem. Using too much power caused the nanites to heat up, potentially frying his brain. Thankfully, safeguards were in place to prevent such an occurrence, but it was a good reason to classify people upon meeting them. If they were unimportant, then it wasn't necessary to use his nanites to store data about them.

"Here we are, sir," Corporal Torres said as he parked the Mudcat in a slot outside a squat building only three stories tall.

Albatross scowled. "I need to see the acting governor, not a flunky," he said. "Take me to where he is."

Corporal Torres grinned. "He's in there, sir. The general isn't much for flash or pomp."

Albatross grunted, opening the door and climbing down.

"And sir?" Torres added.

"Yes?"

"He's not the *acting* governor, sir. He's the governor. I'll be here when you're ready to return to the spaceport."

Albatross turned without acknowledging the flunky, making his way through the wind and snow to the inauspicious front door. They slid apart as he approached, bathing him in heat and light. A breeze followed him in, rustling his clothes as the cold air rushed into the warm lobby.

A single desk, barely more than a table with legs, sat in the center of the lobby. A marine, as plain as the desk she manned and dressed in the insufferable gray and white camouflage, smiled up at him.

"Mr. Albatross, welcome to the governor's office. General Remington will see you at your convenience." She pushed a button on her desk and a lift on the opposite wall opened.

Without acknowledging her, he strode into the lift. The doors shut and the lift took him to the third deck. The general's room, though large, was less than impressive and only decorated by a single picture window. Albatross was two steps out of the lift when he realized it wasn't a window at all but a screen showing one of the two Guild-owned fusion reactors.

They were located at each of the poles and almost a kilometer long, its giant exhaust cones spewed water vapor into the air by the millions of cubic meters per day—a process that had run for almost 300 years and would take another 300 before it was finished.

The simple wooden desk held a lone terminal and no decorations. The man behind the desk wore a short-sleeved brown shirt with his name, "Remington," on one side, and "Marine" on the other. A square block of medals and awards was placed neatly under his name. If Albatross focused, his nanites would decipher each one. He just wasn't interested in knowing the names of made-up awards for things he couldn't care less about.

The general stood, extending a solidly muscled arm to him. His brown uniform had the crisp lines of a man who took pride in his outward appearance. He looked to be in his thirties, but in fact, was almost seventy. The anti-aging treatments of the Alliance worked wonders, even if they didn't extend one's life span much past double what it would naturally be. However, for the time they had, recipients could look and feel youthful.

Albatross set his briefcase down and accepted the offered hand. His respect for the man notched up a few places. Albatross was a thinker, and his body was only as fit as necessary for his job. Some would describe him as "rail-thin" because of his gaunt appearance. Many more physically imposing men had tried to take advantage of him and prove their dominance through severe handshakes. In the end, though, physical strength was no match for his intellect. He always won out.

"Mr. Albatross, General John Remington. It's a pleasure to have you here, sir. How can the Alliance Marine Corps help you?" he asked in a deep baritone that wouldn't have been out of place in an opera house.

Albatross nodded and sat in the simple chair facing the desk that matched the office's spartan nature. He lifted his case, resting it on his lap as he opened it. The paperwork inside was for Remington's benefit, as Albatross had the material considerations stored in his nanites. He handed the paper to the general and sat back with a self-satisfied smile.

"The Alliance owes the Terraforming Guild twenty-two point three billion solar dollars, plus interest. Payments are due immediately. Also, monthly payments of three hundred and eighty-three million must resume without delay. If not, a penalty of ten million per day will be imposed. As you can see, it's in everyone's best interest to resolve this matter." He paused, searching for the right word, "ASAP, as you say."

Albatross smiled, leaning back, certain this would restore the status quo and put the Guild back in charge. Remington sat the papers aside without looking at them. The general glanced over his shoulder at the screen behind him, then back to Albatross.

"Mr. Albatross, I am unaware of the particulars of your contract with the former government of Zuckabar, but that government was dissolved. It no longer *exists*. I'm afraid the Alliance has no obligation to pay the Guild for services we didn't request," he said in a pleasant enough voice.

Albatross was surprised the man would take that specific tack. Then again, they always tried to negotiate or claim they weren't responsible for payments.

"General, regardless of who controls this system now, the two fusion terraformers belong to the Guild. If the Systems Alliance wishes to continue its excellent relationship with the Guild, it will pay the arrears and move on."

Remington leaned forward, placing his elbows on the desk.

"And if we don't?" he asked in the same polite tone he'd used since Albatross entered.

"Then we shut off the terraformers and terminate all business with the Alliance. Might I remind you, there are other planets in Alliance space with contracts for terraforming. Rōnin, Ohana, Weber, and Vishnu will all lose their terraformers. I hardly think the Alliance can afford to lose four of its more important planets," he said with a smug air.

Albatross was used to his opponents reacting emotionally, but Remington's stone face gave nothing away.

Silence stretched for long moments before Remington spoke again. "That would be... unfortunate."

Albatross shifted in his seat. Something was going on, something unusual. When he collected payments, the discussion followed a simple pattern. First pleasantries, then shock and denial, followed by anger and, eventually, capitulation.

After all, there was no alternative. If the Guild shut the terraformers down, the planet would become lifeless. It was true in almost every circumstance.

Especially on Zuckabar.

"Mr. Remington—"

The marine interrupted him with an upraised hand.

"General. I'm an officer in the United Systems Alliance Marine Corps, not a civilian," he said with a perfectly pleasant expression.

Albatross froze, unused to being interrupted. "Fine, *General,* perhaps you don't grasp the situation here. Let me make it simple. Pay, or we shut down the terraformers here and in the rest of the Alliance. If I don't leave Zuckabar with payment, your contracts will be considered void, and penalties will be applied. Whether you pay now, or in five years after a lengthy and expensive court battle, you *will* pay."

Albatross folded his arms defiantly, daring the general to counter his argument.

"You misunderstand, Mr. Albatross—"

There it was—the reversal. Albatross smiled as he knew the man would change course. There was always some fool trying to get one over on the Guild. However, their organization predated every current government except Terra. They were more powerful and resilient, with access to far more resources than anyone could possibly understand. After all, almost every government, no matter how *friendly* or *hostile,* relied on their technology and expertise for many of the planets they inhabited.

"I'm not suggesting we would default on any legally owed debt. I'm telling you that we signed no contract with the Guild for Zuckabar. The government that did was dissolved by law. *We* aren't legally liable for any debts they incurred. You will be hard-pressed to find any court that will side with you on this matter."

General Remington held his hand up to stop Albatross from speaking. "Before you ask, I am a lawyer. I have studied the law for the better part of forty years, military and civilian. I'm also a marine, so I do not make idle threats or speak without commitment. We're not paying your Guild a dime for Zuckabar."

Albatross sputtered, losing his composure for a moment. Why did he feel as if the balance of power had shifted to the marine? The Guild had all the cards to play, not the Marine Corps. Not some random general with delusions of grandeur, that was for sure.

"Fine. If you want to play hardball, then consider the services of the Guild terminated. By our calculations, you have," Albatross looked within, accessing his nanite network. "Eight months until the planet becomes uninhabitable. At that point, you will have undone three hundred years of work. Ultimately, you will pay. Either now or in six months. You have five seconds to comply."

With his nanite network open, Albatross triggered the shutdown, set the counter for five seconds and let it run.

The general leaned back with an easy smile. "I'm not accustomed to repeating myself, Mr. Albatross. I would suggest you do what you think is necessary. But remember, whatever happens next, you wanted it," Remington said.

Not one iota of emotion crossed his face or showed in his voice.

The lack of reaction infuriated Albatross. Why wasn't he responding the way he should?

"That's not how the courts will see it, I promise you," Albatross said.

In his mind, the counter reached zero... but nothing happened.

"I'm waiting," General Remington said with a ghost of a smile.

Albatross stared at the screen in disbelief, his mouth partially opening as he searched for a reply. He sent the signal again, and still, nothing happened. He tried to access the terraformers directly, using the communications channels known only to the Guild. No one knew how deeply they had infiltrated Zuckabar's computer systems. No one in the galaxy knew the truth. Was it a trick? Were they showing him a recorded image of the reactors running even though they weren't?

"The situation is slightly more complicated than you think," General Remington said. "Six months ago, when we annexed the system, we discovered a Caliphate spy network here. The quick actions of Fleet Admiral Villanueva destroyed their base. However, because of the infiltration, we couldn't take any chances. The Navy Corps of Engineers moved into Kremlin and took the station's computers apart, chip by chip. What do you think they found?"

Albatross blanched. It wasn't possible. They had success-fully hidden their network for more than five hundred years. There was no way even a detailed audit could detect their intru-sion. He regained some control and cleared his face, determined to be just as stone-cold as the general.

"You found nothing because there was nothing to find," he lied.

Remington tsk'd him as if he was scolding a child. "You shouldn't lie in polite company. Between the civilian Security and Intelligence Services and our ONI, we did find something. We found something in every computer, both here and in the Alliance—to our utter surprise. The irony was that we would never have found it if the Senate hadn't voted to annex Zuck-abar and turn her into a member planet."

Albatross wracked his networked brain, trying to determine what they could have found that would let them block his access.

"Again, General, whatever you think you found has nothing to do with the Guild. We demand you cease your illegal activity and return—"

General Remington's cold façade slipped a micron. His eyes went hard and hot.

"Mr. Albatross, you no longer have the control you think you have. We found your hardwired intrusions because you used the same methods here and in the Alliance proper. Zuckabar purchased the majority of her electronics from Consortium merchants, whereas, because of the last war, the Alliance manufactures its own systems. By law, no imports on critical military and governmental systems are allowed. Now, what are the odds that a computer system designed and built in the Consortium would contain a hardwired molecular chip with identical code to those found in Alliance computers?"

"Let me help you out, the chances are as close to zero as mathematically possible. Once we found that out, it was easy enough to back-trace it all. You spied on the Alliance. You spied on everyone. Worse, you knew about the slave trade through Zuckabar. And even if you weren't certain, you had to suspect the Caliphate base here." Remington stood up, his mask of civility cracking.

For a moment, sheer rage leaked through as he planted the knuckles of both fists on the table and leaned forward. With a sudden desire to flee, Albatross pushed himself back into the chair, his every instinct telling him violence was imminent.

"How many innocent women and children were sold into the Caliphate stocks? Did you work with them or turn a blind eye? Our engineers are going over every piece of equipment, every line of code, every circuit board. If we can't identify where it's from, it's gone. As of this moment, your property on every Alliance planet is seized, your accounts frozen. You will *never,"* he raised his voice to emphasize his point. "Receive another *dime* from the Alliance. You could have stopped this madness with a single message, but you valued *money* over the lives and freedom of Alliance citizens. And that, sir, is not something the founders of the Alliance could ever tolerate."

Albatross didn't know what to say. He wanted to respond, but for the first time in his adult life, his brain wasn't providing him with the correct words.

Remington, however, still had plenty to say. "Mr. Albatross, if you were an Alliance citizen, you would be arrested and shot. All of the Guild's employees would be. If it were up to me, I would have arrested you and carried out the sentence personally the moment you stepped foot on Zuckabar. However, cooler heads prevailed. We have a message for you to deliver to your masters."

He said the last word like a curse, practically spitting it out.

Albatross was unaccustomed to the fear flooding his body. He desperately wanted to move but only managed to eke out a whispered response.

"Message?" he said, hating the weak and pathetic way his voice sounded.

"Yes. A message. You're finished. Once we are sure there are no more infiltrated computers in the Alliance, we're going to share what we know with everyone. Even the Caliphate. We will let them decide your fate."

Albatross clamped his mouth shut to prevent himself from shouting at the man. When he regained control, he managed to stand, clutching his briefcase to his chest like a shield.

"You're going to regret this," he managed to say finally.

"No, sir, we will not. And I suggest you shut your pie hole. Take it like a man, Albatross, and leave. As of this moment, any

Guild employee in Alliance space will be arrested and deported."

Albatross wanted to reply, yell at the marine, or curse him out, but the look in the general's eyes told him that a beating was the likely outcome if he did. Fear of physical pain overrode his sense of injustice, and he fled, wanting to be far away from the death he saw in Remington's eyes.

Despite his fear, he managed to access the emergency protocols built into his nanites as he took the lift down. Maybe the general was telling the truth, maybe not. Albatross still had a mission to complete. At the very least, the rest of the Guild would soon know what had happened.

Once he was back on the shuttle heading for the ship that brought him here, he was much more in control. The shakes had passed, and he even smiled. The Alliance had opened a galaxy of hurt for themselves. The Guild had much more than mere terraformers. Maybe it was time for them to start a more overt form of control.

When the time came, Albatross decided he wanted to take Zuckabar—so he could personally execute General Remington. That thought brought him much pleasure—almost enough to cover up the fear buried deep in his heart.

CHAPTER TWO
THREE MONTHS LATER

Lieutenant Commander Jacob T. Grimm absently swiveled his command chair back and forth as he waited for an update. He glanced between the MFD attached to his chair and the main viewer displaying their position relative to the Tango they pursued.

"ETA, ten minutes, sir," Ensign Owusu said from his position at astrogation.

He had one hand on his ear, listening to the beat of spacetime emitting from the fleeing ship's gravcoil.

"Mac, broadcast, please," Jacob ordered.

"Aye, sir, channel open," McCall replied.

Jacob leaned down to the pickup on his MFD.

"CTV Komodo, this is USS *Interceptor* DD1071, Commander Jacob T. Grimm. By the authority of the Alliance Navy, I am ordering you to cut your engines and prepare to be boarded."

He pointed at McCall, who immediately pushed the send button.

"Sent, sir."

"Astro, distance to target?" Jacob asked.

"Two-seven-zero thousand klicks, sir," Owusu replied.

They were coming at the Consortium flagged freighter from the stern and above, angling two degrees down at them to converge on their plane while avoiding the ship's gravwake. Komodo continued to accelerate at her maximum of seventy-five Gs. Fast for a civilian ship, but not for the shark-nosed *Interceptor*.

Jacob was happy for the distraction; they were at the end of a dull deployment and ready to return to port. He'd hardly had a moment to himself since he returned from Command School on Blackrock. If not for the batch of promotions made in his absence, he could imagine he'd never left.

The old girl looked almost the same as when he first took command. Of course, she hadn't been in the best shape then. He'd expected, foolishly he supposed, that when the yard at Kremlin Station finished repairs on his ship, she would be as good as new. Instead, they had done the bare minimum to make her spaceworthy. After that, it was up to his XO, Lieutenant (SG) Yuki, to do the rest. Thankfully, she was no stranger to hard work or the *Interceptor* in particular.

All in all, he couldn't complain. Unlike the last time, *Interceptor* went without a CO, Yuki maintained discipline this time. She had done a helluva job keeping the ship's crew busy with the repairs and ensuring they were good to go.

They were a month into the patrol, and Owusu, his former midship and current ensign picked up the freighter slipping in from Minsk and bee-lining it for deep space. It could be nothing, but any excitement was welcome. After all, running down a fleeing ship was what *Interceptor* was made for. Not to mention, some short action would give the crew, new and old, a confidence boost.

He pressed the comm button on his chair. "DCS, Captain. Status XO?"

"All systems are nominal, Skipper," she said from damage control.

For leadership continuity, DCS was located fore of the fusion reactor, while the bridge was aft of the mess and fore of the towed array. If any hit took out the bridge or DCS, the ship would still have a commanding officer.

He adjusted his watch cap, covering one ear that had come free. The ship was cold enough to be uncomfortable without the right clothing. Not so cold he could see his breath, but enough, they wore duty jackets and watch caps, all with temperature control nanite tech to keep them warm.

"Well done, Kim. Why don't you gather a couple of marines and meet in the boat bay for a boarding party? Whether they want us to or not, we're boarding that ship."

"Aye, aye, sir. Gather marines for boarding party."

He turned back to the main viewer, eying the distance to the fleeing ship. Any astrogator doing basic math would have told them they couldn't escape. Where were they planning to go? There was nothing along their heading but a few mining outposts and deep space. In his mind, there was no question they were up to no good. What could they possibly hope to gain from running, he didn't know, but he would soon find out.

———

Sergeant Allison Jennings pulled the skin-tight suit over her lithe and muscular form. It was the first layer of nano-tech-infused armor, offering compression and medical aid in wounds or breaches. On top of the first layer went the joint armor for the knee, elbow, and wrist. Then she pulled on her boots, followed by the "space armor," as they called it—a hardened carapace covering her vital organs and other spots that didn't need mobility. Once it was in place, she connected her helmet, a sleek, angular design made to deflect attacks. She'd seen a vid once, set thousands of years in the past, where men on horseback would fight with long spears. The helmeted knights bore more than a little resemblance to her current armor. When almost everything was in place, she put her gloves on. They were the last piece of the puzzle.

"Sarge," Corporal Naki said from beside her. "We're good to go."

At times like this, she wished El-Tee and Gunny hadn't left the ship. However, when the task force was in-system, they were reassigned to the command ship. She was in charge of the three remaining marines aboard *Interceptor*. Not that she would complain about that aspect of it. No, she just wanted the El-Tee around to deflect her dealing with the Navy officers... other than the Skipper, for whom she had a soft spot.

"Okay, Marines. We're going to keep this simple. Naki and I will make up Alpha team. Owens, you and Cole are Bravo. Alpha goes for the bridge. Bravo, you take engineering. No shooting unless you're fired on. The ship is running, and the skipper will want to know why. Questions?" Jennings asked.

Owens raised his hand. "Corporal—sorry, I mean Sergeant Jennings? If we have to take prisoners, what do we do with them? Tag and tie or escort them back to the Corsair?"

"Tag and tie," she told the Marine with the bright red hair. "Once you have engineering and we have the bridge, the XO will initiate a deceleration, and we can go from there."

She decided against chastising him for forgetting her rank as she'd like to forget it herself. The other three marines nodded, their sharply angled helmets making them look like birds pecking at the ground. Jennings' stifled a chuckle as she'd never thought of the helmets like that before.

"Okay, Marines, who are we?" she asked.

"Killers," they shouted back as one.

"Damn straight. Let's go!"

———

"Intercept, sir," Chief Suresh said from her position in The Pit.

"Thank you, Chief. Match velocity and inch us in close. I want a good picture of their ship before we send the boarding party," Jacob said.

"Aye, aye, Skipper. Proceeding to one klick," Suresh replied.

Jacob tapped his finger on the arm of his captain's chair. Why hadn't the other ship responded? Even if they were blind, they could look out a porthole and see *Interceptor* pulling up on them. The light from the gravcoil wasn't bright enough to be seen from more than a few klicks out, but it was enough.

Yet the Komodo still accelerated.

"McCall, can you laze them?" Jacob asked.

"On it, sir," McCall said as his hands flew over the panel to activate the laser.

Every ship had multiple small optical receptors for exactly this instance. Only the freighter holding a steady course allowed them to make the attempt. Even the slightest evasion would make an optical connection impossible.

"Got it, sir," McCall said. "No response."

"Well damn, I don't want the Corsair taking our people over there while their drive is active. They could run, and we would have to recover before following. Or worse, they could collide," he said.

Jacob had a decision to make. They needed a warning shot —something to force the freighter to heave to and allow themselves to be boarded. The regs called for a coilgun shot across their bow. Close enough for passive sensors to pick up.

"Carter, weapons hot," he ordered.

"Weapons hot. Aye, sir," Lieutenant Carter Fawkes replied.

"One round, five hundred meters in front of their bow," Jacob said.

"Aye, sir. One round. Five hundred meters in front of their bow." Carter held one hand to his ear.

"Turret two, swivel starboard zero-eight-five degrees."

The computer could easily conduct the targeting, but it was good for the crew to practice manual firing whenever possible. Computers could go down in combat, and it was essential to be able to run the turrets manually.

"Downward seven degrees," Carter said into his microphone.

On Jacob's MFD, the turret followed suit. A projected course of the round lined up exactly where he wanted it to go. Since they had matched the velocity of the tramp freighter, all they had to worry about was not aiming at the ship.

"Ready, sir," Carter said.

"Execute," Jacob ordered.

"Firing in three, two, one." Carter depressed the button.

The *Interceptor* shuddered almost imperceptibly as the turret fired its twenty-millimeter payload. The round shot out, crossing paths with the ship at ten thousand KPS. A decent ship's sensor would register the fast-moving projectile and alert the crew.

Jacob waited. Realizing he was holding his breath, he forced himself to breathe normally.

"Any change?"

"Nothing, sir," Ensign Owusu replied in his accented voice. "They are still accelerating at point-five KPS squared."

Jacob resumed swiveling his chair back and forth. He had one more call to make before he had to send his marines over. There was inherently more risk in it, though.

Decision made, Jacob spoke. "Tactical, ready a torpedo."

The bridge hushed as all eyes turned to him.

"Say again, sir?" Carter asked.

"One torpedo, set to detonate one klick in front of the ship. There's no way they can miss that much energy releasing at once," Jacob said.

"Aye, sir, one torpedo. Detonate one klick fore," Carter said. "Torpedo room one, prepare one Mark-Twelve with live payload."

Jacob knew the crew was running efficiently when they signaled the weapon was loaded thirty seconds later.

"Torpedo in the tube, Skipper," Carter said.

"Open the exterior hatch," Jacob ordered.

"Aye, sir. Opening hatch," Carter replied.

Every step was designed to give the freighter more time to realize what was happening so they would hopefully come to their senses and decelerate, or at least cut their engines. They had to see the bow hatch opening. Even a minimal radar scan would pick it up.

"Comms, anything?" he asked McCall.

The spacer shook his head negative.

"Open a channel," Jacob said.

The spacer activated his panel and tuned the radio. He swiveled his chair to face the captain and pointed.

"CTV Komodo, this is Commander Jacob T. Grimm of the USS *Interceptor*. This is your *final* warning. Power down your gravcoil or I will be forced to escalate. Please respond."

Jacob stood up, walking around behind his chair to lean against it. The ship was in "action stations" for an emergency, but they weren't in suits, and they didn't have to be harnessed to their chairs.

"No response, Skipper," McCall said with a sigh.

"Understood," Jacob replied.

He spun the chair totally around, then stopped it when the back hit his hands. "Carter, fire at will."

Carter gulped. Firing a live warhead was stressful in training, let alone in action. He pulled up the firing screen, double-checked the coordinates, and readied himself.

His console's screens showed various calculations and threats. On his right side were the fire controls. The weapon release for the torpedo was under a shield to keep it from accidental depression. He flipped the shield up and pushed the button down with his thumb.

This time, the shudder was more noticeable. A two hundred and forty millimeter wide, four-meter-long torpedo ejected from the ship, fired from the coil accelerator built into the tube. At a kilometer distant from the ship, its own internal micro-gravcoil kicked in and accelerated the projectile.

When it reached the requisite range, the warhead detonated with the fire of a small sun. All twelve plasma pellets ignited simultaneously, consuming the torpedo in a savage exhibition of light and power.

Interceptor's screen darkened to protect her crew from the brilliant destructive energy.

"Anything?" Jacob asked.

McCall snapped his hand to his ear as the comms came to life.

"Yes, sir. Master Tommy? I think that's how he said his name. He's requesting to know *our* intentions, sir," McCall said with a grin.

"I guess there's nothing like an anti-ship torpedo to get their attention. Tell him to cut his engines and prepare to be boarded."

McCall nodded. "Aye, sir, relaying message."

While the comms man worked, Jacob hit the button on his chair.

"Boat bay, Captain, prep for launch and standby."

The line clicked, and Chief Warrant Officer Boudreaux replied, "Aye, aye, sir. Prepping for launch."

"Sir?" McCall said with a frown. "The master of the vessel is declaring we have no authority to board him. For what it's worth, Skipper, he's got a thick accent. He may not understand what we're saying."

Jacob dropped his chin to his chest and squeezed the back of his chair from where he stood.

"It's a Consortium flagged vessel. Does he sound Consortium?" Jacob asked.

"I'm sorry, sir. I'm not familiar enough with their language to know," McCall said.

It was a fair point. It wasn't as if there were a massive mingling of the populations. With virtually no tourism, the only thing the two nations had between them was the trade treaty... until the wormhole came along. Once it was up and running, Jacob fully expected tourism to skyrocket; people were starved for new things to see, and the Consortium people were exotic enough to deliver that experience. Not to mention, some of their worlds were darn near paradisaical.

Jacob sat in his chair and adjusted the MFD until it showed his shoulders and head.

"Put him through," Jacob said.

"Aye, sir."

The image shifted, and an older man with blue skin and a silver-streaked beard appeared on the screen. His eyes glowed a dark orange, giving him an ethereal appearance. The only other people from the Consortium Jacob had met were similarly styled.

"Good afternoon, sir. I'm Captain Grimm of the *Interceptor*. You are in Alliance space. You are ordered to heave-to and submit to a customs inspection—"

The master of the ship began to protest, but Jacob sped up,

cutting the man off. "We will do everything we can to make it quick and painless and get you back on your way."

The older man looked off-camera for a moment then turned back to Jacob and gave him a sharp nod.

"They've killed their engines, Skipper," Owusu said. "No power to their gravcoil."

"Excellent," Jacob replied. "Boat bay, Captain. Launch the boat."

———

"...Launch the boat."

Jennings and her three marines were harnessed in. Space armor wasn't powered and weighed almost twenty kilos. It would crush the person inside of it if thrown about the cabin.

"Thank you for flying Air Boudreaux. Please ensure all your seatbacks are upright and your possessions are stowed," Chief Boudreaux said over the intercom with her French accent.

"Our travel time will be approximately one minute. I hope you didn't have a big breakfast."

Owens groaned. It was no secret that Boudreaux liked to give the marines a rough time when transporting them in the Corsair. It was a point of pride for Corsair drivers to make their passengers puke—as long as those passengers were of lower rank and marines.

In preparation, Jennings exhaled and clenched her formidable abominable muscles.

"Marines, you *will not* puke in your helmets. Understood?" Jennings growled.

"Yes, Sergeant," they yelled back as one.

"Doors open," Boudreaux's voice came over the intercom. "Release clamps."

Lines keeping the ship in place retracted as the large bay

doors beneath her unfolded outward like storm shutters. The Richman field snapped into existence, holding the ship's atmosphere in while allowing the Corsair to exit. The dropship shook once more, then fell.

Boudreaux, ever willing to practice her skills, executed a combat departure, with thrusters pushing her out of the boat bay at six Gs. The Corsair dropped out of the ship like a rock off a building. Five hundred meters out, she flipped, and the grav-coil kicked in, rocketing the ship forward at six Gs of acceleration for thirty seconds, followed by a sudden reprieve as she flipped the ship over again.

Jennings knew high g turns back-to-back were what led to vomiting. To prevent it, she sucked in a breath, then blew it out and tightened her abs. While she had never experienced a kick from a mule, she imagined it felt the same way.

Sure enough, Cole puked.

At the end of thirty seconds, the gravity let off, and she felt the clang of metal through her feet as the two ships came together. It was standard practice to treat every boarding as a combat boarding. The atmosphere in the Corsair was drained until they could confirm the atmosphere in the target ship existed. Too many marines in the early years of the Alliance lost their lives boarding ships they thought were friendly.

She was glad to be alive in her time rather than hundreds or even thousands of years before. How her distant ancestors even managed to survive getting off Earth was beyond her. Of course, they had technology and training that put them light-years, figuratively and literally, ahead of those early years of travel and colonization.

Jennings shook her head. It was unusual for her to think so deeply about a subject. She had spent six years in the marines so far, two of those as a corporal. She *liked* her rank. Ever since she was promoted—after the *Madrigal* action—she'd found herself with something new to consider. A life and a career beyond taking orders. She was a leader now. An NCO. She was giving the orders, not just following them. It had her examining her life in a way she hadn't before. She didn't like it.

Her life before the marines wasn't what she called easy. MacGregor's World was a tough, nasty place to grow up. She might be exceptionally strong off her planet, but on her planet, she was slightly above average. Since she joined the marines, she'd found a level of confidence she'd never thought possible on her homeworld.

No matter how much Gunny Hicks assured her that she would do great, she had yet to prove that to herself.

"Owens," she shouted. "Check it."

PFC Owens hit the release on his harness and charged over to the airlock, hitting buttons on the panel beside it to make sure there was atmosphere on the other side.

"Clear, Sarge," he replied.

"Chief, give us some air," she said to the pilot.

"Roger, Sergeant, atmosphere incoming."

The lights on her heads-up display turned green, showing they had air to breathe and wouldn't blow up the moment they opened the hatch.

"Cole, get your helmet off and clean it up," she ordered.

"Aye, aye, Sergeant," he said with a groan.

The hatch partitioning the cockpit from the hull section slid open, and Lieutenant Yuki, the ship's XO, walked out in her ghost-white ELS suit. The Emergency Life Support suits were designed for high visibility on the off chance a spacer went overboard. It was rare, but it happened.

Across her chest were YUKI and NAVY written in block letters. On her collar and underneath the helmet, her rank insignia was clearly visible. *Interceptor's* shark insignia adorned her shoulder. Around her slim hips, she wore a gun belt with the standard-issue MP-17 holstered.

"We good to go, Sergeant Jennings?" the XO asked.

"Aye, ma'am. We just need a moment to confirm the conditions on the other side of the hatch."

Though she could see Yuki's expression through the clear faceplate built into the ELS helmet, Jennings' face was hidden. Yuki raised one eyebrow, glancing over at the hatch that read "Clear."

"All right, I'll check in with the captain," she said as she turned around and made the call.

Jennings glanced back at Cole. He didn't need to see her face to know he was in for a shaming when they returned to the ship.

As fast as he could, he unsealed his helmet, dumped out the puke into a receptacle, and then slammed it back on. He gave her a thumbs up when the seal was in place.

"Good to go, ma'am," Jennings said.

Yuki turned around and pointed at the hatch. "Lead the way."

———

Yuki followed the marines in, keenly aware of the necessity for their abundance of caution. Once *Interceptor* had started engaging pirates and smugglers in earnest, they learned there was no barbarism criminals wouldn't do to escape capture and punishment. She still had nightmares about what Nadia Dagher had endured. She swore if she were ever in that position she would die before she let someone slap a collar on her.

Resting her hand on the butt of her pistol and holding her NavPad in the other, she followed the hulking armored forms in as they cleared the airlock before Owens hit the button on the internal hatches.

The large metal hatch slid open with a hum, revealing two men with blue skin and glowing tattoos waiting for them. They glanced at the heavily armed marines and immediately stepped back, raising their hands and shouting at them in their native language.

Yuki grew up on Rōnin, the only world in Alliance space where the original settlers came from old Earth's Asian countries—specifically Japan. Something like ninety-three percent of the original colonists came from the island nation. Her mother, an artist, was a strict traditionalist, insisting her daughter learn all the traditional arts and speak their native language.

Like Rōnin, the Consortium was founded and populated by primarily Asian peoples. Unlike Rōnin, however, over the six hundred years since the colonists left earth, the mishmash of Korean, Chinese, and Japanese had formed a new language—one she didn't speak. There were several high-end commercial translators that could do the job in real time, but they were rare and expensive. With the Navy's budget ever shrinking, translation tech wasn't high on the admiralty's list of things to provide *Interceptor*.

"You understand what they're saying, ma'am?" Jennings asked.

"They mean us no harm. Lower your weapons," she replied.

Jennings patted the air, indicating for the marines to lower their guns.

"Glad you came along. I didn't understand a word of it," Jennings said.

"Me either, Sergeant. But them raising their hands in alarm was a pretty good indication."

Jennings grunted in reply.

Yuki pointed at the right-hand man. "Take us to the captain. You understand 'Captain?'" she asked in traditional Japanese.

The man nodded, turning and moving down the hatchway to the ship's fore.

"Marines, move out," Jennings ordered.

"I thought you said you didn't understand them?" Jennings asked over the private channel.

"Sergeant, my home has kept the traditional Japanese language pretty much frozen for six centuries. Meanwhile the Consortium is a hodgepodge of languages, most of which I don't speak."

"I'll file that away for future use," Jennings said.

Yuki, Jennings, and Naki followed the men up narrow stairs while the other two Marines went below to the engine room. Civilian ships used actual stairs instead of ladders, and Yuki found the confined space nerve-racking.

The slim XO had no problem moving through the narrow passageways. She glanced behind her, noting the marines in their bulky space armor had to go single file to make their way. Most ships were a tight fit for armored marines because every-thing had to be made as narrow as possible to fit inside the gravcoil's field. The larger the coil, the larger the ship, and the more power required to run it. For merchants, that meant more money just to keep the lights on.

They reached the bridge deck, and Yuki frowned. Yes, the ship was clearly older, but there was no excuse for a non-opera-tive hatch on the bridge. The most minor meteorite strike, and the whole crew could die. She added it to her notes on the NavPad. They weren't exactly there for a health and safety inspection, but any hazards to the freighter were potential hazards to Alliance shipping lanes.

The seven men on the bridge were of a variety of ages and

builds. The captain, an older man with a silver-streaked beard, turned in his chair to face them. His face crinkled, and Yuki thought he was sneering at her.

"I have papers," he said in broken standard while pointing to the locker against the far bulkhead.

"Would you show them to me, sir?" Yuki asked.

As the man moved past her, she felt the two marines spread out to cover the area. The crew didn't seem hostile, but their ragtag appearance and the fact that no one spoke standard was off-putting. Even for small trading vessels—and Komodo wasn't small—it paid to have at least one crewman who spoke standard.

Something wasn't right. She kept her eyes on the captain, following him and trusting the marines to watch her back.

The captain stopped at a locker, glancing at the marines as he fumbled with the lock to open it. He cursed, punching in the code again.

Yuki took a step toward him—

"Gun!" Jennings shouted.

CHAPTER THREE

ELS suits offered protection from the vacuum of space, padding for blunt force, and minimal armor. They weren't designed to absorb weapon's fire.

Lights danced on the bridge as beams of energy flashed back and forth. A panel next to Yuki exploded. She dived for the deck, hitting her knee on the corner of the console. A single maser struck her back and an intense pain blossomed as heat bloomed around her. She screamed as the weapon cooked her inside the suit.

Jennings leaped in front of the stream of microwave radiation, putting her back to the assailant, absorbing the beam on her armor. Naki shouldered his MP-17, firing the 10mm rounds in short bursts. The slugs took the first man in the chest, neck, and face, sending him flailing backward over a console.

Yuki scrambled on all fours, doing her best to ignore the pain, and crawled for the hatch. Sergeant Jennings rushed forward, her armor glowing from the incoming fire. The enemy captain had a pistol in hand and brought it up to shoot the marine.

He wasn't fast enough.

Jennings slapped the weapon from his hand before smashing the palm of her armored glove into his nose. He grunted, head flinging back to bounce off the locker.

"Contact bridge, hostile targets," Yuki said over the radio.

Her voice warbled, speaking through the pain in her back. Naki took down a second target with a precise shot to the head. There were still assailants scrambling for cover and firing their masers in the enclosed space. Computers exploded as the deadly beams superheated everything they touched.

The captain came at Jennings again, swinging hard. She blocked with both forearms then shoulder-checked him. He slammed into the locker again and Jennings grabbed his shirt, flinging him over her with a twist of her hips. He screamed as he flew across the room—until one of his allies' weapons flashed across his head, silencing him forever.

The remaining four had their pistols and were popping up from behind consoles, focusing their fire on Jennings. Her armor glowed bright red from the heat with waves of energy rising from her like a mirage on a hot day. Yuki pulled herself into the corridor behind Naki, who used the hatch as cover. She fumbled through the pain to pull her MP-17 pistol and held it out as steady as she could, covering the big marine's back.

"Naki, kill these mother f—" Jennings' order was cut off as a maser struck her in the helmet, knocking her back.

Lance Corporal Akolo Naki didn't hesitate and pulled a grenade from his belt.

"Proximity detonation," he said to the computer.

He leaned around the corner and hurled the explosive into the far corner. It sailed through the air until it was above the huddled men, then detonated with a deafening boom. An eerie silence fell over the compartment, broken only by the groans of the survivors.

"Bravo team, report," Jennings said as she regained her feet.

As the heat faded from her armor, the normally muted camouflage pattern was a mess of warped metal and blackened patches.

"Owens here, all secure. No survivors, though. Sorry," he said.

Jennings shook her head. "Don't be."

Yuki tried to stand. After all, if the marine could get up, surely she could. Her legs wobbled as she rose. Tremendous agony ran through her, bringing her to tears, but she refused to stay down.

"XO, what the hell do you think you're doing?" Jennings said as she marched past Naki.

"I'm not going to sit this out, *Sergeant*," Yuki replied with all the strength she mustered.

"Uh-huh," Jennings replied in her laconic way.

She took the lieutenant's arm and hit several buttons on the computer built into the suit.

"You look a lot worse than I feel," Yuki said by way of excuse.

"I'm wearing armor, XO, you're not. Nighty-night," Jennings said.

Jennings had activated the nano-tech meds in Yuki's suit. Her objection died in her throat as the nanites killed the pain receptors in her back, and she almost collapsed with relief. Then she really did collapse. Jennings and Naki caught her and started hustling for the Corsair.

"*Interceptor*, this is Bravo-Two-Five. We need immediate medevac. Multiple hostiles encountered. Ship isn't secure. I say again...."

———

"...Ship isn't secure," Jennings' voice came over the comms.

"Mark?" Jacob pointed at his ops officer. "Put together a boarding party, one engineer at least. Get over there and help the marines secure the ship."

His second officer leaped up. "Aye, aye, sir. Boarding party with one engineer," he said as he exited the bridge.

"McCall, send a packet to command with everything we know up to this point," Jacob ordered.

"Aye, sir. Packet to command."

Jacob leaned back, tapping his fingers on his command chair in an attempt to alleviate his worry. Medevac was a message no CO wanted to hear. It meant one of his people was possibly dying over there, and there wasn't anything he could do about it.

———

Petty Officer First Class Desper made her way to the boat bay, running through the hatchways yelling, "Make a hole," whenever she encountered other crew.

In medical emergencies, seconds counted. The ship's newest complement, Lieutenant Krisper, the fresh-faced surgeon straight from fleet medical, ran behind her, carrying his bag. The two spacers assigned to sickbay would meet them there with the stretcher.

Desper slid down the last ladder, feet hitting the deck with a thump. She sprinted through the large hatches just as the boat bay lights flashed yellow and the big bay doors on the deck yawned open.

Spacer First Class Whips and Spacer Second Class Eggers had the anti-grav stretcher already set up, along with the bags of medical nanites she would likely need.

Desper's MedPad beeped as telemetry from the XO's suit came in.

"What are we looking at, PO?" Lieutenant Krisper asked.

"Third-degree burns on most of her back," she said.

Bringing up her pad, she pointed at the diagram of Lieutenant Yuki's wounds. "Possible spinal damage from the maser fire as well. If Allison hadn't overridden her suit and put her in a nanite-induced coma, she would have likely died from shock within minutes."

Burns were bad. Cuts, bruises, bullet holes, and other forms of physical trauma were a cinch to heal compared to them. Even with nano-regenerators, growing new nerve endings and skin would take time.

"Attention, attention, attention. Corsair is docking," a voice crackled over the speakers.

The Corsair rose like a wraith out of space and hovered even with the ship for a moment until the doors closed underneath it. Landing skids extended down, and the ship came to a gentle rest as her pilot put her down. The side doors immediately opened.

"Go-go-go," Desper yelled.

They ran into the ship to find Yuki strapped in, face down. They quickly freed her from the straps and slid her onto the AG stretcher, careful not to aggravate her wounds. Burns were a fact of shipboard life, but these... bad didn't *begin* to describe the hell inflicted on the XO's back.

Eggers moved with lightning efficiency, hooking up the bag of IV nanites meant to supplement the temporary ones supplied from her suit. There was always a balance with regenerative nanites. They were miracles of modern technology but had downsides. Too many. They healed the patient too fast, often causing a form of shock only seen in dehydration and trauma. When regenerating the human body, it was 'slow and steady wins the race.'

Krisper gagged when the smell of cooked flesh hit him.

Desper didn't have time to be amused at the officer's lack of stomach.

"Move it, Whips," she growled.

The spacer fumbled with the controls to the AG stretcher before guiding it toward the exit.

Lieutenant West, Chief Petty Officer Redfern from engineering, and several spacers she didn't recognize kitted out with ELS and weapons ran by them toward the waiting dropship.

They were barely out the hatch when the Corsair dropped out of the ship, heading back to the Komodo.

———

Jacob leaned back in his chair, doing his best to appear calm and patient. The desire to tap his fingers or fidget in his chair was almost overwhelming. Almost. It was the curse of command: a desire to know what was happening and try, somehow, to control the outcome while also knowing that micromanaging his people would lead to disaster. He could guide, advise, and direct, but if he tried to ride herd on them, it would ultimately lead to worse performance.

"Sir, Sergeant Jennings on the line," McCall said.

Jacob pointed at his MFD. The screen flickered, showing the diminutive blonde Marine with a dirt-smudged face. It took Jacob a moment to realize she wasn't wearing her helmet.

"Allison, what's the situation?" he asked.

Her lips stiffened and her eyes narrowed at his casual use of her first name.

"Ship's secure, sir. No survivors."

He waited for her to provide more details but realized, in her laconic way, she wasn't going to.

"Sergeant," he said more formally, "what happened?"

She glanced off-screen and nodded to someone he couldn't see.

"I wouldn't want to presume, sir. We boarded. They appeared to comply. When the XO asked for the ship's log, they tried to distract us then opened fire with masers."

Jacob glanced over at Lt. Fawkes manning weapons. The young man raised an eyebrow.

"It's an odd sidearm for them to have, but if they were from the Consortium, it makes sense," Fawkes said.

"Then what?" Grimm asked.

"Lieutenant Yuki went down. We covered her and killed the bridge crew. Bravo team led by PFC Owens went to engineering. They had the same experience, though they were able to take down their assailants without any injuries."

Jacob racked his brain about masers. He made a note to ask Lt. Fawkes to look into it for him.

"Captain," Naki said from off-screen. "Want to see something cool?"

"Not now, *Corporal,*" Jennings said in a frigid tone.

"Show me."

The camera zoomed out revealing Jennings whole form. The bridge went deathly silent. Her armor was blackened and warped. Pieces were missing, and Jacob saw her ruined helmet off to one side.

"What the hell. Why didn't you come back with the XO?" he asked.

She shrugged. "I'm fine, sir. The armor did its job, and I would like to keep doing mine."

Of everyone on board, Jacob had a special affinity for Sergeant Jennings and Corporal Naki. They had survived close combat together when criminals on Kremlin Station had tried to murder them while they were attempting to recover the ship's missing gravcoil.

"Negative, Allison. I mean it. Get back here when Lieutenant West arrives. I want a full medical workup," Jacob ordered.

She looked like she was going to argue, then acquiesced. "Yes, sir."

As the image faded, he heard her say. "You're dead, Naki."

"Sir?" Fawkes said to get his attention.

"Go ahead, Carter," Jacob replied.

"Jennings had armor, and it looked like bread left in the oven too long. The XO didn't have anything but the ELS," Carter's voice trailed off.

As shipmates they had served together for over a year, it was natural for him to worry, but Jacob couldn't let them focus on *maybes*.

"She's in good hands, Carter. Right now, we have a job to do." He stood up and pointed at the main screen, using the excuse to hide his concern and maintain his image as the unflappable captain.

"I want a computer hook up to their ship. Let's learn everything we can about them. I want to know where they came from, what they're carrying... hell, what they had for breakfast. Got it?" he asked not just Fawkes but the whole bridge.

"Aye, aye, sir," they said in chorus.

Once they were busy making his orders happen, he walked forward and knelt next to The Pit.

He pitched his voice low so only she could hear. "Devi, in your time in the Navy, have you ever run into a freighter crew-carrying similar weapons?"

"Negative, sir. Masers are military grade. They also take more training than a coilgun or ion pulse weapons. They aren't 'point-and-shoot.'"

Jacob agreed. However, he had a hard time believing he'd just killed a crew of Consortium black ops infiltrating the Alliance. What possible motive could the Consortium even have? The vast majority of shipping was lined up in Praetor, waiting to use the wormhole instead of the standard route across the Corridor. Even the loss of months from the delay would be gained back by using the shortcut.

Something was going on, but what?

CHAPTER FOUR

Admiral Wit DeBeck stared out over Anchorage Bay from his office on the twenty-seventh floor of Alliance Military Command. The waves rolled in easily and he could almost feel the cold from the light flurries of snow falling on the other side of the window. Alexandria's coastal climates were brutal in the winter. The snow falling was just the beginning.

He had more than weather to worry about, though. Watching the waves crash on the rocks helped him stay calm when he wanted to yell in frustration and anger.

All the work they had done to annex the Protectorates, with the pure luck of finding the wormhole—the single greatest discovery of their lifetimes—and Congress still wouldn't issue a formal budget for the Navy to leave TF-121 in-system. In the end, they were lucky to establish a permanent base and form a picket squadron. One light cruiser and three destroyers were hardly a defense, though.

He loved his nation. He'd served the Alliance his whole adult life and would likely serve until he died. Sometimes, though, he wished the politicians could be shown the door.

After discovering the wormhole and subsequent detection of the activities of the Terraforming Guild, Zuckabar needed a fleet stationed there, not a tiny marine garrison and a handful of light ships. Yet as long as the anti-Navy faction controlled the house, that wasn't going to happen. He could not push public opinion to the point where the politicians had no choice but to act, like when they annexed the Protectorates.

He turned away from the window and gazed at his empty office. His desk was bare. The walls held exactly thirty-six pictures—all headshots of men and women in uniform going back to 2881.

The pictures were of every ONI agent who'd lost their lives in the line of duty since the end of the last war. It was a stark reminder that intelligence came at a cost.

Lives.

However, as an ancient freedom fighter said, "The tree of liberty must be refreshed from time to time with the blood of patriots and tyrants."

If it had to be his blood, he would gladly give it. Ideally, though, it would be from their enemies. Liaisons with the Department of National Intelligence kept him up to date on the matter with the Terraforming Guild. With zero military involvement, he could hardly butt in. At least not officially.

Zuckabar and the wormhole were his primary focus. Not only were they about to clear travel through the Bella Wormhole, but it was also going to open a direct lane to Consortium space—which would inevitably bring the two nations closer together. Even with nine hundred light-years separating them, they had managed a robust trade. When the total transit time between their trading hubs was a matter of hours instead of months, they would be closer still.

The Caliphate was desperate for space; an empire like theirs lived and breathed conquest. They would never get the chance if they didn't make a move on the Consortium soon. The thought of having the Caliphate in control of half the wormhole was keeping him up at night almost as much as what the Guild was hiding.

"Admiral," his assistant, Ensign Prague, said over the intercom.

"Go ahead."

"Nadia Dagher is here, sir."

Wit smiled to himself. Maybe he could kill two birds with one stone.

"Send her in," he said.

A moment later, she walked through the door, looking considerably healthier than the last time he'd seen her.

"Nadia, you're looking much better."

She stopped in front of his desk and snapped to attention. "Reporting as ordered, sir."

He waved her to a chair, which she ignored.

"Psych has given you a clean bill of health." He watched her reaction carefully.

The doctors had told him that she was a gifted liar—that it was possible they were wrong, and underlying trauma could surface in unusual ways.

She replied with a brief nod.

"I want to hear it from you," he said.

Her face didn't change, nor did her body. Not so much as a flinch.

"Admiral, I'm good to go. Let me back in the fight," she said in a flat, even tone.

He sighed and sat in his chair, leaning forward with his elbows on the desk. "Nadia, if you're not up to this, I need to know. Don't BS me. If you're ready, I'm sending you back to Zuckabar."

If she were going to react, this would be it. She did, just not the way he expected. For the first time since she entered his office, a bit of color returned to her face, and her lips spread into a slow smile.

"Is *Interceptor* still there?" she asked.

Wit hesitated, not because he didn't know the answer but because he was curious about the question.

"Yes," he said after a moment of examining her.

"Good. I'm ready, just point me in the right direction," Nadia said.

He studied her carefully for a moment, conflict warring deep within. She was his best agent. He needed her. Deep down, though, he knew she wasn't fully healed. Would she ever be?

"I take it you're fully briefed on the business with the Guild and our computer systems?" he asked.

"Yes... I've read all the reports. Do you think they are in league with the Caliphate?"

He shook his head, reaching for his coffee and pausing the mug centimeters from his lips. "No. God help us if they were, but no. I think they are making a move in Zuckabar. What bothers me, what keeps me up at night, is that they successfully hid their infiltration for centuries. We have literally no intel on them, and that has to end now."

"I'm not sure what this has to do with me; I don't know anything about the Guild," she said.

"None of us do. But, you know the system and the people in it better than almost any of my other agents. I need you to go there and figure out what the Guild is up to and report back to me," he said.

Nadia's countenance darkened. "I was under the impression we would be going after the Caliphate, sir."

Wit looked hard at the commander. Her skills as an agent were undeniable, but he worried her experiences would prevent her from doing the job he needed her to do. "The time to go after the Caliphate will come, Nadia, but this is where I need you now. Every penny of our official budget is spent on the covert war against the Caliphate. I need you in Zuckabar, and I need you to look into the Guild. Are you ready?"

Wit cared deeply about her. If he was honest, he thought of her as more of a daughter than an agent. His deepest fear was having her join the collection of photos on his wall.

"Yes, sir, I'm ready. I'll be honest—I would rather go after the Caliphate, but if this is where you need me, then this is where I'll go," Nadia said.

"Excellent. Your cover ID as Commander Dagher is in full effect. Records have you assigned to Logistics. Your flight is waiting for you at the spaceport. Good luck, Commander."

"Thank you, sir. Whatever they are up to out there, I'll figure it out, you; you can count on it."

CHAPTER FIVE

J acob turned his chair to face his second officer and returned to the bridge. He still wore his ELS suit to his credit, having come straight from the boat bay to report.

"Carter," Jacob said to his weapons officer. "You have the con. Mark, with me."

He stood up and headed for the ship's sole briefing room located to the stern.

"Aye, aye, sir. I have the con," Lieutenant Carter Fawkes said as the captain exited.

Jacob marched through the perpetually broken open hatch that led to the conference room. Generally, a hatch would never be left open, but he made an exception in this case. The room was used far too often to have a sentry open and close the hatch every time it was needed.

He found his chair at the far end of the conference table. It was painted with the ship's logo, a grinning cartoon shark with the words "First to Fight" on the top, and the ship's designation, "DD-1071," on the bottom.

"Have a seat and report, Mark," Jacob gestured to the chair opposite of him.

Mark sat down. Placing his helmet on the table, he seemed to deflate somewhat. They had searched the detained ship stem to stern for the last six hours, looking for anything to explain the crew's desperate attempt to escape boarding and their sudden violent attack.

"How's the XO?" he asked first.

Jacob stifled his grimace. It would do no good for anyone to know how worried he was about his number one. Part of his job was keeping morale up and presenting a positive face for the crew to rally behind.

"Still in surgery. I'm sure Lieutenant Krisper will let us know when he can," he said.

"What did you find?"

Mark frowned as if he were hoping for better news. "That's the weird thing, Skipper. We can't figure out what drove them to attack the boarding party. The cargo bay is full of random crates of electronics. The most expensive piece was a prefab fusion reactor. The kind they use on new colonies. Enough power to light up a space station."

"Weird" was an understatement. Why would a crew from a friendly nation suddenly decide to open fire on his people? Even if they had succeeded in killing the boarding party, *Interceptor* could have—would have—blown them out of the stars.

"Any ID on the crew?" Jacob asked.

Mark shook his head. "Besides the XO, PFC Owens is the closest thing to a computer expert on board. He's going over their log and data, trying to see who they were. The IFF appears legit. In fact, the whole ship is legit. The only thing strange, besides their behavior, was the ragtag appearance of their clothes."

Earlier, Jacob had watched the footage from each boarder's helmet cams. Especially Jennings. Her heroism in diving in front of the maser to protect Lieutenant Yuki was undeniable.

He would put her in for a bronze star with a "v" for combat. Her quick thinking likely gave Yuki a fighting chance. Along with Jennings, he recommended the rest of the boarding team for a combat action ribbon.

Action aboard ships in friendly space was rare enough that few people had such ribbons. However, if the rumors he was hearing over the Navy channels were to be believed, activity was picking up.

The Komodo crew had looked like refugees, not professional spacers. Maybe pirates who took the ship from the original owners?

"Mark, we can't store the bodies aboard ship, so make sure you recover enough genetic material to properly identify them."

"Aye, sir, we will. As well as detailed pictures of their faces." His face turned slightly green. "At least those who still have faces."

Jacob grimaced at the state of the bodies. He had forced himself to watch the footage and he knew the state the remains were in.

"Remind me never to be in an enclosed space when a grenade goes off. Corporal Naki's quick thinking likely saved Sergeant Jennings. It left a helluva mess, though."

Mark shook his head, his eyes going hollow for a moment. "Good lord, Skipper, I never want to see anything like that again."

Jacob gave him a moment. Having seen some truly horrific things in his time in the Navy, he sympathized with the man's need to come to terms with it.

"You did well, Mark. All our people did. Now get out of that suit, get some grub, and supervise the programming of Komodo's beacon."

Mark stood, tucking his helmet under his arm. "Aye, aye, sir."

After Mark went about his orders, Jacob pulled up his NavPad to type a report to his new CO back on Kremlin. He wasn't looking forward to the man's response. At least he wouldn't have to hear it for several hours.

Jacob had liked it a lot better when *Interceptor* was on her own.

When he returned from Command School on Blackrock, he was surprised to find only a light cruiser and two destroyers in-system. With the discovery of the wormhole, he thought TF-121 would become a permanent fixture.

The admiral had said there was political maneuvering going on. He'd hoped the necessity of the Navy in Zuckabar would be obvious to anyone, but all they had managed to do was replace the picket with a squadron. A small one at that. An LC would be more than a match for any non-military threat but would offer little protection against a serious strike force.

Which brought him to one Captain Oberstein—who was less than thrilled with his current assignment, let alone having Jacob under his command. Oberstein hadn't even met with him, issuing orders via his comm officer and sending Jacob on his way.

He finished up his report and hit send. It would automatically attach itself to the next packet. With light lag it would be hours before the report was received. What he wouldn't give for Faster-than-light comms.

Leaning back, he looked at the situation, bringing up a small holographic map of the system and highlighting their location. They had three more days on their scheduled patrol, then back to Kremlin Station, where they would resupply and give the crew some much-needed time off. The other two destroyers in the system were currently stationed at the wormhole, which nominally rested one and a half billion klicks from the binaries and in between the relative locations of the two major starlanes.

Jacob stretched, yawning. He heaved himself up and decided to go for a walk—something he loved doing on his ship. Of course, it didn't take very long to walk the keel of *Interceptor*. Each Hellcat was big and advanced for their time, but that time was forty years past. Jacob wasn't even alive when they were built.

As he left the room, he slid his hand along the table, admiring the artwork of the shark. There were advantages to smaller ships. The larger ones made it more impersonal, impossible for the captain to walk the entire ship and know the crew. In the time since he returned, Jacob had nearly memorized the entire roster of a hundred and thirteen crew, two shy of her full complement.

He stopped at the double hatch leading to the bridge.

"Fawkes, when everyone is back on board, resume Condition Yankee and previous course. If you need me, I'll be at medical," he said.

Lieutenant Fawkes turned in the center chair and acknowledged him. "Will do, sir. Previous course and Yankee."

"Good man," Jacob said as he headed for the ladder down.

"Now hear this," Fawkes's voice said over the loudspeakers. "Prepare for Condition Yankee."

———

Jennings collapsed on her rack, body aching from the bruises running up and down her back. She stared up at the underside of Lieutenant Yuki's' bunk and let her mind drift. The doctor had given her some painkillers, but they sat unused on her small bathroom sink. Bunking with the executive officer had a few privileges—like a private head.

She went over the fight again, what happened, and her response. Komodo's crew were too nervous—it should have tipped her off to a problem. Her reaction time was good, but it almost wasn't good enough. Another full second and Lieutenant Yuki would have died.

When the maser hit, her suit alarms had screamed at her, but she hadn't moved—not when she felt the heat cooking her, and not when Naki's grenade had tossed her around the bridge like a rag doll. That hurt more than the maser.

Her instincts told her to act, and her instinct served her well. Lying there in her bunk, though, she realized something. Instincts were well and good when the crap hit the fan, but she needed more than that. She needed to cultivate a tactical and *strategic* mindset. Start thinking three steps ahead instead of just one.

She wasn't just a grunt anymore but in charge of others' lives. In the end, though, the captain would approve, she decided. The way he'd leaped to shield her from the criminal on Kremlin Station shooting at them had shown her what kind of officer she was. If risking her life to save her charges was what it took, then so be it. Even if she did feel like a tenderized turkey.

"Ow," she muttered as she rolled over.

While her birth world's oxygen-rich atmosphere, higher pressure, and stronger gravity had gifted her with denser bones, muscles, and cells, it did nothing to make injuries any less painful.

When sleep didn't come, she pulled herself off the rack with a grunt and headed for the showers. If she couldn't rest, she could at least use her ration of hot water to relieve some of the pain. Maybe if she got the water scalding enough it would take her mind off of the fight.

———

Chief Suresh watched the plot as *Interceptor* sped away and the freighter disappeared behind them, noting the location in her personal log. She had a contact at Fort Kirk who did salvage; if the ship were still out there in two weeks, she would let him know. There was nothing in the regs against helping out salvage companies. She couldn't make money from it, but other forms of compensation were perfectly legal.

It wasn't that she didn't expect a big fat retirement check from the Navy someday. Even with genetic rejuvenation, the day would come when she would be forced to a desk position, training recruits on how to do the thing she loved. No, she couldn't do that. Couldn't just stop flying because of the arbitrary number of her age.

After a few minutes, the freighter disappeared from the short-range sensors and showed up on the long-range scope. Something about that freighter bothered her, but she couldn't quite put her finger on it. All the time she'd spent in space, she'd relied on her gut to guide her through—her true north, so to speak. Right then, it was telling her something was going on, but what?

"Chief, come starboard two-one-two mark zero-nine-four, ahead standard," Ensign Owusu said.

"Aye, sir. Starboard two-one-two, ahead standard." She typed in the course, locking the coordinates and adjusting their acceleration. "Course laid in."

She glanced at the little mirror on her station, angled to see whoever was sitting in the center seat.

Lieutenant (JG) Fawkes looked back. "Execute," he said.

"Aye, aye," she said with a grin.

Commander Grimm had no idea how much he'd impacted his crew. The newbies would take some time to understand, but the officers who served with him before would drag themselves naked over hot coals for the man.

She would too.

Interceptor banked as her gravcoil powered up, accelerating to three hundred gravities and pushing out a gravwake that disrupted space-time in a cone behind them. The crew leaned as the ship's two competing gravity sources temporarily fought for dominance.

Chief Suresh checked the coordinates, ensuring the computer followed the ones she entered. Glitches were rare, but her sense of duty didn't allow her to slack off.

———

Lieutenant Max Krisper leaned against the bulkhead, wiping the sweat from his brow and taking in a deep refreshing breath. He'd spent seven hours in a touch-and-go operation, guiding the nanites around the XO's body, trying to kick start the healing process and keep her from losing more of her tissue than she could regenerate from.

They'd filled her with liters of building blocks, the protein-laden fluid the nanites used to repair cells when the host body ran out of resources—which was the XO's case before they could even get her back to the ship.

PO Desper peeked in the hatch to his office, she somehow managed to look fresh even though he knew she had worked as hard as him. "Sir, you need anything?"

"No, thank you. Just... I need a minute." Exhaustion seeped through him as he spoke. He hardly recognized his own voice.

She nodded, stepping out of the room to start cleaning the surgical theater.

He'd only come aboard a month before, so he didn't know the crew or the people he worked with. Having a woman burned half to death wasn't what he anticipated when NavPer ordered him out here from the Fleet Hospital on Fort Kirk.

However, he was the nearest doctor, and the ship needed one. He was a lieutenant, for Pete's sake. He'd hardly call himself a doctor—not with Navy med school only a few months behind him. Yet here he was, on a ship, performing nanite surgery, feeling ready to have a heart attack himself.

This situation wasn't what he was promised when he signed up.

"Four years on a ground station or major hospital before you will be stationed as an assistant on a heavy cruiser or battleship." That's what they had told him. The smaller the ship, the more experienced the doctor. Given that there was only one on a destroyer he felt wholly inadequate for the job.

His MedPad interrupted his thoughts, notifying him of a message. "Lieutenant Krisper, sickbay," he replied.

"Captain here, Krisper. How's our XO?"

He racked his brain, trying to figure out where to start.

"Where are you, sir? I can come to you," he said.

"Mess. When you're ready," Commander Grimm said.

"Aye, sir. I'll be there in ten," Krisper said.

———

Jacob used the time to file some of his unending paperwork. It turned out command school *did* teach officers how to deal with the immense number of reports they had to read, write, and sign. Instead of doing it all himself, command school had taught him to delegate.

Nearly all of it.

It made him smile as he gathered all the forms and requisitions and sent them off to Lieutenant West to read and approve. Anything unusual or important would come back to him, but West would handle everything else.

Which he thought was a treat. Requisition forms and status reports were as fun as an EVA without a suit.

"Skipper," said Spacer First Class Josh Mendez while holding a plate of Jacob's preferred breakfast, steaming eggs, potatoes, and sourdough toast, and a fresh glass of the orange flavored drink.

"You see, Josh, this is why you made first class," Jacob said.

"That was the plan, sir. I'm shooting for PO next year," Mendez replied with a grin.

He set the food down in front of his captain before moving on to the next table to clean it and remove the dishes left by the morning crowd.

Only then did Jacob realize the eggs were fresh, not freeze-dried.

"Son of a gun," he muttered.

Mendez must have put some food aside for his skipper. Part of Jacob wanted to feel guilty about having fresh food when the rest of the crew was on the freeze-dried rations. However, rank had its privileges—and it wasn't like he ordered the young man to do it.

He cleaned his plate eating every morsel before sitting back and enjoying the last bit of buttered toast when Lieutenant Krisper entered.

Jacob eyed the man as he walked to the table. His slight frame reached a hundred and sixty-eight centimeters, but it wasn't his build that bothered Jacob. It was the way he purposely avoided touching anything. As he walked into the mess, a group of spacers exited, and the lieutenant practically climbed up the bulkhead to avoid coming in contact with them.

It might be nothing, Jacob decided. After all, this was his first shipboard assignment, but it was worth keeping an eye on.

"Sir," Krisper said by way of greeting.

"Max—" the lieutenant flinched at the use of his first name.

"I prefer *Doctor,* sir," he interrupted.

Jacob liked addressing his officers and crew informally. Technically, by *The Book*, it would be lieutenant, not doctor. Tradition, however, allowed the ship's medical professionals more decorum.

"As you will, Doctor. How's my XO?" Jacob asked.

"I did everything I could. When they brought her in, she had third-degree burns over eighty percent of her back and shoulders. Fourth-degree burns around her spine. I performed debridement of the dermis, using the nanites to—"

Jacob held up his hand. "Doctor, if I wanted a play-by-play, I would read your report. *How is she?*" he asked.

Doctor Krisper blinked several times. "I was telling you that, *sir.*"

"No, you were telling me what you did. I want to know how she is right now. Alive? In pain? What's her condition?"

He'd read the doctor's jacket. His last CO rated him as competent, if impersonal. Above all else, he was young, five years younger than Jacob, and with zero shipboard experience. Which meant it was Jacob's duty to teach him how to be an officer and a shipmate.

Confusion crossed Krisper's face, and he leaned back, crossing his arms.

Jacob noticed the defensive response. While he was lost in self-pity aboard *Bethesda*, something had happened to his navy, something he intended to help undo. Everyone was so focused on avoiding blame they weren't doing their damn duty. Krisper would be with him for a while, though, giving him time to crack the man's hard shell.

"She's in stable condition, for now. We're consuming an enormous amount of our protein stocks, keeping her nanites fueled. The next few hours will tell," Krisper said.

"Good to know. I'm sure you did everything you could—"

"Yes, I did. I also noted in my log the inefficiencies of the sickbay and the lack of supplies."

Jacob put aside the man's interruption for the moment and focused on the alarming news. "This is the first I'm hearing of this. Have you spoken to Chief Pierre? He's you're number two in sickbay."

Krisper glanced around the empty room, leaning in when he was satisfied no one would overhear. "Sir, I don't think I need to consult with an *enlisted* man for my needs. Surely I can come to you or the ops officer?"

The shock of those simple words hit Jacob like a blow as he processed the meaning behind what the doctor said. He held very still, turning his expression to stone. He certainly didn't want the lieutenant to see the disgust he felt in his heart. He would've thought it was a joke, except for the sincerity on Krisper's face.

There were always officers who thought they were better than the enlisted. They were as wrong as Krisper. Every man and woman had a vital role to play aboard ship. For things to run smoothly a hierarchy was established. As captain he was in charge of that hierarchy. It made him important, but no more valuable than Josh Mendez running the mess. In some ways, less valuable.

"Lieutenant," he said in an overly serious tone to emphasize the importance of what he was about to say, "Chief Petty Officer Pierre has more time in the Navy than both of us combined. He's spent the last twenty years assigned to sick bays, training young doctors to be assets to the Navy. This is why we have *Chiefs*. They show us how to behave. I want you to think long and hard about that."

He let his stone façade fade with some effort. He had great respect for the men and women who served under him. Pierre had proved instrumental in keeping the people they had rescued from *Madrigal* alive. He and Desper were tremendous assets and he would be dammed if he let them be disrespected.

"Yes, sir," Krisper said.

He had the decency to look somewhat ashamed, so Jacob was willing to chalk it up to youth and ignorance.

"May I ask a question?" Krisper said.

"By all means. Ask away."

Jacob lifted his glass, taking a sip as he waited for Krisper to find the words, giving himself an excuse to shield his face while he did his best to let the negative feelings go.

"I don't mean to pry, sir, but I have noticed virtually all of the crew have served on the ship for... longer than normal. Is that usual for destroyers?"

Jacob placed his glass down, fidgeting with it for a moment to find time to respond.

"Doctor, how long have you been in?"

"Three years in a few months," Krisper replied.

"Have you heard of the incident at Pascal?"

Krisper shook his head. "Before Navy med school, I was pre-med at the University of Alexandria. I didn't have time to keep up on Navy matters."

Jacob made a note to ask the doctor why he joined the Navy when he didn't seem overly fond of her.

"Well, I was in an... incident. I did nothing wrong, but it looked bad. Nine months ago, I was in another one here. We uncovered a massive human trafficking ring, not to mention the wormhole," Jacob said evenly as if the galaxy-changing phenomenon was absolutely normal.

Krisper's eyes widened. "That was you? Why wasn't it in the Navy Times?"

Jacob let out a short chuckle. "I'm still not a favorite son, because of that, the crew who served with me on the last tour are here for the foreseeable future. But don't worry—you're a doctor and a good one from what I can tell. A little wet behind the ears, but good. The Navy can't afford to put good sawbones out to pasture."

He couldn't be sure, but Jacob suspected his words hadn't put the young lieutenant at ease.

CHAPTER SIX

Albatross shielded his face from the bright sun of Babylon's red primary. It cast a harsh light on everything and everyone on the planet. How the people of the Caliphate had traveled thousands of light-years only to find a world resembling the deserts of their ancestral home was beyond him.

He tapped one finger to his temple, activating the polarizing lenses in his eyes and soothing the pain of the unusual light. The nanites woven into his clothes circulated the heat away, cooling his skin to a more comfortable temperature.

"This way." The dark guard punctuated his order with a shove.

Albatross complied, knowing the precarious position he was in. Like every other nation except the Iron Empire, the Caliphate owed the Guild. He alone had the power to reduce their payments, which was the only reason he was alive.

The Caliph's palace stood as a monument to their empire. Massive painted domes, spires, and towers spread throughout the complex, and intricate murals on the walls all spoke of an excess of wealth spent on construction.

Two more guards joined the first.

"This way," the leader said.

He shoved Albatross down a corridor hidden between two statues. Albatross followed him, keeping his eyes forward. What he didn't see, he couldn't report on.

He swallowed hard, trying to keep his nerve. Usually, it was easy for him, but the incident with General Remington had not only infuriated him, but also shaken his confidence.

They entered through an arch, and he almost stumbled. A large, circular, sunken room filled with pillows lay at the bottom of short stairs. A line of women clad in shreds of clothing and silver chokers stood on their tiptoes, with their heads up and shoulders back. He saw Consortium, Terran, and even some that looked like they came from the Iron Empire. A dangerous gamble considering how possessive the Empire was of its people.

Albatross was fully aware of the Caliph's use of the obedience collars, but to see it in person turned his stomach. He focused on what was ahead and tried to do his best to put the vapid expression of the dozen women out of his mind.

Lounging on the pillows was a stout man with a thick black beard. A naked serving girl knelt next to him, filling his cup whenever he handed it to her.

"Mr. Albatross," he said with a smile. "It's a pleasure."

"Admiral Rahal, thank you for seeing me." Albatross made his way down their stairs and stopped before the admiral, bowing.

Rahal laughed. "Excellent, you know your place. You may call me Kasseem. What can I do for the Terraforming Guild? Are we behind in our payments? Perhaps I could persuade you with an *alternate* form of compensation?" He gestured to the young, blue-skinned woman at his side.

Shock rolled through Albatross. Unlike the girls on the stairs with blank expressions, this girl knew exactly what was happening to her.

As if he could read his mind, Kasseem said, "Yes, she knows. It takes some time for the collar to... how you say? Break their minds, yes? Once it has, they are pliant. Until then, there is a little fight left in them. It is truly a joyous moment when you see that hope fall from their eyes, and their mind and body are yours to do with as you please." Kasseem reached over and pried her mouth open, sticking one finger past her lips.

Albatross stifled the queasy feeling in his stomach. He knew this was happening on paper. After all, they had access to the Caliphate's computers as well. To see it, though, turned his stomach more than he thought it would. Even the Guild, though they worked their people like slaves, didn't force them to endure rape and degradation.

"Thank you for your generous offer, Admiral, but I'm afraid I have to decline. And no, I'm not here for payment, but with an offer."

He thought he saw relief in the slave's eyes.

Kasseem sat straight up, snapping his fingers and pointing to the girl. "Take her to the barracks, a reward for my brave men."

Two of the guards led her away.

"Now, what is this you have to offer my Caliph and me?" he asked.

Albatross put the girl out of his mind and refocused on his purpose. Part of their arrangement with the Caliph of Hamid was to protect the Guild's employees from such fates. What he would do here would continue to ensure Guild dominance for the foreseeable future. A future the Guild intended to be unending... as long as the Caliphate didn't find out they were being spied on.

"I believe we have a mutual problem. The new wormhole in Zuckabar and Praetor?" Albatross asked.

Admiral Rahal frowned, mirth fleeing his face in an instant.

"I'm afraid I do not know of what you speak," he said.

"Don't play coy with me, Admiral. With the wormhole in Zuckabar, the Alliance can bring their warships to your door in a month instead of six. We know how you raid Consortium planets and the other neighboring systems. You are conquerors. And why not? To the victor go the spoils. Am I right?" Albatross said.

Kasseem broke into a toothy grin and laughed. "You are wise, my friend. Of course, we are conquerors. As you say, this wormhole does present a problem. If we could find one of our own it would be less of a problem?"

Albatross knew what he was hinting at, but it wasn't possible. Professor Bellaits, the man responsible for the discovery, had yet to release how he found the astronomical anomaly. The Guild had many resources, but a large fleet wasn't one of them. However, they were offering a generous bounty for information leading to other wormhole locations—through appropriate intermediaries, of course.

He shook his head. "I'm afraid that isn't possible at the moment."

"Then I don't see what we have to discuss. With our own wormhole, we could attack the Alliance and destroy their pathetic navy," Kasseem said.

He held up a grape and crushed it, letting the juices run through his fingers.

"Quite. I do have something to offer you, however. Can you contact your planetary defense network?" Albatross asked.

Kasseem raised a bushy eyebrow but retrieved a small communications device all the same. He spoke rapid-fire in his native language. They responded the same way.

"I have them," Kasseem said.

"A ship is about to appear in orbit; please do not fire on it," he asked.

Kasseem shook his head and laughed. "Appear in orbit? You have lost your mind, Mr. Albatross. This is the home of our Caliph; we have the most advanced detection network in the known galaxy—"

A burst of static filled the air, and the soldiers on the other side of the line yelled in unison.

"Don't fire," Kasseem yelled. "Do not fire!"

Albatross stifled a joyful expression at their panic. It restored some of his lost confidence. The Guild had technology no one else in the galaxy dreamed of. It was about time they started using it to further their own goals.

"You see, Kasseem, we do have something to offer," Albatross said with a savage smile.

"A stealth ship?" Kasseem said in a hushed tone.

"A stealth ship," he confirmed.

Kasseem's level of awe was deeply satisfying to Albatross on many levels.

"Well then, Mr. Albatross, if you are offering us the ship, then my nephew, Captain Istam, will command her, and you can personally accept the Alliance's surrender!"

For all his caution, Albatross hated the Alliance with a passion; the idea of forcing them to capitulate was worth the risk of trusting the Caliphate.

He decided, *no risk no reward.*

CHAPTER SEVEN

J acob didn't see the blow, but he sure as hell felt it. It took him in the jaw, deflecting off the padding and spinning him around to slam face-first on the mat. A dull numbness spread over his face, forcing him to blink several times.

With a slow deliberateness, he pushed himself up to his knees, panting as he tried to catch his breath.

"Don't get fancy, sir. Keep your hands up, protect your face," Jennings said.

"What... about... my stomach?" he asked as he climbed to his feet, breathing hard.

Jennings shook her head. "You've got size and reach, sir. Don't let them get in close. If they do, exhale like I showed you, and your stomach will be fine."

Jacob jumped up a little, shaking off the fog.

"It doesn't feel like I have anything on you," he said with a grin.

As a tall, broad-shouldered man, Jacob rarely had to defend himself physically. As he towered over ninety percent of his peers, and outweighed them by twenty kilos, people only took confrontation so far before they backed down.

"Remember, sir, exhale when you attack. That way, when you're hit, it's just muscle damage. When you're fighting, you need to be looking for an exit. If you are up against anyone with even a little bit of skill and experience, no matter their size, you're going to get your ass kicked, sir."

Her face was dead serious but Jacob thought he detected the hint of a smirk.

"Fight defensively, then?" he asked.

She shook her head.

"No, sir. If you're going to fight, you have to commit. What I'm saying is, commit to the fight, commit to the goal. But your goal isn't victory—it's escape."

Jacob looked down at his hands and arms. It was hard for him to reconcile his size, strength, and mass with the idea of falling back. However, he was keenly aware of his deficiencies.

"One more round?" he asked.

"If the captain wishes," she said.

Jennings cracked her neck, rocking up on the balls of her feet. The tank top she wore revealed the ugly yellow remains of the bruises that lined her back from her boarding action. Jacob's workout clothes were drenched, and he felt like he'd gone through a washing machine. Putting his hands up in front of him and dropping down in his stance, he made himself ready.

"Okay, go!"

Jennings marched right at him. He jabbed at her, trying to force her back. Exhaling with a sharp cry as he did so, she batted his hand aside and drove her other fist into his stomach. His muscles clenched with the impact, feeling it through the padded torso protection. Her other hand came back around and hit him in the side of his head... again.

The result was the same.

He went down.

"I think that's enough for now, sir."

She reached down and helped him up.

"Thanks, Allison," he said.

She stiffened at the use of her first name. "Captain's prerogative, Sergeant."

"Aye, sir. Just remember—" she patted the side of his face gently. "—guard your head."

Jacob pulled off the armor with care. His ribs ached, and his face pulsed with a dull pain as he lifted the helmet off. He shuddered to think what she would do if she hit him full strength and he *wasn't* wearing armor.

"Allison, can I ask you a question about your homeworld?"

"As the captain said, it's his prerogative," she replied.

She walked away, bouncing on the balls of her feet to stay limber.

"My biology is a little rusty... or maybe just non-existent," he said with a grin. "Isn't MacGregor's World one-point-four Gs?"

"Aye, sir." She turned, pushing her back and shoulders through a series of stretches.

Inwardly, Jacob chuckled at her laconic response. Sergeant Allison Jennings was born in the wrong era, he decided. She would have fit right in on a frontier planet. Her stoicism was unusual for women, but then again, MacGregor's World was a harsh, unforgiving place. Growing up there probably had more of an impact on her than inherent biology.

"That means you're forty-percent more massive and stronger... but you seem tougher than that?"

She grabbed a towel from the rack and wrapped it around her neck before wiping her face.

"Have you ever visited MacGregor's, sir?"

He shook his head negative.

"The average altitude of the colony is two kilometers above

sea level. The atmosphere is twice as dense as human standard," she looked away at something he couldn't see, her bright blue eyes shimmering before she shook herself, "Needless to say, sir, we don't get a lot of new colonists."

"Were you born there?" he asked.

Jacob grabbed his towel, needing quite a bit more to wipe the sweat from his brow.

"Yes, sir. My family are dirt owners," she said.

Navy files tended to have everything a captain needed to manage his crew, but the little pieces of history, like their heritage, weren't included. Dirt owners... her family was one of the original settlers three hundred years ago.

"Oh," he said.

She grinned, something he didn't see often. He wasn't sure it was altogether pleasant.

"Aye, sir. The survival rate of those first few generations was on the low side."

That was an understatement. If he recalled his history correctly, The MacGregor's World original colony ship had over a million souls. When the Alliance formed a decade later, less than a hundred thousand people lived on the planet. Those that survived were tough as nails—and strangely refused to leave or accept any terraforming help.

It wasn't long after discovering the colony that nano-med-tech exploded as a field and offered treatments to reverse many of the ailments the higher Gs caused them. Even with that, life on the planet was brutal, but their population stabilized. It was still only a few hundred thousand, but they were hardy and fiercely independent.

He was about to respond when the comms interrupted him.

"Captain, Bridge. Ensign Hössbacher."

Jacob nodded at his top marine before limping over to the bulkhead and hitting the comms button. "Go ahead."

"Call from *USS Corvus*, sir. Captain Oberstein," Hössbacher said.

"Delay?"

"Two seconds and change, sir. *Corvus* is parked outside Kremlin Station." Hössbacher said.

"Put him through," Jacob replied.

He glanced over his shoulder at Jennings as she strapped twenty-kilo weights to her wrists and ankles.

He shook his head. *Madwoman.*

"Commander Grimm, this is Captain Oberstein. I understand you're returning to Kremlin?"

"Yes, sir. We're scheduled for leave and resupply."

The delay aside, the captain didn't respond immediately. Jacob's hand hovered over the comm button, but he resisted asking Hössbacher if the captain was still on the line.

"According to your logs, you still have two weeks' worth of provisions aboard?" Oberstein asked.

Jacob hesitated, wracking his brain for the last report from Mendez on the food stores. He wasn't sure, but that sounded right.

"At least, sir," he said.

Behind him, Jennings moved in deliberate slow-motion through a martial arts form complete with kicks and punches, while her muscles quivered from exertion.

"Good. One of the outer mining stations, Gamma-7, sent a distress signal. No message, just their emergency beacon. I want *Interceptor* to head out there and find out what's going on. Render aid or facilitate evacuation at your discretion. *Corvus* out."

The line clicked dead.

The sudden cessation of the conversation surprised him. Oberstein didn't wait for him to acknowledge the orders. It was... *odd.* Despite the *Interceptor's* heroic actions, he was still persona non grata for many of the Navy. If Oberstein wanted to treat him that way, it was fine as long as he did his duty.

Jacob leaned against the bulkhead for a moment, debating how to proceed. He had no say in the assignment. *Thunder* and *Apache* were both orbiting Zuckabar; he had to wonder why Oberstein would send his ship when there were two other destroyers available.

He keyed the comms button again. "Astro, what's the distance to Gamma-7?"

"Astro, Ensign Owusu, sir. One moment," he said.

He glanced over at Jennings completing her form with a flourish of punches and kicks. The final move was a slow-motion spinning round kick that she stopped mid arc, holding her leg out at a seventy-degree angle.

"Sir, Gamma-7 is a mining platform on the far side of the system from Kremlin. Rough guess... fifty hours. I can have an exact course for you in a few minutes," Owusu said.

"Plot it. I'll be up in ten minutes, Captain out." He slapped the button ending the call.

He went to the stern ladders from the gym and made the long trek up to his cabin. Every rung reminded him of Jennings' lesson. Don't fight; escape and evade. At least he was handy with a sidearm as long as he remembered to use it.

Small unit tactics and unarmed combat weren't heavily taught in the Navy. While enemy boardings happened, they were rare. The navy still mandated drills to cover the unlikely event. Marines acted as the enemy boarders and relished their trouncing of the Navy types.

His only other concern about delaying their return to port, was Yuki. She was confined to sickbay, and Doctor Krisper had recommended a full workup when they returned to port, which wouldn't be for another five days, minimum, depending on what they found out there. Oberstein wasn't making his job easy. Then again, what CO ever did?

———

Half an hour later, Jacob entered the bridge dressed in a clean uniform and sporting a fresh bruise on the side of his face.

Lance Corporal Naki grinned at his captain like an idiot. All too aware of how the officer got his bruises. "Captain on the bridge," Naki said.

The duty officer, Lieutenant Mark West, jumped up. A far cry from the first time Jacob came on board. They were a long way from that disorderly, undisciplined crew, and he couldn't be prouder of the men and women who served on *his* ship.

"Mark, what's the situation?" he asked.

"Sir, the distress beacon was received three hours ago. It's automated. No details other than the emergency," West said.

Jacob took the center seat.

"I have the con," he said.

"Captain has the con," West replied.

With no follow up message he had to assume no one on Gamma-7 was able to respond.

"Astro, show me the system, please," Jacob said.

"On main viewer," Owusu said.

Zuckabar Central's unusual orbital map appeared. The planet held a roughly circular orbit at seven hundred million klicks and change—well outside the Goldilocks zone for a habitable planet. It was the only survivor of the supernova that turned the binary star into a white dwarf and a pulsar. The interior planets were obliterated in the explosion, leaving vast fields of asteroids out past Zuckabar Central's orbit.

The largest concentration of asteroids on the farthest out

system orbit was almost two billion klicks from the sun and currently on the opposite side of the system from *Interceptor*.

A blinking red dot showed their current location. As Jacob watched, a dotted yellow line representing their proposed course curled out with the ecliptic of the system, diverging as it spread to the farthest orbit until arriving at Gamma-7. White letters flashed the time: fifty-two hours and seventeen minutes.

"That's a long time to wait for help," Chief Suresh said from The Pit.

"Don't I know it," Jacob said.

He wished there was a faster way. He checked the numbers Owusu supplied on his MFD, and they were solid. He couldn't have plotted a better course himself.

"Ensign Hössbacher, all hands please," Jacob said.

The young man hit a switch on his console and pointed at his captain.

Jacob took a deep breath, knowing his next words would reach every ear on the ship.

"Now hear this. We have received an automated distress signal from mining station Gamma-7. We don't know the situation out there. I know everyone aboard was looking forward to some much-needed leave, but I also know, if it were any of us floating out there in the black in need of help, you would want the fastest ship riding to the rescue."

He paused for a moment. He truly hated telling the crew they had to spend another week, possibly two, without leave. Not that they couldn't endure, but when people had their hearts set on leave, it hurt morale to have it delayed, possibly canceled entirely.

"*Interceptor* is that ship. We will proceed to Gamma-7 at flank speed. Set condition Zulu, action stations," Jacob said.

The alarm immediately sounded throughout the ship. Jacob

could imagine the crew rushing in an orderly fashion to their emergency posts, closing bulkhead doors, checking outlets, and securing the ship for flank speed. They wouldn't proceed the entire way in action stations, of course. However, as they approached port they had been preparing the ship for resupply, and a lengthy stay. Action stations would ready the ship for whatever came next.

Lieutenant Mark West watched his ops panel as every station turned green, reporting their readiness.

"Skipper, the ship is secured for action," West said.

Jacob nodded to Owusu. "Ensign, call the ball."

"Aye, sir. Astro has the ball. Helm, come starboard, zero-eight-three mark zero—"

Owusu hesitated, glancing at his captain for confirmation. Flank speed was rarely used; generally, the Navy stuck to eighty percent power, which was more efficient and gave the ship a comfortable safety margin in case of secondary gravcoil failure. Flank speed left no room for errors. In Jacob's opinion, the lives of the people on Gamma-7 justified such risk.

"Flank speed confirmed," he told the ensign.

"Aye, sir. Helm, accelerate to flank speed," Owusu finished.

Chief Suresh copied the course over from Owusu's station before confirming. "Come starboard zero-eight-three mark zero and accelerate at flank speed, aye. Course ready," Suresh said.

Jacob leaned forward, gazing at the stars twinkling in the main viewer. Anything was possible. Deep down in his soul, he thanked God for his chance to be where he was, captain of a ship, master of his destiny. There was nowhere he would rather be.

"Chief... execute."

———

Yuki flexed her hands uselessly. She wanted—needed—to be at her duty station down in damage control or on the bridge, not lying face-first in sickbay while nanites regenerated her damaged body.

"Doc?" she said. "Anyone there?"

Chief Pierre's face appeared. The older man had more stripes in the Navy than anyone on board, except the COB. Chief Suresh had spent a quarter of a century serving the Alliance. Pierre was only five years behind her. Not that she could tell—the anti-aging treatment the Navy provided froze everyone at a ubiquitous thirty years old.

"What can I do for you, ma'am?" he asked.

He had the drawl of a New Austin native, and Yuki knew from experience that people underestimated him. He could be a doctor with all the knowledge he had, but like most non-comms with as much time in service, he preferred the role of mentor and guide to that of leader.

"Chief, I can't stay here. Tell me I can get up and walk out?" she pleaded.

"I'd love to, ma'am, but you know what needs to be done. You've got a minimum of eight more hours. Can I get you a NavPad? At least you could work or watch a movie?"

"Thanks, Chief," she said. It was hard to hide the disappointment in her voice. She wasn't in any pain. Surely she could do her damn job?

"It's normal, ma'am. People of action do not like to be inactive. It's why you're an excellent XO," he said.

She opened her mouth to respond, but his unexpected compliment stole her words. By the time she recovered, he'd moved away.

If she couldn't stand watch, the least she could do was catch up on work. Then she wouldn't have to think about what led to her current predicament.

CHAPTER EIGHT

Captain Rod Beckett (ret.) gazed out of the large bay window at his exclusive view of the interior of Kremlin Station. The rest of the station was a mishmash of modern and niche buildings, but the Russian heritage of the unique architecture was on full display around the governor's tower. Hundreds of aircars flashed through the air, weaving in and out of the spires that carried workers to the zero G repair facilities at the center of the station.

He had his hands full, and that was an understatement. The previous governor had an entrenched network loyal to his family. When the Alliance announced they were taking over the station, there were riots, murders, the lot of it. It took months to restore order and get the station back to "business as usual."

The Navy had chosen him because of his experience in the system and his knowledge as an engineer. Kremlin Station was a wonder of old and modern technology fused together in impossible ways. A non-engineer wouldn't begin to be able to run the place efficiently. However, they had replaced the ineffective station police with a new civilian security force led by Navy shore patrol. They had to train tens of thousands of personnel while also doing their job. He had the problems of a military base, a massive city, and a space station all in one.

"Rod?"

Rod turned to the source of the voice. Anya entered his office. With sparkling green eyes and straight blonde hair she took his breath away. With her wafted in the mouth-watering scent of cooked beef in the form of pelmeni dumplings.

He stood motionless for a moment, drinking in the sight of her and breathing in deep.

"My dear Anya Ivanova," he said with a huge grin.

For some reason, the young woman had taken a liking to Rod from the first day she met him. He'd almost forgotten what it felt like to be infatuated, and the spring in his step and the lightness in his heart were visible on his face.

"We have a lunch date. Or did you forget?" she said in her heavily accented voice.

"I could never forget you," he replied.

From outside his office, his assistant called him. "Governor Beckett, there's a Commander Dagher here to see you?"

Rod glanced at Anya with a shrug. "I won't be long, Anya. Would you mind waiting outside?"

"Not at all," she said.

Anya pulled a fresh slice of Medovik from her basket and placed it on his desk.

Rod swallowed at the sight of the honey bread.

"You're an angel."

"In case you get hungry while you have your little meeting," she said with a coy smile.

Anya stood on her tiptoes and placed a gentle kiss on his cheek. Her face broke into a deep crimson as she hurried out, brushing past a dark-haired woman in the uniform of a naval commander.

Nadia Dagher clasped her shore cap under one arm and a

briefcase in hand. She nodded to Anya as the woman left Rod's office, then came to a stop in front of his desk. He walked over from the window to sit behind his desk. Even though the doctors reassured him that he could not know the difference, he could tell that they weren't his original feet. Especially when they pained him.

"Commander Dagher?" He held out his hand.

She took it in a firm, well-practiced grasp.

"While we've never met, Governor Beckett, we have bled in the same sickbay," Nadia said with a smile.

Recognition dawned on him as he realized she was the commander of the freighter *Dagger*.

"Please, don't apologize. I think I've had enough of that, and if I'm right, you probably have too," she said, glancing down at his feet.

"You are right, of course. I'm glad you're doing better, and back in the Navy, I see. I thought you were a chief petty officer, though?"

Nadia glanced down at her uniform, her cheeks blushing the barest of red as she sat down.

"Technically I am. However, for this mission I'm a Supply Officer, counting beans. Makes it easy for me to move around and no one gives me grief."

She sat her case down on the table and pressed both locks at once, holding them down for five seconds before letting go. The case morphed, in the manner that nanite-formed objects often changed shape. One second it was a standard black leather briefcase, the next it was an advanced computer with sensors and readouts. He could tell it was a privacy screen based on the antenna and the electromagnetic wave scanner.

With a push of a button, it sprang to life. Light flashed out, scanning the room, then it hummed in the background but did nothing else.

"Impressive laser show," he said.

"Thank you," she replied. "ONI can't be too careful these days. May I call you Rod?"

"I wish you would." He gestured for her to take a seat, and he followed. "What do the spooks at ONI want with my little corner of the universe?"

"You know about the commotion with the Terraforming Guild, and you know about the Caliphate base here. Zuckabar has gone from a nowhere system run by a dictator to the most important port-of-call in the Alliance."

Rod couldn't disagree with her. He was slammed from rebuilding the station's computer network and police force to keeping the repairs on ships moving on schedule.

"Don't I know it? I've got a million things to do, and the least of them is managing the hundreds of ships scheduled for repair."

"I sympathize. While I've never run anything quite as large as Kremlin, I can't imagine it's any easier with size," Nadia said.

"The work never seems to end, that is for sure," he replied.

"I'll be blunt, Rod. I need access to everything. Unlimited access. No barriers. The admiral—" Rod knew she could only be speaking of the head of ONI.

"—has intelligence that there will be another attempt on the system. We don't know what kind or when, but he suspects soon. Possibly before the wormhole is fully active."

The former chief engineer leaned back, absorbing what she had told him.

"Is this what passes for intelligence these days?" he asked, slightly sour.

"Excuse me?" she asked with open mouth disbelief.

"I'm an engineer, Commander Dagher, not some fancy spook or politician, and even I could have told you that. Of course, the Caliph is going to try and take the system. The *Bella* wormhole is the most important discovery of our lifetime, possibly ever. Do you know what the geniuses back in Congress authorized to safeguard it?" he asked.

It was hard for him to stay calm about the mess they had dumped on him. He loved his job, the Navy, and the Alliance, but the people who ran it left him wondering which side they were actually on.

She shook her head.

"A lousy light cruiser and three destroyers. This station only has point-defense for taking out asteroids, and that was built in the last century. Talk about emboldening our enemies. Why didn't we just hand over the lease and let them take over the system?" he asked her.

"The admiral agrees, or I wouldn't be here. If we can find some solid evidence of a threat, he can force Congress' hand and move a task force here like we should have in the first place," she said.

Rod was all for more help. He wasn't kidding about his ability to defend the station. Technically, it was up to the good Captain Oberstein to defend the system. He had no doubt, though, if overwhelming forces showed, the captain would leave them to deal with it on their own. Not that he could blame him. All it would take was for a Caliph battle group to show up, and the system was theirs. Their only real protection was distance: it was simply too far away for the Caliphate to hold the system, at least until the wormhole was active. The nightmare scenario, the one keeping him up at night would be if the Caliphate controlled both sides of the passage.

"Sorry, Commander, I didn't mean to take that out on you. Of course, your offer to help is appreciated. What can I do to assist?" Rod asked.

Nadia's shoulders sagged and she looked tired to him, almost like the act of walking and talking was a weight on her.

"Thank you. I need access to your mainframes," she said it so matter-of-factly Rod almost missed the enormity of her request.

"If you're looking for people, that's going to be a lot," he said. "We're talking Millions."

"Tell me something I don't know," Nadia replied. "My freighter stopped here several times a year. We have to start somewhere and checking names off a list is the first step."

Rod leaned back, tapping his fingers on the polished desktop. "Why do you think that will work?" he asked.

"The Guild may have been deceiving the Alliance for a long time, but that doesn't mean they are good at it. They were able to perpetrate the fraud because we weren't aware of it. Now that we are, the game has changed. More than one mole hunt has been successful because someone in enemy intelligence got cute with the cover IDs," she said.

That thought hadn't occurred to Rod. "Interesting. I guess this is why I'm an engineer, and you're counterintelligence. I'll have my assistant set you up with access to the computers and some quarters. Would that do?"

"Yes, that would be great and thank you. You're very kind."

She hit several buttons on her device, and it reformed into a briefcase she clasped under one arm.

"My pleasure, Commander. I'll make sure Petrov has the necessary access for you ASAP, Rod said.

She stood to leave but stopped at the closed door and turned to look at him.

"Oh, Rod, I almost forgot. I was told *Interceptor* was in-system, but I didn't see her when my ship came in. Is she nearby?" she asked nonchalantly as if inquiring about his afternoon plans.

He didn't miss the sudden fluctuation of her voice when she

said the ship's name. Was she really interested in his old boat, or the man who skippered it?

"I'm afraid not. She was tasked to answer a distress call and won't return for at least a week. I believe, though, when she is back, she's scheduled for some leave time."

He couldn't tell if the news made her happy or sad. In the end, she nodded to herself and walked out.

CHAPTER NINE

Tapping away on his NavPad, the cold crept into the tips of Jacob's fingers. The quiet business of the bridge enveloped him as he stood watch, using the time to complete more of the paperwork West had kicked back to him for final approval.

"Passing a hundred thousand klicks, sir," Ensign Owusu said.

Jacob's head popped up. For the last twenty-five hours, they had decelerated in their approach toward Gamma-7.

"Hail them, Roy," Jacob ordered.

"Aye, aye, sir." The ensign spoke quietly into his mic for a moment. "If they're there, sir, they're not responding."

Gamma-7 was close enough to offer lag-free communications. If anyone were on the station, they would hear *Interceptor*. Which meant they were either unable or unwilling to respond.

"Good enough, Roy. Monitor the emergency frequency. You better get your second up here and have him do a complete EMR sweep just in case we missed something obvious," Jacob said.

"Aye, sir, on it." Hössbacher flipped a switch on his panel. "Now hear this. Spacer First Class McCall report to the bridge."

"PO Tefiti, hear anything out there?" Jacob asked.

He turned to Ensign Owusu and his second, Petty Officer First Class Tefiti. Like a few other members of his crew, Tefiti hailed from Ohana. The dark-skinned native of the island planet came with perfect fit reps across the board. Jacob was surprised the PO requested service on the *Interceptor*.

Tefiti had the space-time headphones on, listening intently for the slightest gravitic vibration that would signal they weren't alone.

"Sir?" he asked as he freed one ear to hear better.

"Anything?" Jacob asked.

"Nothing yet, sir," Tefiti said.

"You know the pulsar can play havoc with the gravitic sensors," Jacob said in what he hoped was a helpful tone and not that of an overbearing CO.

"Aye, sir. Ensign Owusu and PO Oliv have given me the rundown. I have to say, as gravitic interference goes, the pulsar is the most interesting star I've listened to. It's almost like music. If one were into shouting and beats," Tefiti added with a smile.

"Good to know. As you were," Jacob said.

While they could "see" the platform with light-speed sensors, they didn't have a visual on it yet. Lieutenant West had given them all a detailed briefing on Zuckabar's furthest mining platform, and Jacob had commended his thoroughness.

"As you can see, sir, they aren't the typical mining outpost. Neither an old cargo ship retrofitted as a mother ship nor a hollowed-out asteroid. Instead, they went with a station-keeping platform with its own refinery and a one-kilometer-long magnetic rail for delivering the goods to Zuckabar," West said.

Newly released from sickbay and able to resume light duty,

Yuki piped up, "How many potential casualties are we looking at here?"

Jacob would leave the questions to her unless he felt like West or Yuki were missing something important.

"The manifest they filed with Kremlin Station says thirty-five. However, it's a few years old, and new management hasn't updated their databases yet, ma'am," West said.

Yuki chewed on the thought for a moment. "If they do have more than that and we have to make multiple trips, we can always convert the boat bay into a triage station. That way, we can offload any casualties without moving them through the ship. The really bad ones we can carry up to sickbay... what say you, Doctor Krisper?"

Krisper's head shot up as if he weren't paying attention. He coughed a little, adjusted his position, and tapped the table.

"Excellent idea, Lieutenant. I'm sure we can make that work," he said in a formal tone that nearly made Jacob frown.

Yuki turned to Fawkes. "Any sign of violence?"

"Negative, ma'am," Lieutenant Fawkes answered. "We've got good radar returns on the station, and I haven't seen anything to suggest a hull breach or any other external damage. No debris or frozen atmosphere. No other ships within three hundred thousand klicks, either. They could be out there, though—there's a reason Gamma-7 is here after all.

"When the sun went supernova, the force of the explosion expelled the stellar material out here. Which is why it's such a popular place to mine. This orbital plane is packed with enough material to make several planets," West said. "All the debris gives plenty of sensor shadows for ships to hide in. If there is a ship and they are moving around on reaction thrusters only, we wouldn't know it."

Jacob was impressed with his crew. They were on top of it,

and he hardly had to ask any questions during the entire briefing. A sure sign they had done their homework.

He pressed the coms button. "Boat bay," he said.

"Boat bay, Baxter here, sir."

"Is the Corsair ready to fly?" Jacob asked.

"The chief is doing a last-minute check, but yes, sir, she is. Medical has their people down here along with two marines."

Spacer First Class McCall hustled onto the bridge and took the second position at comms.

"Good job, Baxter. Captain out," Jacob said.

He leaned back, watching the numbers count down as they approached the mining facility. His people were ready, and they knew their business. Anything more on his part would just be to assuage his own feelings. One of the downfalls of command, he supposed. At the end of the day, he was just one man on a ship of many.

"One-zero-zero kilometers per second and falling," Suresh said.

Her hands were on the manual controls as she watched the three monitors showing her everything she needed to guide the destroyer into position.

"McCall?" Jacob asked.

"I've got limited power and heat emissions, sir, but no signals other than the beacon. It doesn't appear anyone is home," spacer McCall replied.

In space, about the only way to "see" anything was through electromagnetic emissions. While Hössbacher focused on communications, McCall scanned the EM bands. With a full station, there would be "noise," just from daily life. Instead, they had nothing.

Minutes passed as they drew closer. It would be nice if they could go in full speed and do a fly-by, but with the sheer amount of asteroids in the area, it wouldn't be safe.

"One-zero KPS, twenty seconds to relative," Chief Suresh said.

He fervently wished the station inhabitants were simply experiencing a mechanical problem. Even if they had no radar or comms, *Interceptor* was close enough to signal with running lights.

"Zero-one KPS..." she said.

"Gravcoil at zero power," Suresh said.

"Close the iris, Mark," Jacob ordered.

With as much debris as they detected and the amount pinging off the hull, he'd rather not risk something getting lodged in the gravcoil.

"Aye, aye, sir. Gravcoil iris is closed," Lieutenant West replied.

"Five-zero-zero MPS," Suresh said as she continued to ride the thrusters, slowing the ship down.

"On screen," Jacob ordered.

High-powered cameras on the bow of the ship activated, replacing the ship's status on the main viewer with a crystal-clear picture of the stars beyond Zuckabar. With the pulsar and white dwarf behind the ship, they had an interference-free view of the outer system.

Hössbacher fumbled with the controls for a moment before hitting the right one. The screen zoomed in, and the platform took center stage.

"Sorry, sir," he said.

"It's okay, Roy," Jacob said.

Roughly five times the volume of *Interceptor*, the mining platform had four boom-like arms in the shape of an "X" extending from each corner, enabling it to unload/load four ships at a time. The central structure was dome-shaped, with multiple pipes, fittings, and other offshoots.

"The comms gear appears to be there, sir," Hössbacher said.

He pointed to the image and zoomed in to show a series of dishes and antennas extended from the upper side of the facility.

"Good eye," Jacob said to the young man.

"Devi, you think you can dock with her?" he asked the coxswain.

"I'd rather not, Skip," she said.

Focused as she was, Devi didn't take her eyes off the readout to look at him as she spoke. "If they do have problems, I'd hate to be lashed to her."

"Understood. Carry on," he said.

"Aye, sir. Parking orbit in two-zero seconds. Five meters per second... four... three..."

Her skilled hands brought the ship to a halt relative to the station.

Jacob sat in his chair, leaning back and staring at the station for a second. He sipped his tea, running through the hundreds of possible reasons why their emergency beacon would broadcast and they wouldn't respond to a hail.

"Comms, try a laser," he ordered.

"Aye, aye, sir. Locating..." Hössbacher moved the camera around, looking for the laser port.

Every ship, station, and life pod had a laser port for direct communications.

"Found it. Slaving," he said.

Invisible light lashed out from *Interceptor*'s laser emitter and anchored to the station's receiver.

"I don't get it, sir," Hössbacher said. "I've got a solid lock on the mirror but no response from the system."

"That's damn peculiar," Jacob muttered while he rubbed his jaw. "Why did the beacon turn on?"

Mining this far out from the planet and station wasn't

without risk. Usually, though, the dangers were mitigated by technology. He activated comms.

"XO to the bridge," he said.

While he waited for her to climb up from DCS, he examined the station.

"Carter, could the pulsar kill everyone aboard while leaving the station intact?" he asked.

"I don't think so, sir. We're pretty far out. Even with the focused gamma and x-ray emissions, the station's shielding should have proved more than enough to deal with it. Not to mention all the asteroids randomly between the stars and here. The odds of a gamma flare hitting this spot but bypassing Zuck-abar's detection are pretty low. Not impossible, but unlikely."

"If anyone can tell me what they think might have happened, I'm open to suggestions." He made sure to look around the bridge to assure them he was serious.

"Hull breach?" McCall asked.

"Negative," Ensign Hössbacher said. "A small hull breach wouldn't kill everyone on board, and a large one would show on radar."

"Oh," McCall said.

He seemed to shrink into his chair next to the ensign.

Jacob appreciated the courage it took for an enlisted spacer to speak up on a bridge full of officers. "It was worth a shot, Mac. I was thinking the same thing," Jacob said.

The young man brightened, smiling at his CO. "Yes, sir."

Chief Suresh glanced in the mirror on her console, allowing her and the captain to see each other.

"Sir, the railgun delivery arm... do you notice anything strange about it?" she asked.

He pulled up the schematics on his MFD and compared them to the current position. The railgun delivery arm was separated from Gamma-7 by five hundred meters and stretched out a kilometer long. It was loaded via rail from the station and aimed and fired by computer. Somewhere in orbit around Zuckabar Central, a matching arm waited to "catch" the cargo, decelerating it the same way it was fired. The generator and operator controlled the arm from a boxy enclosure at the far end.

After a long moment, Jacob shook his head, not getting the clue.

The COB smiled like a school teacher explaining the basics to her most dense student. "If they're out here mining, sir, then they should be delivering their payload to Zuckabar Central, correct?"

Of course they would. The only way this situation was profitable was to stockpile the precious metals these planetary fragments consisted of and send them out en masse. The area was too crowded with asteroids for a big M-class freighter to come out here and collect it all. He glanced at the plot, and it hit him.

"Oh," he said.

"Aye, sir," Chief Suresh confirmed. "If they're mining, why is the railgun pointed *away from the planet*?"

She was right. The railgun's trajectory was almost in the opposite direction it should be.

This was a mystery... and Jacob hated mysteries. He wasn't any good at puzzles. As a child his family would play puzzle games and he always lost. In the Academy, when the rest of the class would go on leave to gaming palaces, Jacob would spend his time reading. The most popular games of the day were all puzzle games. His brain didn't work that way. Instead, he figured things out by relating them to history and myths.

"What we have here is a Roanoke," he said as a memory tickled his brain.

"Sir?" Yuki asked as she walked onto the bridge.

Her uniform was modified by a medical vest that monitored

her vitals and kept the nanites working until she was one hundred percent. It was the only way Dr. Krisper would let her out of the sickbay.

"XO, glad you're up and about," he said.

"Me too, skip. I tell you, masers are nasty," she said with a grin. "What's a row-note?"

Jacob pointed at the main screen. "Roanoke. It was a colony that vanished. The only clue to what happened were words carved into a tree on the island."

She raised an eyebrow. "Tree, sir?"

He grinned. "Yeah, it was a long time ago on Earth. Fifteen hundred years or so."

"As the captain says. Do you want me to assign someone to lead the shore party?" she asked.

Crew assignments were the primary duty of a ship's exec. Her job was to manage the morale and crew problems and only bring them to the captain's attention when needed. He knew she loved leading the boarding actions, but she was off the roster until her back healed.

"Who's up on the rotation?" he asked.

She made a subtle nod at Ensign Owusu as she turned her back to him.

"He could use the experience, sir, but..." she whispered.

Jacob tended to agree. Owusu was an excellent astrogator, but he needed experience in other areas. Leadership only came through action. He couldn't quite put his finger on it, but something in his gut told him the situation was more serious than they were seeing.

"Owusu, anything on the scope?" he asked.

The young man checked his radar and lidar screens, followed by a glance at PO Tefiti, who shook his head "no."

"Negative, sir. If there is another ship out there, she's running silent," Ensign Owusu said.

Part of the duty of a commanding officer was giving his Ensigns opportunities to shine. However, he also didn't want to unduly risk the success of the mission. Shore missions just didn't come around enough for him not to send Owusu.

An idea hit him.

"I've got it, XO," he said. "I'll go and take Owusu with me."

Yuki's eye's narrowed. It was every officer's duty to lead boarding missions. The majority of the burden fell on the XO, but there was a rotation for a reason. Just as officers served as department heads for different divisions, it was vital for them to have a wide range of experience. Hyper-specialization was what the warrants were for; officers needed to know how everything worked.

However, it was also her job to protect the captain... sometimes from himself.

"Excellent, Captain," she said. "I'll monitor the situation from here."

"Privilege of rank, XO. I think I'll stretch my legs. Owusu, you're with me." Jacob headed for the hatch. "XO, you have the con."

"Aye, sir. XO has the con," she said as she slipped into his still moving chair.

———

Only a slight bump told Jacob the Corsair had docked with Gamma-7.

"Dang, Chief Boudreaux, that's some excellent flying," he said over the open comm.

Sergeant Jennings, PFC Owens, Ensign Owusu, PO Desper, and the two medical assistants heard his compliment. It was important for the CO to recognize excellence and reward it with praise. Nothing killed morale faster than a commanding officer who was stingy with praise and liberal with criticism.

The radio clicked, and her electronic voice came back. "Thank you, Skipper. You be careful in there."

He pointed to Jennings, who nodded. Her space armor made her look like a hi-tech knight from a movie as she moved to the hatch. She placed one hand on the panel, pausing for a moment.

"The station is operating on emergency power. Owens, burn it," she ordered.

All the Marines wore their space armor, and if not for the ranks on their shoulders, it wouldn't have been possible to tell them apart. The PFC opened the Corsair's hatch, pulled an optical cable from his wrist and plugged it into the exterior hatch controls.

"Ten seconds," he said.

"Roger," Jennings said. "Sir, I've got point. You come in after Owens. Ensign Owusu, take the rear."

"Is all this necessary, Sergeant?" Petty Officer Desper asked.

"I'm going to pretend you didn't say that PO," she said without looking at her.

Owusu chuckled at the exchange. This was the young man's first boarding action, and so far, he was handling it well. Jacob had known ensigns who couldn't move past the hatch unless prodded. Owusu didn't look like he would have that problem. He also wasn't too eager—another obstacle new officers had. No one needed to go in guns blazing. That was what the marines were for.

Jacob glanced at the medic and shrugged. The Navy people wore their ELS suits, which were flat white, skin-tight, and would keep them alive in the vacuum of space. Their name and rank adorned their chest like a normal uniform. Jacob's stood out, with his red helmet and stripe running down the side.

The interior hatch slid open. Owens dodged to the side, and Jennings' rushed through, MP-17 in carbine mode with the barrel up and the stock shouldered.

Inside Gamma-7, lighting blinked intermittently, casting deep shadows on the bulkheads that moved like they were alive. Jacob's hand reflexively hovered over the pistol on his hip, reminding himself it was there.

Owens followed Jennings, drawing his weapon as he moved. The advanced sidearm reconfigured in seconds from pistol-sized to a carbine.

Maybe it was the unpredictable lights that reminded Jacob of every horror vid he'd ever watched, or perhaps it was his gut, but something was wrong. More so than just the mystery of the beacon.

"Owusu, stay here with the crew while we check it out," he said over the open comms.

Aye, sir," Owusu said.

Jacob switched to the command frequency. "XO?"

"Aye, sir," her reply came.

"Something feels off. Maybe it's nothing, but better safe than sorry," Jacob said.

"Sounds like an excellent time for a battle stations drill, sir," Yuki said.

He could hear the grin in her voice. They led the fleet in drill time, and he knew it was a point of pride with her and the crew. He appreciated how much she mirrored his thoughts.

"I concur. Set condition Zulu, battle stations," he ordered.

"Aye, sir," she said.

Her voice sharpened as she confirmed and issued the order. "All hands, set condition Zulu, battle stations. This is not a drill."

The klaxon rang as her commlink disconnected.

He was confident he'd made the right move. It cost them

nothing to be cautious and it could cost them everything to ignore the feeling he had.

"Sir," Owusu asked over the private channel.

"Yes, Ensign?" he replied.

"When was the last time a Navy ship was attacked in Alliance space?" he asked.

Jacob racked his brain for a long moment. Almost all the ship losses of the last hundred years had happened in neutral ports or non-aligned systems.

"We're in uncharted territory, Ensign. Zuckabar is only nominally Alliance territory. I hate to make history as the first captain to lose his ship in Zuck," he said with a grin. "Especially after how hard we worked to keep that from happening last time."

"Aye, sir. Understood," Owusu said.

Jacob moved through the hatch, drawing his pistol as he did. The two marines were already at the first intersection, and he wanted to catch up. Once his glove came in contact with the butt of the weapon, his HUD showed him how much ammo he had left. He made sure the safety was on and worked to catch up with the two combat experts.

As spacers went, he'd seen more firefights than most officers, but he wasn't eager to repeat that experience.

———

Jennings agreed with the Captain that something felt off. While the ship was his domain, CQB was hers. She trained night and day for combat, and she refused to be caught by surprise. She knew exactly what an ambush in close quarters could do.

The only thing out of the ordinary, besides the missing crew, was the lack of main power. The lights operated on batteries, which were failing as they blinked on and off. The panels next to the hatches had power, but the reactor was offline.

"Owens, get on the first panel we find and hack it," she ordered.

Step by step, they moved forward. Her HUD generated a map using a form of echolocation as they moved through the station. She couldn't shake the feeling that something was wrong. Her mind fleetingly recalled the slaughter her fellow marines had inflicted on the mercs in the hold of *Madrigal*. She refused to allow her people to fall prey to something like that.

"Owens, four-way coming up," she said.

"I've got left," he said.

"Jennings," Captain Grimm said, let's go right to the command center."

"Aye, aye, sir," she replied.

She liked the captain, and she was glad he wasn't trying to micro-manage the boarding action. Letting her do her job was a sign of a good officer.

"Plot route, command center," she told the computer.

The map blinked, and a transparent yellow arrow appeared on the corner of her HUD, showing her which way to go at the next intersection. They hit the four-way, Owens covering left while she covered right, and the captain hung back.

She froze, holding still and letting the suit listen for any signs of danger. Passive sensors picked up every sound, light, and motion. The flickering light threw off her vision but the sound sensors were solid. She lifted her hand off the carbine and pointed toward the command center to the right. Jacob took position directly behind her, and Owens covered their six, walking backward as they moved.

"Sir," she said. "Switch your sidearm to wide-area."

She saw him look down at his weapon from the three-sixty camera and then back up to her.

"Remind me how to do that?" he asked.

She stifled a sigh, stopping for a moment to wait for him.

"Push the activation button and then select wide-area on your HUD," she said.

He fumbled with the pistol for a moment. Jennings was forever grateful for the safety systems that vastly reduced the number of friendly fire incidents. Barring a freak accident, the weapons wouldn't fire when pointed at an ally.

He found the right button; the pistol expanded to carbine size but with a large barrel at the end, set to fire flechettes of hardened silicate slivers in an adjustable two-meter-wide pattern. He shouldered it but wisely kept the barrel pointed at the deck.

"Good job, sir," she said.

She knew how fragile officers' egos were, and it was helpful to reassure them they could find their butt with both hands and a map. Even if very few of them could. The arrow on her HUD changed to "up" as she moved along the hatchway. After six meters, she found the ladder leading up and down, connecting all the levels. Unlike a Navy ship, which didn't have any ladders leading through more than one deck, civilian designs lacked such precautions. This one ladder covered all four decks of the station.

She edged up on the hole, carbine pointed up, and she ducked in twice in rapid succession, jerking back each time.

"Clear-top," she said.

Repeating the process for the bottom netted the same result. She had Owens cover the bottom, slapped her carbine to her back and heaved up the ladder.

They needed deck two which was only one deck up. Something nagged at her as she climbed. Call it paranoia or good instincts; she decided to pop up and let her three-sixty camera look before exposing herself.

Examining the image, she frowned. The arrow on her HUD indicated the command center was twenty meters away on deck two. However, the image from her camera showed a long hatchway interspersed with stacked cargo crates and unused machinery.

"Sir, I'm going to move to the next level. Follow me close. Owens, ready a screamer," she said.

She didn't like having the skipper in tow. Anyone on the mission could be injured or killed without repercussion. If the CO were, though, there would be hell to pay. Jennings hated to think her decision-making process was affected by the idea. It shouldn't be, but... when had "should" ever had anything to do with anything?

"Aye, Sarge, one screamer," Owens replied.

He yanked the sonic grenade from his belt. She hauled herself up and stepped onto the cargo deck, a five-meter-wide compartment stretching twenty meters in either direction. It was the definition of fish in a barrel. A metal crate lay wedged against the bulkhead at the end of the five meters, reaching halfway up. It would be the perfect cover on either side. Someone could hide behind it. Or she could.

The captain came up next, Owens right behind him. She motioned for the PFC to wait out of sight at the top of the ladder. With her carbine shouldered and the barrel pointed toward the command center, she moved, step by step, in the indicated direction. As if sensing her intent, the captain walked backward, guarding her six.

"Maybe it's nothing, Sergeant," Owens said.

Whispering it over the secure radio told her he didn't believe his own words. No, she was sure. Someone was here. Maybe not in the room, but on the station. She could feel it, and—

Motion caught her eye as a grenade flashed through the air.

Small, black, and hand-thrown, it flew in a lazy arc and Jennings *knew* she was dead.

Commander Grimm launched himself toward the grenade. Wielding his rifle like a club, he smacked the grenade, sending it flying back. He crashed into her, sending her sprawling behind the metal crate, leaving himself in the open.

Fire erupted from the explosive, sending a shockwave rolling through the compartment in a deafening roar. Jennings' watched in horror as her captain flew across the room to slam face-first into the bulkhead.

CHAPTER TEN

Lieutenant (SG) Kimiko Yuki itched to be on the boarding assignment instead of the con. Or maybe she just itched from the new skin growing on her back.

"Status, Mac?" she asked the comms assistant.

"Nothing on passive, ma'am," McCall said.

"Tefiti?" The PO from Ohana had one hand up next to his helmet, pushing in the external space-time detector to seal against his ear.

"Nothing, ma'am," he said.

If the skipper was wrong, then the worst thing they did was make everyone practice the drill. If he was right, then any second, a ship was going to come out from behind one of the many asteroids in the area and fire at them.

Red emergency lighting bathed the bridge, giving everyone a hard-edged shadow. They all wore their ELS suits, helmets, and all. If there was a battle she was taking no chances.

Yuki checked the mission clock: almost twenty minutes since she called battle stations. She drilled her fingers on the side of the chair, willing something—anything—to happen.

Resisting the urge to ask again or check on the department

heads, she pursed her lips together, clenching her jaw. Everyone knew their jobs, and they were ready.

"XO," Hössbacher said.

He leaned away from his console to look at her. "I'm picking up something from the station, a short burst—"

"CONTACT!" Tefiti yelled, "Three-one-five, mark one-eight-zero. Range, three-zero-five klicks. Designated Tango-zero-one."

"Chief—" The word barely left the XO's lips when the COB threw the *Interceptor* forward with a surge of gravitic acceleration.

A second later, alarms wailed as the computer detected weapons fire. Energy blazed on the electromagnetic spectrum, passing through the spot the ship had held a second before.

"Roll and return fire!" Yuki ordered. "Weapons free."

Excitement surged in her, but she held it in check as her training kicked in. A hundred drills replayed in her mind, and she went on automatic.

"Aye, weapons free," Lieutenant Fawkes replied as he flipped up the shield covering the fire control button.

As much as Yuki wanted to order full speed ahead, Suresh couldn't risk it. The dense asteroids floating in the area were too massive for the gravwake to brush aside. However, the ship wasn't a big, slow hunk of iron, but a nimble destroyer, and Chief-of-the-Boat Devi Suresh was the best coxswain in the fleet if she did say so herself. Which she did—often. Twenty-five years of experience let her move the ship with nary a quiver in her hand. Every twitch of the stick and nudge of the throttle were made with all the considerable skill she had.

Interceptor's gravcoil shed wake as she leaped forward at twenty-five Gs of acceleration. Barely a second later, the destroyer rolled on its roof and angled down. The sudden change in direction forced the crew to lean forward as gravity fought with itself.

Four turrets tracked as one. The moment their crosshairs lined up, Fawkes depressed the firing stud. At three hundred klicks and near-zero velocity, there was no need to lead the targets.

20mm tungsten-reinforced nano-steel rounds fired at ten thousand KPS. Each barrel recoiled into the turret, absorbing the force of the firing coil while loading another shot. Behind the barrel the now empty capacitors rolled, clicking fully charged ones in place while the old ones recharged.

The turrets were designed for close combat and torpedo defense. The cobbled-together ship emerging from the asteroid only three hundred klicks from the ship wasn't prepared for the hell unleashed upon them.

Two of the rounds burst through the cargo section punching fist sized holes through and through. Superheated hull fragments sprayed into six crew working on a portable fusion reactor. They burned alive, unable to scream as the superheated air cooked their insides.

The third round hit the bridge, vaporizing the captain and obliterating the control systems. That alone would have done the ship in, but the fourth round went for the heart, plunging into the artificial sun of the fusion reactor—a one-in-a-million hit, freeing vast amounts of energy from containment in an uncontrolled overload.

A small explosion rocked the ship, cracking it in half, consuming parts of the vessel in a ball of fury. A moment later, a second explosion, a hundred times the size of the first, vaporized the last of the ship and sent out a wall of radiation in a globe.

"Holy hell."

Yuki didn't know who said it, but she agreed. Even three

hundred kilometers away, the double explosion was a giant sphere of angry radiation. It was only the second time in her career she had witnessed the destruction of another ship and the first time she was responsible. Men and women, no matter the caliber of people they were, had died and she was the reason. Would it ever get easier? Would she want it to?

"Why were there two explosions? That ship wasn't big enough to have a second reactor?" Spacer McCall asked.

"Mac, get me a line to the Skipper. We'll worry about that ship's demise later," she said.

"Line open," Mac said.

"Skipper, we came under fire, but—" Yuki began.

"XO, Jennings. Grimm's down. We're under fire," Sergeant Jennings said.

Yuki's heart caught in her throat. The captain? Dead?

———

Jennings fired with one hand while she dragged Grimm's limp form to the metal crate he had inadvertently knocked her behind. He wasn't moving, and she didn't have time to check his vitals. The only thing she saw was the crack across the length of his faceplate.

She raised her MP-17 and blind fired over the crate.

"Owens, screamer," she said.

She didn't raise her voice; years of training taught her to stay calm in almost any situation. The screamer flew overhead, emitting a devastating sound at two hundred decibels, enough to clobber unprotected ears. She surged forward, feet pounding the deck and head down like a bulldozer, aiming for the next crate closer to their assailants.

Lights flashed as they fired a mix of gas-powered and laser weapons. Rounds pinged off her armor. Alarms wailed as the lasers heated her limbs. She dropped, sliding the last meter on her butt in a shower of sparks and ignoring the glowing red armor that absorbed the energy weapon's fire.

"Flash!" She leaped up as twelve million lumens burst to life, blinding the ambushers. They wore a mix of gear and as far as she could tell, were nothing more than ragtag mercenaries.

Ragtag except for the six million dollars worth of tracked combat drone powering up behind them.

"Owens. Combat drone. Evac the skipper," she said.

"On it."

Owens charged up the ladder into the hold.

Jennings leaned out from the side of the crate, firing her carbine on full auto. "Suppressing fire," she announced.

Owens slid into position next to the captain, grabbed the handle on the back of his ELS suit, and gave Jennings a thumbs up.

She toggled her selector switch to hyper-velocity. It wasn't suitable for long firefights, but she needed to cover the PFC Owens as he pulled Grimm to safety.

She sprang up from cover, held the firing stud down, and swept the barrel across the far end of the room like she was hosing down a fire. The mag emptied as the weapon flung five hundred silicate slivers downrange in the span of a few seconds.

Sparks flew from where they exploded against metal. Men and women screamed as the darts shredded exposed flesh. Her suit screamed an alarm when a bullet the size of her thumb struck her chest plate, knocking her down to land on her backside and bang her head against the deck.

Without missing a beat, she dropped the expended mag from her rifle and popped in a new one. The counter flashed green as the full magazine registered. Wailing and sobbing broke the silence. She glanced back at Owens, watching as he disappeared down the hatch, having already pushed the captain through.

"Grenade, proximity detonation, high-explosive," she said as she pulled the hand-thrown weapon from her side.

Using an HE grenade in close confines was a risk, but she was confident her armor could take it. On her HUD, the grenade flashed ready. She needed to disable the drone and as many Tangos as she could.

"Did you get her?" a man asked.

"I saw her go down. What about the others?" a woman replied.

"They have nowhere to go. By now, their ship's a cloud of expanding gas," the man said with savage glee.

Jennings didn't believe for one second that these two-bit space pirates got the drop on *Interceptor*. Not that it mattered. They were the enemy; she was a marine and marines killed the enemy.

She waited two more seconds for them to get comfortable, then tossed the grenade like she was aiming for a wastebasket across the room. The half-a-kilo of high-explosive flew up in a tall arc, then down out of sight.

"What's that—"

The explosion ripped through the room, flinging bodies away from the point of impact. The metal crate she used for cover blew apart, and a piece the size of her arm banged off her helmet, sending her spinning.

She rolled, overcoming her momentum and leaping to her feet with her rifle ready.

A man stumbled from behind the boxes. She fired, and his head fragmented, spraying blood against the bulkhead. Servos whined to life loud enough to alert her that the drone was active.

If anyone else was alive, they didn't move. The drone's "T"

shaped chassis carried two coilguns and a box of dumbfire missiles. Not something a sane person would use on a space station. Against the coilguns, she might as well be wearing tissue paper.

"Crap," she muttered as it opened fire.

———

Ensign Owusu advanced down the passageway, running as fast as he dared in the unknown quarters. PO Desper and her two medical ratings were right behind him. They'd taken off the moment they heard Jennings' call come over the radio.

"Right, Ensign," PO Desper said from behind him as he went to go left at the four-way.

"Thank you," he said.

Correcting his turn, he wheeled around the corner to come face to face with PFC Owens—who practically threw the captain's limp form at him.

"Get him out of here," Owens yelled.

Turning around, he charged back the way he'd come.

"You heard him," Desper said. Kneeling, she plugged her suit into the captain's.

Owusu was torn. If the marines were in trouble, he wanted to help. Duty and courage warred within him; duty won. He knelt and secured the grab handle on the CO's suit.

Weapon fire erupted with an ear-splitting whine. Lights flashed, and every ELS suit on the station instantly displayed a red danger sign on their HUD.

Hull breach.

Owusu froze. He wanted to duck and run at the same time. Faced with two conflicting choices, his brain went with option three—nothing.

"XO?" Ensign Hössbacher asked.

"Did you get through to them?" she asked.

"No ma'am, just what you heard, then a wall of electronic noise slammed down on us like a hammer. I thought it was the ship, but if it was..." he finished with a shrug.

There was no way for it to be still jamming them with the ship gone. They had come around a full circle, giving the lateral sensors a good long look at the wreckage of the enemy vessel while also making sure there weren't any other surprises waiting for them. She desperately wanted to recall the Corsair to send reinforcements, but if the landing party was in trouble, it was their only avenue of retreat.

"Then what?" she asked, stifling her irritation.

"I'm getting some weird readings from the station. It's like something inside is—"

He slammed his hand down on the comms button, yelling into the mic. "Charlie One-One, break-break-break! I say again, break-break-break!"

Boudreaux banged her hand down on the emergency departure, not waiting for confirmation. The light on her console turned green, and she jammed the thrusters forward, rocketing away from the station at fifteen Gs of acceleration. She grunted, breathing hard as she desperately fought to stay conscious.

Not a moment too soon.

Gamma-7 went from a football field-sized mining and refining station to a cloud of spinning fragments as her superstructure disintegrated with the men and women of the *Interceptor* still on board.

CHAPTER ELEVEN

Silently, almost reverently, the crew listened as debris bounced off the hull. Most were tiny fragments, but a few were large enough to hit with a thunk or scratch the ship as they rebounded off her armor. The steady ping reminded Yuki of the monsoons her homeworld experienced annually.

Interceptor crawled into position on thrusters, unable to use the gravcoil for risk of flinging one of their missing crewmates out into space, never to be found.

"We're here, ma'am," Suresh said from The Pit.

"Right, all stop," Yuki ordered.

"All stop," Suresh said.

She pulled the throttle to zero, giving the forward thrusters a slight tap to arrest their momentum. The numbers counted down until the ship was at rest relative to the system primary.

"Hössbacher, all hands," she said.

The comms officer threw a switch on his panel, nodding for her to begin.

"Now hear this. We're beginning search and rescue for the captain and the boarding party. All hands to their search stations. I want every eye, every ear, everyone combing space for our comrades. We're not going home without them. Get to it."

She wished she felt as confident as she sounded.

"Chief," she said after a moment. "What are their chances, do you think?"

She hoped the COB would comfort her, reassure her that the Navy's excellent survival tech would see them through.

"Ma'am, if anyone can pull through, it's the skipper," Suresh said.

Yuki felt a stab of pain in her heart. She would agree if he were merely overboard, but who could survive the station's disintegration?

————

Jacob opened his eyes and wondered why it was dark. No. Not dark, just....

"Oh crap," he muttered.

He was floating in space, he had no idea where he was. Not that he would know regardless. One didn't spacewalk using visual flight reckoning. More worrisome than his location, was the long crack vertically up the center of his faceplate.

"Distance to the ship?" he asked the computer.

Nothing.

His head ached, and his body felt like he'd tangled with a spider-bear and lost. He closed his eyes, trying to get his bearings. There was a grenade, and he had swatted it like an idiot. In retrospect, Jennings' armor probably would have protected her.

It just wasn't in him to do nothing.

Surely, though, a grenade wouldn't have destroyed the station? He tapped the buttons on his wrist. Nothing. If the suit were out of power, he'd never have woken up. But it had clearly taken damage in the blast since he had no HUD and the computer wasn't responding.

Reaching down hurt like hell, but he managed to reach his boot and feel for the emergency beacon. It should have activated the moment he hit hard vacuum. It pulsed under his fingers reassuring him that it was broadcasting.

"Hello? Anyone there?" It was a shot in the dark. No comms.

At least air wasn't leaking out of his faceplate. The ELS suits were good for twenty-four hours. He told himself that all he had to do was relax and wait for rescue. Yet no matter how hard he tried to convince himself, he knew it wasn't true. A million things could go wrong, and if any of them did, even a little bit— he was a dead man.

———

"Charlie-One-One, this is Bravo-Two-Five, copy?" Jennings said for the nineteenth time.

Her suit had no EW suite installed, and she couldn't tell if someone was jamming her or if *Interceptor* just wasn't out there. She hoped it was jamming. The thought of dying out in the black, with no one to ever know what happened to her, wasn't pleasant.

"Owens, you copy?" she said.

Jennings' current residence was a section of metal that made up the hallway she'd clung to when the drone had opened fire with its coilguns and missile barrage.

The panel hurled through space, flipping lazily like a tossed coin. Her suit's magnetic seal kept her clinging to it, and it would be pointless to let go. If nothing else it added to her signature.

"Ensign Owusu, you copy? Does anyone copy?" she said again.

It was time to stop. No one was listening. With any luck, *Interceptor* already had the captain back, and they were busy looking for everyone else.

Her suit was relatively unscathed, with some cosmetic damage but nothing significant. She could last twenty-four hours waiting for rescue. Not something she was overly fond of.

Waiting.

———

Chief Warrant Officer Vivienne Boudreaux nudged the Corsair ahead on thrusters alone, accelerating at a timid point-five Gs for ten seconds. As the clock ticked down to zero, she came to a full stop. Once motionless, her EW crew scanned the area. Chief Redfern and Spacer Beech were attached to the outside of the hull in gorilla suits, ready to rescue anyone they found.

Emergency beacons should have lit off like fireworks when the station fell apart, but something was interfering with their communications, jamming them with power the suit's built-in comms weren't able to pierce. Without comms or an active beacon, finding something as small as a suit was like looking for a needle in an expanding haystack. Every minute that ticked by the debris—and her crewmates—spread farther and farther away.

Corsairs were multi-role dropships, and search, and rescue was at the top of the list, hence the abundance of sensor systems. If they were close enough, the ship's multi-frequency radar, combined with the infrared sensors, could find a person floating in space.

If they were close enough.

PO Baxter and spacer first-class Nessie were glued to their consoles, looking for any signs of life. Any anomaly which could guide them to their shipmates.

The odds were against them, though, and she knew it. Boudreaux checked the mission clock, inwardly reminding herself who they were looking for. No one expected *Interceptor* to beat a *frigate,* and they had. The captain could buck the odds like no one's business. He could survive this.

"Anything," she said over the ship's internal comms.

"Chief, if I had anything, I'd shout for joy," PO Baxter said.

She knew he would; asking was her way of dealing with the anxiety. "Moving to sector three-seven-alpha," she said.

———

Jacob sighed with relief as his suit's HUD booted up. He'd taken an awful risk, fiddling with the computer built into the suit's forearm. However, at least an hour had passed since he'd awoken, and every minute he wasn't rescued he drifted farther from the ship. Dying in the vacuum of space wasn't how he wanted to go out.

In truth, he didn't want to go out at all. At least not until he got to see Nadia again. That thought made him smile mostly because he pictured Nadia's mischievous grin and soft brown skin.

"All right, Commander, all the more reason not to give up," he said.

He hit another button on the suit, and the limited attitude thrusters sprang to life. The suit's computer should have automatically stopped his spinning, but again, nothing worked the way it was supposed to.

Navy S&R doctrine called for spacers to talk to themselves while working through a problem. Jacob always thought it was silly, until now, when he found himself in that very situation. Hearing his voice went a long way to giving him hope.

He touched the thrusters, and the slow spin turned into a

gut-wrenching loop. Groaning, he hit the reverse but overcompensated, slamming to a halt then flipping back around the other way, almost costing him his lunch.

His vision dimmed from the Gs, and he struggled to put his hand back on the control. A touch of the button slowed him and another brought him to a halt.

"Okay, tap-tap, don't hold," he said.

He swallowed hard, keeping the vomit down. Jacob was years from his last weightless experience, and he wasn't terribly skilled at it to begin with.

He pressed his comm button. "This is *Interceptor*-Actual, does anyone read?"

A spike of energy appeared on his HUD drowning out his comms.

"Jamming. Great," he muttered.

Whatever was causing the interference was likely keeping the ship from picking up his beacon.

If he were being jammed, it had to have a source. If he could find the source, maybe he could take it out.

With a deft touch, he manipulated the thruster controls to spin him slowly. He watched the jamming signal on his HUD looking for any fluctuation in strength.

When it leaped up, he stopped. There was no way he was going to find the jamming with his MKI Eyeballs. He was going to have to rely on the computer.

All the stars, unfiltered by atmosphere, shone in the night like diamonds. An overwhelming weight pressed down on him as he took in the majesty of space.

"You can be poetic on your own time, Mister Grimm. Get to work," he said in his best imitation of his Academy drill instructors.

With a nudge, he pushed his suit in the direction of the spike. As he moved, the energy fluctuated, forcing him to alter course. Theoretically, if he followed the energy it would lead him to the jamming device.

Theoretically. He could just be flying himself off into deep space.

"Bravo-Two-Five, this is *Interceptor*-actual, do you read?" he said.

There was little chance anyone could pick up his broadcast, but if another suit were close enough... perhaps it would work.

"*Interceptor*, this is *Interceptor*-actual, do you read? I am trying to locate the source of the jamming. I'm on a heading of —" he pulled up the suit's navigation system— "Two-eight-zero mark zero-nine-zero... if my suit is to be believed."

Adjusting his course, he pushed forward, the EMI growing with each passing second. Lights flashed, alerting him to a problem. The ELS suits were designed for twenty-four hours of survivability but his available atmosphere had fallen to twelve hours?

"Crap."

According to his clock, only four had passed since they entered Gamma-7. Which meant the crack in his helmet was leaking air, and he only had four hours to find help, not twenty.

Though lost in space himself, he wouldn't give up trying to find the source of the jamming. If he found and neutralized it, the emergency beacons would work, and *Interceptor* would find him.

———

Jennings had given up on the radio a half hour before, deciding it was pointless for the time being. She may not have an EW suite installed, but she could tell there was interference. Otherwise, where was the ship?

"Give me an enemy to kill," she growled.

Sitting helpless wasn't her idea of a good time. At least in combat, she could take fate into her own hands. What could she do here? All her training told her to stay put, which absolutely conflicted with her instincts to explode into action and do *something*.

In this case, though, she knew her training was right. There was simply nothing for her to do. Training was about overcoming natural instincts to survive unnatural situations. In civilian life, her impulse to charge forward and attack her problems had served her well. In the marines, she followed her training—even if she hated every second of it.

The only saving grace to the situation was that she got the skipper to safety. Owens had enough time to get him back to the Corsair. Commander Grimm was probably sipping OJ in sickbay at that very moment.

Her radio kicked in, spitting static in her ear for a second.

"*Interceptor*, this is *Interceptor*-Actual, do you read?" the skipper's voice said, peppered with static.

She groaned. "*Interceptor*-Actual, this is Bravo-Two-Five, copy?"

The static vanished.

"Jennings?" Commander Grimm said.

"Aye, sir. Am I to assume you aren't on the ship?"

The line clicked with static several times.

"Define 'ship,'" he said.

She heard the mirth in his voice. One thing she had to give the captain—he was steadfast.

Jacob heaved a sigh of relief tinged with disappointment. Part of him had hoped everyone else had made it to safety. However, he was glad to have company. Not the most talkative company, but at least he wasn't alone.

Her signal grew stronger with each second allowing him to triangulate her position the same way he was tracking the jamming. She had to be close, though—otherwise, the suit's comms wouldn't have worked through the interference.

He filled her in on his current status, including the air leak, as he swiveled the suit, looking for her.

"Damn, sir. You don't do anything the easy way, do you?" she asked.

Jacob let out a short laugh. "That's an understatement, Allison. I seem to have an inherent ability to find the single most difficult path, then proceed to line it with obstacles."

Her signal was clean—she was close. His instruments were all he had until she was close enough to signal him visually.

"You sound clear, sir. You have to be within a hundred meters. I'll light off a flare."

He tapped the controls, putting himself into a slow spin. Stars shifted around him, and a second later, he saw the white light burning bright in the darkness.

The Navy used self-oxidizing potassium perchlorate magnesium sticks for emergencies, even in space. A bright blinking light could work, but a spacer could carry a hundred tiny flares or just a couple of lights. Since the flares worked fine and cost a tenth of what the lights cost, the Department of the Navy went with the low-cost option. For once resulting in a superior outcome.

The only downside to the flares was their lack of combustion time. In space, they only burned for three minutes. In atmosphere, they lasted an hour.

"I see it, Allison. One sec," he said.

Adjusting course, he lined up the suit with the shining light.

Once the computer told him he was on course, he tapped the forward thrust.

Ten meters out, he saw the rotating deck plate she clung to with her magnetic boots. He clenched his jaw as he got close enough to see the fist-sized dent in her breastplate.

"You wanna tell me what happened?" he asked.

"They had a combat drone, sir," she said by way of explanation.

Four meters out, he brought his suit to a relative stop.

"When you come back around, I want you to detach your boots and gently push off."

"Aye, sir," she said.

"Allison, *gently*."

She rotated out of view. White light flashed as the flare sputtered out, consuming the last of its oxidizer.

Her helmet appeared as the plate rotated up. Detaching from the metal, she leaped out toward him, floating across the distance.

She banged into him, sending them both into a spin. Magnetic clamps locked down, sticking them together. Once he knew she was locked on, he tapped the thrusters to stop their spin.

"You throw up in there?" he asked her.

"Being shorter has its perks, sir. I can take more Gs."

"Figures," he said. "I always tested right on the line of failure for G-force training. No one ever mentioned it might be my height."

He had her move around behind him and attach to his back like they were cuddling, with her arms wrapped around his chest to keep them as close together as possible.

"What's the plan, sir?" she asked.

"Normally, we sit tight. However, something's jamming the beacons. If we don't find it—"

"—*Interceptor* won't find us," she finished for him.

"You got it. I'm working on its position and backtracking the source. Hang on and try not to shift your weight while I fly us around."

"Roger, sir" she said.

He tapped the controls, aligning them back on the jamming source before pushing ahead.

"On your left," he said in his best mimic of a tour guide, "you will see stars."

She grunted, which he counted as a win.

CHAPTER TWELVE

Lieutenant Mark West couldn't decide between watching the mission clock or the comm's panel. He made himself dizzy trying to switch between the two every few seconds. Between desperately hoping for some sign of the captain, and knowing they were running out of time, he was working himself into a sweat.

The XO had sent an update to Captain Oberstein six hours earlier. Assuming fifteen minutes to compose a reply, they should receive an update any minute. He dreaded what it might say. No way was he abandoning the captain.

Interceptor held its station next to the dispersing remains of Gamma-7. On the main screen, a blinking green light showed the Corsair's location, along with the yellow helix of their course as they searched for the crew.

Mark glanced over at Spacer Gauge again. "Anything?"

He shook his head. "Sorry, sir. Nothing. I—"

Gauger turned, pushing a button on his panel. "Incoming transmission, sir. It's from *Corvus*."

Mark pulled the MFD up and hit the button to view the transmission. Captain Oberstein's face filled the screen. Mark hadn't ever met the man in person, but he had a fastidious look to him, with his perfectly groomed mustache and hair. While that kind of attention to detail could be a boon, something about the man rubbed him the wrong way. Perhaps it was his exact way of speaking or his short conversation habit, so different from the skipper.

"Lieutenant Yuki, I've received your transmission. I'm sorry to hear about your crew overboard and the loss of the mining station. That is unfortunate. Use your discretion on search and rescue. Unfortunately, with the distances involved, we can't get anyone else out there to assist you in time to do any good. Please update me at the twenty-four-hour mark. Captain Oberstein out."

Mark tapped the acknowledge button on the screen before forwarding the message to the XO's NavPad. She was taking a thirty-minute power nap, and he didn't want to disturb her with anything non-urgent.

———

Boudreaux stifled a yawn as she pushed the Corsair to the next way-point. Baxter climbed the ladder leading to the cockpit and handed her up a hot cup of coffee.

"*Merci*, PO. You're the best," she said.

Her exhaustion brought out her French language even more, and she had to fight to stay in English. On her home world of Monde Vert, every child was taught French first as their native language and the official language of the colony. Even though standard, with its mishmash of languages was the official language of the Alliance.

"I aim to please, Chief," he said as he descended.

They were going on seven hours of continuous operations, and even the most seasoned pilots had to take breaks. Even the

Corsairs couldn't operate indefinitely without resupply. Sooner rather than later, she would have to pull off the search to head back to the ship and undergo several hours of maintenance.

Her leg cramped up, forcing her to massage the muscle until it stopped. She glanced out of the cockpit and bit back her complaint when she saw Chief Redfern in his gorilla suit. He had it far worse than she.

"Chief, I got something on the scope. Check out zero-three-zero mark one-one-five," Baxter said from below.

She punched the numbers in on the console. A path lit up on the HUD, showing her how to maneuver the ship on that approach.

"Range?" she asked over the comms.

"Seven point three klicks."

It was far—almost at the edge of the search pattern. She tapped the stick with her forefinger, deciding if they should continue on the path or deviate. If she deviated, it would mess up the search. Yet if she didn't check it out, by the time she came back, it would be too late to find whatever the scope had detected.

"Don't be wrong," she muttered.

With the flick of her wrist, the Corsair's attitude thrusters kicked in, and the ship rolled to one side before she pushed the throttle forward.

"Sending transponder ping," Baxter said. Even with the jamming, they would be able to pick up the signal at their current range.

RF energy leaped out in a focused beam along the same line as the radar. However, instead of bouncing off any material, it activated transmitters. The range fell, klick by klick, with no response. Boudreaux's brow furrowed as she eased back on the throttle until they were moving at only ten meters per second.

"Boudreaux, is that you?" PO Desper said.

The relief in her voice was palpable, and Vivienne Boudreaux almost cried when she heard her shipmate.

"We got 'em!" she yelled out.

———

Yuki stood in the boat bay as the Corsair rose into the room, its folded tail stopping a half meter from contact with the deck above.

Docking only took thirty seconds, but Kimiko felt like it was forever. The bay doors swung up beneath and sealed shut. Amber lights turned white, and the hatch on the side of the Corsair finally hummed open.

Yuki leaped forward, assisting PO Baxter as he helped Desper ease Owusu out of the ship. She suppressed a gasp at the sight of his badly burned suit.

"Desper, where's the skipper?" Yuki asked.

Desper reached up and pulled her helmet off and shook her head negative, her sweat-soaked hair matted to her forehead. "We were separated, ma'am. Jennings and the captain are still out there."

Yuki checked the clock on her NavPad; they still had time and—

"Ma'am," Owens said from above Desper. "The captain dove in front of a grenade, and... well... he was pretty banged up and—"

"And what, PFC?" she demanded.

Owens looked down, dropping his voice to a whisper as if he were afraid to speak.

"His faceplate had a crack, ma'am."

"Secure that negativity, PFC. If there's one thing I know about Commander Grimm, he doesn't know how to fail," she said. "And neither do we. Roger?"

"Roger that, ma'am."

Yuki backed out of the way, letting Dr. Krisper and the medical team rush Owusu to sickbay. She watched the young officer go and silently begged her ancestors to look after the shy ensign.

"Boudreaux, fifteen for food and the head, then back out there. Got it?" Yuki yelled as she backed away from the ship.

"Fifteen, ma'am? I'll do it in ten," Boudreaux said.

"Good woman," the exec said as she turned and marched for the hatch.

She wished she could be out there searching herself, but that wasn't her role. What she needed was something to do. The entire crew needed something to do—other than waiting around for news. They still couldn't move the ship, just in case, but... maybe they could do something.

She depressed the comm stud outside the boat bay with her fist. "Bridge, XO. Have Astro run a trace on the rail arm's direction when we arrived. I want to know what's out there and how it connects to the system."

"Aye, ma'am," PO Tefiti said. "I'll get with PO Oliv, and we'll look into it."

So far, Tefiti had fit in well. She couldn't figure out why he had come to *Interceptor,* but she was darn glad to have him.

The fact that hardly anyone had transferred off in the time since their last action in Zuck wasn't lost on her or the crew. It was highly unusual to stay with a ship as significantly damaged as *Interceptor* was. Usually, the ratings and PO's would be dispersed to the fleet. Even some of the officers would have gone.

However for *Interceptor,* that wasn't the case. A handful of people, including Lieutenant Bonds and Gunny Hicks, had moved to other ships, but the rest had been put to work helping the yard repair her.

When the captain returned, she'd already spent a month in-system, acting as a ferry for the incoming marines. Then Captain Oberstein arrived and immediately sent them on a three-month long patrol of the system without even so much as a single face-to-face meeting.

She wanted to give the station CO the benefit of the doubt. Maybe he didn't realize snubbing Grimm was impolite and undermined Oberstein's authority in the eyes of the *Interceptor's* crew?

Or maybe he didn't care. He was hard to get a read on since she hadn't met him in person or even had a lag-free conversation with him. All his messages and orders were perfectly reasonable.

Most people were right up until they tossed you out the airlock.

———

"Jennings, we have a problem," Jacob said.

The blinking warning in his suit was insistent about his rapidly depleting atmosphere. He only had a few minutes left, and they still hadn't found the source of the jamming.

"Go ahead, sir," she said.

"I only have about fifteen minutes left."

He resisted the urge to turn around and face her. It would accomplish nothing—it wasn't like he could see her face through her space armor.

"Once I run out, I want you to keep on this heading. I'm pretty sure whatever is causing the jamming is in this direction. We've moved at ten meters per second for the last three hours, so it has to be close. Push off my body, and then you keep going."

He found himself remarkably calm, contemplating his

looming asphyxiation. Death by falling asleep didn't sound so bad. As long as he could give Jennings a fighting chance to find the jamming, then it would be okay. With the moment upon him, though, he regretted not having the opportunity to tell the crew how proud he was of their actions and conduct since he took command.

Warning lights flashed as the atmosphere line detached from his helmet.

"Jennings, what the hell? I'm not dead yet," he said.

"If the captain would please stop talking nonsense and hold still," Jennings said as she fiddled with his helmet.

"What are you—" the seal re-engaged, and air hissed into his suit.

The timer blinked rapidly as it changed, going up to one hour. "Sergeant, re-attach your hose immediately. You have sixteen hours of atmo left. That's plenty of time for *Interceptor* to find you."

She didn't reply.

"Corporal Jennings, re-attach your hose. That is a direct order."

He felt her move to his left. Turning, he looked at her armored head. She tapped the side of her helmet, indicating her comms were down. Then she gave him a thumbs up, followed by her pointing at her wrist.

"We're going to talk about this when we get back to the ship," he muttered.

Once she was back in position, he used the micro-burst thrusters to put them back on course. He bit his tongue, not wanting to waste the time she'd given him by talking. If he kept his breathing even and didn't exert himself, he might be able to stretch a couple of extra minutes out of the situation. It bothered him, though, having her sacrifice for him.

"Sir, I think I know what's causing the jamming," she said.

"Oh, so your comm is working again?"

"For now," she said. "I think the combat drone that destroyed the station is up ahead."

"You see it now?"

If it was a military-grade combat drone and not some piece of mining equipment cobbled together and armed, then it was a legitimate threat. Powered by fusion batteries like the Mudcat, it could run forever and was only limited by its available ammunition.

"Got it in one, Skipper. It shines like a flare on thermal," she said.

He depressed the thrusters for a few seconds, slowing them down to zero relative to the drone.

"What the plan, Alison?"

"You're not going to like it," she said.

She shifted around on his back, and the barrel of her weapon appeared.

"Can you hurt it with your MP-17?"

"Negative, sir. We don't load APDS when boarding stations. However, I have one grenade left, which should do it," she said.

"What's the play?" he asked.

If they were on a ship, he would be in charge, but they weren't and he wasn't novice enough to think he knew better in this particular situation.

"We get close enough for me to see it I throw the grenade and boom goes the fusion," she said.

"There's something to be said for the direct approach." Jacob nudged the thruster power up. "Are you sure you can hit it?"

"No sir. I don't see we have many options though," she replied.

The initial acceleration elicited a grunt from him. Once he was up to speed, he eased off the throttle and let the suit coast.

Indicators on his HUD shot up as the source of the jamming approached.

"We're almost there. Can you see it?" he asked.

"Aye, sir. Fifteen seconds, then throw it in full throttle reverse."

He grunted in reply. A flash of light glinted off metal in the distance. Too far for him to see clearly. Warning lights flared, alerting him to danger. More light flashed. "

It's firing at us!"

"That's what they do, sir," she said without missing a beat.

At least the drone's primary function was ground combat. As they closed, Jacob could make out the hulking tracked monster spinning slowly through space. Every time it faced them, the barrels of its coilguns would fire.

Jennings counted down from three. When she hit one, she threw the grenade as hard as she could, throwing her weight backward and sending them into a spin. Jacob pushed the thrusters to full, rocketing them away as fast as the suit would allow. She grunted over the comms, and they were suddenly spinning in a completely different direction, spiraling out from the drone.

"Jennings?" he asked.

Nothing.

"Allison?" Her hands slipped off, and he gripped her leg as she started to pull free.

There was no flash, no sound. One moment jamming pervaded the radio waves; the next it did not. He spun around, trying to assess her injuries when he saw it.

Jacob keyed his mic. "Mayday-mayday-mayday. This is *Interceptor*-Actual. Please respond."

CHAPTER THIRTEEN

On the desk in her spartan room, Nadia's NavPad swiftly scanned every name of every arrival on Kremlin Station for the last year. While it searched, she fought.

Nadia struck the bag with all her might, reveling in the pain blossoming on her flesh hand as she punched the coarse fabric over and over until her knuckles bled.

She stopped, leaning her forehead against the bag, sweat dripping down her brown skin. She stayed that way for a long moment; eyes squeezed shut as if she could undo time itself and make everything go back the way it was. Her burden, temporarily relieved by the weariness she felt, shifted and slithered, threatening her from a distance.

Nadia pushed off the bag, breathing hard as she reached for a drink. A loud squeal of alarm snapped her head around. Fatigue forgotten, she darted over to the NavPad as its holographic display resolved a single name.

She double-checked the settings to make sure it was correct. Her intel had borne out; some morons in the Guild thought bird names would be the way to go for their operatives, but not just any bird names, seabirds from old Earth.

A "Mr. Albatross" was one thing, but a "Mr. Pelican" arriving the same week was a little much especially since Pelican was still on the station.

She had them. Of course, knowing who they were and figuring out what they were up to were two different things.

CHAPTER FOURTEEN

"Status," Jacob asked, waving Private Cole to silence as he walked onto the bridge.

"Good to have you back, sir," Lieutenant Yuki said. "We've recovered every one. Ensign Owusu is in post-op with some serious bruises—he took a beating from the debris. Doctor Krisper is still operating on Jennings."

"Still?"

It took the Corsair a half hour to return to the ship and that was four hours ago. Nanites in the suit had sealed up the gaping hole in her torso where a round had torn right through. That stabilized her, but they needed nanite fuel and a surgeon's guidance to do more.

Once they were back on the ship, he'd wolfed down some chow, slept for three hours (Doctor Krisper had threatened him with drugs if he didn't), and changed his clothes. In the meantime, he'd ordered *Interceptor* to hold position. If possible, he wanted to find out who attacked them and why—neither of which they could do if they headed back to Zuckabar.

"His last report was twenty minutes ago, sir. I don't think

bothering him for updates will produce a more desirable result," Yuki said.

She was right, he admitted to himself. As much as Jacob wanted to march down there and demand a status update, he needed to let the man do his job. The hands-off approach to leadership was frustrating, especially when it involved things he desperately wanted to turn out his way. He couldn't control the outcome through micromanagement.

"You're right. Let's focus on the task at hand."

He looked over at the astrogation station where Petty Officer Tefiti held the gravity detecting headphones over one ear while monitoring the sensor returns.

As it was needed to find the missing crew of the *Interceptor*, they hadn't been able to send the Corsair to investigate the debris cloud from the destroyed ship. Now, the remains had long since dispersed.

"Tefiti? When we arrived, the railgun was pointed away from Zuckabar. Did we record the bearing before it was destroyed?" Jacob asked.

"Let me double-check the sensor logs... Aye, sir. Two-eight-five mark zero-two one. Almost one-eighty from where it should be pointing according to the data."

If Captain Oberstein had sent two destroyers, one could maintain position while the other investigated the direction the arm was pointed. Instead, they were in it alone. He drummed his fingers on the back of his chair in annoyance.

He reminded himself to have good thoughts about his commanding officer. It was too easy to start blaming the man for every wrong. Worse, if he slipped around the crew, it would set a bad precedent. The Navy was the Navy; he didn't get to choose his COs any more than a spacer's apprentice.

"Tefiti, plot me a course along that bearing. Let's go see what's out there," he said.

"Aye, sir. Plotting course on two-eight-five," Tefiti replied.

"What are you thinking, Skipper?" Yuki asked.

She'd waited patiently, rigidly posed beside his chair, her hands behind her back.

"I'm thinking two of my crew were hurt, and I want to know why. Set for Condition Yankee, XO."

"Aye, sir, Condition Yankee," she replied. She hit the all-hands button. "All hands, this is the XO. Set Condition Yankee. Prepare for underway. Set Condition Yankee."

Her voice echoed throughout the ship, and Jacob could almost hear a collective sigh of relief from the crew. Sitting around for hours in their ELS suits was no fun. The Navy recommended no more than twelve hours in the skin-hugging survival suits while on duty. And for every hour of wear, there were ten minutes of maintenance to perform.

"Bridge, engine room, Lieutenant Gonzales."

"Go ahead, Lieutenant," Jacob said.

"Can you come down to engineering, sir? There's something I need to show you ASAP," he said.

His tone was even, but Jacob sensed an undercurrent of tension. Maybe fear? If his chief engineer was concerned, then he was concerned.

"On my way." He headed for the hatch. "XO, you have the con."

"Aye, sir, XO has the con," Yuki replied.

———

Yuki sighed in disappointment. Fresh-dressed replacements would show up any moment, allowing everyone on the bridge fifteen minutes to return to their cabin and switch out of their ELS suits. With the captain gone, though, she was in charge, and she would have to wait for one of the other officers to return before she could get out of her own.

"Don't worry, XO, I'll hurry," Mark West said as he bustled out.

"Thanks, Mark. You read my mind."

"No one likes to be in the skinnies any longer than they have to, myself included," Mark said.

———

Jacob slid down the ladder, hitting deck five with a thump. From the ladder he saw straight into main engineering and through the large hatch into the fusion room.

He'd heard rumors of a new kind of reactor—half the size but twice the power—were on the drawing board. Not that he'd ever see such a thing in *Interceptor*. Forty-year-old destroyers from obsolete classes didn't receive such upgrades. Hell, he was lucky they even repaired her, considering the damage she'd taken in their battle with the pirate frigate.

He couldn't help but notice the scar on the bulkhead where the hatch had blown off and severed Commander Rod Beckett's feet—along with his navy career. Rod was too old to remain in the Navy with such a severe injury. However, it had worked out —Beckett was the new Governor of Kremlin, in charge of the station and the drydock.

He certainly missed the man's wisdom. Beckett had spent more time in the Navy than Jacob by a factor of three. The only other person on board who had a similar time in service was the COB. While he valued her input, there was always the noncom-officer relationship.

Chief Redfern stood next to the fusion reactor control console, holding a toolbox and a NavPad for diagnostics. Lieutenant Gonzales was half-buried in the console's guts. Jacob admired an officer who was willing to get his hands dirty.

"Chief Redfern," Jacob said as he came to a stop next to the broad-shouldered man from Blackrock.

"Skipper. The Lieutenant has discovered a problem he would like to tell you about, sir," Chief Redfern said.

Redfern's tone elicited some concern from Jacob. He'd only met his Lieutenant Gonzales one-on-one when he first came aboard, and Jacob felt a stab of guilt. He should have sought the man out and spent more time getting to know him beyond just briefings with the officers.

Gonzales was a late arrival, assigned to *Interceptor* just before Jacob returned. The man's file was impeccable, with clean FitReps from all his past COs. The only blip was the young lieutenant's continued request for a ground station. With two degrees from the University of Alexandria—one in electrical engineering and another in nuclear physics—he certainly had the knowledge to be of use at R&D. However, he was a ninety-day wonder of sorts. A recent graduate of OCS and newly promoted to lieutenant JG, he'd spent less time in the Navy than virtually any officer with his rank. If he were to succeed in the navy, he would need a lot more experience.

Jacob liked to keep an eye on newbie officers. They tended to be know-it-alls, explaining "how things were" to others with more experience and actual knowledge. He trusted Redfern to keep the kid in line and go to the XO if there was a problem. From the pained expression on the chief's face, though, Jacob was getting the feeling he was about to have one of those moments.

"Lieutenant?" Jacob said with a cough to clear his throat

"One second, sir. I've almost got it," he replied from within the console.

"Watch the discharge as the board comes out, sir," Chief Redfern said.

"Thank you, Chief Petty Officer, I'm fully aware of the—" light flashed followed by sparks leaping out of the console.

Lieutenant Gonzalez jumped, bumped his head on the console and yelped as he pulled out, his hand clasping a fried and smoking optical board.

"Do you know what this is, sir?" Gonzales asked as he stood up. Not even acknowledging the chief's warning was correct.

The engineer had a wiry build and brown skin and the look of someone who desperately wanted to appear older than they were—which was probably why he had a thin regulation mustache. Jacob imagined Gonzales as an angry Academy instructor demanding to know why the cadet hadn't completed his paperwork.

"I'm afraid not," Jacob replied.

Like all officers, Jacob had spent time as an engineer, but it was more of the "commanding the engineering department" variety than actually fixing things.

"It's the feedback board for fusion control. Or it was. It's fried beyond repair at this point," Gonzalez said, tossing the board into a pile container full of spare parts.

"Do we have replacements?" Jacob asked.

"Oh, we do, sir, but we have to return to Kremlin Station immediately," Gonzales said.

A silent groan ran through Jacob. He intended to take the ship after whoever had attacked them. However, if the engineer November-Golfed the reactor, they would have to make for port ASAP.

"Walk me through this, Enzo?" Jacob asked, using the lieutenant's first name.

"I prefer formal rank, sir," Gonzales said.

"And when you're the captain, your preference will matter. Now explain?" Jacob asked.

If they were going to scrub the mission, he needed a rock-solid understanding of why. The lieutenant pulled up short.

"I see... Yes, sir. It's really quite simple," he said as he pulled his NavPad from the side pocket of his uniform pant. "Here is the flow control for the fuel line feeding fusion-one."

He pointed to the schematic showing the intricate pattern of flowing energy around the ship. It looked to Jacob like veins carrying blood. He was familiar with the schematic—it was one of the many screens he had access to on the bridge. However, he was willing to give the young man leeway to explain the problem his way.

"This board, and others like it, control the amount of fuel sent to the reactor. Her sister boards control the power regulation, distributing power to the supercapacitors and other systems as needed."

Jacob glance at Redfern again, hoping for some help. The chief, though, smiled like a patient father and motioned for the captain to wait for it.

"Are you saying the reactor can't control the amount of fuel entering the furnace?"

It was a huge problem. Runaway reactors weren't typical, but they could happen, especially if the ship took a hit. He'd read the report of what happened to the ship *Interceptor* had taken out while he was floating in space. They had hit the reactor of the pirate vessel, and it exploded like a bomb.

His mind raced. He would have to belay the current orders, send out a distress signal and—

"Well, no. Not yet, sir. But if one board is bad, then there might be more. We have to replace them all," Gonzales said.

He blinked, staring at his captain, waiting for the order.

"Wait," Jacob said. "How many primary and secondary boards are there?" he asked.

Redfern winked discreetly, and Jacob felt the tension start to flow out of him. He appreciated Redfern's reassurance, but the cortisol punch the lieutenant's words had shot through him wouldn't be erased with a wink.

"Three hundred primary, a hundred and fifty secondary, and seventy-five redundant ones. We need to replace every single one. I ran through the logs, and all of the boards are past their replace by date. We need the yard to replace a few thousand meters worth of optical cable. Most likely we'll have to cut through the hull to get at the reactor and—"

Jacob held up his hand to stop the engineer.

"Enzo, have you ever served on a destroyer before?" Jacob knew the answer, but he wanted the young man to realize the problem.

"Well, no, sir. As I'm sure you're aware, this is my first shipboard assignment."

"What might you surmise about the age of this ship?"

Turning, Jacob ran one finger over the top of the console, pretending to inspect the cleanliness.

"I don't follow, sir."

Some officers would be resistant to this kind of education. Many young officers, *Ensign Jacob T. Grimm* included, thought they knew more than their superiors. Jacob had no doubt the young man was a world-class engineer in his field of expertise, but this was a destroyer—not a shiny new heavy cruiser or the fleet flagship. There was a "way things were done" in the fleet, and then there was "The Book." The Book might say to replace a certain piece by a certain date, but what worked on paper rarely worked in practice. The Book was great in the yard with infinite supplies.

"Enzo, *Interceptor* is forty years old. Her last hardware refit was five years ago. If we RTB every time a wire needs replacing, we'll never leave port. I understand the problem you're facing. You need to do what a doctor with too many patients does. Triage. Sit down with Chief Redfern and go over the critical components, figure out what needs to be patched, replaced, or overhauled, and then do your best with what you have onboard."

Lieutenant Gonzales glanced at Chief Redfern then back to Jacob. "Sir, I'm telling you, we need to return to port and do a complete overhaul. I understand no captain likes to hear his ship won't function but—"

"Lieutenant Gonzales, listen to me carefully," Jacob said as he headed toward the fore hatch. "Get it done."

Ready or not, they were going after whoever did this. The lieutenant would just have to find a way to keep his ship running.

CHAPTER FIFTEEN

The railgun from Gamma-7 fired packages at thirty percent of the speed of light. Ninety-thousand KPS was several times *Interceptor*'s top speed. The intended recipient could be anywhere from a few hundred thousand klicks away to a few billion.

Interceptor charged through space at five thousand KPS, pulling her towed array. With the kilometer long cable deployed it tripled their active and passive sensor envelope while allowing them to see directly aft.

Two days into their current course and they had yet to see anything, though. Gamma-7 was already on the outskirts of the system and they were adding millions of klicks by the hour. They were looking for a needle in a haystack, and he knew it. It was a fusion-powered needle, though, and if they just got close enough, there would be no way to hide it. In a military ship, those sorts of emissions could be concealed or disguised. Civilian equipment wasn't run that way—a fusion reactor out here would light up like a sun on the infrared. All they had to do was keep their own reactor output low and make sure they had the thermal scanners manned at all times.

Jacob took a sip of his orange drink when Sergeant Jennings hobbled into the mess hall, followed closely by PO Desper. Jacob waved at her. She stiffened noticeably, trying to turn away, but it was too late for her to pretend she hadn't seen him.

Afternoon watch was ramping up, and the mess hall had gone from packed to empty a few minutes before. Spacer First Class Mendez hurried through the mess, cleaning the dining room in preparation for the second lunch that would roll through soon.

Jacob's NavPad beeped at him for attention. Glancing down at it, he hit the "accept" button to read Captain Oberstein's response to the update: "*Keep me posted.*"

Just three words. Jacob couldn't figure out if he were happy the CO wasn't meddling with his work or upset he wasn't more interested. Either way it didn't matter. Good or bad the man was giving him room to operate. He picked at the remains of his fries and something that could be best described as chicken nuggets. Though he seriously doubted they had ever seen the insides of a chicken.

At least frying potatoes was nearly foolproof, and delicious. The limited food choices came down to their resupply schedule. Every cook aboard ship knew what their crew liked and didn't like, and they tried to save the less popular food for the end of the tour in the hopes they would return to port early and not have to use it.

Jacob was pushing their provisions to the very limit. Technically, they had five days left, but he could stretch that to ten by busting out the S-rats. Survival rations for emergencies. They tasted like ash, but they would keep a spacer alive.

He glanced up and noticed Jennings heading across the room away from him. There were no other marines in the mess and he was mildly offended she didn't want to sit with him. Though, to be honest, who wanted to sit with their CO during a meal? During his weekly lunches on Bethesda Station, Jacob had eaten like an automaton, never wanting to spill anything or make an odd sound.

He decided to let it go. She was an excellent marine, and if she wanted to be by herself, then so be it.

Just as he planned to go over and say "hi" before heading to his cabin, the intercom crackled to life.

"Captain to the bridge. Captain to the bridge," Yuki's voice boomed over the loudspeaker.

He leaped up, heading for the hatch, stopping only to drop his tray in the recycler. Mess was two levels below O-deck, and it would only take him a minute to climb the ladders.

When Jacob arrived at the bridge, there was excited commotion around the astrogator's console.

"Captain on the bridge," PFC Owens said as Jacob passed the threshold.

Lieutenant Yuki waved him over from where she stood next to PO Tefiti. The rest of the bridge didn't acknowledge him, nor did he want them to. They had enough work to do; they didn't need to stand every time he came up. Only the watch officer need acknowledge him.

"What have you got, Kim?" he asked.

She pointed at Tefiti's screen. "No thermals, Skipper, but Tefiti picked up something just at the edge of passive. It might be nothing, or it might be something."

Whatever it was, Jacob realized, was way the hell out there. "PO, what are you thinking?"

"Not sure, sir," Tefiti said. "The reading is faint. I think we're getting a reflected return off someone else's short-range collusion radar. Their signal is bouncing off a stray rock toward us."

Jacob leaned over to examine the scope. He saw something, but it could just be the reflection of random EMR bouncing around out here on the edge of space... where nothing was supposed to be, which meant Tefiti was likely right.

"Something's better than nothing. Good job, PO," Jacob said and clasped the man on his shoulder.

"The question is, Skip, what do you want to do about it?" Kim asked.

"Range to contact?" Jacob asked.

"If it's actually there, and not a reflection from something farther out, one-point-five million klicks, sir," PO Tefiti said.

Jacob smiled as the man covered his butt with his explanation, he just didn't realize Jacob wasn't the kind of CO to come down on his crew for errors. Either way, though, he had a decision to make.

"I have the con," he told the XO as he moved to the center seat.

"Skipper has the con," she said. "I'm going to head down to engineering and see if I can be of assistance," Kim said.

Jacob gave her the go-ahead as he pondered the question. Could he risk it? What if it was just an asteroid or a comet?

He switched the MFD to navigation mode and examined their current location. There wasn't anything near them on the charts, and any asteroid big enough to reflect radar at over a million klicks would be mapped as a prime target for mining.

Bottom line, they were running out of time. If it turned out to be nothing, then they would have to RTB anyway.

"Tefiti, plot the course to the helm. We're going to check it out," Jacob said, making his decision.

"Aye, sir. Plotted. Helm, come to zero-five-one mark zero-zero-four. Throttle to four-zero-zero gravities," Tefiti said.

"Mark, rig for silent running," Jacob ordered.

"Aye, sir. Silent running." Mark leaned into his console. "Now hear this: All hands, rig for silent running. All hands, rig for silent running." The order echoed throughout the entire ship. Hatches were sealed, computers turned off, anything and everything that generated unnecessary heat was shutdown. Not even hot water would be available until after they resumed normal duty.

Jacob leaned back and let his bridge function, focusing on his screen. He was gambling a lot on the minuscule signal they'd received—on top of the initial gamble that there was anything at all out this way, to begin with. It was entirely possible the railgun arm had malfunctioned, or a thousand other reasons for how it ended up pointing away from Zuckabar Central. Jacob had only his gut telling him that something wasn't adding up.

"Course laid in, sir," PO Collins said.

"Execute," Jacob said.

———

Jacob swiveled his chair back and forth a few centimeters to each side as the distance counted down. It was a bad habit and showed how nervous he felt. The moment he realized what he was doing he planted his feet on the deck.

Interceptor ran silent as she decelerated in her oblique approach to the unknown object to avoid hard radar returns. So far, only weak and sporadic radar pulses appeared. Whatever the object was, it barely showed up on passive sensors and didn't seem to have any active emissions at all. If they hadn't deployed the towed array for a larger detection area, they would have never found it.

"Twenty seconds to zero, Skipper," Chief Suresh said.

As usual, whenever he manned the bridge, she found a way to be in The Pit. Not that he minded. She was the best coxswain in the Navy as far as he was concerned.

Yuki entered the bridge, stopping next to him. She still wore dirty work coveralls since she came directly from engineering.

"Let's see what we can see," Jacob said.

"Helm, turn the ship five degrees to port," Ensign Owusu ordered.

"Aye, five degrees port," Chief Suresh replied.

Jacob admired his crew. They had worked hard, trained hard, and the fruits of their labor were paying off in skill and efficiency. In the words of one of his academy instructors, "They jelled."

"Passive is building a picture now, Skipper. Main viewer," Owusu said.

The main screen blinked, and empty space was replaced by a pentagram shaped superstructure with no navigation lights. It was dark enough that they barely made it out, and parts of the image were missing—obvious parts.

"Is radar malfunctioning?" Jacob asked.

"Negative, sir. All systems are nominal," PO Tefiti replied.

"Stealth coating?" Yuki asked.

"Possibly. It's not a ship, whatever it is. I don't see why anyone would want to coat a platform. If the goal is to hide, then they couldn't use magnetic shields to protect from radiation. One solid gamma-ray burst from the pulsar, and they're toast."

Everyone on the bridge knew exactly what he meant. Solar radiation would kill a crew faster than a railgun and in a much more unpleasant way. It was rare, but it happened.

Something about the stealth coating tickled his memory. He pushed the comm button.

"Engine room, bridge," Jacob said.

"Engine room, Lieutenant Gonzales."

"Tap into the viewer, Gonzales, and tell me what you think we're seeing."

"Aye, sir. One moment." There was a brief pause as the engineer examined what the bridge saw. "It looks like a station, sir."

Jacob glanced up at Yuki, who matched his grin.

"Lieutenant, I know it's a station. What I'm asking is why we can't see all of it?"

"Well, I don't know, sir," Gonzales said.

"Save us from uptight lieutenants," Yuki muttered for her captain's ears only.

Jacob took a deep breath and let it out slowly. He resisted the urge to show his annoyance and kept his mannerisms carefully neutral.

"Enzo, there's no wrong answer here. What could cause parts of the station to be invisible on passive, with no return at all?"

"I... well...." The man clearly wasn't used to brainstorming or guessing.

Jacob could understand his unwillingness to go out on a limb. However, he needed something to go on, and his chief engineer was the only man aboard who could make an educated guess.

Finally Gonzales spoke, "When I was at university, we worked with special nano paints that could absorb EM waves. Everything from light to thermal. However, as good as it was, it wouldn't work on anything other than stable platforms in special conditions. Even then, it had to be refreshed regularly. Maybe this is something like that? I can look into it if you like, sir."

"Good man. Get back to me when you have something. Bridge out," Jacob said.

It had taken a moment, but he felt like the engineer ultimately understood what Jacob was trying to accomplish. Working on a ship was vastly different from a ground station. Crew had to stay flexible and keep an open mind. With the way the navy had treated its people, though, Jacob understood why an officer would be unwilling to stick his neck out.

"Okay, people. If Enzo is right and it requires regular maintenance, let's play dead and see if anyone comes calling," he said.

Lying doggo watching a target wasn't much fun, but it beat a shooting match, and everyone aboard knew it.

CHAPTER SIXTEEN

A ship could only run silent for a relatively short period, depending on the heat generated. Lying doggo, with her engines off and minimal internal activity, best case, the Hellcat class destroyer could achieve fourteen hours with zero thermal radiation. All other emissions were completely controllable; it was the heat they couldn't block forever. Heat sinks would eventually reach their tolerance, and then the ship's temperature would increase. With all the radiators retracted, there was nowhere else for the thermal radiation to go but to the heat sink.

If *Interceptor* were brand new, maybe she could make the fourteen-hour mark, but she was forty years old. Nothing in her worked the way it had when she was fresh off the assembly line.

"Skipper, we're approaching tolerance," Yuki informed him.

As she spoke, the mission clocked ticked over to ten hours. Jacob dragged his arm across his brow, clearing the accumulating sweat. They had passed thirty degrees Celsius a few minutes earlier. It was approaching critical. If they used any of the main systems, though, like the gravcoil or weapons, they would need to load a new heat sink first lest they overheat the ship to disastrous impact.

"Astro, anything?" Jacob asked.

Ensign Owusu manned the radar/lidar console next to main gravitics where PO Tefiti sat hunched over listening for the tell-tale sound of an approaching gravwake.

"Nothing yet, sir. We still don't have a complete picture of the station or any idea what she's for," Owusu said.

The mystery of Gamma-7 had led them to the stealth station. It was the only clue they had in their search for the thirty-five-missing Alliance citizens.

"Maybe thirty more minutes, skipper. Then we're going to have to eject," Yuki whispered next to him.

"I know," he said. "I won't push the heat sink too far. It would be nice to catch them with their pants down, though."

The dim light on the bridge made it easy to see the illuminated consoles and controls, but it also left him feeling tense, as if they were hiding and one breath would reveal their location. The rest of the crew felt it too. They whispered and moved carefully as if their silence would somehow help the ship.

As far as their passive sensors could tell, there was nothing living on the station. It either didn't have a fusion reactor, or it wasn't on. Which meant there was no one aboard. If it was related to Gamma-7, then someone had to come check it out soon. If for no other reason than to find out what happened to the mercenaries. At least, he hoped.

"Contact," Tefiti whispered, "designation Uniform-One-Alpha, bearing one-niner-zero, mark zero-four-four."

"That doesn't make any sense," Owusu said. The officer checked the readings on his station.

"I know, sir," PO Tefiti responded to Ensign Owusu. "Regardless, there they are."

Jacob pulled the astrogation screen over to his MFD, high-lighting the sensors to see what exactly Tefiti was looking at. Sure enough, an unknown contact had appeared at the ten million klick mark, the spot where they could reliably detect a strong gravwake. With light-lag, the image they were looking at was a minute old, but the plot would update to real-time as it drew closer.

"Are they heading for the station?" Jacob asked softly.

"I need a minute for a good reading on heading and speed," PO Tefiti replied.

Jacob let the man work, taking a moment to go over any options that popped in his head. They were so far out of the system that he had a hard time imagining what a legitimate ship could be doing so far out. Not to mention coming from a heading, which was essentially deep space.

"Strange," Jacob muttered.

"I've got a solid bearing, sir," Tefiti announced. "Their heading is right for the station. Velocity, one-one-five-zero KPS, and decelerating. Power levels match a civilian grade gravcoil. Best guess, it's a light freighter."

Jacob played with the math in his head. If he fired up the *Interceptor* immediately, he could run them down... probably. Not knowing anything about the ship wouldn't leave a margin for error. The odds of them having a higher acceleration than *Interceptor* were low, especially if they were a civilian ship. The Navy could afford to spend a hundred million on a gravcoil. Civilians were more about expenses, safety, and a return on investment.

Every second they waited the unknown contact drew closer into *Interceptor's* pursuit envelope. Once they were deep enough in, they couldn't escape no matter how fast they were for a civilian.

"XO, best guess on a zero intercept?"

"Another half an hour tops. It'll be close, but by the time they see us, they won't be able to escape," Yuki said.

It was a race, the kind Jacob hated. Could the heatsink last another half hour before systems failure? As if the ship itself was aware of his thoughts, the internal temperature clicked over to thirty-one degrees Celsius.

This ship could be their one chance to find the missing miners and figure out what happened.

"Astro, assume current course and speed and plot us an intercept in three-zero minutes," Jacob said.

"Aye, sir. Intercept in three-zero minutes," Owusu repeated.

Jacob leaned back, the easy part was over. He hated waiting, but no amount of wishing would change the situation. Patience and dedication would win the day.

Twenty-five minutes later, as the temp increased to thirty-five degrees, the unknown ship was clearly inside their engagement bubble. Spacer Mendez ran a continuous line of cold drinks to the bridge, and sweat dripped off every forehead. They had even broken out the towels to help keep the perspiration out of their eyes.

The time had come, though, and the math didn't lie. The only way the contact could outrun *Interceptor* was with a military-grade gravcoil.

"That took forever," Jacob muttered.

"I'll head down to DCS, sir," Yuki informed him.

"Astro, intercept course. Ops, drop the sink and cool the can," Jacob ordered.

"Aye sir, dropping the heat sink and cooling the can," West said.

Jacob triggers his comms for ship wide. "All hands, now hear this. It's about to get considerably cooler. Watch your stations for adverse impact. Report any problems immediately."

Ensign Owusu responded immediately, as he had updated

their intercept course as soon as the captain made it clear he intended to engage.

"Helm, five degrees up-bubble. Come starboard two-one-one, accelerate to three-zero-zero gravities."

"Aye, aye. Five degrees up-bubble, starboard two-one-one at three-zero-zero gravities," Suresh responded.

Besides dropping the heat sink, the fastest way to cool the ship was to cycle the air. Specially designed micro airlocks bled hot air into space, taking all the heat stored with it. A light breeze blew through the ship, rustling hair and cooling the ship by ten degrees within seconds—enough to send a shiver down Jacob's spine as the sweat instantly cooled.

"Helm, execute," Jacob said.

"Aye, aye, Skipper," Suresh said.

She smiled with glee, pushing the throttle forward. *Interceptor* vibrated as power flooded into the gravcoil, sending the destroyer surging ahead. Within seconds they were traveling at hundreds of KPS.

"They'll see us in three... two... one," Owusu said.

Sure enough, the plot updated and showed the unknown contact turning away from *Interceptor*. On Jacob's screen, a yellow oval showed *Interceptor*'s current overtake envelope and the unknown contact was well within.

"Acceleration?" Jacob asked.

"Two hundred and twenty-five gravities, sir," Owusu said. "It's unusually high for a civilian ship, but not impossible."

Jacob leaned on his elbow, rubbing his jaw as he considered the problem. Even with their unusual acceleration they couldn't hope to escape.

Once the contact realized the situation and heaved to and cut their engines, it would still take over thirty minutes to intercept. He was tempted to launch the Corsair with the marines to board the station. Jacob didn't like the idea of separating his forces or leaving the marines without backup. A million things could go wrong, and ultimately, the ship with the answers they wanted was running away from them.

He tapped the MFD, bringing up Yuki in DCS. "What do you think, XO?" he asked.

"We could blow by them, let them know how ridiculously slow they are. Once they see us at four-eighty Gs, any smart skipper would heave-to," she said.

Jacob nodded. Although a smart skipper wouldn't be involved in something illegal or run when a Navy ship approached.

"Roy?" Jacob asked Ensign Hössbacher at comms. "Give them the line."

"Aye, aye, sir," Roy said with more than a bit of glee.

The line consisted of an order to stand to and prepare to be boarded. Communications wasn't a hotbed of activity when a ship was deployed far from port. In combat, comms controlled the EW systems in conjunction with the weapons officer. However, those situations were few and far between. The young man took joy in extending his captain's order.

"Unknown ship, this is Alliance destroyer USS *Interceptor,* heave-to and prepare to be boarded," Hössbacher announced over the radio.

The distance between the two ships was vast for a planet but minuscule for lightspeed. It took less than eight seconds for the message to reach the fleeing ship. Jacob watched the clock tick away on the corner of his MFD. A small asterisk noted the time the message was sent. Once three times as many seconds had passed, he assumed they had received the message and chosen to ignore his orders.

"COB, take us to four-hundred gravities if you please," he ordered.

"Aye, sir. Four hundred gravities," Chief Suresh replied.

"New time to intercept, two-zero minutes, sir," Owusu said.

"Very good," Jacob replied.

He was interested in how the contact responded. *Interceptor* was accelerating at almost twice the tango's rate—and it was still far shy of the destroyer's maximum. Even if the freighter managed to pull more Gs, they wouldn't outrun a Hellcat for long. She might be old, but she was the fastest destroyer in the fleet.

"No change in bearing and—" Tefiti stopped, holding up his hand, cocking his head to one side. "Sir, I'm getting an anomalous gravity reading, I uh, I don't know what to make of it. I've never heard anything like this before."

"Owusu?" Jacob asked.

"I'm running it through the computer, sir. Nothing. The frequency of the disruption doesn't match anything on record." The ensign frowned.

Between the two of them, they had more knowledge and experience with gravity waves than any one on board. For them to hear something new was worrisome in its own right.

Gravcoils emitted waves behind a ship. When those gravity waves passed through detection apparatus, they disrupted them at a specific frequency, resulting in the sound a ship's crew could pick up on their headphones. Computers assisted in determining the source and type of disruption, but a spacer with a good ear could detect variances the computer couldn't reliably distinguish.

"Could it be a malfunctioning gravcoil?" Jacob asked.

The PO shook his head. "I don't think so, sir. Besides, if their coil were malfunctioning, they wouldn't be running."

He had a good point. The unknown contact accelerated at a constant two-twenty-five.

"Roy, battle stations."

"Aye, sir." Ensign Hössbacher pressed the button on his

console, and red flashing lights lit up the bridge. "All hands, set condition Zulu, battle stations. This is not a drill. I say again, battle stations. All department heads signal readiness."

Ten minutes to weapons range, and another five after that if they wanted to come relative to the ship.

More than enough time for his crew to don their ELS suits.

"Mark," he said to the ops officer. "You have the con."

Jacob leaped up and headed for his cabin. It would only take him a few minutes to change.

"Aye, sir, I have the con," Lieutenant West said from his station.

Since he still had to perform the logistic duties of ops, he didn't move to the center seat.

Jacob stepped into his cabin a few seconds later, shedding his clothes, glad to be out of the sweat-soaked garments. He longed for a shower, but there was no time.

"Captain, XO." Yuki's voice pipped in over the cabin speakers.

"Go for Captain."

"Sir, something's fishy about this, and I don't just mean the anomalous gravity readings. I'm running the ship's power curve through the computer, and I can't find anything that matches it, civilian or military. The kind of readings I'm seeing, I would expect a warship. The fusion reactor output is on the same spectrum as a heavy cruiser, but we have solid radar returns. We know for sure that she is forty meters longer than us, but overall less tonnage."

That was odd. He could think of no logical reason to put a giant fusion reactor on a small ship. Even *Interceptor*'s MK III reactor was more than enough energy. Power generation was never the problem; moving and storing it was. The gravcoil's limiting factor was mass, which encouraged designers to put the smallest reactor possible on a ship. Putting a larger reactor on a smaller ship meant the gravcoil had to scale up proportionally. For what? If the contact could accelerate faster, they would have already.

"Good work, Kim. Keep looking into it and let me know," he said.

"Aye, sir."

———

Director Parsons frowned. When he was given the mission to Zuckabar, the organizing committee had assured him it was planned out to the last detail. He let out a low growl at whoever had missed the "detail" chasing their stern. An Alliance destroyer had no business this far out on the rim, and it couldn't be a coincidence. Someone, somewhere, had screwed up, and it was up to him to fix it.

He ran his fingers over his sleek command chair arm. *Aethia* was too valuable to risk losing, and he absolutely couldn't let it fall into enemy hands.

When he saw the ship on the plot, he turned and ran, which was a mistake he realized. He should have checked the computer first. If he'd waited a few minutes, he could have drawn the ship in and destroyed her. In his haste, not only did he tip them off, but he also led them in the direction of his exit vector.

"Helm, time to exit?" he asked.

"Eight minutes, sir. However, protocol—"

He snarled. "I damn well know what protocol is."

The whelps upper management sent him were infuriating. He had the most advanced ship they could build, and they staffed him with inexperienced, snot-nosed brats.

If they couldn't outrun the Navy ship and they couldn't use the exit, then they had to fight. If he engaged, though, the

Alliance vessel had to be destroyed with all hands and no traces.

"Range?" he asked.

"One-point-two million kilometers," the man at sensors said.

Parsons nodded. Standard Alliance Navy engagements began at one million klicks. If the destroyer intended to fire on *Aethia*, they would open with torpedoes first. However, once they were within two light-seconds the battle was over.

Aethia needed to survive that long. She was armed with state-of-the-art ECM and torpedo defense, but only one weapon. One was enough, though.

"Power the weapon," he ordered.

———

"One million klicks, Skipper," Lieutenant Carter Fawkes announced from the weapons console.

The crew wore their ELS suits and were ready for action. Jacob pulled his helmet on, securing the seal. The rest of the bridge crew took his cue and followed suit.

"Comms, put me on," Jacob said.

"Aye, sir," Hössbacher said. "You're on, sir."

Jacob tapped the screen, centering himself in the image for a moment. "Unknown ship, this is Captain Jacob T. Grimm of the USS *Interceptor*. You are in Alliance territory. I order you to heave-to and prepare to be boarded. We will fire on you if you do not comply. Do not make me destroy your ship."

Hössbacher nodded. "On the chip, sir."

"Send it," Jacob ordered.

At a million klicks, they only needed three seconds and change for the message to arrive.

———

"…Destroy your ship."

Parsons frowned as the message played. If it were him, he would've just opened fire, but the Alliance Navy had their protocols and couldn't fire on a ship that wasn't firing on them, which he could use against them.

"Helm, full stop," Parsons said.

"Sir?"

"You heard me." Parsons swiveled his chair over to his support officer. "Turn on the Alliance IFF."

"On," came the reply.

Parson cleared his throat, shook his hands out, and then let a relieved smile overtake his face. He pushed the comms button on his seat.

"*Interceptor*, phew. Are we glad to see you. When our computers picked up the power curve, we thought you were pirates!"

———

"With whom am I speaking?" Jacob asked.

"Orval Parson, master of *Aethia*."

The man on the screen appeared to be in his late thirties. With his clean jawline and perfect teeth, he reminded Jacob of a salesman, groomed to perfection.

"Mr. Parsons, when we went active, our transponder clearly showed us as Navy. Why did you take so long to obey?" Jacob asked.

"You can't be too careful operating out this far on the rim of Zuckabar. You Navy types never come out here. I'm running on a shoestring budget—I can't afford any damage, let alone losing the ship and crew."

It all seemed reasonable. A small ship running cargo for a far-off station, but what was the station doing out here to begin with? What cargo were they running?

"Understood. I'm afraid I will have to board and inspect you, sir. Please refrain from using your engines or adjusting your attitude," Jacob said.

"Of course. Happy to have some company, to be honest. Can't wait to see you," Parsons said.

"I look forward to meeting you in person, Mr. Parsons," Jacob said and killed the line.

He leaned back, the familiar tingling feeling in his stomach telling him something wasn't quite right.

"XO?" Jacob asked.

"Skipper?" Yuki replied from the small section of his MFD dedicated to his first officer.

"Anything seem odd about that?" he asked.

She chortled. "Everything. I mean, he's not wrong. I would've run too, but why are they out here, and who are they working for? And why are they so happy to have us delay them while we search their ship?"

Jacob smiled, glad his astute XO picked up on the same questions he had. For whatever reason, NavPer wasn't transferring his people to other ships, and they should be. When they eventually decided to get their collective heads out of their aft section, his people would make a positive impact on the Navy. They were professionals and damn good at their jobs.

"Stand down from battle stations?" Lieutenant West asked.

Jacob shook his head. "Maintain readiness. Something about this feels off."

"Aye, sir," West replied.

"Owusu, what's out there?" Jacob waved his hand in the direction they were traveling.

"Sir?" Ensign Owusu asked.

"Where was he going?" Jacob asked.

Owusu shrugged. "I have no idea, sir. Gamma-7 is the only registered station this far out, and the second base is not registered. As far as the charts are concerned, we could go in this direction forever and not see anything. There isn't even another star system for well over the starlane limit."

There were pressing questions Jacob wanted to ask Mr. Parsons, and as soon as he was aboard, he would.

Closing on an unknown ship was the most dangerous part of any encounter. If an enemy were going to do something, they would do it soon. Jacob hoped his crew's general level of readiness would allow them to respond before they were destroyed.

Despite knowing *Interceptor* was a warship, designed to close on the enemy and tear them apart with her turrets, something nagged hard at Jacob. A gut feeling to pull back. There were too many inconsistencies.

"Sir?" Tefiti said. "Those grav readings? They're increasing."

Jacob hit the button on his con, transferring the readings to his MFD.

"Something about this looks familiar," he muttered.

He pushed the comms button and sent the readings to the chief engineer's desk as he spoke.

"Engine room, Bridge. Lieutenant Gonzales, would you look at your screen please?"

"Aye, sir. What am I looking at?" Gonzales asked over the comm.

"That's what I wanted you to tell me. What's does it look like to you? I don't need an exact definition, but something about the power curve looks familiar."

"Sir," Owusu interrupted. "Their maneuvering thrusters just fired. They're pivoting on their axis."

"I don't know, sir," Gonzales said. "Without some context, it could be any number of weapons."

"What?" Jacob said, leaning down to the MFD to speak. "It's a weapon?"

"Obviously, but I don't know what—"

"Helm," Jacob yelled. "Hard over!"

———

Parson's watched the distance tick down from green to yellow to red.

"Helm, bring us about, slowly. We don't want to give away the game," he said.

"Yes, sir. Swiveling," helm replied.

The ship swung around to line up the weapon with the oncoming Navy destroyer.

He glanced up, watching the targeting vector line up perfectly. The nature of the weapon required the ship to point directly at her target, not unlike an Alliance ship's main guns. Except the Guild Defense Force's weapon was something the Alliance had never seen before—and wouldn't see again since he was about to obliterate that troublesome destroyer. He would be the first captain in the Guild to down an enemy ship.

"Full power," the operator informed him.

Parson waited a few more seconds, ensuring there was no chance the range would be a problem.

"Fire," he ordered.

———

Chief Suresh didn't question the order, she acted.

"Hard over," she said as she rolled the ship to port.

Gravity shifted, and their stomachs' sank before—

Interceptor lurched as if struck by an asteroid. Alarms wailed, and harnesses clamped down like vices, holding the seated bridge crew in place and protecting them from the sudden and violent gravity disruption.

The ship shook like a can in a paint mixer. Even with the harness, Jacob had to force his eyes closed to keep from losing his lunch. Others were not quite so lucky as he heard retching from ops.

Then it was over, and *Interceptor*'s lights flickered and died. Emergency lighting—self-contained battery-powered units—clicked on all over the ship. Smoke filled the bridge from fried circuits and overloaded panels.

Jacob shook his head, trying to clear his vision and restore his wherewithal. His stomach rolled as dread seeped into him.

Whatever had hit them was unlike anything he'd ever heard of before—and it was immensely powerful. He feared they were readying for a second shot.

"What?" He coughed, sending pain lancing through his ribs. "The hell was that?"

With no power flowing to it, his MFD sat dark. He tapped his NavPad and connected his comms to Yuki down in DCS.

"Damage Control Station, XO Yuki," she said in a hoarse voice.

"Captain here. What's the situation?" he asked.

"One sec."

She devolved into a coughing fit and cut the line. After a few seconds, she returned.

"Sorry, sir. Damage reports are rolling in from the starboard side, along the keel. We've got hull breaches from frame seven through forty on deck six. I don't even know what this reading is, sir, but the gravcoil is down, along with gravity in the fore-deck. I'm dispatching repair crews now. As soon as I know, you'll know."

"Roger that. Get to it."

He cut the line and switched to engineering as he eyed the

weapons panel. Fawkes sat dazed, holding his head, trying to refocus. Jacob knew the feeling.

"Carter, you okay?" he asked.

"Aye, sir. Just, uh, trying to get it together," Fawkes said.

Jacob's depressed the com button. "Engineering, bridge."

"Engineering," came Gonzales' slurred response.

"We need power to the bridge asap," Jacob said.

"Aye, sir, I'm on it," Gonzales said.

"Good man," Jacob replied. He pressed the emergency release for his harness, stumbling forward to kneel next to The Pit. "Chief, any ideas?" he asked.

Even Suresh, who he was sure had seen her fair share of strange, shook her head.

"I have no idea, Skipper. I can keep us moving with thrusters, but nothing else," she said.

"Roger that. Try to keep us moving in a lateral direction. With the gravcoil down, at least we're harder to spot."

"Aye, sir, lateral thrusters," she confirmed.

Jacob pushed himself up and stumbled his way to astrogation. Lights blinked on the panels, and fans hummed as they kicked on, clearing the smoke.

"Good job, Gonzales," Jacob said.

He patted Owusu on the shoulder. "Lay it on me, Ensign. What can you see?"

Owusu rebooted the radar; the screen in front of him flared to life and formed a picture of the space around them.

"Not much, sir. Whatever hit us took out radar one and two, along with our forward gravity sensors," Ensign Owusu said, his voice shaky from the hit.

"Call the ball, Owusu. Get us so we can see the freighter," Jacob ordered.

"Aye, sir. I have the ball. Helm, roll starboard, eight degrees. Change heading to one-three-five mark zero."

By presenting the port side to their target, they could use the undamaged radar/lidar arrays, as well as the other gravitic sensors, to "see" their aggressor.

"Tefiti?" Jacob asked the PO.

"Sir, I'm okay, but with the forward array damaged, our gravity sensors are going to be hampered," he said.

Jacob nodded. "Understood. Do your best."

"Aye, sir."

Once he had visited each station and made sure everyone on the bridge was uninjured, he returned to the con and tried his MFD. It had power but still no display.

"Damn," he muttered.

They were still alive, though, which meant *Aethia* either couldn't fire a second time, or she couldn't see them.

CHAPTER SEVENTEEN

Parsons shouted at his crew. "What do you mean, you can't find them? They were six-hundred thousand klicks away. We had a solid bead. Ships don't just disappear!"

Nothing had exploded. That was the problem. And they had to confirm there were no survivors—they couldn't just guess. It was too important to leave anything to chance.

"Sir, there's no distress signal, and I'm not picking up anything on gravitics. They're just not there," his astrogator said.

"That's not good enough, Stefan. We can't return to Omega Base and tell them we 'think' the Alliance Navy ship was destroyed. Helm, reverse course. If their ship was wrecked, the debris would continue on right at us, and we should see it in a few minutes. If not, we find the hulk, and we hit it again."

"Yes, sir," Stefan said.

———

Thirty minutes of back breaking work later and the *Interceptor* wasn't even close to full operation. Yuki stood beside the skipper, her helmeted head touching his. After engineering restored power and they were sure no one was stranded without a helmet on, he ordered everyone to seal their suits and then drained the can. Repairs with no atmosphere were much less complicated.

"We got lucky, sir. We lost the forward computer node, six berths in the crew quarters, and the rec room, but they were all unoccupied during the alert."

Yuki held out her NavPad with a blueprint of the ship with the damage highlighted. The loss of the forward computer node would hurt the ship's ability to track and identify targets. Not to mention the loss of two forward radar/lidar stations and the gravity detectors.

Jacob shook his head. "Lucky" was an understatement. A hit like that just a few meters up would have killed everyone in sickbay. The whole reason sickbay and the crew quarters were there was that the Prow gravwake was strongest around those areas, meaning a shot was far more likely to deflect around it. Also, the armor was thickest there because it was where the gravcoil connected to the hull. Statistically, it was the second safest place on the ship.

As they consulted, more lights flickered on around the bridge.

"Hooray," Suresh said with a deadpan. "I can see again."

The Pit's controls were active, and the hum of the gravcoil vibrated through the deck.

"Weapons are back," Fawkes said.

"Astro as well," Owusu added.

"It lives," Jacob said with a grin.

"Contact, two-one-zero-zero klicks bearing one-eight-three mark two-five-one," Tefiti said.

"Confirmed grav wake, Uniform-One-Alpha. It's the same ship. They're practically on top of us, sir."

For them to be that close, they would have had to decelerate. Maybe they thought they could help, but Jacob didn't buy it. Whatever had hit them wasn't an asteroid or other accident. He knew that in his gut. They had turned and fired on his ship. "With what?" was the question.

A question he might never know the answer to. *Interceptor* had gotten lucky once, but she would not survive a second hit. He could not allow them to fire again.

"Weapons, lock on with the turrets. Suresh, keep us on their flank, whatever that weapon is, they apparently have to aim in line with the ship," he said.

"Aye, sir," Fawkes replied. "Turrets two and three, swivel zero-nine degrees."

"Accelerating," Suresh said.

"Owusu, do they see us yet?"

A moment of doubt surged through Jacob. What if they had hit a natural phenomenon? The Alliance had nothing capable of disrupting a gravcoil and causing as much damage as they had taken—at least not without leaving some trace of where it came from. It wasn't a directed energy weapon; the damage was kinetic. If he destroyed their ship without giving them a chance to surrender, then he would be in front of a board of inquiry, and that would be the end of his command.

Grudgingly, he admitted, at least to himself, he had to give them another chance. "Comms, open a channel," he said.

"Sir?" Ensign Hössbacher said with an edge of disbelief.

"Skipper. Jacob," Yuki said from next to him, "if we open a channel...."

She didn't have to finish, he knew the risks.

"If I'm right, Kim, he has to turn the ship to fire. I think whatever caused the anomalous gravity reading was their weapon. If he so much as twitches, we fire. Understood?"

"Aye, sir." She turned to Fawkes. "Weapons free. If they turn four degrees, you fire, Carter. Got it? Don't wait for my order. Four degrees."

"Aye, aye, ma'am. Fire at four degrees, copy," Fawkes said as he turned to his panel and watched the readings with hawkish intensity.

"Roy," Jacob said, nodding at Ensign Hössbacher. "Put me through."

"Aye, aye, sir. Channel open," the young man said with a gulp.

It was a risk, but the evidence all pointed to it being an acceptable one. If the bogie had fired on *Interceptor*, they had done so only after pointing the ship at them. If it hadn't been their weapon, then there was no problem.

"*Aethia*, this is Commander Jacob T. Grimm. Do not alter course or bearing. If your ship so much as vibrates, we will obliterate you."

———

Parsons swore. He couldn't believe the stupid destroyer had survived a hit that would take out a battleship. They had a solid lock when they fired. There was no possibility they missed.

"Can we fire again?" he asked.

"Yes, but we have to turn."

"Are you stupid? Of course, we have to aim the weapon. Helm, prepare to execute a hard turn. I want the line-up locked into the computer. As soon as we have a location, turn, and fire. Don't hesitate."

"Yes, sir," his helmsman said.

———

"*Interceptor*, you're okay? When you went off our screens, we feared the worst," Parson's voice crackled over the speaker.

Jacob wished he could see the man's face and judge him, but his screens were still dark.

"*Aethia*, do not move. Do not engage your weapons. Shut your engines down immediately," Jacob said. "We have a solid lock on your power readings. You have five seconds to comply."

Jacob glanced over at Owusu, who held his hand up, ready to signal when the reading changed.

———

Parsons couldn't let them board *Aethia*, and if he shut off power, he couldn't stop them.

"We have a location, sir, and a lock."

"Do it," he said.

———

"They're turning," Carter yelled.

He did as he was ordered, flipping the safety cover off the switch and smashing the red button. Both starboard side turrets fired, the barrels surging back and slamming another round in place, then firing again.

20mm rounds sliced through space at ten thousand kilometers per second. The first volley struck *Aethia* just as the second volley fired. Their beam was in full view, providing *Interceptor*'s turret teams with a large silhouette. *Aethia* wasn't huge, barely twenty-five percent larger than *Interceptor*, but at such a range it was a chip shot.

Turret two had fired a millisecond before three, her round

hitting first, smashing through the stern just above *Aethia*'s mess hall. Tungsten-reinforced nano-steel blasted through the chairs, tables, and people, right into the supply room opposite, then out the other side.

Turret three's projectile struck midship. Rounds designed to penetrate military armor punched through *Aethia*'s civilian hull like a pencil through wet paper. Seventeen crew died instantly as the explosive power of the round superheated the passageways like a miniature sun before sucking everyone behind it out the other side.

Aethia heaved, her turn interrupted, and the pause proved fatal. Had they kept turning, the next two rounds would have missed, but when turret two caused an explosive decompression, the ship hiccupped. Two more rounds blasted through the ship as a third volley fired from *Interceptor*.

They needn't have bothered with the third volley. Turret two's second-round burned through *Aethia* at an angle. Halfway through the ship, it struck the fusion control stations and obliterated all twelve members of her engineering crew.

Without the computer controlling the fusion, the reactor overwhelmed its containments, eating the ship from within until only melted scraps of hull remained. The reactor floated away, burning bright for a few more seconds before its fuel was spent, and it vanished in the darkness.

Jacob balled his fist and slammed it down on his armrest. "Damn fine shooting, Fawkes."

"Aye, sir. Thank you, sir," Fawkes replied.

Jacob detected a sense of remorse from the young man. "It was us or them, Carter," he said softly.

"I... I know, sir, but..." he shook his head.

"Astro, what do you have?" Jacob asked, changing the subject.

Owusu hunched over his controls, going over the readings. "It's weird, sir."

Jacob smiled. "Is that a technical definition?"

"No, sir. Sorry, sir. It's just, the reactor was five times more powerful than they needed. It simply wasn't required to operate that ship."

It gave credence to Jacob's theory that they had some kind of new weapon.

"Any sign of survivors?" he asked.

"No boats launched, sir. It happened too fast," Owusu said.

Jacob leaned back. They had to figure out where *Aethia* was heading, but *Interceptor* was lamed, a broken ship. There were hours of work ahead before that could happen.

CHAPTER EIGHTEEN

Nadia followed the dark-haired man through the mass of people. Years of training allowed her to slide through the congestion without drawing attention.

The large crowd of tourists and workers on lunch weren't her problem; the location was. Why was her target visiting the museum of Kremlin Station? For the last ten minutes, he had stood in front of the onion-shaped building, looking up at the outside display.

Her glasses shifted, showing her the aerial view from the micro drone hovering above. It had a laser lock on her target and would follow him wherever it could.

No one approached him, he wasn't transmitting anything, and he didn't *do* anything but look up at the display. After another ten minutes, he turned around, taking in the governmental buildings near the museum. A moment later, he joined the crowd and headed toward the nearest air-taxi station.

If he followed the same pattern he had the last three times, his next move would be to return to his hotel in the main district. Normally she would follow him, watching whom he spoke to and interacted with, making sure he returned home.

Something about the situation made her gut tighten. While the Guild had made a mistake in their cover IDs, she didn't want to assume they were idiots. That would be the path to a miscalculation that could cost her everything.

But why was he on the station? Why visit the outside of the museum and not even go inside? Her target was still in the taxi heading away. There would never be a perfect time. She leaped up and headed for the building.

Inside, the climate-controlled atmosphere sucked the moisture from her skin and raised goosebumps all over her exposed flesh. The station's temperature stayed at a balmy twenty-two, but inside the museum it was kept intentionally colder. Much like the hardy people who colonized Zuckabar, the museum was filled with practical exhibits interspersed with larger-than-life statues of their national heroes.

Nadia appreciated the record of their accomplishments. As an agent, knowing the history of a people proved invaluable. From their earliest days facing the dangers of the pulsar to the installation of modern anti-asteroid support weapons, all of it was there to read. She could have spent hours learning it all.

She reminded herself that her target hadn't entered the place even once since she started observing him. Nadia stopped at the last exhibit on the first floor, an architectural concept of the original station. Hard as it was to believe, the early pioneers had planned on making the station six times as large, capable of sustaining the population of an entire planet on its walls. Upstairs, she walked around the large display room, examining random objects: a wrench, a spacesuit, and a pre-grav booster engine. Nothing registered, nothing clicked. Whatever the spy was doing, she decided, it wasn't inside the museum.

She walked across to the balcony facing the row of governmental buildings. Immigration, drydock, Space-Traffic Control. Nothing stood out. Any one of them could be a target, but without knowing the Guild's endgame, it was impossible to guess.

————

Albatross dodged to the side as the Caliphate crew swarmed past him. So far, their mission was going exactly as he and his handlers had hoped. The Caliph Navy jumped at the chance to use the Guild's stealth ship for a daring mission that would bring the Alliance to their knees and secure the wormhole for the Guild.

If only he could personally accept the surrender of General Remington on Zuckabar Central. That honor would go to someone else, however. Assuming there was anyone left alive on the planet to surrender.

With an errant thought, he accessed the nanite computer map in his brain, and the timeline for the mission in Zuckabar popped up to his field of view. While it was nearly impossible to plan missions to run concurrently, there were workarounds. The Outrider group should have completed stage one of their plan. By the time they had completed the final stage, there wouldn't be an Alliance left to undo the Guild's conquest of Zuckabar.

Captain Istam appeared from a side passage, giving a friendly smile and wave. It was hard not to like the slightly overweight man. With his barrel chest and full beard, he had a fatherly appearance.

"Mr. Albatross, would you care to join my officers and me for dinner? We toast the coming success."

Albatross didn't believe in superstition, but he didn't want to make a mistake because he thought they had already won. Still, one drink wouldn't hurt.

"It would be my pleasure," he replied.

CHAPTER NINETEEN

Jacob rapped his knuckles on the conference table to start the meeting.

"Come to order," he said.

Things had heated up somewhat since the destruction of the *Aethia* two days before. Work crews had managed to seal up the hull with temporary plating, but there were still problems to fix, and time was a factor.

Lieutenant Yuki and the other officers were elbow-to-elbow in their chairs, the lone exception being Bosun Sandivol, the only NCO who routinely sat in on meetings. As he was the logistics and supply coordinator for the entire boat, he needed the heads-up on the command crew's decisions. They would eventually be trickled down to him in some form anyway; he might as well get it from the shark's mouth.

Once everyone was silent, Jacob signaled Lieutenant Yuki to start. She looked around the table, taking a moment to meet each officer's eye. Yuki's youthful appearance, partly because of her strong Asian genetics and partly because she was barely thirty years old, left her looking out of place in charge, but the hard set to her eyes left no doubt who was running the meeting.

"Mark, talk to us about ops?" she asked.

Lieutenant (JG) Mark West had the sandy brown hair and tanned skin often associated with natives of New Austin. With many bodies crowded into the small room, even with the broken hatch open, it was warm, and Mark cradled his black watch cap in his hands.

"Ma'am, all personnel have returned to duty. We're a hundred percent in that respect, but...."

Jacob frowned. "What happened?"

"Well, sir," Mark turned to him. "When the ship took the hit, we lost the starboard storage and about half the remaining fresh food, plus all the emergency rations."

He finished with a nervous glance around the table as if he expected people to blame him. A ripple of concern washed over the room. It would take *Interceptor* at least three days to return to Kremlin Station. When they left port, they carried two weeks of food. They'd already spent six days out—which would leave them with just enough supplies if they turned around and started accelerating for Kremlin immediately. Something Jacob didn't want to do.

The *Aethia* had come from somewhere and was probably headed back there when she ran. If it were just pirates, he'd turn for home, but there were Alliance citizens out there counting on a rescue.

Where they were, was something no one had the answer to.

"What if we rationed?" Jacob asked.

The officers settled down and waited for Mark's response.

"The crew's good, sir, but we can only stretch what we have left for maybe five or six days more before we start feeling the effects," Lieutenant West said.

Jacob glanced up at Bosun Sandivol. "Bosun, can you see to that? The mess is going to need to get creative."

"Aye, aye, sir. Stew is the official menu of the day until we return to port," the bosun said.

"Good man." Jacob nodded.

"Okay," Yuki continued. "Thanks for the update, Mark. I guess I'll need to ration my chocolate." Several people chuckled, and she let her smile shine. "Weapons?"

Lieutenant Carter Fawkes worried Jacob. The young man hadn't bounced back from destroying the freighter. He sat in his chair, sunken-eyed and a little pale.

"Ma'am, uh, one sec."

He pulled up his NavPad and scrolled through his report to find the notes he needed.

Jacob decided he needed to ease the tension. Everyone was under a lot of pressure, and they didn't need their CO adding to the burden.

"It's okay, Carter. Just tell us what you can remember and submit the report later".

Carter looked up from the NavPad, bleary-eyed but with a smile of relief. "Thank you, sir. Turrets are online and good to go. The number four torpedo tube, however... I wouldn't trust it until we can have the yard check it out. We've used eight percent of our twenty mike-mikes so far, and the Long 9 is good to go."

"Thank you, Carter," Jacob said.

Yuki glanced over at Lieutenant Gonzales. "Engineering?"

"I'm not sure what you want me to report. Everything I've done is detailed in my log."

Jacob wasn't sure, but he felt like the lieutenant was challenging Yuki, daring her to call him out.

"Enzo," Jacob said, deliberately using his first name.

"The purpose of these briefings is two-fold. One," he raised his finger to make the point. "Is to highlight the most important aspects of your department."

Jacob added a finger. "The second is to give us a general feel for how things are down there. So please, stretch your imagination and give us a broad overview version of your report. Understood?"

Lieutenant Gonzales chafed under the CO's rebuke. He shifted uncomfortably, trying to move, but it was impossible to do so without bumping into his neighbors with the room so full.

"Yes, sir," he said. "We have access to eighty-five percent acceleration. The hit rent the forward gravcoil housing, and I don't recommend going full power—the entire assembly could rip off the ship. We sealed the breaches using nano-paste. If we had more time we could fabricate interlocking plates. When we get back to Kremlin, we're going to need to dock and have the yard fix it more permanently since the forward section lost nearly one hundred percent of its armor."

Jacob's concern over the armor was minor compared to the gravcoil. *Interceptor*'s advantage in almost any situation was her speed. The little ship needed it to survive. With only—he did some quick math in his head—four hundred and sixty some Gs available, their efficiency would be way down.

"Is there anything you can do to increase that?" Jacob asked.

"There's no provision for repairing the gravcoil housing while underway, sir," Enzo replied.

Jacob gave the young lieutenant, what he felt like was a fatherly smile. One reserved for deliberately obtuse children.

"Enzo, I didn't ask you what 'The Book' said. I asked you if there is anything you can do to shore it up."

Lieutenant Gonzales stared back at him with a blank face.

"Sir?" he said. "I just told you, there is no—"

Jacob held up his hand and cleared his throat.

"Lieutenant Gonzales," he began.

The rest of the officers knew the engineer was in for it when the captain started using rank—it was a reminder of who was in charge. "I am under the impression you have two degrees, correct? One of which is from the University of Alexandria's physics department, correct?"

Jacob hated to publicly call the man out, but he felt it was necessary to wake the engineer up. He needed something, anything, to make him realize he wasn't at university or the Academy but in the real world. In the real world, problems needed solutions, not excuses.

Gonzales straightened up at the use of his rank, his back going stiff.

"Yes, sir. Electrical engineering and nuclear physics, to be exact."

Jacob carefully moved his own NavPad a centimeter to the right to give himself some time to think.

"And then you studied at the Naval Academy on Blackrock station for...?"

"Two years, sir."

"And what did you study there?" Jacob asked.

"Sir?"

"What classes did you take?"

"I don't understand what that has to do—"

Jacob interrupted him again. "Indulge me, *Lieutenant*."

"Fusion reactors, quantum electrical conduction, coilgun technology, and gravcoils." He paused for a moment before adding, "sir."

"Suffice to say, then, of all the people on this ship, with perhaps the exception of Lieutenant Yuki, you are the most educated person aboard ship," Jacob said.

The engineer blinked, glancing at the XO as if he hadn't known. Then it finally dawned on Jacob what was going on.

Gonzales didn't feel the education the Navy provided for

officers was equivalent to the engineer's private schooling. Jacob's education was entirely Navy. His mother's sacrifice had bought him a ticket to the Naval Academy when he graduated from high school.

While the Naval Academy on Blackrock station was equivalent to a bachelor's degree from any university, it wasn't exactly the same. Yes, they learned about history, science, math, English, all the usual subjects. However, instead of spending time on electives, spare time was used to understand more about Navy traditions, ranks, customs, and procedures. Jacob could write an excellent report, but he doubted he could tell any kind of story with his writing.

His lone creative pursuit was playing the guitar, a tradition he picked up from his mom, Master Chief Melinda Grimm. Whenever she was home on leave, she would drag out the same instrument that sat in his quarters and play old and new songs for him.

Jacob needed to play again. He'd buried it under duty and grief, but it was time.

He blinked hard to clear his mind and refocus himself on the situation at hand. He would have time to reminisce once they were back in port.

Lieutenant Gonzales sat back, running a finger over his pencil-thin mustache. "Sorry, sir. I think I understand. I'll get with the XO and see if we can't figure out a solution."

Jacob nodded to both him and Yuki. "Good. You'll find the XO knows more about the *Interceptor* than anyone else aboard."

Yuki turned to Ensign Owusu, the head of astrogation. "Ensign, what have you found about the possible destination our friends were heading for when they ran?"

Ensign Owusu squared his shoulders, the line on his jaw clenching. He was very good at his job, but he was young. Barely a year out of the academy. Destroyers like *Interceptor* were fantastic for training crews, and they'd stuck the youngest, least experienced officers on her.

"I have PO Tefiti down in stellar cartography searching for answers. He's the most qualified person to figure this out. I'll continue to look as well, but I think he's our best shot."

Jacob smiled at the admission. Many a young officer would be tempted to boast of their abilities and skill, but Owusu was solid. He would give credit where credit was due, which was a sign of an exceptional officer in the making.

"Thanks, Owusu," Yuki said. "Moving on, we have to—"

The rest of the meeting went with no striking revelations or surprises. They were on their own, with a broken ship, more than a billion klicks from help. The safest course of action would be to immediately head for Kremlin Station, but they weren't out here to be safe. He still had a job to do. *They* still had a job to do: Find the missing personnel from Gamma-7, figure out what's going on out here, and put an end to it.

No, not a job, a duty. If they couldn't answer a simple distress signal, what good were they out in the black?

———

Petty Officer First Class Tefiti sat cross-legged on the couch in stellar cartography. Three holographic screens surrounded him, each with a different star system highlighted, including Zuckabar. It was his job to decipher the puzzle, but he felt like he didn't have a picture to reference.

Unfortunately, he was running on hardly any sleep. Between repair parties and trying to find the answer to an impossible question, he was exhausted. He pressed the comm button.

"Mess hall," he said.

A second later, the ship's computer connected him to the duty watch in the mess. "Mess hall, Spacer First Class Mendez."

"Mendez, this is PO Tefiti down in cartography. Can you send someone down here with a pot of coffee, black and strong?"

"Sure thing, PO. I don't have anyone available this time of night, but as soon as I can, I will," Mendez replied.

"Thank you, Spacer, you're a lifesaver," Tefiti said.

He disconnected and went back to studying the stars. As best he could figure, the problem was one of destination. After *Interceptor* was spotted, *Aethia* had run a reciprocal course strongly indicating they were trying to return to wherever they came from.

It was just that there was nothing even remotely close on that heading. Galactically speaking, starlanes were common. However, in practice, they were rare. People spent their whole lives trying to discover new ones. Most discovered starlanes ended up serving very little use. Occasionally, though, one would be found that made the news around the galaxy.

Star charts of the area showed multiple scouts passing through, and none of them reported finding a starlane. Maybe he was on a wild goose chase?

Tefiti glanced at the hatch, leaned back, and rubbed his face again. He appreciated the solitude. There were more problems than just solving the mysterious heading for him to ponder. All the nasty rumors about Commander Grimm could be true, but his crew seemed to revere the man. Admittedly, Tefiti liked the commander and tended to trust his NCO sense about officers, which told him the skipper was the real deal.

Jacob Grimm had a sense of honor about him, a calm resolve to do his duty, without all the yelling and screaming some captains did. Grimm wanted to inspire his people, not threaten them. Tefiti admired that.

Yet then there were Pascal and Zuckabar. The media said he'd murdered children in Pascal through his reckless cowboy aggressiveness, shooting before he even knew what he was shooting at. As for Zuckabar, any accomplishment he might have made there was buried when Professor Bellaits discovered the wormhole. Something no one thought would ever be found, Tefiti included.

Even if it meant hurting his career a little, Tefiti couldn't pass up the chance to observe not only a true binary star system but one with the first wormhole ever discovered. He had pull with NavPer, worst case, he could transfer off if things looked bad. Which they kind of did. It was highly unusual for no personnel to transfer off-ship after a tour, especially one involving combat. Yet everyone who hadn't transferred in with Tefiti was from the previous voyage.

The doors slid open, and a short marine with blonde hair pulled in a tight bun walked in. Her camouflaged greys said, "Jennings" on the name tag. She had a thick muscular neck and shoulders that made her otherwise curvy frame appear top-heavy. What mattered most, though, were the two empty coffee cups in one hand and a pot in the other.

"Mendez said you wanted some coffee?" she said, holding up the cups.

Tefiti smiled. "Thank you, Sergeant."

In the marines, she was an E-5, the same grade as a Petty Officer second class in the Navy. He outranked her by a few years, but it didn't matter as much since he was Navy and she a Marine.

"Were you coming down here anyway, Sergeant?" he asked.

She nodded, handing him a cup before pouring his coffee.

"I like to look out there," she said.

"Me too. Have a seat. I wouldn't mind the company while I try to figure out where that ship was going," Tefiti said.

She took a seat on the other end, sitting ramrod straight as she mechanically sipped her coffee, blue eyes gazing forward at the viewscreen showing the stars in front of the ship. Sipping his coffee, he lost himself in the screens, flipping back and forth, looking at the stars from different angles. Starlanes moved, but not much. As long as the two systems stayed within a hundred and fifty light-years, they connected via gravitic manifolds—condensed conduits of space-time that a ship's gravcoil could attach to and ride like a rail.

Yet there was nothing out here. He sighed, waving his hand and closing the windows before leaning back and looking up at the overhead.

"Giving up?" Jennings said.

Her sudden speech startled him. She didn't move other than to sip her coffee, so he'd almost forgotten she was in the room.

"Not so much giving up as out of options. Wherever they were going had to be another ship; there are no bases out this far and certainly no starlanes," he said.

"Are you sure?" she asked.

"About what?"

"Gamma-7's cargo rail pointed in this direction," she said.

"Well, yeah. That's what led us to the stealth base back yonder."

"It has no life signs, no lights. It's not a base. It's a retrieval cargo rail with an automated platform. I would ask myself 'why there?'"

He shrugged, pointing at the visual in front of the room. "It doesn't matter. There's nothing on this course. No ships, no bases, no far-off moons. Scouts have looked this sector up and down; there's just nothing out here."

"Nothing they found or nothing you found?" she asked.

"Well, yeah, nothing I... Oh Jennings, you genius!" Tefiti leaped up, knocking his NavPad on the deck.

He scrambled to pick it up as he ran out the hatch.

After he left, Jennings laid down on the couch. Resting the coffee on her chest, and watching the stars until sleep claimed her.

CHAPTER TWENTY

"You've got to be kidding me?" Jacob said from the command chair.

PO Tefiti shook his head. "No, sir, I'm not."

He was in the astrogation chair with the gravitic array head-phones around his neck. "I actually got the idea from Sergeant Jennings. She came down to cartography with some coffee and mentioned the possibility that I hadn't looked for everything. She was right. I used the charts and didn't bother looking for a starlane since there were several scouts registered who had looked and reported nothing."

"You're telling me there is a starlane out here, and it's not on the charts?" he asked.

"Aye, sir," Tefiti grinned. "I have no idea why it isn't charted, but it's here, strong and stable. Either the scouts missed it or—"

"Or the cartography for the area was falsified," Yuki said. "Which would make sense if someone wanted to hide a starlane."

The bridge went silent as the crew listened intently. Hiding a starlane was unheard of. Their locations often sold for millions, sometimes more. Even the ones that went nowhere were useful for research.

"I'll be dammed. Where does it go?" Jacob asked.

"That's the strange part, sir. There isn't a system close enough. The grav strength of this lane reads a star system no farther than 5-10 light-years. Walking distance, really. The other lanes out of Zuck are much longer."

Roughly speaking, a light-year in a starlane translated into an hour of travel. There were very few lanes longer than a hundred and fifty light-years, as the gravity between the stars beyond such a distance was too weak to hold the manifold together.

When the lanes were first discovered, travel to most destinations took five times as long. As gravcoils became more refined and denser, their velocity down the lanes increased. Jacob didn't pretend to know the math, so he trusted what the charts said. Except out here there were no charted lanes.

"What are you thinking, PO? A secret base on the other side of a hidden starlane?" he asked.

"Pretty much, sir. This ties in exactly with where they were heading," Tefiti said.

Jacob leaned back, glancing down at the mirror that allowed him to see Chief Suresh's face.

"Devi, you think you can fly it?" he asked.

"Pshaw, Skipper. I'm insulted you feel the need to ask," she said with a feigned look of disgust.

"Right." Jacob tapped the comm button. "Engineering, Captain."

"Engineering, Lieutenant Gonzales speaking."

"Enzo, we've discovered a hidden starlane—"

"Surely not?" Gonzales said in shock.

"I know. What we want to do is go through it. Can the gravcoil take the stress?" Jacob asked.

There was a pause as Gonzales checked his computer. sir, I think so. Starlane travel is a little smoother than act acceleration. As long as there aren't too many bumps, w should be okay."

"All right then." Jacob cut the connection. "PO Tefiti, you have the ball," Jacob said.

He pointed at comms. "Mac, give me all hands."

"Aye, sir," Spacer second class McCall said, activating the system. "You're on, sir."

"Now hear this," Jacob said. "This is the captain speaking. Our encounter with the armed freighter has led us to an uncharted starlane. I know we're low on food and that you've all done a remarkable job holding the old girl together. I need to ask more from you now. I don't know what's out there, but I do know thirty-five of our fellow citizens are counting on us to find them. The evidence points to this starlane, and my gut agrees, so we're going through. Set condition Zulu, action stations."

The klaxon wailed as the computer repeated in its automated voice. "All hands, action stations. Set condition Zulu."

"Helm, come two degrees starboard and five degrees up bubble, at zero-zero-one gravities for five mikes then full stop," Tefiti said.

Suresh switched on the HOTAS.

Gripping the stick and throttle, she cracked her neck and responded in an even tone, "Aye, starboard two degrees. Five degrees up bubble. Set throttle to zero-zero-one gravities."

Finding a starlane was tricky business, as was locking onto one for travel. Since it was an unknown lane, they weren't rushing it. They had more than enough time to swap out their uniforms for ELS suits.

By the time he was back on the bridge and encased in the stark white suit with the blood-red stripe and red helmet, the rest of the crew had also changed. Switching into the suits was hard work but important—one of the most essential drills they could do. With a hull breach, seconds were the difference between life and death.

"Full stop," Chief Suresh said.

Tefiti was back in the secondary chair, with PO Oliv in the primary and Ensign Owusu standing behind them, holding the grab bar above his head. He needed the experience but going through an unknown starlane wasn't the time for him to learn.

"Scanning," Tefiti said. Minutes ticked by. "Found it. Relaying."

"Engineering," Jacob said.

"Engineering, Lieutenant Gonzales."

"Is the coil ready?"

"Aye, sir."

"Good man." Jacob killed the connection. A thought occurred to him. "Ensign Owusu, you have the con."

Owusu's eyes bulged. "Me, sir?"

"Yes, you. You can do it, Owusu," Jacob replied.

He moved out of the way and gestured to the chair. Owusu hesitated before standing and shook nervously as he took the center seat. Jacob took up the first officer's position, sealed his boots to the deck, and grabbed the bar above his head.

Ensign Owusu cleared his throat. "Uh, I have the con."

Jacob waved it away. This wasn't the time to chide the ensign on the regulations and protocol of a command switch. The look in Owusu's eyes said he wouldn't forget the formality of taking command again.

"Helm, increase the aperture," Ensign Owusu said.

"Aye, sir. Aperture open," Suresh said.

On the ship's bow, the gravcoil intake widened to twice normal size. Lasers inside the ship narrowed as the gravity manifold leading to the other star system triggered a vibration in their beams.

"We have a lock," PO Oliv said in her lightly accented voice.

"Excellent," Owusu said. "DCS, report?"

Yuki didn't hesitate or ask why it was Owusu. "Damage control reports all hands ready."

Owusu glanced up at his captain. Jacob waved for the man to continue. "You have the boat, Ensign. You tell me."

"Aye, sir," Owusu replied.

He rubbed his hands together, took a deep breath, and leaned forward as if he was trying to find anything he'd forgotten.

"Helm, full power on my mark."

"Aye, sir. Full power on your mark," Chief Suresh replied.

Outwardly, Jacob was as calm as a cucumber. Inwardly, his gut churned. Entering a starlane felt like falling from a tall building, looking down and knowing you wouldn't survive the impact.

"Helm... execute," Owusu said.

Chief Suresh slammed the throttle forward. The full power of the MK III fusion reactor flooded into the gravcoil. The gravity went crazy, and restraining harnesses locked down on the crew for a split second, protecting them from the acceleration.

Jacob forced himself to keep his eyes open lest he vomit—something he didn't enjoy under any circumstances, let alone in front of an audience, and in his suit.

For a full minute, the feeling persisted. On the screen, stars flashed and widened until there was nothing but bright white light and no sense of movement at all.

"Starlane achieved. Velocity is stable," Chief Suresh said.

She gingerly took her hands off the controls and locked the stick down to prevent accidental activation. In the lane, the ship could move, but anything more than a three percent variation in course would result in a violent expulsion into real space with no way back to the lane.

"Time to exit vector, three-point-seven hours," Oliv said. Once in the lane, they were able to determine the precise length.

"Stand down from condition Zulu," Owusu ordered.

Jacob patted the ensign on the shoulder. "Keep the chair, Owusu. I'm going to my quarters. Call me if you need me."

"Aye, sir, and um, thank you," Owusu said with gratitude.

Jacob gave him a thumbs up before exiting the hatch. Lance Corporal Naki fell in behind him and took his place outside the captain's quarters when Jacob went in.

Jacob left his ELS suit on and crashed. A couple of hours of shut-eye would do him some good. He needed to be prepared for whatever they found on the other side of the lane.

———

Operator Tier-Three Harmon despised his boss the way he hated all middle management. His supervisor had about as much personality as a slug, but he could live with that. No, it was the unending tidal wave of useless crap he came up with for him to do that rankled Harmon so.

If it weren't for Guild Base Omega's proximity, he'd lose his mind. As it was, he only had to spend three days out of every six on the space station guarding the starlane.

As if it even needed guards. Harmon dropped his tired feet on the panel and leaned back. They knew when every ship was coming and going. *Aethia* wouldn't be back from its mission for another eighteen hours.

He stretched, trying to keep himself awake. The only saving grace about this shift was the time—the middle of Base

Omega's night. He could watch vids or play games, and no one would interrupt him for another three hours.

Harmon flipped over to the entertainment screen, sliding through the various vids employees had downloaded on to the computer over the years. The Guild had their own entertainment, but it was all corporate crap, designed to sell the company and engender loyalty. The really good stuff came out of the Alliance and Consortium. He passed over the section reserved for the explicit Caliphate vids—those turned his stomach.

From the chatter on the boards, a lot of the everyday folk weren't happy about the Guild's involvement with the slavers of the Caliphate. Harmon himself hadn't realized how bad it was until the bootleg vids became available.

He was pretty sure there weren't any Guild women there. From what he'd heard, the higher-ups had an arrangement with the Caliph himself to return any Guild employees who found themselves on the wrong side of an obedience collar.

Skipping over those, he found the latest action movie out of the Consortium. A cyborg samurai fighting the evil genetic monsters. Good popcorn fun. Just as the movie's opening credits ended, red lights flashed all over his console. A blip appeared on his screen, and alarms wailed as unscheduled traffic popped into existence on their side of the starlane.

He froze with shock, his heart pumping as he tried to do three things at once.

"This isn't possible," he muttered.

His brain kicked in, and training took over. He told the computer to identify the ship and its location and distance. Due to the nature of starlanes, ships had relatively predictable exit vectors of only a few million cubic kilometers. However, to ensure the Guild observation post could see any ship, they had built the station more than a million klicks away from the possible entrance vectors.

Harmon's hand hovered over the button that would call his boss. If he called him, the supervisor would undoubtedly take his frustration out on Harmon.

While he silently debated his decision, the screen flashed words he wished weren't there:

Possible unknown ship contact. Condition Three, contact your supervisor.

———

"Skipper," Yuki said, gently shaking Jacob.

His eyes popped open. "Yes," he said.

He blinked several times—a blank fog filled his brain. Reality snapped forward, and his first officer's presence hit him like a slap in the face.

"What are you doing in my cabin?"

"Sir, there's a problem. We tried to wake you over the comms, but you weren't responding." she said.

"What is it?" he asked, the last of his grogginess vanishing with a shot of adrenaline.

"I think you need to see it for yourself, Skipper."

Thankfully, Jacob still wore his ELS suit. He'd collapsed into his bed out of exhaustion and hadn't bothered to take it off. He took the proffered hand and heaved himself out of bed, grabbing the red helmet as they walked out.

Lance Corporal Naki was gone, replaced by PFC Owens, who snapped-to as the captain passed him before falling in step to relocate outside the bridge.

"Captain on the bridge," Owens said as he dropped into parade rest outside the hatchway.

"I have the con," Jacob said.

"Captain has the con," Ensign Owusu replied as he stood up from the center seat and headed for astrogation.

"Sitrep?" he asked.

Yuki took her position beside him, one hand holding the grab bar above her. "Sir, we came out of the starlane earlier than expected," Owusu said.

"How much earlier?" Jacob's scanned the readout on the MFD attached to the chair.

"Thirty minutes. So far, we can't explain it... and that's not the only thing," Yuki said.

Starlanes generally hovered out from a star around the eight hundred million to one billion kilometers, depending on the gravity of the system's star. Zuckabar's were farther out than normal because of the binary star system's pulsar, but here...

"Where's the system's sun?" he asked, certain there was some kind of mistake.

"That's the problem, Skipper," Yuki said. "We don't... uh, we can't find one."

"What?" he blurted out before getting control of himself.

He ran through all the possibilities, coming up empty, and looked around the bridge, hoping for an explanation. For there to be a starlane, there had to be a star. Besides black holes, it was the only natural phenomenon with the requisite gravity. If there were no sun, then they were stranded and he couldn't consider that possibility.

"Black hole?" he said, doing his best to restrain the fear in his voice.

PO Tefiti shook his head, "No, sir. Singularities have a very specific gravitic frequency. I'm not picking that up. I'm hearing the gravity of the main-sequence star but without the corresponding evidence of one. I'm at a loss for how... there's nothing wrong with the equipment, and we have nothing on the charts. As far as the Alliance cartography is concerned, we're in the middle of nowhere. Dead-space."

Dead-space was what the Navy called the area in between star systems. Dead, because if a ship found themselves outside a system, they were as good as dead. The gravcoils were amazing tech, but they weren't FTL—only starlanes were. No entrance, no FTL.

"XO," Jacob said as his mind whirled through the different possibilities. "Rig for silent running. Let's proceed with caution."

"Aye, sir. Rig for silent running." She hit the all-hands comms.

Her next words were revibrated throughout the entire ship. "All hands, now hear this. Rig for silent running. I say again, rig for silent running."

———

Harmon hesitated, hand hovering over the comm's button when the contact vanished. Did he report it? Or just log it? He thought about the tirade his supervisor would go into if he were awakened in the middle of the night over nothing. However, if it ended up being important, Harmon could blame the computer for its lack of definitive return. If pressed, he could tell upper management that he'd tried to confirm the contact, but since it disappeared, he had nothing to confirm.

It wasn't like the computer was flawless. Sometimes the software didn't know how to classify unusual natural phenomena. Maybe it was an asteroid that got sucked into the gravitic well of the starlane. It could be anything, really.

Regardless, he wasn't going to risk the wrath of his supervisor over a computer error. Instead, he cleared the emergency code, returned his movie to the screen, and did his best to forget all about it.

———

"The passives are picking up a few things, sir," Ensign Owusu said.

"Excellent. Any signs of a planet?"

"I think so, sir. This whole system is confusing. Gravity says there is a star out there, but we can't see it—and I don't know how that's possible."

Jacob understood the young man's dilemma. A ship could hide in space, but a star? However, something remote tickled the back of his mind.

"Mac," Jacob said to the spacer manning the comms panel. "Would you have Lieutenant Gonzales join us on the bridge?"

"Aye, sir." Mac hit a button on his console. "Lieutenant Gonzales, report to the bridge. Lieutenant Gonzales, please report to the bridge."

The computer would route the request to the specific compartment where the crew member was located. If the person speaking said "now hear this," or "all-hands," then the computer knew to direct the next words to the whole ship. Officers were tracked by their NavPads. Petty officers had a cut-down version, and the rest of the spacers were assumed to be at their duty stations or in the mess, showers, or rec room.

A few minutes passed, and Jacob was about to order Mac to page Gonzales again when the disheveled Lieutenant stumbled through the hatch, one hand futzing with his sweater and the other holding a thermos of coffee.

"Sir?" he asked as he came to a stop next to the con opposite Yuki.

"Sorry to wake you, Enzo. We have a problem," Jacob said.

"No problem, sir. Just grabbing some shut-eye. How can I help?" Gonzales replied.

Jacob made a mental note to praise the engineer for turning around his attitude.

Yuki said, "Somewhere out, there is a star we can't see. PO Tefiti has the gravity reading, but the star... isn't there. We can't figure out how. What do you suggest?"

Enzo grinned. "Seriously?"

"Yes, *Lieutenant. Seriously,*" Yuki said, a slight annoyance registering in her voice.

"Sorry, ma'am, I meant no disrespect. It's just... I thought you were pulling my leg... uh, ma'am." Gonzales turned to astrogation. "Ensign Owusu, pull up a thermal image of the system."

Jacob glanced up at Yuki to see if she knew where the engineer was going with the idea. She shrugged. Thermal radiation was relatively short range and they wouldn't need it to see a star anyway.

"Aye, sir, one moment," Owusu said.

He looked into his scope as he adjusted the dials that shifted the screen's overlay.

"Hmm," Enzo said. "Dial-up the sensitivity ten percent."

"Aye, sir. Ten percent," Owusu replied.

Red, yellow, and white splotches appeared on the screen in a vaguely circular shape in the center. It could have been a disruption on the lens as far as Jacob knew. Enzo reached past the ensign and adjusted a dial.

"I don't see what you're—" Jacob froze mid-sentence.

The screen shifted, and he saw it. A massive star, easily larger than Zuckabar, or even Alexandria's main sequence star, was twice as large as old Earth's sun.

"*Chikushō,*" Yuki said under her breath.

Jacob grinned up at her. "I'm going to assume you said, 'holy crap,' and I agree completely."

Yuki flushed. "Yes, sir. That's *exactly* what that means."

"What is it?" Jacob asked.

Yuki looked at Lieutenant Gonzales. When he didn't respond, she said, "I think, Skipper, it's a dark star."

CHAPTER TWENTY-ONE

"What exactly is a dark star?" Jacob asked. He wasn't asking anyone in particular, he was happy to have anyone answer.

"This is more Lieutenant Gonzales's field, sir. I can only give you the cliff notes," Yuki said.

Gonzales, in the meantime, gazed at the astrogation monitor, his coffee thermos forgotten.

When Gonzales didn't answer, Jacob cleared his throat. "Enzo, care to explain?"

Gonzales shook his head, blinking several times.

"I... sir... it's not possible," he whispered.

Jacob grinned at the response. He'd felt the same way about the wormhole when he first heard of it.

"Assume, since we're looking at it, that maybe it is possible," Jacob said.

"Aye, sir, it's just... well... if such a thing existed," he didn't look away from the console as he spoke. "I think we would have found one already. We've explored something like three-thousand star-systems, and between the five major powers and the hundred some-odd independent worlds, we've seen brown dwarfs, black holes, and everything in between, but no one, sir —I mean *no one*—has ever discovered a dark star."

"That's great," Jacob said. "What's a dark star?"

Enzo pointed at the screen, "That is, sir."

"Listen, if one of you doesn't explain to the rest of the class what a dark star is, I'm going to start dropping some letters of reprimand," Jacob said.

"A dark star," Chief Suresh started. "Or more accurately, a dark *matter* star is a star in Newtonian mechanics with a gravitational pull strong enough to hold its light in but not strong enough to form a black hole. It's a white whale, Skipper. Theorized but never found to exist."

"How do you know that?" Lieutenant Enzo asked.

"These rockers don't mean stupid," she said. "It means I'm smart enough to avoid promotion because I like hard work and low pay... sir."

Chief Suresh's deadpan tone and complete lack of emotion were flawless. Jacob ignored his coxswains sarcasm directed at the junior officer. It was a chief's job to keep such officers in their place.

"Remind me never to play cards with you, Chief," Jacob said. He imagined she could bluff an empath.

"Aye, sir. Don't fleece the skipper," she replied.

"Is she correct?" Jacob asked.

Enzo finally pulled his eyes off the screen to look at his captain. "Yes, sir. One hundred percent. It explains why we came out of the starlane earlier than the computer predicted. It also explains why we can *see* it on thermal but not visual. It's massive, with a tremendous heat index, but nearly invisible at this distance."

The bridge quieted as everyone absorbed the magnitude of what they were witnessing. When the professor discovered the Bella wormhole, *Interceptor* was in-system but there was nothing to see. A dark star encounter, though, was something everyone aboard was a part of. When Jacob was younger, he imagined joining the Alliance Exploration Division, but the agency was all but dissolved after the Great War.

Here he was, present for not one but two epic stellar discoveries. He didn't even have to join the exploration corps to do it.

Elation turned to puzzlement. Technically, they hadn't discovered the dark star. The freighter had headed this way. Which meant they already knew... but... why would anyone hide such an amazing astronomical phenomenon? Who could hide it?

Jacob stiffened, leaning back as his pragmatism took over. "Chief, bring us starboard ninety degrees, ahead ten gravities. Astro, deploy the towed array. Mark, drop an anchor, just to be sure."

"Aye, aye, sir. Ninety degrees starboard, ten gravities," Chief Suresh said as her hands flew over the controls.

"Anchor away," Mark West said.

The towed array unspooled behind them. The one kilometer long, one-centimeter-wide line was stored in the ship's stern just above torpedo rooms five and six.

"What are we looking for, Skipper?" Owusu asked.

The ensign asked a good question. They were here to find thirty-five missing miners from Gamma-7 station, but it turned into so much more than that.

He prayed those miners were still alive and weren't on either of the ships *Interceptor* had destroyed. Until he knew for sure, it was *Interceptor*'s duty—no, their *sacred* duty—to find them. Jacob T. Grimm wasn't going to be the captain who bucked thousands of years of naval tradition and left people to die alone in the black.

Not him.

"PO Tefiti," Jacob asked. "Any sign of other ships or anything odd?"

Tefiti shook his head. "No, sir. However, it's hard to say definitively. This dark star has some seriously weird gravity pulses coming off of it. I don't really know how to explain it sir."

"Take your time," Jacob said with a grin. "It's only a hitherto unknown stellar phenomenon. You can have a few seconds to figure out how to describe it."

Tefiti let out a long breath forcing himself to relax. They were all incredibly blessed to witness such a fantastic sight, and everyone on the bridge understood.

"You see, sir, gravity generally sounds like a drum beat. Fast, slow, irregular, but always a drum beat. Zuck is the most unique star I've ever heard. This though, it sounds like a hundred drums beating at the same time, and slightly out of sync."

"Understood. Don't hurt yourself listening, PO. It won't do us any good if you can't hear at the end of the day," Jacob said.

Tefiti slipped the headphones back on. Out of curiosity, Jacob switched over to the gravity frequency and listened. Tefiti wasn't wrong about the beat. To Jacob's untrained ear it sounded like one long base line. Worse, since the computer had no idea what it was listening to, the software couldn't filter it out as background noise.

"Ops, do we have a solid lock on our anchor?" Jacob asked.

"Aye, sir. We should be able to find our way back, no problem," West replied.

"XO? You think you can do something to filter out the star's noise so we can have a better look at the system?"

"Aye, Skipper. I'm on it." She turned about, heading for the hatch.

Yuki was the ships computer expert. She could adjust the software on the fly at Tefiti's direction if it was needed.

"Let's see what we can see," Jacob said, leaning back in his chair.

————

Director tier two Cardinal flipped through the screens of his workers. Despite every advantage in the world, the people corporate sent were constantly trying to slack off. Was it too much to ask they worked their twelve-hour shift with exuberance? He had to stay on them like flies on honey.

"Worthless," he muttered.

Omega Base held two thousand personnel. Two hundred of them were Guild Security Forces. Of the remaining eighteen hundred, half were there to run and maintain the equipment. The other half were spread out over the planet, supervising food production via the beans and rice rovers. Any one of the giant machines could produce enough per square kilometer, per month, to feed one person for life.

The Guild had nine hundred such machines, running over millions and millions of square kilometers. Omega Base was their primary food producer. The total Guild population galaxy wide was an industrial secret, but Cardinal had guessed somewhere in the hundreds of millions. Otherwise, why run the automated farms all the time?

The men and women assigned to run the harvesters were the capable, reliable ones. The dregs they sent him for labor required constant watchdogging.

"Sector seven," Cardinal said as he spotted one of the laborers entering minute nine of his seven-minute bathroom break.

"Security, Sector Seven," came a gruff voice.

"Employee Mike-one-five-alpha has exceeded his daily bathroom time. Go get him."

"On it," the gruff man said.

A few minutes later, security forces dragged a half-naked man out of the bathroom. Cardinal watched the man plead with them. They always begged.

Cardinal checked the particular employee's record; he had a habit of visiting the bathroom far too often. The computer flagged him for punishment. Security hauled him to the maintenance chamber where he worked. Punishment was useless in private. All his fellow drones needed to see the results of ducking their responsibility. A pole rose out of the floor in the center of the maintenance bay. Security cuffed the whimpering and sobbing man to the device.

Cardinal keyed his pickup and broadcasted his words all over the maintenance bay.

"Mike-one-five-alpha, you're a disappointment to the Guild. You claim to want to work hard and do a good job, yet you constantly shirk your responsibility. I'm afraid we have no choice. You will be sterilized and punished."

He hated listening to the pathetic attempts to change his mind. He didn't decide who was punished. They did. If they really wanted a family they wouldn't be lazy. The employee manual was quite clear on the matter—hard work would be rewarded, tardiness punished.

Cardinal couldn't hear the man's screams as the pole shocked him or the sobbing as he was injected with medical nanites that would prevent him from ever having children—or any desire to copulate—ever again.

To a certain point, the reward of sex and family motivated some, but past that point, it was easier to remove the desire from them entirely, leaving them with nothing but the work.

The last thing the Guild needed was more worthless people reproducing and saddling the Guild with more mouths to feed.

———

Lieutenant (SG) Yuki and PO first-class Oliv were crowded shoulder to shoulder over the screen, coding the software to block out the erratic hum of the dark star.

Oliv pointed at the last line. "I don't think that's going to work, XO," she said. "We can't use predictive coding on this."

"But the computer is showing a standard rhythm," Yuki replied.

"The computer is good, ma'am, but there are frequencies the human ear can pick up that no machine the navy has can." Oliv closed her eyes and cocked her head to the side, listening. "There's an irregularity here. It's hard to notice, and I think Tefiti probably figured it out before me, but it's like... the star has a beating heart. Instead of thump-thump-thump like you would expect, there is a hiccup... but I can't detect a pattern. Here... like this."

Oliv tapped her fingers on either hand, one for the main beat the other for the offbeat.

"It's so weird that space-time has a sound," Yuki said.

"Not that weird, ma'am. Everything has a sound. Metal, rocks, people. Gravity beats space-time like a drum. As gravity passes through light, it disrupts the light in harmonic ways. We read that disruption as sound."

She paused, tapping out the rhythm. Oversized headphones covered one ear, the other was free to hear the XO. Yuki went back to coding while Oliv tapped out the pattern. Yuki was excellent at puzzles, which was why she took to coding. She'd spent four years at Rōnin's Academy of Computer Science while she was in the Navy's ROTC program. They paid for the upscale school as long as she kept her grades up. That was never a problem.

Yuki shook her head, remembering her mother's abject

horror upon announcing her intent to join the Navy after she graduated. Her mother was an artist, a modest profession, and appropriate, at least in her mother's mind, for a proper Rōnin woman.

Kimiko Yuki took to art about as well as a toddler rolling through paint. Coding, though, made sense to her. Art did not.

"*Oy vey,*" Oliv muttered. "I think I've got it."

She pressed the comm button. "Bridge, PO Oliv. Can I speak to PO Tefiti, please?"

"One sec, PO," Mac replied.

"Go for Tefiti."

"Tefiti, it's a seven-one-four with a third mixed in," Oliv said. The excitement in her voice brought her light accent out even more.

"Son of a—" Tefiti stopped himself. "Good job, Oliv!"

She closed the line and wrote out the pattern.

"I don't get it..." Yuki said.

"It's hard to explain. It repeats seven beats, then one, then four, each one changes to the fourth one—" she paused as Yuki's eyes glazed over.

"Never mind, just program the computer to do it this way," Oliv said as she sketched out the proper beat followed by the mathematical formula to show Yuki what she meant.

"That's a thing?" Yuki asked.

"Aye ma'am, it's a *thing.*"

———

"Holy shi—" Tefiti jumped up, stopping his prohibiting obscenity at the last second.

Jacob swiveled his chair, careful not to spill the cup of tea he held. They were going on twelve hours on duty, but he hesitated to turn over the bridge under the circumstances. He couldn't risk it until he knew exactly where they were and what danger they were in.

"PO?" he asked.

"Sir... I... *there's a planet out there,*" Tefiti said. He toggled the main viewer, and consequently, the powerful optical camera built into the shark's nose to a specific location.

Empty space.

"Are you sure, PO?" Lieutenant West chimed in.

"Aye, sir. I don't understand. One second." Tefiti hunched over his console, the whole bridge watching him as he worked.

As amazing as the dark star discovery was, having a planet orbiting it would prove a scientific bonanza. Jacob heard the lift doors open, paying them no mind until Spacer Second Class Josh Mendez showed up with fresh coffee for everyone. Jacob glanced at the mission clock. It was twenty-three hundred hours, well past the young man's duty time.

He turned to Jacob last, taking his half-full cup and replacing it with a fresh, steaming mug of mint tea.

"Josh?" Jacob asked. "You're on the morning shift in the mess, aren't you?"

The spacer smiled as he juggled the empty mugs he'd collected. "Sir, if you're on duty, I'm on duty."

He walked off the bridge with the tray tucked under his arm.

Officers often forgot how hard a crew worked. Not that the officers didn't also work hard, but it wasn't the same kind of work. The crew was often sweaty and physically exhausted from strenuous physical labor at the end of the day. While Jacob was often exhausted, it was more from stress than labor.

"Chief," Jacob said in a subdued voice, leaning forward to keep it between them.

She glanced in her mirror, meeting his eyes.

"Skipper?" Suresh asked.

"Mendez." He jerked his thumb at the crewman. "Is he a go-getter all the time, or just with me?"

It was an important question. Sometimes, though not often, a crew member would suck up to the captain; it could be difficult to tell who was genuine or fake.

"I'll talk to his PO and get back to you, sir," she said.

As the COB, it was her duty to know everything about the enlisted crew.

"I'd appreciate that."

Jacob wanted to reward the kid if he were truly working hard. That kind of initiative was worth praising. He certainly endeared himself with the bridge crew by bringing them fresh coffee.

"I've got it!" Tefiti shouted.

He hit a button, and the screen resolved to show what his instruments knew was there.

A planet.

Jacob stood up in disbelief. "You got to be kidding me."

"I'm gonna take a wild stab, sir," Chief Suresh said. "And say no, he is not."

Either the people on this planet were the luckiest bastards who ever lived, or they had technology the Alliance hadn't even dreamed of.

CHAPTER TWENTY-TWO

Senator Talmage tidied up the last of his desk. A month felt like a long time, and he looked eagerly for any excuse to delay departure as long as he could.

At least, he mused, he could take Eva with him. Any trip was bearable if she came along. As it was, she had boarded the *Alexander* hours before. He still had to finish up the last of his work and hand everything off to his assistant, Charles, before leaving. He didn't want to go, but when President Axwell asked, yes was the only possible answer.

The trip to Zuckabar wouldn't be all bad, he decided. Plus, the privilege of witnessing the first passenger ship through the wormhole would be exciting. Something he could tell his kids about one day... when he and Eva decided to have one.

He sent the last file off, closed the connection, and stood to leave. Something nagged at him, a feeling that he shouldn't go. However, as the man who led the annexation charge—and who signed off on Commander Grimm's award—he had a responsibility. If he stayed behind, it could be seen as having no faith in his idea. No, he had to go. He just wished the haunting feeling that he was making a mistake wouldn't go with him.

CHAPTER TWENTY-THREE

After almost three thousand years of studying astronomy, humanity was still nowhere near figuring out how big the universe was. However, there was one thing they could count on in the Milky Way galaxy, and that was stars. Lots and lots of stars. There were hundreds of billions of them in their galaxy alone.

Not every star was a main sequence like sol, or even the binary of Zuckabar, but every star *could* have planets. Mathematically, if even one percent of those several hundred billion stars had planets, and only one percent of those planets were habitable, then there were several *million* habitable planets in their galaxy alone.

Of those planets, though, very few of them fit into the 'Goldilocks zone'—perfect for humanity to live on, which was where terraforming came in. Need it hotter? Colder? Fixing a planet's average temperature was the first step. Seeding with the right flora, bacteria, and oxygen mix came next. A hundred different scientific disciplines were involved, and each required massive amounts of expertise and equipment.

Left to the individual colonies, every terraforming process

would need to re-invent the wheel, each time starting from ground zero. Enter the Terraforming Guild. They were experts, had the equipment, and were *theoretically* non-partisan. They had no respect for persons or borders. They would work with the Caliphate or the Consortium.

This gave them, and by extension, everyone, an advantage. Hundreds of otherwise uninhabitable planets sustained life, including in the Alliance and, of course, Zuckabar Central. Though Zuck Central wasn't exactly life-sustaining, that process would take many more centuries.

Which was why Lieutenant Commander Jacob T. Grimm of the USS *Interceptor*—along with the rest of the bridge crew—stood in open-mouthed disbelief at what they saw on the main viewscreen. It wasn't just any planet but a garden world—a verdant sphere teeming with natural resources.

"Enzo," Jacob said. "I... have many questions."

"You and me both, Captain. This isn't possible. The planet get's heat but no light for things to grow. Not to mention the distance isn't right." Lieutenant Gonzales checked the astrogation console over Owusu's shoulder. "Something like 400 million klicks from the sun—well outside the Goldilocks zone."

Jacob sipped his tea, standing for a long moment looking at one of the rarest sights in the galaxy. Even the rare verdant worlds of the Alliance, of which there were only two, required terraforming, and those were in the Goldilocks zone.

"Run silent status?" Jacob asked.

Mark West checked his screen before replying. "One hundred percent sir. No emissions. At our current speed and output, we would have to run over a buoy for them to detect us."

"Astro, distance?"

Owusu shook his head, looking at his equipment as if he

couldn't believe the readings. "Sir, they're one-seven-five million klicks from the starlane entrance."

"Better and better. If we remain on silent running, how long to orbit?"

Jacob heard someone suck in a breath. He'd be dammed if they would come all this way and not do their level best to find those missing miners. There was only one possible location, and it was staring them right in the face.

"At two-zero Gs constant acceleration, I can have us in orbit in say—" Owusu tapped the keys in rapid succession, doing calculations on the fly.

"Call it one-seven hours, sir. If we maintain silent running and are able to refresh the heat sink."

Jacob sat down and pulled up the system map they had managed to piece together so far. He drew a line with his finger from the starlane to the planet. It was a moving target, but it looked like the planet's orbit would remain relatively close to the starlane for the next few weeks. They were fortunate the orbit wasn't on the other side of the star, they never would have found it.

"Owusu, let's avoid this corridor, even if it adds time," he said. With a flick of his finger, he sent his projections to the astrogator's console.

"Aye, sir. Recalculating."

Jacob changed the screen over to comms selected Yuki from his menu.

"XO here, sir."

"Kim, I want a staff meeting for 0900 hours. Please have Sergeant Jennings attend."

"Aye, sir. Zero-nine-zero-zero with marines. I'll make sure the coffee is black."

She cut the line, and he noticed Owusu was ready with the course.

"Two-three hours, sir. Cutting it close, but if we assume we can return at our current max acceleration, only three hours back."

"Call the ball, Owusu. Put us in a high parking orbit."

"Roger, sir."

"Mark, you have the con. I'm going to get some rest."

"Aye sir, I have the con."

There were days when he never left the chair, and he had to admit that he vastly preferred those days to those where he never sat in it.

———

United Systems Alliance Marine Sergeant Allison Jennings took one step into the briefing room, immediately sidestepped and dropped into parade rest beside the hatch.

Half the ship's officers and Chief Warrant Officer Boudreaux were at the table with their painted shark logo. Grimm looked up at Jennings and smiled.

"Allison." He gestured to a seat next to him.

"Aye, aye, sir," she said, snapping to attention then briskly marching to her seat.

She didn't miss the smiles and eye-rolling from some of those in attendance—she was a marine, she missed nothing.

Officers on a ship, with the notable exception of the skipper and his XO, didn't often run with the devil dogs of the corps. She knew he understood. Precision and excellence in everything they did were required. Not just for some arbitrary standard, but because one day, the lives of everyone on the ship could depend on even the lowliest marine private performing without flaw.

"Settle down, peeps," Grimm said.

In a way, the marines aboard ship were outsiders. Their

mission was wildly different from the rest of the crew. In ship engagements, they served as damage control and search and rescue. On the ground or aboard other ships, their mission was to kill the enemy before they were killed themselves. Jennings knew Boudreaux, the captain, and the XO had all been there with her when the stuff hit the fan. She respected them.

"Okay, Kim, why don't you give us the heads-up on what we're seeing," Grimm asked.

The XO hit a button on her NavPad, and the holographic feature came to life, showing a verdant world.

"Since it really shouldn't exist, we're calling it 'Wonderland.' The closer we get, the more info we're gathering. Chief Suresh has us crawling along and doing a great job of keeping us hidden from any passive or active scanners."

"Question?" Mark West raised his hand. "The heat sink is close to tolerance. What's the plan for that?"

"Good question, Mark," Grimm said. "We're going to cut acceleration and drop it directly behind us."

"The angle Owusu has us coming in on should shield their sensors from any thermal radiation until it's too late. Since the gravwake will be down, it won't shatter and draw attention," Yuki continued.

Allison zoned out slightly. This was all "Navy" business. She wasn't even sure why the captain requested her. Clearly not to guard the hatch like she initially thought. Still, she made sure her brain filed away what they were saying in case it became important later on.

"Here's what we have on their infrastructure," Yuki continued.

The camera zoomed in, and what Jacob initially thought was perhaps a planetary ring turned out to be thousands of "X" shaped satellites. The readings on the hologram showed the satellites had four massive extending arms, each over a square kilometer in size.

"Wow," Grimm said.

"Indeed, Skipper," Yuki replied. "There are *thousands* of these in orbit. They circle the planet, and from what I can tell, they're the planet's light source. Like giant sunlamps powered by dark energy, bathing the planet in constant sunlight and absorbing the reflected light. If PO Oliv hadn't figured out a way to compensate for the dark star's wonky gravity, we would never have seen it."

"Wait," Lieutenant Gonzales said. "Are you saying the planet is invisible?"

Yuki shook her head. "Not so much invisible as difficult to detect. Between the gravity of the dark star, the satellite system, and its orbit, Wonderland was near impossible to see. Which leads us here," she said, hitting a button and displaying a station connected to the planet by a long tube.

"A space elevator?" Grimm said.

"Yes, sir. A gravcoil powered space elevator," Yuki said, letting the monumental statement sink in.

"Who has this tech?" Gonzales asked in amazement.

The XO keyed her NavPad and brought up the Universal Terraforming Guild symbol.

"But they're just a corporation. How can they hide an entire star system?" Gonzales continued.

Jennings tuned out their conversation as she examined the elevator. The station itself was oblong, fitted with a moderate-sized gravcoil on top. Which meant if one were standing in the station, they would be looking 'up' at Wonderland.

She frowned. That meant the elevator had to have some kind of mechanism to swivel the passengers. It sounded complicated to her. From the size of the place, she expected no more than thirty personnel tops, maybe less. The docking clamps on the side of the station looked like they were set up for freighters like *Aethia*—which meant they could dock the Corsair, assuming the captain wanted her to go in from above.

Seemed logical. They might have ground-to-air defenses or maybe even ground-to-space defenses. A small marine unit in the Corsair could infiltrate and take over the elevator, find and rescue the hostages, and evac before the people on the ground even knew what hit them. If the hostages weren't on the elevator, then her marines could use it to go planetside at little risk.

"Jennings, did you catch that?" Grimm asked.

"Skipper?" she said.

Glancing up, she realized the XO and engineer were both looking at her.

"Sorry, sir. No. I was formulating an infiltration plan. Please continue."

"That's actually what we were getting at. Kim thinks that once we're on the station, she can locate the hostages. From what we can see, only one central base connects the elevator to the ground. It's possible the hostages are on the station, but it doesn't look big enough to have a permanent population aboard."

Mark West raised his hand. "Sir, about that. One of my girls in ops, PO Third Class Patel, is from Vishnu. She grew up on a farm. We were looking over the power output, and she happened to see one of the structures down there and said they looked an awful lot like harvesters her family used. Just, you know, a hundred times bigger."

"Tell her 'good eye' for me, Mark. Well done. So it looks like the Guild is using this as a farming planet."

Lieutenant Fawkes spoke up for the first time. "That begs a whole other question."

"That being?" Yuki asked.

"Well, ma'am, how many planets like this do they have that they can use this one just for farming?"

Stunned silence hit them.

Having grown up on the hellhole MacGregor's' World, Jennings couldn't imagine having such a lush garden world to live on and using it for something as mundane as farming.

"They have better ones," she said. "That's the only explanation, Skipper. If you have a racing aircar, you don't sweat when your compact is trashed."

"This world being awesome by our standards, and them having spent what appears to be *trillions* on it... is just MacGregor's World to them?" Grimm asked.

Jennings' lips went thin in a tight smile. Her history with her home planet was... complicated. With its high gravity and high-pressure atmosphere, the conditions there were severe. It had given her a unique physiology, for sure, with more upper body strength and thicker back and neck muscles than a five-foot-tall woman from any other planet.

She had left on her eighteenth birthday and had no desire ever to return. Not that she didn't have plenty of leave saved up, she simply never wanted to step foot there again.

Both a strange pride and deep resentment were associated with the Alliance's treatment of MacGregor's World. Because the small population of the planet couldn't hope to field their own Navy, they had joined the Alliance for mutual defense. They appreciated the military and medical help but resented any social intrusion.

When the Alliance built Fort Kirk in orbit, MacGregor's World received more visitors, but not many. For the most part, the Alliance ignored the planet—except for the Marine Corps, who did everything they could to recruit from the population. But that strange combination of pride and resentment kept most people bound to the planet.

Except for Jennings. She hated the place with a passion and refused to end up as someone's fourth wife. She closed her eyes for a second and wiped those thoughts away.

"Yes, sir. If they needed Wonderland to live on, they would use it," she said.

"Damn," Grimm muttered, surprising the table.

He looked up with a grin over his faux pas of the regs for swearing. "None of you better report me."

They chuckled. The Navy's annoying regs on swearing aside, Jennings had dropped a massive bomb. Only using a lush world like Wonderland for farming seemed criminal. Billions of people could live on its surface.

"Are we sure it's the Guild?" Chief Boudreaux spoke up, her light French accent cutting through the joviality.

"Markings on the station are consistent with Guild identifiers. They don't have IFF that we can detect," Yuki said. "But it's their system, and no one knows about it."

"So *Aethia* was theirs?" Boudreaux asked.

"Looks that way, Viv," Grimm said. "Which fits, considering we have no idea what they hit us with other than it damn near destroyed *Interceptor*. Clearly," Grimm said pointing at the hologram, "they have more advanced tech than we thought possible."

"What do we do, Skipper?" Fawkes asked.

"Our job," he replied. "Thirty-five Alliance citizens are counting on us, and I intend to find them. I don't know what orbital defenses the Guild has or what kind of detection apparatus, but they have some high-tech crap."

"Agreed," Lieutenant Gonzales said.

"Jennings, we could come to a stop three million shy and deploy your team in the Corsair?" Yuki asked.

Jennings shook her head.

"Allison, you disagree?" Jacob asked.

She bristled inwardly at his use of her first name, but he was the captain—and he had saved her and Corporal Naki, so she cut him some slack.

"Even running silent, the Corsair is too big, sir. They'll shoot first, and that will be that, especially if they have more of those guns," she said.

Heads nodded around the room.

"Thoughts, then?" Yuki asked her.

"Yes, ma'am. Blow out—four marines in Raptors. Once we're on the hull, we'll find our way in and take the station. Then you come aboard in the Corsair for exfil when we find the hostages."

Everyone around the table wore puzzled expressions—except for Grimm, whose face went stiff. "Allison, if we're off by a single half percentage point..."

"I'm confused," Lieutenant Gonzales said. "What's a 'blow out.'"

"Crazy marines being crazy," Chief Boudreaux replied.

Commander Grimm answered Gonzales but looked directly at Jennings.

"It means we load the marines up in their power armor, attach them to the hardpoints of the Corsair, then rev it up to a few hundred Gs and shoot them at the station like missiles."

Another round of stunned silence hit the table. Jennings's face reflected zero emotion, except for the slight ghost of a smile on her lips.

"Oorah," she said.

CHAPTER TWENTY-FOUR

"I don't mean to question your judgment, Sergeant Jennings, but are you sure about this?" Lieutenant Yuki asked.

The two were alone in the armory as Yuki plugged in the code to access the morgue where the powered Raptor armor was stored. Security required one ship's officer and one Marine, unless the ship had Marines who were officers, which at the moment, *Interceptor* didn't.

"Yes, ma'am," was her only reply.

She didn't miss the sideways look the XO gave her. The morgue hatch rolled up out of the way with a deep hum.

"Come to mama," Jennings whispered.

Where the Marine space armor made them look like medieval knights preparing for a duel, the Raptor armor was altogether different—it looked more like a bipedal dinosaur than a man.

Yuki whistled. "Hard to believe each of these things cost almost as much as a Corsair," she said.

"Worth every penny," Jennings replied.

The suits were sleek, with long "feet" that ended in an ankle a half meter up, granting the Marines the running ability of a cheetah while wearing them. Hunched down in storage mode, the suits were only two meters tall and two-point-five wide.

"All suits, activate," Jennings said.

A computerized voice that sounded half like a growl replied. "Identification verified. Squad Sergeant Allison Jennings. Confirm authentication code."

Jennings glanced at the XO.

"It's voice-keyed, Sergeant. Knowing it wouldn't help me," Yuki said.

Jennings frowned. The XO mistook her hesitance for secrecy when, in reality, it was a flicker of embarrassment—something she hated feeling.

"Fine," she grumbled. Clearing her throat, she said, "Let your plans be dark and impenetrable as night, and when you move, fall like a thunderbolt."

Yuki's eyebrows went up in surprise. "Sergeant, that's beautiful. Did you write it?"

Jennings shook her head once. "Sun Tzu."

"Code accepted, access granted," the growling voice replied.

As one, all four suits stood up and stepped one massive foot forward, then knelt, and the front of the suit opened like a double door.

"I'll let you get to it," Yuki said.

"Ma'am," Jennings replied.

They had three hours of prep work to get the suits ready. Technically, they were *Romeo-Zero-Five suits, Assault.* Marines just called them Raptors.

"Naki, Cole, Owens, clock's ticking," she said.

The three other marines rushed by the XO as she left.

———

Jacob swirled his beef and potato stew around his bowl with the Navy issue spoon. Though it was flavorful, he wasn't hungry, but as the captain, he had a duty to set a good example. Especially with the worsening food situation on top of almost a solid day of running silent. The bowl had all the vitamins and nutrients he would need, which was important when they had nothing else to eat.

"Mind if I join you, sir?" Lieutenant Fawkes said holding a tray with stew and a cup of coffee.

"I wish you would," Jacob said, gesturing to the empty seat across from him.

Jacob had his NavPad next to his bowl, reading the daily briefings and reports from the different department heads. There was no end of paperwork, and a captain's job was never done.

He watched Carter adjust his bowl, spoon, and coffee several times. Clearly, the young man wanted to talk, and Jacob happily gave him the space and silence to find the words.

"Sir," he whispered. "How did you deal with *it* after Pascal?"

Jacob respected the amount of courage Carter had come up with to ask his captain such a delicate question.

"Do you mean how did I deal with the Navy turning on me, or the consequences of me being the one who gave the order?"

Carter looked down at his lap as if it were the most interesting thing in the world at the moment. "Maybe both, sir... the latter, sir."

It wasn't as if *Interceptor* hadn't seen combat before, but there was a stark difference between a warship bearing down, and a sudden battle where the other ship was destroyed in the blink of an eye.

Jacob suspected, though, that it wasn't what Fawkes had done so much as whom he had done it to. Firing on a warship was a lot different than firing on a freighter. Something Jacob could certainly empathize with.

"I wish," Jacob said after a moment. "I could tell you it will get easier, but it won't. This is the job, Carter. In some ways, we're no better than our ancestors living on pre-industrial Earth. It's kill or be killed out here. You did exactly what you were supposed to do, and you saved all our lives."

"By taking theirs, sir? I mean... it was a freighter. They weren't pirates or Caliph or... they were just... people." He said the last word barely louder than a whisper.

Jacob thought for a moment, hoping to find some inspirational words. "After Pascal, my tactical resigned her commission. She was a sweet girl, and I can't imagine the pressure on her. She did exactly what she was supposed to do, just like I did. I never did get to talk to her before she left, but I know the impulse she felt. I felt it too."

Carter looked up, genuine sorrow in his eyes. "You, sir? You were going to quit?"

Jacob chuckled. It wasn't all that long ago, but it *felt* like a lifetime. "There was a moment where they had me in this room for like a day, and they kept coming at me and coming at me about what happened, trying to get me to admit my guilt. But I didn't have any guilt to admit. I did nothing wrong. In fact, I did several things right."

Jacob glanced at the crew filling into the mess for lunch.

"PO Hanz," Jacob said to one of the damage control crew.

"Sir?" Hanz said, coming over.

"The stew is good, but I'm not hungry," Jacob said.

"Thank you, sir!" Hanz took the bowl and returned to his seat a few tables away.

Carter leaned forward. "What kept you going, sir?"

"I found a reason to motivate myself, Carter. I can't tell you what reason you need to find, but I couldn't end my career like that. I needed to be known as something other than the guy who gave the order to fire on children."

Carter deflated slightly as if he expected some piece of wisdom that would make him feel better about destroying the faux merchant vessel. There was none to be had.

Jacob's NavPad beeped, letting him know it was time to launch the Corsair.

"I'll tell you this, Lieutenant," Jacob said as he stood. "You're one hell of a weapons officer. A credit to the Navy and an invaluable asset to *Interceptor*. You. Saved. Lives. All of our lives. More importantly, you did your duty with honor. Don't forget that."

"I won't, sir. Thank you, sir."

Jacob scooped up his NavPad and headed out. He hoped the young man figured a way to be at peace with his actions.

———

Interceptor's boat bay was in the aft-most part of the ship, with the bay doors opening to space above and astern of the gravcoil. Above the boat bay was the aft ammo storage and torpedo rooms five and six.

The sleek black Corsair took up two-thirds of the bay, leaving barely enough room to muster maybe twenty personnel, plus the little control room. The spot for the Mudcat against the portside was empty, since FleetCom had removed theirs while *Interceptor* was under repair.

As Jacob approached, reinforced double hatch doors slid open with a hum, revealing four marines in Raptor armor. Currently, they were a non-reflective flat black that sucked in the light around them.

"Jennings, good to go?" Jacob asked.

The suit growled in response, lights flashing on the inset helmet. "Good to go, sir."

"Scary much?," Chief Boudreaux said from beside him.

She was dressed in her stark white flight ELS, cradling her helmet in one hand. The hatch opened again, and eight crew marched in, led by Lieutenant Yuki. They all wore soft armor over their white ELS suits, MP-17s in carbine mode, and sober looks. The station couldn't hold more than thirty people. With the Raptor armor and the Navy personnel, they had a good chance of taking it without casualties.

He looked over the six men and two women going on the mission. Besides his XO, he knew CPO Redfern and PO Oliv. The other six were spacers he was aware of but not familiar with.

"Bring 'em to order, XO." Jacob walked toward the Corsair, did an about-face, and came to attention.

"Chief," she said.

Redfern nodded. "Detachment, atten-shun!"

The marines did an about-face in their armor, shaking the deck. The Navy members of the boarding team snapped to attention facing the captain.

"Chief Boudreaux," Jacob said, "You may begin your departure checks."

"Aye, aye, Skipper." The lithe woman practically skipped to her Corsair and climbed up the small external ladder to the cockpit.

"Detachment, stand at ease," Jacob said.

They relaxed, dropping into a less formal posture.

"Every year, citizens of the Alliance put their lives on the line, heading out into the black for profit, for our nation, and for each other. Some go to provide for their family, others because it's what their family has always done."

Jacob turned to the Corsair as Boudreaux started her preflight. Panels whirred to life, and the little ship hummed as power flooded through the small craft.

"We put on this uniform and go into space for all the same reasons, save one... we are making a statement. *This we'll defend.* Freedom of the starlanes, our fellow citizens, each other. Nothing is more important than the lives and freedom of our people." Jacob paused, letting his meaning sink in.

"Thirty-five Alliance citizens are counting on you to bring them home to their families and loved ones. You are counting on me to guide us forward. Let's none of us let the other down," he said. "Godspeed and good luck."

"*Interceptor!*" Chief Redfern bellowed.

"First to fight!" cried the spacers.

"XO, you may begin," Jacob said.

"Aye, aye, Skipper. Chief Redfern, let's load up and move out!"

———

Chief Warrant Officer Vivienne Boudreaux cracked her knuckles and neck as she waited for clearance to depart. She tugged at her pilot's ELS, which was essentially the same as a standard suit except for the modifications which allowed her to stay conscious up to nine Gs.

"Chief, you're clear to drop in ten," Baxter said from his position in the command booth.

Yellow lights flashed alerting the bay occupants to stand clear. The large bay doors beneath the ship swung open into space. In her mind, she counted down with Baxter. At one the gravwake emanating from the stern of *Interceptor* vanished. She hit the hat switch under her thumb, activating thrusters and pushing the ship out of the *Interceptor* at three Gs for fifteen seconds. Boudreaux grunted, breathing hard and forcing the blood to stay out of her head as best she could. The blood rushing to her head rather than her legs, these negative Gs were always harder for her.

Once the computer gave her the green light, she cut the thrusters, rolled the ship, and pushed the gravcoil up to twenty Gs. Compared to the *Interceptor*'s coil, it was tiny and insignificant.

They were still looking at five hours of acceleration, followed by three hours of deceleration before they would be in the right position to "fire" the marines at the space elevator. On top of eight hours attached to the ship, it would take the Raptor armor's attached ion drives another six hours to slow them to survive impact on the station.

Boudreaux shook her head at the insanity of the maneuver. However, if it failed, it wouldn't be because of her. The poor marines were stuck inside their Raptors, unable to move more than an inch for the next fourteen hours. The rest of the personnel, on the other hand, were secured in the passenger compartment, able to stretch out, sleep, watch vids, even eat or use the bathroom if they needed.

She flipped the comms switch to check on them.

"Bravo-Two-Five, Charlie-One-One, status?" she asked.

"Charlie-One-One, Sergeant Jennings is asleep, Chief, but don't worry about us; we're good," Lance Corporal Naki said. "Let us know when we're half an hour out."

"Roger, Bravo-Two-Five. Wilco at zero-three-zero minutes from target. One-One out."

Boudreaux suppressed a grin. Why was she even worried? Of course, they were sleeping.

———

Jacob watched the little ship vanish from the passive sensors at the ten-thousand klick mark. Even with its active acceleration, she was too small to pick up. He hoped and prayed this was also true for the space elevator's sensors.

In the meantime, he updated his log and checked to make sure the emergency buoy was in place. If anything happened to them, he wanted to make damn sure that someone, sometime, would figure it out.

Once he'd confirmed the fate of the miners, or rescued them, they would high-tail it back to Zuckabar and let fleet command know there was a hell of a lot more going on out here than they could have imagined.

CHAPTER TWENTY-FIVE

Controller third-tier Vesper glanced around the control room. The other six controllers were busy with their own work, no one spared him any attention. He was more concerned about the supervisor, though. The control room's linear layout allowed the supervisor to look at each screen without much effort.

However, the current supervisor was snoozing, with his feet up on the console and a half-eaten dinner in his lap. It was against company policy to sleep on duty, but what was a lowly controller going to do to a supervisor? The only people on the ladder he outranked were the laborers, and there weren't any in the control room.

The other controllers on duty had their responsibilities, monitoring the heat build-up in the elevator lane, checking on the laborers unloading the cargo, and seeing to security. Vesper's glorious job? Guiding incoming traffic to the appropriate dock. Which he did once a week when the cargo ship from Zuckabar departed and arrived. If it weren't for the particular dense metal the outer asteroid belts of Zuckabar had, he wouldn't even have that little task. As it was, the only other thing to do was watch the radar/lidar returns and occasionally blast an asteroid with a plasma round from the swivel-mounted weapon on the central ring.

If Vesper were a dedicated and obedient cog in the Terraforming Guild corporation, he would drink his stimulant, take his happy pills, and do as he was told. *If* he were an obedient cog.

Which he wasn't.

Vesper's father had shared with him a secret, one his father had shared with him. It had taken Vesper years to figure out how to use it, but once he did, it made his life infinitely more enjoyable.

When he was fourteen, right before leaving home forever to go train for his future job, his dad had taken him aside and whispered something to his boy. In a life of complete monitoring, where even going to the bathroom was observed, his father had taken a great risk.

"Promotion," he whispered. "Is the *illusion* of reward."

It was true. Vesper had watched his contemporaries strive for a single tier, working their fingers to the bone for a point-two-five percent increase in basic income adjustment, not even bothering to ask why they set the B-cola low to begin with?

And the mythical promotion to middle management? A supervisor tier five? He could forget about it. Why would they ever promote a person who was good at his job? His fellows worked and worked, desperate to go from controller to operator and then supervisor. They actually believed the corporate propaganda.

Every six months, they were transferred to a new duty station. In eighteen years of work, he'd never served with the same people twice. Once, he'd seen someone who looked vaguely familiar, but he couldn't be sure.

However, when people transferred out, some supervisor tier

five would come out with a cake and declare so-and-so had made promotion to a new tier, and if the rest of you just worked harder, you could too.

At first, he'd believed it. But the words of his father echoed in his brain.

His life wasn't as bad as the laborers, of course. Those poor bastards' only hope was maybe a weekend at the entertainment rooms, or possibly someday entering the family lottery.

Nearly half the low echelon employees attempted suicide, though very few succeeded. Between pills, brain waves, nanites, and old-fashioned conditioning, the Guild kept its people alive and working.

Hell, Vesper had never met anyone above Supervisor Tier-Three, anyway. It was the highest rank his lowly position came in contact with.

Once he knew the truth—that there was no escape, not even in death—his focus changed from "promotion" to "do the least work possible without punishment."

The Guild had spent a good amount of money teaching Vesper to program computers. He used this skill to make his life easier, erasing his inadequate evaluations, deleting footage of his work time, covering up his gaming on the job, hiding all of his illicit activities. As long as his immediate overseers didn't catch on, there was almost nothing he couldn't do.

His next step was to find a way to transfer to a planetside base with actual places to go and people to see. He'd kill for a girlfriend, but that would have to wait until he found a base that had women. With the way the Guild segregated the sexes, the only time he saw women were in illegal vids.

His thoughts were interrupted by flashing red lights on his console. Years of reflexes kicked in, and he hit the mute button before pulling up the readings. Radar picked up four objects heading for the central ring of the elevator. They were tiny, barely the size of a fist, but they were decelerating.

Vesper had thirty seconds to decide how to classify them. If he marked them as a threat, his supervisor would come over and want to look at his work, which wasn't ideal, considering he was hacking the shipping list on his secondary screen to have more contraband sent his way. If the supervisor wanted to see what he was working on, he wouldn't be able to hide it.

Besides, the objects were small. If they even hit the central hub, they'd just bounce off. No, he couldn't risk being found out over something that was probably nothing.

He marked them as "no threat" and closed the screen, and went back to his real work: making hell more livable.

————

Raptor armor plunged through space, their external, fusion-powered electromagnetic ion drives slowing their velocity to something the Marines could survive on impact.

"Fifty KPS," PFC Owens reported.

Jennings had one eye on the same screen and the other on the threat detectors. The armor's systems were the most advanced the Alliance could produce, but they were limited by size. While ideal for zero-G and ground combat, they weren't spacecraft. The attached EmDrives were for limited thrust, not enough to stop them from a velocity created by a gravcoil powered ship, which was why they had spent the last eight hours decelerating.

Jennings cracked her neck, relieving some of the tension. She yawned, taking a long moment to loosen up her head before activating squad comms.

Raptor armor operated off a mix of autonomic, manual, verbal, and computer-assisted controls. The armor relied on the marine's nervous system; whatever they did, the armor did. In an effort to keep the suits simple they only had two triggers to squeeze. The right trigger fired their multi-barrel coilgun mounted on their shoulder. Once engaged, the weapon rotated on an articulating arm, tracking the operator's pupil for targets. Marines could choose between full-auto, burst, and single-shot. As the squad sergeant, Jennings could choose for them; in this case, they were all set to single shot, except hers, which was on full-auto.

On their left hand were the grenades. They had access to a wide variety, from stun to high-explosive and everything in between. Again, Jennings had the override set to stun. While the Marines trained for any situation, the Corps found it easier to tell them when to pull the trigger rather than decide which trigger to pull. The last thing they needed was a confused private firing off a thermite round inside a starship.

The suit's onboard computer handled everything else, from active camouflage to ECM. All the operator needed to do was put their Raptor in the right mode.

"Ten KPS," Owens said.

Jennings watched the velocity trickle down with the range of the elevator's central hub. They could make out the massive structure on their optical sensors twenty klicks out. The planet filled the background, blocking out everything else. A blue-green jewel, it was how she imagined how old earth looked before she was covered in cities from pole to pole.

The "X" pattern of the satellites spread out, visible even at such a long distance. The hub, though, was what she focused on.

She'd imagined it would be circular, but it was more of a flat rectangle, with pyramid-like protrusions on the wide side and docking clamps and bays dotting it. The elevator itself was missing, which meant it was in transit. Up or down, she had no idea.

"One hundred MPS, five klicks," Owen's reported.

"Roger," she said.

"Identify tether point," she told the computer.

A yellow line appeared, dotting out from her point of view to a red circle on the station.

Tether locked, the computer flashed on her screen.

It counted down until she felt the vibration of the discharge. A hyper-thin line, strengthened by nanites, fired out from her shoulder and the other three Raptor suits at the same moment. They hit exactly where they aimed.

Her armor whirred as the line reeled her to the structure. Armored feet three times as big as her own clamped down on impact. The joints in the legs flexed to absorb the slight remaining momentum, and the three-toed claws beneath the digitigrade ankles magnetically locked on.

"Touchdown," she whispered.

A laser connected all four suits, allowing for instantaneous and undetectable communications.

"Owens," she said. "Burn it."

"Rog," he replied.

The space black suit knelt and pressed a four-fingered hand against the deck.

"It's too thick, Sergeant. We'll need an airlock."

On Alliance stations, emergency airlocks were located in precise positions dictated by law. She frowned. This wasn't an Alliance station, and no safety inspector from any government had ever looked at it. However, the basic need for emergency airlocks had to be the same.

"Fan out, advance by two, shoulder to shoulder," she said.

They acknowledged with a click of their mics and spread out, ten meters apart, two advancing while the other two guarded the rear. Jennings kept an eye on her threat meter. They were exposed, and the longer they were there, the more likely they would be discovered.

"Found it," Private Cole said.

A beacon appeared on their screens, and the other three Raptors homed in on him.

"Good job," Jennings said.

She remembered Gunny Hicks was always liberal with his praise, especially to the privates who needed constant assurance they were doing it right—and was an absolute hammer on their heads when they did it wrong.

"It's encrypted," Owens said. "Gonna have to burn it, and that is going to set off all kinds of alarms."

"Do it," she ordered. "We can deal with those when we're inside."

The Raptor armor's angular, almost lizard-like helmets clamped shields over their visors as Owens' plasma torch sparked to life. It cut at over twenty-thousand degrees and burned through the outer hatch like it was butter left out in the hot sun.

Atmosphere vented with explosive force, sending molten fragments into space. Pieces of the hatch banged off Owens' armor, which he ignored. The torch recessed into its housing, and Owens grabbed the cooling edges of the lock with the claw-like hands and heaved. The remains of the hatch sheared off, and he tossed it into space.

Red lighting spilled from the interior.

"Naki, go," Jennings ordered.

———

Alarms screamed in the control room, surprising everyone. Vesper jerked in his seat as the hull breach sounded, followed by intruder alert.

An ice-cold dread filled him, clenching his stomach as he realized it had to be the four contacts he didn't report. But how? They were too small and moving too slow to puncture the hull.

The massive screen on the bulkhead blinked away from the planet to shift to an interior airlock. A bright light burned through the center of the hatch, turning the reinforced nano-steel to slag. While it still glowed from the heat, a four fingered giant metal claw punched through the hatch and ripped it right off the housing.

Monsters out of some kind of mechanical nightmare burst through, heads bobbing like murderous chickens as they lumbered through the hallways. Then he caught a glimpse of the second one's chest: USMC RPT-01

The computer flashed on the big screen: "*United Systems Marine Corps Raptor Powered Armor.*"

Alliance Marines here? How? Why hadn't the starlane outpost communicated the arrival of their ship? How did they even see the planet? These were all good questions, and they flew through the mind of every single Guild employee on the elevator terminus—yet they had no answers.

———

Clad in his ELS suit like the rest of the crew, Jacob slid into his center seat as the alarms on *Interceptor* flashed.

"Breach initiated twenty-seven seconds ago, sir," Lieutenant West said.

"Thank you, Mark," he said.

With the marines on board, it was time for the *Interceptor* to give the people on the elevator terminus something else to think about it.

"Chief Suresh, go loud," he said.

"Aye, sir, going loud." Her grin was visible in the little mirror they used to see each other.

Lights switched on the panels as silent running disengaged. Ops immediately cycled the heat sink, which by itself would draw attention. However, Chief Suresh pushed the throttle forward and revved the acceleration up to three hundred Gs alerting every gravity sensor in a ten million klick radius.

"How long until they see us?" Jacob asked.

"Fourteen seconds, sir," Ensign Owusu replied.

Jacob didn't want to count on them having only the super-weapon *Aethia* used. From what they could piece together, *Aethia* had needed to change course to fire, not unlike the Long 9 mounted in the bow of *Interceptor*. However, a station could mount hundreds of other weapons, including torpedoes, short-range missiles, area effect guns... the list went on. They needed to be ready.

Jacob counted down from fourteen to zero in his head when he knew they would see the destroyer.

"ECM full, evasive maneuvers," he ordered. "Comms, commence jamming."

———

"What the bloody hell is going on?" Supervisor Krzywicki screamed.

They had their hands full between the breach and intruder alarm, trying to guide security services to the incoming threat. Then Vesper's computer detected a massive gravity wake emanating a little over four million klicks away.

Vesper only ever saw the known contacts and desperately

tried to recall how to identify unknowns. He smashed several buttons before querying the computer correctly. The color drained from his face, and his stomach clenched even tighter as the machine identified the threat.

"Mr. Supervisor, sir, it's an Alliance destroyer. The computer says Hellcat-class. She's on bearing perpendicular to us at a current speed of six thousand KPS and accelerating at three hundred gravities," he shouted, unable to keep his voice at a normal tone.

"One Alliance destroyer?" Krzywicki said. "Just one? You're sure?"

Vesper double-checked the computer. He also took an extra moment to close his non-work screen to keep his supervisor from tapping into his system and seeing what he was really doing with his time.

"Yes, sir. No other contacts. I'm linking in with the outpost and trying to get a better picture," he said.

Krzywicki hit the button that brought the space elevator to combat stations. "The intruders are the priority. Weapons, assign banks one through five to alternate fire on the ship. Let the computer handle it. I doubt we'll need more than one volley."

The weapons officer, a petite man with overly long hair, clapped his hands together and went to work.

"All security personnel, converge on access way one-five-two," Supervisor Krzywicki said.

———

"Junction," Jennings pointed out.

She hunkered her suit down, facing the way they'd come, her shoulder-mounted gun guarding their six.

"Roger," Owens said.

He lumbered up to the computer junction and jammed his clawed hand into the electronics. Nanites streamed out of his fist, resolving the connection between the base's computer and his Raptor suit.

"I've got limited access."

"OPFOR?" Jennings asked.

"Closing. Thirty seconds, port side," Owens replied.

"You've got the lights?"

"Yes, Sergeant. I do."

"Kill them," Jennings ordered.

On a space station, the only source of light came from within. Few people experience true darkness, and the marines knew that oh so well. Every light in the station blinked twice and turned off, plunging the inside into absolute blackness.

Shouts of confusion echoed down the hatchway as the opposing security force was suddenly blind.

"Advance," Jennings ordered.

As large as the Raptor suits were, they didn't look like they should move fast. However, they could run up to a hundred kilometers an hour on open ground and jump ten meters straight up. In the confined halls of the elevator base, their massive, armored shoulders bounced off the bulkheads, and their clawed feet tore chunks out of the deck.

Eight armed men with light body armor and shock rifles lined the hatch. They could hear the Raptors but not see them.

Jennings arrived first.

"Flash," she said, then pulled the trigger in her left hand.

A magnesium flare launched from her shoulder, lighting up the hallway like a miniature sun as it burned the strobing pulse into the enemy's corneas. She charged behind the projectile, knocking bodies aside with ease. Men crunched into the hull, bones breaking and skulls bouncing off the metal.

The security force was reduced to a scattering of moaning men and dead bodies within a few seconds.

"Don't step on them," she said as she proceeded.

The computer mapped their progress, comparing it against the external layout and showing her the most likely course to the command deck.

"Contact rear," Naki said. His coilgun barked twice, followed by the shriek of shredding metal. "Defense drones eliminated."

They weren't the problem, however. The security force's first responders were lightly armed and easy to take out. Drones were the second wave and not much tougher. Next, she expected heavier armed troops with weapons capable of damaging the Raptors.

"Naki, take Cole and head to the elevator. Owens and I will continue to the command center."

"Semper Fi, Sergeant," Naki said, lumbering off to the starboard, with Cole following him.

Jennings continued, releasing the safety on her coilgun. With the safety off, the computer could auto-fire at explicit threats. Ahead, the motion sensors showed something large coming their way.

"Movement," she said.

Owens broke right, slamming his suit against the hull while she went left. Two men in heavy armor came around the corner armed with large plasma rifles.

"Contact front," Owens said.

"Flash," Jennings said.

Another flare fired out of her shoulder, bouncing off the side of the hallway and twirling through the air. These men wore helmets and were likely unaffected by the darkness or the flash grenade. Sergeant Jennings didn't enjoy killing, it was simply her job, to be done when needed and at no other time. If she could take down the enemy any other way, she would.

She squeezed the trigger on her coilgun. The barrels rotated, raining fire down the passageway. The first armored opponent blew apart as five-millimeter rounds tore him to pieces. The second one squeezed off a plasma stream a half-second before Owens' coilgun hit him twice in the chest, dropping him like a stone.

Superheated plasma splashed off Owens' armor, dripping down onto the deck in molten puddles.

"Status?" Jennings asked.

"Operational. Armor's scorched, but I'm good."

Jennings acknowledged with a mic click and took off, lumbering down the hatchway. The computer had a good read on the station layout. Between power distribution and thermal variance, she was sure they were going in the right direction.

Rounds pinged off her armor from the side. She turned, seeing a security man with a projectile weapon firing at her.

"Bean bag," she said and fired.

A half-pound of hardened gel shot out and took the man in the chest, sending him flying into the bulkhead.

"This is the hatch, Sergeant," Owens said.

A large hatchway with double doors made of reinforced metal had the words "Control Room" stenciled on them. She took three lumbering steps, lifted her leg, and kicked the center of the hatch with all her powered armor might.

———

"Torpedo launch... second launch, torpedoes inbound, two-seven-zero-zero acceleration.

"Damn, that's fast," Lieutenant Fawkes muttered.

"All batteries, fire," Jacob ordered.

Outwardly, Jacob showed no reaction to the revelation that the Guild's torpedoes accelerated four times as fast as the Alliance's Mark-XII's. Inwardly it sent chills down his spine.

"Flank speed," he ordered Chief Suresh.

"Aye, sir, flank speed." *Interceptor* shot forward, piling on the KPS, giving the guns a few seconds longer to engage the incoming projectiles.

Vesper panicked when the gunfire started. It was one thing to see a gunfight in a vid, but hearing it right outside the hatch was unnerving.

He desperately tried to stay calm, even as his heart pounded in his ears and his mouth went dry. The rules stated that no one was allowed to leave their station during an emergency. With sudden clarity, Vesper realized the rules weren't designed to keep the employees alive so much as doing their job until they died at their station.

"Arm yourselves," Supervisor Krzywicki said.

He pulled out a particle beam pistol Vesper had no idea the man had.

"With what?" Vesper shouted back.

Everyone in the room had watched their state-of-the-art plasma rifles slide off the armored marines like so much water. Then the hatch clanged, and the room shook. Vesper leaped out of his chair, ducking behind his console.

"We need to blow the station," someone yelled.

Vesper knew, at least intellectually, that the Guild policy was never to allow bases to fall into enemy hands: a policy written by people who never had to actually follow through with it. Then the hatch clanged again, and a three-toed appendage burst through. Clawed hands replaced it and pulled the hatch apart as if unwrapping a treat.

"Fire," Krzywicki said as he pulled the trigger.

Blue beams of accelerated electrons lanced out, striking the armor. The lead monster rushed in, shoulder-mounted weapon spitting fire. Vesper hit the deck, hands over his head, screaming as the cannon ripped through the room. After a moment, the firing stopped.

He opened his eyes. The large screen was demolished, covered with a red liquid he didn't recognize. It was blood and other organic matter. Vesper puked. When he looked up, the body of the man next to him was shredded, half his skull missing. Everyone was dead. Turned into dogmeat where they stood.

"Surrender," a voice growled.

A rotating barrel filled his vision. A menacing mechanical reptile stared down at him, and he sputtered his surrender while aspirating his vomit.

CHAPTER TWENTY-SIX

J acob hit the button on his MFD, bringing up the communications from Sergeant Jennings. Sweat matted her face, and she wiped a bare arm across her head. She wasn't in her Raptor armor, which Jacob didn't blame her for. They'd spent almost twenty hours inside the suits.

"Sitrep?" he asked.

"We have control of the station. No casualties on our side. However, sir, aside from the six-security personnel who were wounded, only one surrendered on their end. The security people have no idea how to run the elevator. The only operations person is a man named Vesper. He's volunteered to help us. Unfortunately, sir, there's no sign of our citizens here. From what we can tell, no one lives on this station."

Jacob scratched his head. His helmet was off, but he still wore the suit. They'd managed to shoot down the two incoming torpedoes, but it was close. Thankfully, Jennings and the Marines had taken control before they had to face any more of the deadly weapons.

It struck him as odd that no one on board knew how to use

the elevator. How did they operate it if not from the station? It was also unfortunate that the missing miners weren't there.

"Can I speak to Vesper?" Jacob asked.

"Yes, sir." Jennings left, returning a second later, holding a thin, pale man by the collar and jerking him toward the screen.

"Mr. Vesper, I presume?" Jacob asked.

"Y-yes," he said.

His eyes darted around, and fear was plain on his face.

"I'm Lieutenant Commander Jacob T. Grimm of the Alliance destroyer USS *Interceptor*. My marine tells me you surrendered?"

"I don't want to die," the man replied.

His eyes shot back and forth and his voice trembled with fear. Jacob guessed he was in his early twenties.

He didn't know the situation, but he was curious to know why so few had surrendered to such an obviously powerful opponent. "Fair enough. First, thank you for your offer to help. We appreciate it. Can you tell me where the Alliance prisoners are?"

Vesper glanced around, eyes widening. "You... you did all *this* because of those miners?" His mouth opened and closed like a fish.

"Alliance citizens were taken, Mr. Vesper, and I want them back. We don't leave our people behind," Jacob said.

He watched the man work through the statement as if the idea had never occurred to him.

Vesper swayed. "I'm sorry. We're very compartmentalized, so I don't have the information—"

Jacob sighed. He'd hoped this was a lead.

Vesper dropped his voice to a whisper and continued, "—I can guess, though. About a week ago, a transport ship came through. They moved them through the station down to Omega Base... uh, the planet."

Jacob's eyes widened as he realized the situation.

"Mr. Vesper, how many planets like this *Omega Base,* does the Guild control?" Jacob asked.

On paper, the Guild had one planet, positioned outside the "northern" border of the Terran Republic. They were supposed to be more like bankers than a governmental force. Jacob struggled to recall anything he'd learned in school or Academy about them. He knew they controlled the terraforming tech, like the fusion reactors spewing water vapor on Zuckabar, but beyond that he had no idea.

"Well, I've only ever seen the planet I was trained on and this one. We transfer a lot, though, and don't usually see the same place or people twice. I wish I could be more helpful."

Jacob gave the man a reassuring smile. "You are, sir, you are. Thank you for your help. May I speak to Sergeant Jennings?"

"Sure," Vesper said. He hesitated a moment. "Captain Grimm? May I come with you when you leave?"

"We're not a taxi, Mr. Vesper. I can't just take you and drop you off—"

"No, I mean, can I request," Vesper struggled for the word. "Asylum?"

Jacob stopped, stunned at the request. If the tables were turned, he couldn't imagine asking an enemy for asylum. He glanced at Lieutenant West.

"I don't know the protocol, sir," West whispered.

"I will look into it and get back to you," Grimm said.

"Thank you," Vesper replied before disappearing off camera.

Sergeant Jennings' crystal blue eyes pierced the camera with an unwavering and unnerving gaze. Jacob reminded himself she was on their side.

"Skipper?"

"The Corsair's on the way, ETA three hours. Secure the elevator until it arrives, then plan for an assault on the planet. I want our people back."

"Aye, aye, Skipper," she said.

A second later, the screen went black. Jacob leaned back, worry furrowing his brow. It was going to be a long three hours.

"Carter, you have the bridge. Chief Suresh, would you be so kind as to summon your relief and join Lieutenant West and me in the briefing room?" As he spoke, he headed for the hatch.

"Aye, sir," Fawkes said. "I have the bridge."

"Aye, aye, sir" Chief Suresh said.

A few minutes later, Jacob looked across the table at his second officer and the COB. He tapped one hand on the table while looking over everything the Alliance had in the database about the Terraforming Guild. Silence filled the room as he scanned the files. It wasn't much.

"Chief, I asked you here because you've got the most time in service. Do you know anything about the Terraforming Guild that isn't in the record? You lived on Vishnu, they're one of the planets using the service."

"Yes sir, I grew up on Vishnu, but I don't recall hearing anything about the Guild beyond we owed them money for our atmosphere scrubbers."

"I was stationed at Bethesda for a year. Vishnu is a pretty planet," Jacob said.

"Thank you, sir. I grew it myself," Suresh replied.

Mark coughed, covering a chuckle.

"Nothing you can think of that will help out?" Jacob asked.

She shook her head, "Negative, Skipper. The Guild is... aloof at best. They don't interact with civilians."

"I'm starting to see why," he said.

"Sir?" West interjected.

"Based on my conversation with Mr. Vesper, it doesn't sound like they engender much loyalty from their people. The downside is they have a lot more people than we ever imagined. Multiple planets and, of course, ships. It is vital we return this information to the Alliance. Understood?"

"Yes, sir," they both said.

"COB, get with Owusu and program us a course back to the starlane. I want to evac with a moment's notice if needed."

"Aye, sir. I'm on it," she said, heading to the bridge.

"Mark," Jacob looked at his second officer. "We need our acceleration situation fixed. What's the status there?"

Mark tapped his NavPad and brought up a miniature hologram of the ship in blue, with sections on the forward starboard hull in red. He flicked his fingers, and the hologram leaped to the table's projector and expanded to 1/50th scale.

"Lieutenant Gonzales got with the XO before she departed, and they brainstormed some ideas. He pitched them to me, but I think the best solution is for—"

Jacob settled in, letting Mark talk him through the technicalities of the repairs on the forward section. He trusted his people to do the job. Now he had to do his and return them home safe.

———

Air hissed as the Corsair mated with the station's main airlock. The Navy personnel had their suits sealed and weapons ready, just in case. Yuki was in constant contact with Sergeant Jennings, but there was no need to be careless.

The hatch hummed open, revealing Jennings in her gray marine tank top and shorts, soaked in sweat from her time in the Raptor armor.

"Don't shoot," she said, nonchalantly holding up her hands.

They lowered their weapons, and Yuki stepped out, pulling off her helmet. "Sergeant, report?"

Jennings saluted and then turned around, walking for the control tower. Yuki fell in next to the short marine.

"We have seven prisoners. Two of them are critically wounded," she said, glancing over her shoulder at Desper.

"Where are they?" the medical PO asked.

Jennings let out a sharp, ear-splitting whistle as they approached an intersection. The bulkhead moved, and RPT-02 towered over them, a burned streak of metal etched down the front of his armor like the trail of a molten tear.

"Owens, take the Doc and whomever she needs to the prisoners."

"Aye, aye, Sergeant," his filtered voice came back.

The reptilian armor gave a very human shrug and turned toward where they had the prisoners lying on the deck. PO Desper peeled off two of her people and shifted her bag around as she followed the immense powered armor.

"We estimated at least thirty people on the base. What happened?" Yuki asked.

"You'll see, ma'am," Jennings said.

Yuki followed the clearly exhausted marine sergeant down another corridor. After the time in the armor and another three here on guard duty, who wouldn't be worn out?

Jennings pointed at a ramp down.

"Cole and Naki went to secure the elevator, ma'am, and... well..." Jennings stopped. "Chief Redfern, can you take the rest of the shore party up that way."

She pointed to the shattered control room hatch. "That's where the technical stuff is, and... well, I hope none of you had a large breakfast."

Yuki noticed a few of the spacers blanching but hid her grin. Dead bodies were part and parcel of the Navy. It was sad, but it was the job.

"Roger that, Sarge," Redfern said.

He waved his troops forward, giving Yuki a knowing wink as they passed.

Jennings bristled at Redfern referring to her as "Sarge."

She filed it away for future reference. Not that she wanted to bother her roommate. As bunkmates went, Jennings was first-rate. She made her rack, didn't leave anything lying around, and always did her fair share of cleaning. Talkative; however, the marine was not.

As Yuki stepped past the marine to go down the ramp, Jennings put one hard hand on the XO's shoulder. "Ma'am, just remember, we were forced to do this. When we moved to take the elevator entrance, things went sideways fast."

The look on Jennings' face, the fact that there *was* a look on her face, unsettled Yuki.

She nodded and continued down the ramp. "Understood, Sergeant, the Raptors record everything anyway and—"

The smell hit her first, like a public head left uncleaned for too long. Then she realized the bulkheads weren't painted black, they were covered in dried blood.

"What the fu—" she stopped mid-word to bend over and vomit the remains of her breakfast over the deck.

"They wouldn't surrender, ma'am, and they had weapons," Jennings whispered.

What Marine power armor had done to the poor bastards wasn't something she wished on her worst enemy. They'd never sort out the remains of who was who. They were all just... exploded all over the space elevator doors.

"Why?" Kim gasped when she could breathe again.

She turned away, suddenly envious of the spacers sent to the control room.

"Vesper says the security forces won't surrender. We only captured who we did because they were unconscious. As for the rest, I guess the station manager is supposed to blow the place if it falls. We were quick enough to prevent that from happening, obviously."

"What do you mean?" Kim asked as they crested the ramp back up into the passageway.

"We forced the hatch and immediately took fire. After the plasma burn on Owens' armor, I didn't want to take the chance of them getting lucky, so we sprayed the room."

Kim didn't think she could puke again, but her stomach was going to give it a hard try. The control room wasn't as bad as the elevator entrance, but it was littered with the shattered, blasted, and exploded bodies of the previous occupants'.

"Sergeant?" a man's voice said.

Yuki didn't recognize it. She turned to see a thin, pasty young man with dark hair, fidgeting with his hands in front of him.

"XO, this is Controller Vesper. He's the one who agreed to help us. He'll fill you in, ma'am. If it's okay with you, I'm going to rotate my people out to get some rack time."

"Semper Fi, Marine," Yuki said.

Jennings raised one eyebrow as if to say, "Don't pretend to be a Marine." She snapped to, saluted, and exited in a brisk walk.

"Okay, Mr. Vesper, I'm Lieutenant Senior Grade Kimiko Yuki, *Interceptor*'s XO. You want to tell me what's going on?" she asked.

He turned, expecting her to follow as he carefully moved across the deck, trying not to step in any of the puddles of sticky blood. Sitting down, he pulled up the screen showing the station's status.

"We run-in twelve-hour shifts, and we were a couple of hours in when your marines... arrived. In another three hours, the lift will arrive with the replacement crew, expecting everyone on the elevator to swap out for the two-hour ride down to the planet."

Yuki nodded, keeping up. "What you're saying is that you don't control the space elevator from here?"

"No, ma'am... I mean yes, ma'am. Err, correct," he finally said.

"What do you do up here?" Yuki asked.

"The laborers were here to unload or load cargo from the Outriders. Security kept an eye on the laborers, and the bridge crew was here for Space-Traffic Control. My boss—" he started to look toward the center of the room, then stopped. "He was here to keep us on task."

"Mr. Vesper, you're in an uncharted system, on a secret base that's almost invisible. Who exactly are you resupplying out here?" she asked.

He shook his head. "Well, uh, Lieutenant?" Yuki nodded, letting him know he'd said it right. "All I know is that twice a week, an M-class freighter comes from starlane Violet—that's the lane leading to Zuckabar—and departs via starlane Gold. Every week like clockwork, one of the Outriders dock and resupply. I don't know where they go or where they come from, though."

Yuki blinked several times as the information hit her like a slap in the face.

"Are you telling me there's another starlane out there?" she asked.

"Well, yes. I don't know where it goes, but Gold is the other lane out of the system. We monitor the ships coming and going when they're in close orbit."

Yuki slapped her hand on his mouth to force him silent. She put one finger to her ear to activate the suit's comms. "Baxter, do we have a tight beam to the ship?" she asked.

"Aye ma'am," PO Baxter said from where he was nestled safely in the belly of the Corsair.

"Patch me through. Any delay?" she asked.

"Patching. The delay is less than a second, ma'am," he said.

She waited while the laser hit *Interceptor* almost three hundred thousand kilometers away.

"Foxtrot Two-Zero to *Interceptor*-Actual," she said.

It seemed the only place free of human remains was the overhead, so she looked up, waiting for the response.

"Foxtrot Two-Zero, this is Indigo One-Five. Actual is asleep. Is it urgent?"

Kim thought about it for a second. The captain was running himself on the ragged edge, on the bridge at all hours when he wasn't pacing the ship talking to the crew.

"Negative. Inform Astro there is another starlane. I don't have a vector yet, but be on the lookout at—" she glanced down at the display screen Vesper pointed to. "Zero-four-five to zero-six-zero. There could be a ship out there."

"Aye, aye, ma'am. Will relay. Indigo-One-Five out."

Kim felt better with the ship warned. One problem down, untold millions to go.

"Okay, Vesper, let's assume our people came in on one of those transports. Where would they be?"

The computer tech brought up another screen showing the base on the planet below.

CHAPTER TWENTY-SEVEN

Despite being the busiest hotel on the entire station and booked out with the full twenty-five hundred guests, the main lobby of the St. Regis hotel was a ghost town in the middle of the night.

The air in the lobby shimmered, but the handful of employees staffing the front desk never looked up. Nadia stepped lightly, moving through the luxurious wide-open space with a mixture of speed and care. She was dressed head-to-toe in a blackout suit, designed to render the wearer invisible to the electromagnetic spectrum. Sound, however, was still being produced, so she had to be careful.

She dodged one drunken couple as they walked to the bank of mag-lifts leading to the lower rooms. Those weren't the rooms Nadia was interested in: she needed the special VIP rooms that started at three hundred feet. The higher-up ones had a lower gravity and were reserved for the richest clients. Like a certain Mr. Pelican. Another rookie mistake in the spy game. No one likes to slum it, but Nadia could go months on any planet without leaving any trace of her passage simply by sticking to the places people didn't look.

It would seem, she decided, that the Guild wanted to keep their agent in luxury while he completed his mission on Kremlin Station. A dead giveaway that amateurs had planned and executed the Op.

The doors to her target room open, and she darted forth, dodging past a limping man as he exited. Once inside, she detached her NavPad and pressed it against the computer. Nanites flowed from the device; seizing local control of the lift, the pre-programmed routine sent it flying up. In moments, it came to a halt exactly where she needed to be. Nadia stepped out, following the ping on her HUD to the door where her target slept. One more application of her NavPad, and the door slid open like a whisper. She had to be careful lest she alert her target to her presence.

Nadia had spent some time in luxury hotels, but this suite was opulent. She ignored the spacious front room with its zero-G tub and total immersion entertainment center and headed right for the bedroom.

She took a risk, she knew, entering the target's apartment while he was home. However, she needed intel, and just following him around wasn't doing the job. He was there for a reason, and it wasn't to spend every day looking at a museum before returning to his hotel to gamble.

Entering his domicile at all was a considerable risk, but it was a risk worth taking if she found what she was looking for. It wasn't, though, a risk worth taking more than once.

Her NavPad made quick work of the secondary lock on the bedroom door. She slipped noiselessly inside, taking each step with premeditated care. The target's chest rose smoothly, signifying the depth of his sleep. Nadia moved to the far wall, where a work desk was attached. It was empty, but Nadia checked it anyway, looking for a sign of what the Guild was up to. She frowned. Nothing.

In fact, other than the man sleeping and the built-in hotel computers, there wasn't a single piece of computer tech in the room. She'd expected to find a computer she could infiltrate to discover their plans. Everyone in the universe used a computer. Where was his? After each movement, every glance or breath, she checked to make sure he still slept. One errant step, and it would be over.

Determined not to go home empty-handed, she switched her goggles to thermal vision. The room turned into a collection of dark blues and purples with splotches of red and... white?

Mr. Pelican's body radiated the temperature of a sleeping human, except for his head. Around his forehead and scalp, white plumes, like tiny little mushroom clouds, exploded around him in bursts.

Then it hit her. Tricky devils must have invented some kind of nanite computer system and implanted it into the brains of their agents. Nadia risked taking a few steps closer, raising her NavPad as she approached. EMI picked up considerably with every step. It was enshrouding the sleeping man like a shield.

His eyes popped open an instant before he bolted upright, hand coming up with a hidden weapon. The lights flashed on, illuminating every square inch of the room. Nadia froze, not moving, not even breathing. She suppressed her impulse to just kill him. She needed to know what he was doing, what his ultimate goal was, and whether he had allies. None of which she would find out if he were dead.

His shoulders twitched, relaxing slightly before he threw the covers aside. Padding to the bathroom, he walked right past her. The moment he disappeared, she allowed herself a breath. Ten steps separated her from the bedroom door. She took one, then another. The toilet flushed, and she froze again as he came back into the room. For a moment, she thought he saw her as he stopped and looked around the room. The sonic stunner in his hand swayed.

He turned back to his bed, and she took another step. He spun, bringing up the gun and firing. Nadia threw herself sideways as the cone of hypersonic waves flashed by her, exploding against the wall.

She hit the carpet, rolled, and was back on her feet, running like mad for the door. His aim wavered as the blackout suit did its work. He couldn't quite make out her figure. His weapon whined as it repeatedly discharged. The first one missed, but the second grazed her back, sending her flying sideways.

Nadia hit the door jam, bounced, and rolled into the living room. She barely shielded her face in time as the second blast hit her full-on.

CHAPTER TWENTY-EIGHT

From under the comfort of his heavy wool blanket, Director Cardinal frowned. The last check-in from the space elevator was over five hours old. If the supervisor was screwing around on the company network, he'd make sure the man paid hell for it.

Throwing off his blankets, he swore all the way to the bathroom as the cold tightened his skin and froze his toes. Furious, he pulled his work suit out, muttering about being the only person in the system who actually wanted to do his job. Of course, his job was to find fault with the other employees and reprimand and punish them as needed.

Cardinal's foul mood certainly made him like the idea of punishing someone. Hourly status reports were mandatory. Storming out of his room, he accosted the first person he came across.

"Take me to the control room, now," he demanded.

The man squeaked, turned, and practically ran down the hall.

Cardinal wanted to look back over the last six months of reports to see exactly how often the dunderheads on the elevator had missed their hourly schedule. It was just dumb luck he had spotted it this time. He blamed his insomnia. If he hadn't stayed up late, catching up on his work, he would never have noticed the lapse.

"This is the lift, sir," the meek man said.

A large red number on the doors counted down; Cardinal knew it was the time until the elevator returned from the station. He was about to rebuke the man, but it was perfect. The elevator was only seconds away, and he could tear into the station's supervisor in person. Maybe even have the man administratively punished. His lips curled up at the idea.

Dismissing the worthless laborer, he positioned himself in the middle of the doors. Carefully crossing his arms to display the appropriate amount of unhappiness.

He wanted to strike fear into the idiotic supervisor. Make him kneel in awe of his majestic power. He held his hand up, finger pointed to the sky, and prepared himself. As soon as the door opened, he would leap forward, point his hand right at the supervisor's chest, and *demand* answers. The man would be too stunned to lie and would confess his crimes immediately.

Unfortunately for Director Cardinal, when the doors opened, he was so preoccupied with carrying out his plan that he didn't look to see who was actually in the elevator compartment.

He leaped forward. "Ha!"

Then his mind caught up, and he had a single heartbeat to wonder what the hell was in the elevator before the rotating coilgun tore him to shreds.

———

"Cease fire," Jennings shouted.

It was partially an unnecessary order, as there was nothing

remaining to fire at. No one could have expected someone to leap at them as the doors opened, and she could hardly blame PFC Owens for firing. She was fairly certain she would have done the same if she were on point.

"Sorry, Sarge," Owens said.

"Check targets before firing," Jennings said.

"Aye, Sergeant," her team replied.

Jennings pulled up the map Vesper had downloaded to their computers. The base had a few thousand people, including several hundred security forces. They would break into two teams. Alpha (call sign: Downtown-One) would bee-line for the detention facility. Bravo (Downtown-Two) would go in the opposite direction, raising as much hell as possible and heading for Omega Base's power dish.

Since the satellites in orbit provided a near-constant stream of energy, they couldn't stop the incoming power. What they could do was blast the regulator into atoms, and the power would go with it—along with any defenses.

With their orbital defenses down, Boudreaux would provide air support and exfil, not to mention *Interceptor* could make orbit and provide emergency fire support with her batteries.

"Bravo team, go," she ordered.

Lance Corporal Naki clicked his mic twice and took off, with Private Cole right behind him.

Jennings' timer popped up, counting down sixty seconds. It would give Downtown-Two time to be noticed and draw security away from Downtown-One.

———

Naki skidded to a halt, his half-ton powered armor screeching against the floor plates.

"Cole, we're in the elevator building now. Beyond this door

is a courtyard surrounded by the larger complex. Our target is approximately two klicks southeast. We go out here, dump some HE's around us as we run, then over the wall and on our way to the power regulator. As soon as we have confirmation of our target, we go weapons hot, understood?" Naki asked the private.

"Yes, Corporal. Understood," the private confirmed.

"Good man," Naki said, unconsciously mimicking the captain.

Sergeant Jennings had turned over local control to Naki. The corporal set their weapons to full auto and gave the computer complete control. Anything the threat detection software picked up, the multi-barreled coilgun would eliminate.

"Ready?" Naki asked.

"Semper Fi," Cole replied.

Naki lifted one three-toed foot and slammed it through the door. The metal frame buckled with a wrenching sound and exploded outward. Cole ducked down and charged out. Instantly, a high-explosive grenade shot out from a panel on his left shoulder, firing up the side of the space elevator building and detonating twenty meters away to confuse the enemy.

"Downtown-One this is Downtown-Two, go loud!" Naki said.

Click-click came Sergeant Jennings' response.

Leaving the search and rescue to Downtown-One, Naki focused on their task. He followed Cole out the door, firing a smoke grenade filled with chafe to cover them from any weapons fire.

The marines had caught the base completely by surprise.

Naki targeted the main gate, and his coilgun let out a ripping sound as fifty rounds of five-millimeter tungsten penetrators vaporized the steel double doors used for vehicles to enter the compound. He leaped, followed by Cole, their Raptor suits springing them ten meters into the air to land on top of the wall.

Cole's shoulder-mounted coilgun spun on its articulating arm and fired a three-round burst. Naki didn't look to see what had triggered the threat. Speed was their weapon; the faster they went, the more difficult it would be to overwhelm them with superior numbers. Naki was only concerned with armored vehicles or powered armor, and the corporal didn't think they had either. He grinned inside his suit, letting himself feel a little superior in their position.

Raptor armor was the ultimate force multiplier. Except plasma guns, no amount of small arms fire could hurt it. Even those, though, would take time to penetrate the thick hide and reactive armor—time the wielder wouldn't have.

"Radar's clear, no air vehicles," Cole said.

"Let's go." Naki fired another volley of HE grenades straight up; these were programmed to detonate on impact.

Together, the two marines leaped off the wall, their digitigrade legs extending to absorb the impact, allowing them to keep running without pause as they hit the ground.

Outside the walls were the main barracks—several squat buildings almost like factories. Based on the space elevator's computer, it was a little after 0900 hours, and they would be empty, as the day shift was starting and the night shift was finishing with last meal.

"Thermite," he ordered.

Grenade canisters in both suits rotated until the thermite clicked into place.

"Fire."

The thump-thump of compressed air sounded, and four grenades flew off left and right. They hit the buildings six meters apart and burst into a bright, burning flame at over three thousand degrees.

Twin columns of black smoke rose behind them as they departed the immediate area, running at maximum speed. The half-ton, armored, man-shaped reptiles sped up to a hundred kilometers per hour, shaking the ground and carving great holes in the concrete.

———

"What is going on? Where's Director Cardinal?" Supervisor Bevin asked.

No one answered him. He queried the computer, only to have it reply: *Director Cardinal's life signs not detected.*

"Intruder alert!" someone yelled.

"Bring the base to full alert," Bevin shouted to the control room. "All security personnel are to arm themselves with lethal weapons and report to the Central spire. Where are these intruders headed?"

"Straight for the power regulator, sir." Controller Pablo's hands shook as he hit his keys.

A screen popped up, showing several columns of smoke, ruined buildings, and a hole blasted in the wall. Bevins frowned. They simply weren't outfitted to fight a full-scale invasion. There had to be dozens, if not hundreds, of enemy troops to do that kind of damage. If they managed to bring down the regulator, the base could switch to backup power, but it wouldn't last them more than a few hours.

"Put out a distress call to the Outriders. They should be able to respond. After that, call the damn outpost. They should have seen something come through the starlane. And get every available armed person to the power regulators!"

———

The distant explosions brought a smile to Jennings' face.

"Owens, burn it," she ordered.

"On it," he said.

Owens' four "fingers" bent backward, and the cutter tele-scoped out. The tip flared to life, burning bright blue as he ran the monstrous arm down the side of the reinforced door. If Vesper was right, they were outside Omega Base's detention facility. She was surprised to find the outer door unguarded, even with Downtown-Two causing a ruckus. Unless they were civilians, totally unprepared for an assault. If she were an amateur, she could imagine sending everyone to stop a threat to the power regulator. Which was exactly why they did it.

"Thirty seconds," Owens informed her.

The suit's internal display, just like her space armor, gave her a three-hundred-and-sixty-degree view with the field of vision condensed to a hundred and forty degrees. Jennings didn't need to stand with her back to Owens to guard him, but she did out of habit. Not every marine was trained in power armor. The six-week school on Blackrock was considered the second toughest school in the entire Alliance military machine, and the marines who passed were authorized to wear a pin on their dress uniform—a Raptor's head with crosshairs for eyes.

The gist of the training was to rid marines of any bad habits. They needed to be more tactical in armor, not less. Cautious of corners, fields of fire, and other small unit tactics. Yes, powered armor was a force multiplier of at least a thousand, but the time they would spend in the suit was insignificant compared to the time not. Training sloppy in the suit made sloppy marines outside the suit.

Five meters away, two men wearing black uniforms turned the corner. Their sidearms labeled them as security and threats. They froze, eying her massive armor and the giant coilgun swiveling their way. Their eyes went wide, transfixed by the weapon.

"Surrender," she said.

To be heard on the battlefield required a loud, low-pitched sound. Raptor suits automatically enhanced the user's voice, giving it a growl for intimidation purposes.

The one on the right threw his hands in the air. The one on the left went for his gun. Three rounds hit him before it cleared the holster, the first to his pelvis, then his stomach, and the final round square in the sternum. At four times the speed of sound and weighing twenty grams each, his body exploded, coming apart like a bomb had gone off inside, showering the other man with blood and gore.

The survivor stood there in stunned silence, covered in what used to be a human being. A high pitch keen escaped his mouth, and he dropped to his knees, wailing and begging for his life.

"I don't know about you, sergeant, but I find these Guild types to be cut-rate cowards," Owens said.

Jennings didn't reply, but she did agree with him. Killing them didn't sit well with her. For all their advanced tech, the people running the place seemed little more than imbeciles trained to use the equipment—without any desire to excel at their jobs.

"Run," she growled at the groveling man. "Now."

He slid in the blood, trying to stand and run simultaneously. It took him a moment before he vanished around the corner.

"Through—" as Owens spoke, the power and the lights went out.

———

"There she is," Naki said to Cole.

The two men slid to a halt in a hail of dust and debris.

Multiple smaller buildings surrounded the hundred-meter-tall dish. The air above it hummed with transferred energy.

Sirens in the distance, as well as the roar of an aircar closed in on the two marines.

"I don't think we have time to dismantle it by hand," Cole said.

"No, we do not. Mortars," Naki ordered the computer.

The long, multi-barreled coilguns on their backs locked into place as the nanites reconfigured them to fire high velocity mortar shells. In reality, they were grenade innards wrapped in nano-steel. Ten seconds and their weapons were angled to fire on the power station.

"Rapid-fire, fifty degrees spread, alternate HE and Thermite," Naki ordered.

"Aye, Corporal. Fifty degrees spread, HE and Thermite. Ready."

"Fire," he ordered.

The guns thumped and recoiled as they began firing two mortar shells a second. Their computers did complex calculations, re-aiming the weapons with each volley to arrange impact at the same instant. Ten high-explosive grenades and ten thermite grenades hit simultaneously across the dish.

It blew apart, sending a gout of flame a hundred meters up. Fragments of the dish flew through the air in every direction for half a klick. The air above the dish superheated as the beamed energy suddenly had nowhere to go, adding to the destruction.

"Magazines empty," Cole said.

"Same," Naki replied.

They had flashers left, but that was it for lethal grenades.

"Charlie-One-One, this is Downtown-Two, you are clear to start your run."

"Roger Downtown-Two, Charlie-One-One acknowledges. Relaying info to Indigo-Actual," Chief Boudreaux replied.

Naki glanced up—it wouldn't take the Corsair long to descend, but until they were on it with the prisoners, the mission wasn't over.

————

The door fell to Owens' powered claw, and he ripped the remains off the frame and hurled it behind him.

Jennings ran through while he covered her, slicing the pie from left to right. The front room was empty, nothing more than a processing center. Multiple regular doors exited the room, and she found the one labeled detention. Metal shrieked as she shoulder-checked the secure entrance.

She followed the flailing door in, yelling as she did so. "Alliance Marines!"

Magnetic holding cells lined the hallway, six each, and one large one in the back where the prisoners were. The computer counted twenty-four people, including six children. Which meant eleven were missing.

"Who's in charge here?" she growled.

An older man with gray hair and a pronounced bald spot raised his hand as he stepped forward to shield his people.

"I am," he said. "Mining Chief Castigate."

"Owens, find the controls and release them," she said as she marched, hunkered down to avoid damaging the ceiling with his giant armor and dropping potentially dangerous debris on the floor.

Any compassion she had for the Guild employees vanished. The prisoners were dressed in flimsy t-shirts and underwear, nothing else. Her three-sixty visor allowed her to glance either way without moving her head, and she couldn't help but notice there were no women.

Magnetic containment flickered and died as Owens found

the controls. Without the slight glow of containment, the only illumination was the emergency lighting.

———

"Why isn't the backup coming on?" Supervisor Bevin demanded from a man who knew no more than himself.

The radio squawked, "Sir, it's gone... just... gone!"

"What do you mean it's gone?" Bevin demanded.

"They blew it up, the whole thing, it's on fire."

Panic built in Bevin's chest. Backup power would maintain the base, but they couldn't use the space elevator without the power array.

This was no pirate raid or mere incursion—this was a full-fledged invasion, which left him only one option. He glanced at the panel before squeezing his eyes shut. It wasn't fair. He shouldn't have to make the decision.

Yet it was the only option left him. Corporate procedure was clear and the good of the company was paramount. He *had* to do it. Bevin placed his hand on the scanner, opening the panel to the destruct button.

———

Boudreaux guided the Corsair down through the stratosphere, air-breathing plasma engines screaming as she pushed the frame to the absolute limit. Air ignited around the Corsair as it plunged down leaving a trail of burning particles in its wake.

The last thirty seconds of her descent, when she decelerated, would be the tricky part. Anyone with a handheld missile launcher could shoot at her.

"Threat, threat, threat," Baxter yelled over the comms.

"Dammit," she murmured.

She didn't need to tell him what to do—he'd trained for this very situation. If anything, speaking to him would be a distraction. Instead, she twisted the stick over, pulling up to even out their descent. The altimeter flashed from ten thousand meters down to five thousand then one thousand.

"Launch, launch, launch," Baxter yelled.

In response, she pushed the nose down and jammed the throttle forward.

"Time to impact?" she yelled without taking her eyes off the HUD.

"Eight seconds," Baxter replied.

She eyed the flat terrain below, none of which was helpful. The burning tower that had to be the remains of the power regulator was off to her right. She kept going down, but pushed the craft into a shallow turn. With the throttle all the way forward, the ship broke the speed of sound many times over, but the question wasn't if she could outrun the missile—she couldn't. She could, though, fly around the beam of energy currently burning a massive chunk of ground where the power regulator used to be.

"Five seconds," Baxter yelled.

She only needed two.

Engines screamed as she plowed through the air, plasma trailing behind her, burning like a sun as she headed directly for the power beam. Then she did something she was sure the missile couldn't—she pulled hard up, using the thrusters to make her Corsair go vertical to the ground, spreading her wings wide, absorbing the speed and eliciting a grunt from the crew as she piled on nine Gs until the limiter kicked on and gave them relief.

The surface-to-air missile flew below them, failing to pull up after the Corsair. It slammed into the beam of energy and exploded in a flash of light.

The radio crackled to life.

"Dang, Chief, when I said on the double, you really took it to heart!" Lance Corporal Naki said.

———

Jennings had them lined up just inside the door, ready to go the second the Corsair touched down. She popped smoke in the LZ and leaped to the top of the nearest building to provide cover.

"Overwatch," she told her suit.

The computer adjusted the angle of its sensors and looked farther out for threats. What the leader of Gamma-7 had confessed disturbed her deeply. She was a damn Marine and had killed more people in the last year than most marines did in their entire careers, but... it was cold. She supposed the Guild probably thought no one would ever find out, so why not? Who would ever care?

"Downtown-One, this is Charlie-One-One, ETA ten seconds."

Jennings acknowledged receipt with a double mic click. Even if Chief Boudreaux had said nothing, a deaf person wouldn't miss the scream of the plasma engines and the boom of the sound-barrier breaking.

Threat detected. Her suit warned her of an aircar approaching. She turned in time to see the mounted gun on the back of a military style car swivel toward her.

Slaving the coilgun to her trigger, she brought up her right arm, hovering the brackets over the speeding vehicle. She breathed out and squeezed; her coilgun spun to life, and a stream of death roared toward the car. The ceramic frame, meant to protect occupants from crashes or small arms fire, was never intended to deal with the hellfire raining down. The aircar disintegrated, blowing apart and shedding debris across a half-klick of ground, lighting fires along the way.

———

Bevins hesitated. Company policy was absolute on the matter. No exceptions. At the same time, though, he didn't want to die.

"What are you doing? Hit the button!" one of the controllers yelled.

"No, don't! They're leaving!" another said.

"You idiot, look at the signature. More troops are landing," the first said. "Hit the button now. It's company policy."

Bevins wasn't sure. What if they were leaving? But why? Surely, if they were here, it was to take over.

Self preservation warred with his brainwashing and he took too long to make a choice. His fingers brushed the button but he couldn't bring himself to push it. A fight broke out as someone tried to stop him. The two men hit each other and rolled right into Bevin, making the decision for him.

———

Between six prisoners from the elevator, twenty-four miners, and nine ship's personnel, including Vesper, there was no room inside the Corsair for the marines, with or without their armor —which they wouldn't abandon under any circumstance.

"On the hardpoints, claws attach, and let's go," Jennings said.

Owens and Cole leaped up to the hovering Corsair, attaching to the port side like remora on a shark. Naki did the same on the starboard side.

"Go, Boudreaux," Jennings ordered.

Chief Boudreaux didn't hesitate. She pushed the throttle

forward, climbing over Allison Jennings' position. Jennings leaped, clawed hand scraping the hull until it found a hold, and she pulled herself up into the external cradle.

"I'm on!" she shouted.

Boudreaux jammed the throttle forward, sending the drop-ship screaming into the sky.

Five seconds later, Omega Base vanished in a pillar of nuclear fire.

Hard radiation and a concussive force strong enough to shatter steel slammed into the Corsair as she rocketed higher into the atmosphere. Had Boudreaux not punched it when she did, the ship would have suffered the same fate as the base below. As it was, she lost some paint and looked like a toasted marshmallow from the stern.

"You marines okay out there?" Boudreaux asked.

"Let's never do that again," Corporal Naki replied.

CHAPTER TWENTY-NINE

Jacob occupied his usual chair in the packed briefing room. The sound of air rushing through the ventilation punctuated the silence. Dr. Krisper sat next to him, and the miner, Chief Castigate, at the far end. Mr. Vesper stood against the bulkhead, Sergeant Jennings—with her sidearm—stood next to him. Lieutenant Yuki and Chief Boudreaux were there as well as PO Oliv who acted as their guests guide.

Jacob believed his ears. He didn't want to, but he believed them. Chief Castigate, looking considerably better than when he'd come aboard four hours before, had no reason to lie.

"Mr. Castigate, let me express my deepest condolences. I promise you, everyone involved will pay." Jacob looked across the room at a pale-faced, barely standing Vesper. Thankfully, they had the foresight to put him in Navy coveralls. His Guild uniform would have been painful for the survivors and dangerous for him.

"We've had some time to come to grips with our loss, Captain. Honestly, we all thought we were dead. When my wife —" he stopped for a moment to compose himself. "When

Marty hit the emergency beacon, I didn't for one second think the Alliance would come."

"Sir," Jacob said gently. "We're the United Systems Navy. We don't leave people behind. It's not in our nature."

"That sounds mighty good on a recruiting poster, son, but this is the real world," Castigate said. "And in the real world..."

"Well then, how about this. We're the *Interceptor*, and no one aboard her would leave someone behind."

Castigate looked up, tears welling in his tired eyes.

"That I can accept," he whispered. "Thank you."

"One thing, sir, if you could clear it up for us," Jacob said. "When your wife hit the emergency beacon, why did they take you, prisoner? They had to know we would come looking."

"I don't think they intended to leave the station intact, Captain. From what I picked up, they were there for our access codes and the rail arm trajectory. They intended to blow the station once they had what they wanted. You just got there before they finished."

"That explains the ship and the mercs, Skipper," Yuki said from the other side of the table. "They must have hired them as a cut-out to keep their hands clean. If the station was blown when we got there we would've assumed it was an accident and never looked."

"If their plan was to blow the station, why take you prisoner?" Jacob asked.

"When Marty hit the beacon it activated a failsafe that purged the computers. The only person with first hand knowledge of the codes and trajectories... was me. I wasn't about to let them have it. They took us here where they had the equipment to force me to speak, I guess," Castigate said.

Jacob lowered his voice to ask what he had to in the most respectful way possible. "I'm sorry, sir, but I have to ask. Did they get the codes?"

"Yes. Dammit. They did. After what they did to Marty and the other women I wanted to die. But they got the codes out of me."

"Petty Office Oliv, would you escort Mr. Castigate to his people and make sure their needs are seen to?"

"Aye, aye, Skipper," Oliv replied.

She held her arm out for the hatch, and Mr. Castigate stood, despair plain on his face as he turned to leave.

Interceptor was running tight on space and food. Air was the only thing they had plenty of. Having a bunch more mouths to feed wasn't going to help.

"Jennings, would you put your marines on the prisoners? I don't want to take any chances if they're conditioned to kill themselves," Jacob said.

"Aye, sir," she replied and spoke quietly into her comms.

Yuki opened her mouth to speak, but Jacob hushed her with a hand. The hatch of the briefing room was stuck open, and he didn't want Castigate to hear any of their anger; the man didn't need anger. God knew his crew was pissed, but the survivors needed calm reassurance.

"Dr. Krisper?" Jacob asked.

Of all of them, he'd hoped the doctor could keep his emotions cool.

"Sir? Uh, they're fine. A bit malnourished and exhausted, but... who the hell spaces women because they don't have the facilities for them? I mean, what the hell, sir?" Krisper yelled, standing with both fists planted on the table, eyes like lasers, not at Jacob but Vesper.

The Guild employee looked to the deck, unwilling to make eye contact with anyone in the room.

"It's uh, company policy," Vesper whispered. "If we were an all-female facility, the men would have—"

Jacob motioned for the doctor to sit. "Thank you, Max. I

think we know how you feel, and I'm certain everyone here is equally appalled. I hadn't realized the Guild had diverged from our society this far."

"No wonder they turn a blind eye to the Caliphate," Yuki said.

"The Guild doesn't see people, ma'am," Vesper said, a little louder this time. "We're columns on a spreadsheet—one with an infinite number of rows. They dangle carrots in front of us to keep us working, and when we serve no more purpose, our row is deleted."

"I don't get it, though," Boudreaux said. "How do you get people to blow themselves up rather than be taken alive? They nuked their own base?" she asked.

All eyes turned back to Vesper. It was a way of thinking so alien to the Alliance that no one in the room could grasp how it could happen.

"Upper management, ma'am. I'm not privy to their thinking. Though we are taught from birth that the company is more important than self," he said.

"So, how did you escape the programming?" Jacob asked.

Vesper's lips twitched into a small smile. "My father told me it was all a lie. I used my computer skills to make my life... uh... more comfortable, rather than trying for a promotion that would never happen."

"You're a hacker?" Jacob asked.

Vesper shrugged.

"Captain, Lieutenant Gonzales," the engineer's voice sounded from the comm panel.

"Go ahead," Jacob replied.

"Sir, I think we can repair the gravcoil for maximum acceleration, but we're going to have to take it offline and go outside in gorilla suits to fix the housing where the crack is."

"One moment, Enzo." Jacob glanced around the room. "Thoughts?"

Dr. Krisper coughed. "How long, sir? With the added mouths to feed, were down to a few days of food, maybe not even enough to get back to Zuck without missing three or more meals."

Jacob frowned. That wasn't good at all. A hungry crew, even well-trained, wouldn't be efficient. Problems would creep in if they went even a day without food.

"What about the space elevator thingy? Did they have stores?" Boudreaux asked, turning around to look at Vesper.

He shook his head. "No, ma'am. We brought our meals with us. All the food stores we had were blown up with the base."

"Sir," Jennings said, "we're in enemy territory, and there's a possibility of other ships arriving. We can't stay here."

Jacob appreciated her point of view for sure. The science and engineering the Guild used to turn a dark planet verdant was—quite frankly—impossible for him to imagine. He'd love nothing more than to study the place, but Jennings was right, they couldn't stay.

"As I see it, we have two problems," Jacob said, holding up two fingers. "We're running out of food, which we can resolve by RTB."

"And the other, Skipper?" Yuki asked.

"We're the only ones who know about the Guild's masquerade."

Yuki tapped one finger against the conference table. "If there is a possibility of enemy ships, we really should evac."

Jacob leaned toward evacuating back to Zuckabar ASAP. Once through the starlane, he could transmit a packet to command, detailing what they had found, and then go about repairing the ship. Maybe Kremlin could send someone with some supplies to get them through. He didn't see a downside, which worried him. Of course, that was why a good officer met with his command crew and sought a variety of opinions.

"Go ahead, Kim?" he prompted his exec.

"We stressed the gravcoil moving through the starlane. I don't want to bet on a broken ring for the trip back. I know The Book says it won't happen, but practically speaking, I'd rather not be stuck in dead-space."

"Why take the chance?" Jacob added.

"Exactly, sir. Besides that, if we've got to swing from the trees, I'd rather do it closer to the ground than out in space. Not to mention if there are other ships out there, we don't know where they are, and we need every advantage," Kim said.

"What did you have in mind?" Jacob asked.

"We take the ship into low orbit and use the ionosphere as a shield,"

"Use the atmosphere as a shield?" Dr. Krisper asked. "How?"

"You should have been in engineering, Lieutenant Yuki. That's genius," Lieutenant Gonzales said from the comms.

"How so?" Jacob asked his engineer.

"Sir, we can establish a low orbit on the edge of the ionosphere. On a planet this size, it will likely be six or seven hundred klicks up. Even with the gravcoil off, we'll have thrusters to extend our orbit. The electron interference from the solar radiation will mask the ship's signature. Lidar won't be reliable because of the high-energy reactions, and radar will be useless because of the thickness of the thermosphere above us. Should work, sir."

"There's a downside, though," Chief Boudreaux interrupted. "If we're skimming the ionosphere, we will be as blind as the people looking for us."

Her revelation sobered the moment. Jacob glanced to Yuki for confirmation, and she nodded. Regardless, it was his call.

Kim was right. They didn't know where the enemy ships were. If he was going to assume, it was best to assume the worst. He would need every advantage to get his people home.

"All right then, Kim, have Chief Suresh take us in. We have work to do and not a lot of time to do it. You have your orders. Execute."

———

Command Supervisor Tier-one La Mont leaned back, sipping coffee while the quiet perfection of the bridge continued around him. They were far out-system from Omega Base, surveying other possible starlanes besides the two they already knew about.

"Sir," Operator Polanski, a stocky older man with too much gray, interrupted him. "Signal from Omega Base, emergency channel."

That piqued La Mont's interest. "Put it through," he said.

"Outriders, this is Omega Base." The man's voice shook with fear. "We're under attack by some kind of invading force. They're taking out buildings—has to be hundreds of enemies. Return immediately. We need—" the transmission abruptly cut-off.

La Mont frowned, tapping his earpiece then looking at Polanski with questioning eyes.

"That's the whole communique, Mr. La Mont. It just ends," Polanski explained.

"Operator Sneed? Best course back to Omega Base?" La Mont asked.

"Eight hours, fifteen minutes, Mr. La Mont."

"Best speed then, Operator Sneed. Best speed."

———

Chief Redfern desperately forced his eyes forward. Unlike many of his contemporaries, the twenty-year Navy vet enjoyed zero-G. Operating a Gorilla suit was second nature to him. Under normal circumstances he wouldn't bat an eye at going EVA to repair the ship.

However, floating outside the ship, five hundred klicks above Wonderland, he knew—*without a doubt*—if he looked down, he'd blow chunks all over the suit's interior.

"Chief, your vitals are all over the place," PO Desper said via comms.

Regulations required medical personnel to monitor any EVA, and Desper was the duty medic.

"Tell me something I don't know, Doc," he muttered.

Clawed hands scraped along the outer hull of the forward section above the gravcoil to where the unknown weapon had blasted vast sections of hull plating off and, from what the computer told them, wrenched parts of the outer hull away from the gravcoil ring housing.

The cracked hull at the bow looked far worse from the outside. The shattered remains of metal and electronics, like toys smashed with a hammer, were all that lingered.

"What the hell did this, Chief?" Spacer first class Beech asked over the comms. His Gorilla suit was a few meters behind Redfern's, represented by a blinking yellow dot in the Chief's HUD.

"No idea, Beech. Look at the edges... it isn't melted or... it's like we hit an asteroid or something. Honestly, it looks like the kind of damage the Long 9 would do if we loaded her with round shot instead of APDS."

"Do they do that, Chief? Round shot, I mean?"

Redfern chuckled. "You need to read some history, son.

When the Alliance Navy first took to space to protect Alexandria and Seabring, they were unarmored merchantmen retrofitted with cargo launchers—barely more than magnetic slingshots."

Redfern attached his magnetic tether to the hull plating below the exposed deck. He reconfigured the claw to a cutting plasma torch, and sliced a straight edge to attach the patch. He had to slice far enough back that the new plates would connect to undamaged armor.

The one-point-eight metric ton suit was designed to work on the outer hull and repair damage that couldn't be fixed from the inside. Regardless of how well they patched the armor, the ship would still need a month in drydock to make the repairs permanent.

"Fighting the pirates is what brought the two worlds together. We could have made some kind of bizarre monarchy after that, but the admiral of the 'Fleet,' David Alexander, refused to give up on the idea of a Republic. Here we are, three hundred plus years later, still trudging along."

Beech's gorilla-sized arms took hold of the cut plate and pulled. A half metric ton of broken nano-steel pulled away as easy as a kid tearing apart cotton candy. Small thrusters on the suit fired off, glowing blue as they belched ions and pulled the heavy metal away from the ship.

"It didn't take long for those early settlers to realize they needed a full-time navy with real weapons. We had the infrastructure to build ships, just not the knowledge. In many ways, it was a frontier back then. For all the advanced medical tech and computers, there wasn't anyone who could manufacture a gravcoil."

"What did they do? You can't fight with a merchant ship." Beach rotated his suit, sending the broken hull plating toward the planet below. Under normal repair procedures they would conserve the material, but their time constraints forced them to abandon the raw material of the hull. They simply didn't have time to ferry each section back into the ship.

Redfern anxiously looked away, trying hard to focus on what he was saying instead of the nagging feeling of falling.

"Merchant ships have crappy reactors—no extra power for anything—but they have plenty of space. The engineers of the day took the magnetic cargo launchers and refined them into coilguns. Far more energy efficient than a railgun, with the added bonus of not having to replace the coils."

Beech jetted up ten meters to the open airlock where the new six-meter by four-meter hull strips waited. Grappling with his clawed hands, he pulled the first out.

"Three hundred years, and we still use coilguns?" Beech asked.

"Well, you don't account for the lost years, but anyhow, what would we replace them with? Directed energy weapons are power-intensive and easily damaged. Rail guns require an extensive infrastructure for repair and replacement, and plasma weapons are fantastic at close range—but lose potency at long range."

The first plate went over both the upper coil bracket and the main hull. Once in place, Redfern rotated down, angling his body parallel with Wonderland to run the molecular bonder across the edge.

"Oh boy," Redfern gulped.

"You okay, Chief?" Beech asked.

"Yeah. Where was I?" He was not okay, but he'd be dammed if he'd tell a snot-nosed spacer that.

"Round shot?" Beech reminded him.

"Right," Redfern said as he finished the first row of molec-ular bonding.

He only had six more to do. Piece of cake.

"The first guns fired round shots of solid nickel-iron, like some kind of archaic wooden sailing vessel from the fifteenth century. After the first few engagements, the pirates started welding wedged armor plating on their ships. Even at the high velocity of thousands of kilometers per second, the angle of the shot mattered. At least until we developed armor-piercing discarding sabot, or APDS as they are labeled on the box.

"It was by no means a new idea. Armor-piercing rounds went back to the old days of firearms. Back in the twenty-seventh, ships were only lightly armored since the gravcoil deflected particles and debris away from the ship anyway. For merchant ships, that meant no armor at all."

Beech triggered his thrusters, illuminating the side of the hull with blue light as he brought down another layer. Redfern fixed it in place, starting a new row of molecular bonding.

"Because of the low available power and the armor the pirates were using, we had to find something to give us an edge. Lucky for us, some of the colonists were vets and knew the basics of APDS ammo. Similar to what we have today, but back then it was made of straight tungsten or depleted uranium. That did the trick, but once we figured out nano-metallurgy, everything went to the nano-reinforced versions." He knocked on the armor plate he fused to the ship.

"My folks worked for Solar Express. We ran a half million-ton D-Class freighter pretty much my whole life," Beech said.

Redfern frowned. He'd underestimated the young man. His scores were average, and he never seemed to excel in engineering—with his background, he should have stood out a lot more than he did.

"Beech, you wanna tell me why your scores are middle of the road then?" He asked while he held the new panel over the last one and started the bonding process.

"To be honest, Chief, I wasn't sure I wanted to stay in the

Navy. *Interceptor* is only my second assignment, and everyone seemed—"

"Demoralized?" Redfern asked.

"Aye, Chief. That's it. My first post wasn't much better, but then I got here and started to think it was the whole Navy. I know I'm only twenty and have a lot of living to do, but... well, Chief, it wasn't any fun. Not like mom and dad's boat. That is until the captain arrived."

Redfern finished the seal on the last armored plate. "I know what you mean, Beech. He's the way the Navy is supposed to be."

"Aye, sir. He reminds me of my dad. He has this sense of command about him," Beech said.

Redfern knew all too well what the young man spoke of. It was like the Navy chased away the good officers until only the selfish ones remained.

With the last bonded piece in place, he keyed his mic.

"Lieutenant Gonzales, Chief Redfern."

"Go ahead, Chief," Gonzales replied, his voice distorted by the radio.

"You wanna check the seal on the forward hull?" Redfern asked.

He pushed off the ship, using the thrusters to move below the armored plating. It was unlikely, but there was a slim chance when the pressure built, the plating would explode off the ship. Seconds ticked by as atmosphere returned to the ship's forward sections. The armor held. With the outer layer up, engineering crews could get to work reinforcing the hull from the inside.

"What's next, Chief?" Beech asked

"We do the same thing all over again," Redfern said.

CHAPTER THIRTY

L a Mont frowned at the display. It simply wasn't possible.

"Hail them again," he ordered with a snarl.

Repeated attempts didn't change the visual display of the massive nuclear crater where Omega Base used to be.

"Sir, we've received the log," his second said. "They initiated invasion protocol."

La Mont pulled his eyes away from the screen. "That's idiotic. It was never meant to be used out here. Director Cardinal would have waited for us to return and— what?"

"It wasn't Director Cardinal, sir, but a supervisor named Bevin."

That was even worse. Some fool supervisor decided to blow a multi-trillion-dollar investment because he panicked? La Mont had sent many a strongly worded memo to the directorate about the autonomy of supervisors and the incident on the planet proved his point. No mere supervisor should have ever received the authority or even had access to initiate invasion protocol.

"What about the logs? Did they show who was invading?" he spat the words out between clenched teeth.

"Yes, sir. An Alliance dropship hit them."

A dropship? La Mont wracked his brain for information about the Alliance and how they operated. A dropship could mean an invasion. If it was an invasion how did they keep it a secret? They would have sent a battle group—which meant there were likely cruisers in the system.

No. They couldn't hide a battle group. This had to be an accident. Which meant...

He clenched his fist and hit the chair. He knew they should have just blown Gamma-7 when he was there. Getting fancy with the mercs was the directorate's plan, not his.

They were there to rescue the prisoners, not invade the damn planet. La Mont groaned aloud this time. All that money wasted because some stupid supervisor was given command codes to blow the station.

"Any word from the outpost?" La Mont asked.

His second frowned. "No, sir. Their transponder is still on, though."

"Send them an update. Tell them to go active and weapons-free. If the Alliance ship is heading for the starlane, I want them blown to bits before they get away. Also, find out where the hell Outrider Command is and let them know the situation."

———

The last light on the board flipped to green, and Chief Suresh gave Jacob a big thumbs up. "We have access to full acceleration."

Jacob thumbed the comm switch. "Well done, Mr. Gonzales!"

"Thank you, sir," he replied.

Eight hours in orbit was too long for Jacob's taste, even hidden in the ionosphere as they were. While they were hidden from detection, they were also blind to what was above them. The not knowing drove him crazy.

"Astro, do we have a plot for returning to the anchor?" he asked.

"Aye, sir," PO Olive said.

Except for Chief Suresh and himself, second watch manned the bridge. The careful ship handling needed to skirt the atmosphere of Wonderland required Suresh's vast experience and skill. It also meant she was on her third cup of coffee.

"ETA to departure?" Jacob asked via comms.

"I need fifteen to button up the ship, sir," Gonzales said. "Then we'll be good to go."

"Get to it," Jacob said. "Chief Suresh, take ten and stretch. I need you at a hundred percent."

"Aye, aye, Skipper." She hit the button, summoning her standby.

A minute later, PO Collins entered the bridge. The slightly built woman with curly brown hair sticking out from her watch cap took the Chief's place. With the ship this close to the planet, they couldn't deploy their towed array. With their food situation, they couldn't crawl back to the starlane. They had to make best speed.

"Skipper," PO Collins said, once she was done buttoning herself in.

"Yes, Jennifer?"

The Pit was more akin to the Corsair's cockpit than the rest of the stations on the cramped bridge. The coxswain had a molded flight couch that leaned back at a forty-five-degree angle. It helped them remain steady even when out of combat.

All their auxiliary stations were on their left, primary on their right. Between the pedals at their feet, the throttle and stick for their left and right hands, plus the hat switches and different flight modes like docking, and maneuvers, they could fly the entire thing with their eyes closed.

"Sir, I don't know if it's my equipment or what, but... we're taking some chop from an unknown source."

Jacob's first thought was to dismiss her concern since she just came on shift, but... Chief Suresh had sat in The Pit for the last eight hours. She might have missed something—or it could have just started.

"What do you think, Astro?"

Oliv glanced at Tefiti, who shrugged.

"Sorry, sir. This deep in the gravity well of Wonderland, I can't hear a thing," he said.

"It's gone, sir," Collins said. "I think... and I would want to check with Chief Suresh, but I think we just got buzzed by a ship in orbit using their gravcoil to circumnavigate the planet."

Jacob knelt next to Collins as she showed him the interference.

"Of course, we can't see it, but the effect was clear. Watch," she said, replaying the last few minutes from her sensors.

Sure enough, almost thirty seconds after Suresh left the bridge, the keel thrusters kicked in to keep the ship at its current altitude and burned longer than they had the last three times.

"You think a gravwake hit, pushing us down?" Jacob asked her.

"That would be my guess, Skipper," she said.

"Well done, Jennifer," he said, clapping her on the shoulder. "See what you can do about calculating their speed. If we time it right, we can make a run for the starlane while they're on the other side of the planet."

"Aye, Skipper," she said, getting to work.

"Skip," Yuki said from her position next to the captain's chair. She had her NavPad out, making calculations of her own.

Jacob patted Collins on the shoulder and pulled himself up to stand next to his XO. He was tall enough that he felt the need to hunch over when he was on the bridge—he didn't have to, but his watch cap would occasionally brush the lower hanging equipment, and a lifetime of banging his head on objects kept him perpetually hunched. Not to mention when he was standing next to his XO, or just about anyone else, he towered over her.

"I've been going over what Redfern saw on the hull," she said.

Her NavPad showed detailed images of the broken forward section. Jacob let out a sigh. Whatever hit them had done severe damage. If it had struck the gravcoil a few meters below, they'd all be dead.

"What have you got, Kim?" he asked.

She glanced around the bridge and leaned in closed. "I wouldn't have thought it possible, Skip, if not for seeing Wonderland, but I think they're using *gasers*."

Jacob hoped his blank expression would relay the fact that he had no idea what she was talking about—which was starting to annoy him. He wasn't the most scientifically minded person in the fleet, and ever since he had taken command of *Interceptor*, he'd felt the need to go back to school. Wormholes, dark stars, and now gasers?

"Gaser? Do you mean a graser?" he asked.

He was familiar with every weapon used on every ship in the major systems. There were always some outliers using offshoot tech, but it was all pretty standard for the most part. Nations tended to adopt a specific basis for their tech and build weapons platforms off that. Supporting ships required an enormous infrastructure, all of which came at a high cost. Standard-ization of equipment helped keep that down.

Virtually all of the Alliance's offensive tech was built on coilguns—even the torpedoes were fired from coilgun hous-ings. That let them service ships at a lower cost at any number of installations or using UnRep ships.

Kim shook her head. "No Skip, *gaser*. It's a theoretical laser created using compressed gravity. I don't know all the specifics, even if that was what hit us, sir. However, imagine a coherent beam of condensed gravity and—"

"Sonofa..." he muttered. "Wouldn't the power requirements be off the chart for such a weapon?"

"Aye, sir. You would need a fusion reactor with three times our output to run one. When we encountered the first ship, their power output was three to four times what a typical merchant had. And like you surmised, Skipper, they'd probably have to route it through the gravcoil to make it work."

"Which, if it's true, verifies my hypothesis about them having to turn the ship," Jacob said.

"Yes, sir. The only problem I can see with the idea is the range. They're using it as a surprise weapon. I can't imagine it has much more range than our Long 9. Otherwise, *Aethia* would have hit us much sooner."

"Inverse-square law is a killer," he said, happy to remember something of how high-energy weapons worked in space. "Which is why we don't use directed energy weapons."

Kim was shocked for a moment. "Sir? I thought you didn't have a science background."

"I've read a book or two," he said with a roguish grin. "His-tory books, mind you, not science." He sobered for a moment. The implications of the weapon were immense. "If this is the case, and I want you to get with Lieutenant Gonzales on the math, then we have a big problem," he said.

"Aye, sir. We can't stop to go through the starlane, or they'll get close to us, and that will be that," she whispered.

They could try running silent, head the opposite direction then try to circle back around to the starlane. However, the Guild knew where they had to go, it would be just a matter of waiting for them. *Interceptor* didn't have the stores to play that game.

"We're not at war with the Guild," Jacob said. "I'm not sure I can justify firing on them first," he said with a frown.

He certainly *felt* like they were at war. Since they'd investigated Gamma-7, the Guild had done their level best to wipe out *Interceptor*.

"That's a decision you have to make, sir. It's why you make the big bucks," she said with a grin.

"Fair enough. Get with Enzo and let me know."

"Aye, sir," she said.

He watched her leave the bridge, proud of the officer she had become. Before he'd arrived ship's morale was lax. Kim and the rest of the crew weren't screw-ups. They worked hard and did him proud. All they had needed was someone to believe in them.

Of course, even having the best crew in the universe didn't mean they could outfight a ship with a weapon capable of destroying them with a single shot. The Guild miscalculated, though. Probably because they had never fought an actual war. One weapon system, no matter how powerful, made ships less versatile, not more. Once they figured out the weakness of the gaser all they had to do was stay behind the enemy.

Something that was easier said than done.

"Skipper, I've got the math for you," PO Oliv said. "At their current velocity, they will come back around in one-zero minutes and three-three seconds— mark."

He nodded. "Thank you, Oliv."

Ten minutes. He had that long to formulate a plan. He pulled up the planet's orbit on his MFD. Cloning Oliv's console, he tied in her calculations and watched the red dot of the enemy ship draw ever closer.

They could always wait them out, hoping the enemy gave up and went looking elsewhere. Or his ship would run out of food and they would be forced to surrender. Of course, knowing what the Guild did to its female prisoners, he would rather die than allow his crew to suffer that fate. He knew everyone aboard felt the same way. No, either they all escape, or no one does.

Vesper's stone-faced recitation of the value the Guild placed on humanity was like a bucket of ice water. Even if prisoners were the worst scum humanity had to offer, they still deserved a trial and a chance to defend themselves. Spacing prisoners required a level of callous indifference to humanity he just couldn't imagine. He had threatened to space prisoners before, but he wouldn't have sent them out the lock. It was a bluff, and he had counted on them not calling it.

Jacob ran his eyes over the bridge, admiring how his crew did their job despite their situation. They were all thinking the same thing he was, yet their behavior didn't alter one iota.

Chief Suresh walked on the bridge, a coffee in one hand and an orange drink for Jacob in the other. "Skipper, brought you some of that sludge you like from below."

"Thanks, Chief I—" His hand extended to take the drink. Jacob froze as a plan formed fully in his mind.

He couldn't hide the grin. "Oh, this is gonna be good."

"You okay, Skipper?" Chief Suresh asked.

"I think I see a way out of here. Let me fill you in."

CHAPTER THIRTY-ONE

"Mr. Governor, are you okay?"

Rod looked up, one hand rubbing his dry eyes. "Thank you, Vasky. Yes, I'm fine. I'd be better if you could tell me where we are with locating Commander Dagher."

The briefing room's cool, dehydrated air piped in at a constant temperature. Heating and cooling a massive construct was always a game of degrees. Sometimes the temperature would spike without warnings; other times, it would drop. Low humidity was the only consistency.

Nadia was overdue with her check-in, and while Rod knew she could take care of herself, she was still Alliance personnel on his station.

"I'm sorry, sir, I've got nothing new to report," Vasky said. "Every spare person I have is looking for her, which isn't many. There is just no sign."

The rough-hewn man with scars on his face from his fire-fighting days had taken over as chief of security when Rod became governor. While there were many loyalty problems with station personnel, Vasky had proven to be efficient and dependable.

Not having enough people had never been a problem before, however.

"What do you mean? Station security population rivals that of some cities."

A slight sheen of sweat on Vansky's forehead was visible in the dull yellow light.

"In the last twenty-four hours, I've had nearly half my forces suddenly resign. My personnel at the docks tell me that they've never seen such a rush on passenger ships. Hordes of people are taking any available transport leaving the system."

Rod's heart raced. For a moment, he imagined he could feel the blood in his veins bursting to get out.

"Why is this the first I'm hearing of it?" he demanded.

"It's the first *I'm* hearing of it, sir. From what I gather, it started about a week ago. Several key people called in sick and then were reported AWOL after they left the station. From there, it snowballed. No one is saying why, but there can only be one reason."

Rod hated where Vasky was going. Like ships, stations had grapevines. It didn't matter how the message started, as long as people trusted it. If everyone thought war was coming to Zuck, then abandoning Kremlin was the smart thing to do.

He wasn't without his own resources, though. Yes, the Alliance was in a bad spot with the Caliphate and the Iron Empire, but they weren't anywhere near a shooting war. The Admiralty had plans for Kremlin, and they weren't prepared to hang it out to dry. Even if all they did was peel off a light cruiser and a pair of destroyers from the fleet to guard it, Rod was sure the Alliance had bigger forces on the way. They just weren't here yet.

"Assume they know something we don't," Rod said. "What is the most likely avenue of attack?"

"If anyone attacks, whether it be state forces or pirates, they are going to want the station intact. It's too difficult to survive out here without it. I would say boarding parties, which would mean fighting in the streets. However..." Vasky looked away.

"What is it?" Rod asked.

"I've seen a lot of fighting in my life, station fighting, the real close quarters stuff... it's brutal. I think surrendering the station might be a better alternative."

The words hit Rod hard. He'd barely started his tenure on Kremlin, and the idea of surrendering appalled him. If it came to it, though, he would. Two million people lived and worked on Kremlin. Fighting inside the station would risk all their lives.

"Let's hope it doesn't come to that," Rod finally said. "What else could an opposing force do if they wanted to take the station?"

If he had to, Rod would stay up all night to figure out what was going on. He had to wonder, though, was his ex-ship caught up in the matter?

CHAPTER THIRTY-TWO

Wonderland's intense gravity and unusual star made for an incredibly active ionosphere, where electrons slammed into the atmosphere and played merry hell with all forms of EM sensors. If ships weren't infinitesimally small on a planetary scale, the crew of Outrider Five could have looked down and seen *Interceptor* plain as day when they passed over her again.

However, seeing a ship the size of a Hellcat-class destroyer from over a thousand kilometers away was akin to seeing a needle in a haystack from an airplane on a cloudy day.

On the bridge, Chief Suresh knelt next to PO Collins and talked her through the maneuver they were about to execute.

"We're ready, Skipper," Chief Suresh said, with a reassuring nod to Collins.

Jacob felt mildly concerned. When he proposed the idea to Suresh, he'd assumed she would helm the ship.

"No, sir," she had said. "This is exactly the kind of thing Collins needs to do. These opportunities don't come along often, and she can do it, Skipper."

Jacob trusted his crew—Chief Suresh in particular—so if she said Collins could do it, then she could.

It still made Jacob nervous, having his number one helm operator beside the stick while they pulled their surprise. He pointed to Spacer Gauger, who triggered the all-hands button.

"All hands. Now hear this: combat is imminent. The Terraforming Guild thinks their advanced tech and hidden solar system makes them unstoppable. They think they can murder our brothers and sisters with no consequences. They fight for profit. We fight for each other. Follow your training, listen to your POs and *Interceptor* will be victorious. We will show these scumbags what an Alliance warship is all about."

Down in sickbay, Mining Chief Castigate looked up and listened to the captain's words. He had tried hard not to think of his wife while they were still fighting for their lives. Within the relative safety of the ship, he had few excuses. When he closed his eyes, his wife's face waited for him, the look she gave him as the Guild marched her, the other women, and the little girls into the airlock.

"—Warship is all about. Helmets on, man your stations, and Godspeed," he finished.

The speaker went silent and Castigate looked up at the young doctor tending to his friends.

"Dr. Krisper?" he asked.

"Sir?"

"Is your captain for real?"

"I know what you mean, sir. But I assure you, after a month on this boat, he's very real."

Castigate shook his head. "I hope his luck is as good as his speech."

"Me too, sir. Me too."

· · ·

With helmets on, and the atmosphere drained from *Interceptor*, the destroyer was ready to fight.

"PO Collins..." Jacob said, holding one hand up. "Execute."

He brought his hand down sharply to punctuate the order.

"Aye, sir. Initiating maneuver," she said in a nervous, high-pitched voice.

Hands as steady as a surgeon's increased throttle while she used the hat switch on the main control stick to push the *Interceptor* up through the ionosphere. Condensed layers of atmosphere and excited particles gathered around the bow, partially obscuring the painted shark's mouth.

Eight hundred kilometers above, Outrider Five, passed on the same orbital trajectory, using her gravcoil to maintain a high orbit. The wake she emitted was weak compared to full power, but it was enough for the sensitive systems of the Alliance destroyer to detect.

"Contact," PO Tefiti said. "Six-zero-five klicks at zero-nine-zero relative. Same signature as *Aethia*, Captain," he said, turning to Jacob. "If I had to guess, I'd say they were sister ships. Designating new contact, Golf-Tango-One."

Interceptor used as little thrust as possible, rising from the depths of the ionosphere undetected by the Guild ship. Once they were in close quarters, there would be no time for Golf-Tango-One to respond.

"Sir, I have a firing solution," Lieutenant Fawkes said.

"Well done. Can we disable their coil without destroying the ship?"

"Fifty-fifty, sir. There are variables I can't account for," Lieutenant Fawkes replied.

"Do your best," Jacob said.

The range continued to close, and Jacob knew it was only a

matter of seconds before *Interceptor* had to show up on Golf-Tango-One's radar. They were practically out of the ionosphere and had an excellent passive lock on the Guild ship.

———

"Sir," the EW operator of Outrider Five said, "I have something funny on the aft systems. I'm picking up a distortion."

La Mont heaved himself up, happy for the excuse to move. After hours of searching, he was starting to think the Alliance ship had headed for deep space.

"What have you got?"

"It's hard to say. Nothing on gravity, but I think something is behind us."

La Mont frowned. "Focus radar aft, cut the gravcoil, and let's see what we can see."

The EW operator flipped a switch, sending lightspeed sensors shooting out behind them. Of course, at that range, it took less than a second for the image to resolve, and alarms wailed as the computer detected the threat. Comms crackled to life as a message was received from the newly detected ship.

"Guild ship, this is Commander Jacob T. Grimm of the USS *Interceptor*. Heave-to and surrender. This is your only warning. Failure to comply will result in your immediate destruction."

Jacob gambled on them needing to point the ship at a target to fire their gaser. It wasn't a huge gamble, but one all the same. With no official declaration of war, he couldn't in good conscience open fire on a vessel without giving them a chance to surrender.

"Anything?" he asked Gauger.

"Nothing yet, sir."

"Send it again," he ordered.

"Aye, sir, sending."

Jacob drummed his fingers on the arm of his chair. He was more than happy to open fire if they tried anything, but if he could capture them without any undue risk to his crew, he would.

"Power spike," Tefiti said. "Gravity readings are all over the place."

"Acceleration," Oliv said. "Two-zero-zero gravities on an ecliptic course with Wonderland, they're going to try and swing around."

"Pursue them, Collins," he ordered.

"Aye, sir. Two-five-zero gravities pursuit course," she said as the ship surged forward.

Within seconds, *Interceptor* was back in range, and the Guild had no hope of outrunning her.

"Skipper," Yuki said over the comms on their private channel.

"Go ahead."

"Sir, it's possible they have more than one ship, and they're trying to lead us into an ambush."

He hated to think of the possibility, but his XO was right. He'd given them enough rope, and he'd told them one warning only.

"Weapons," he said on the bridge-wide comm. "You have permission to fire."

"Aye, sir," Fawkes replied.

Carter's hands were steel as he adjusted the calculations on the enemy ship. The range was a ridiculous thirty-four-hundred klicks. Had the Guild ships built a single turret gun, they could have fired the instant they detected *Interceptor*.

"Locked on." Fawkes flipped the shield up, prepping the firing button. "Three... two... one... fire."

He depressed the stud, and the ship shuddered as turrets one and two fired their 20mm projectile at ten thousand KPS.

The results were instant. Power dropped suddenly as Golf-Tango-One's gravcoil splintered from the impact. The next hit passed through the stern, igniting the atmosphere inside the ship and wiping out its engineering section.

"Good hit," Fawkes said. "Both rounds. Good hit."

Jacob signaled Gauger again. "Put me on."

"Aye, sir, you're on."

"Guild ship, if you can read me, please surrender immediately."

Tension built in the back of Jacob's neck. He didn't want to leave a ship stranded in orbit, even if it would be better to turn and head for the starlane with haste. It just wasn't in him to abandon people who might need help.

"They're launching escape pods, sir," Oliv said. "Good returns. They're headed for the planet."

Jacob sighed in relief. That was something. So they wouldn't surrender. That was fine. As long as they weren't shooting at him.

"Well done, everyone. Especially you, Collins. That was some fine ship handling."

"Thank you, sir," she said, looking into the mirror as she spoke so he could see the smile on her face.

"Astro, initiate the course for our anchor."

"Aye, sir," Oliv replied. "Helm, come Two-Five-Five, set acceleration to four zero-zero gravities."

Collins repeated the order before bringing the ship around, using thrusters to point her in the right direction. The gravcoil hummed and *Interceptor* shot into space.

"Deploy the towed array," Jacob ordered.

"Aye, aye, deploying the towed array," West said.

The kilometer-long cable with its built-in sensor antenna unspooled behind the ship until it reached the end with a metallic thud that reverberated through the ship.

"Contact," Tefiti said. "Multiple contacts, one-Eight-Zero, range one-five million klicks, and closing."

Jacob turned his chair to look at Tefiti's station. "Say again?" They had just deployed the cable, how could they have a contact that quick?

"They were obscured by the planet, sir, but I can hear them now. They must have come through the other starlane and made best speed. With the planet shrinking behind us, they came on screen suddenly."

"How many?" Jacob asked, his mouth suddenly dry enough to make him cough.

Tefiti held one hand to his ear, listening for the telltale gravity pulses identifying individual ships.

"The range is too great for certain identification, sir, but I would say, at least a half-dozen."

Jacob's face fell. They had barely destroyed the last two. It had taken all the guile he could muster to beat them. But six? Maybe more?

"Helm, flank speed. Recalculate time to starlane," he ordered.

He had no doubt they could make the starlane before the enemy ships, but could they stop and enter before those Guild frigates caught up and wiped them out with gaser fire? Before he made any other decisions, he stopped and prayed. He would need all the help he could muster.

CHAPTER THIRTY-THREE

When *Interceptor* entered the system, they had spent almost a full day sneaking up on the planet at low acceleration. With a fleet of ships chasing them and with no chance for stealth, they had to run full throttle back to the starlane.

No matter how many times he did the math, Jacob couldn't make it work. They would come to zero at the anchor, and six minutes later, the Guild frigates would open fire. *Interceptor*'s speed wasn't enough; all the pursuing frigates had to do was keep going at their current level of acceleration, and they would run right over his destroyer.

"Course change, all contacts, new heading... they see us, sir. Coming right for us," Tefiti said.

With light-lag, all their sensor capability was delayed. Fifteen million klicks rested at the very edge of reliable gravity detection. Once the enemy ships were within two million, they could put the other active light-speed sensors on them.

"Chief, what's our current acceleration and velocity?" he asked.

"Full power on the gravcoil, sir. Acceleration at five-point-three KPS squared. Current velocity on my mark is three-one-zero-zero KPS... mark," Suresh relayed the information like the consummate professional she was.

Jacob switched his comms to the chief only. "Devi, when we arrive at our anchor, you're going to have to do the fastest star-lane entry in history if we want to make it."

"Twelve minutes, twenty-seven seconds is the official record, skip. That was on a route from Sol to Alpha Centauri, in a custom-built ship made for racing the lanes, using the oldest charted starlane ever found."

"Well then, good thing you're the fleet's best coxswain," he assured her.

"Aye, aye, sir," was her only reply.

Regardless, in a little less than three hours, they would find out if she could pull it off.

———

On the bridge of Outrider Command, Director Fargo read the reports coming in and couldn't believe his eyes. Well, he did believe them because the reports were true, but at the same time, he questioned the sanity of all involved.

"Carl, can you just confirm for me that Omega initiated *invasion protocol?*" he asked his second.

"Yes, sir. One moment."

Fargo waited patiently as his man pulled up the records. Having gone to gather the fleet for their assault had proved to be a double-edged blade. Had Outrider Command remained in orbit, it was likely the Alliance ship would never have reached Omega. Having left, however, to commence operation *Broadsword,* the events did happen, and he was the area director responsible for success of the mission.

He smirked at the idiotic mission name. Then again, everything that came down from corporate seemed ridiculous these days.

"Sir, I have confirmation. Supervisor Bevin initiated the protocol. When Outrider Five investigated, her engines were destroyed by a Hellcat-class destroyer, USS *Interceptor*."

That name tickled a memory. He frowned. It was the Guild's lack of foresight that allowed her deeply hidden spy net to be discovered. Had they simply handed the information about the sex trafficking ring to the Alliance as he had suggested, they would have made an ally of the Alliance instead of an enemy. Now it was down to him to fix the situation, and he was trying to do so with the least amount of Guild exposure possible.

"Carl, have we word yet on Achilles? Is it operational?"

His second, a short man well into his forties, with a balding patch, shook his head.

"*Aethia* was on the last check to make sure it was locked on and loaded. However, an Alliance destroyer in the system may mean *Aethia* led them here."

Fargo sighed. Since the capture of any Guild computers or tech was forbidden, the *Aethia* was likely destroyed. No matter what happened next, Operation Achilles had to proceed, and he would make it happen. One little destroyer could not stop him, no matter how insanely lucky they had been up to this point.

———

Spacer Second Class Josh Mendez hurried to finish securing the mess. He'd run down from his Zulu post in the Long 9 chamber to hastily make a hundred sandwiches and send them out in little lunch boxes with juice for hydration and the faux chocolate bars for energy.

The captain was right. They couldn't go another two hours without refreshments after spending the previous day in silent

running. Fifteen minutes into the pursuit, he had ordered
atmosphere returned and food made, along with a shift change.

Mendez had spent two years in the Navy and over a year on
Interceptor. Before *the captain*, he was ready to be done. He loved
cooking and operating the mess on a destroyer was a considerable challenge, but until the captain showed up, it was a daily
nightmare. No one on the boat had talked to each other. They
weren't even shipmates, let alone friends. For a nineteen-year-
old kid straight off the farm, he was hoping for what the
recruitment posters promised: *"Don't read about other worlds, see
them. Join the Navy!"*

So far, the only other world he'd seen was Zuckabar Central.
A frozen wasteland made up of miners and alcohol, it wasn't his
idea of a good time. He hadn't even gotten leave after
completing his training, going straight from advanced weapons
operator school to *Interceptor*.

He was, though, the ship's best cook. Plus, once he realized
how amazing the captain was, he'd tried very hard to be on the
man's good side. Josh was never late, he never talked back to his
POs, and he worked his butt off.

On top of all that, he made sure the captain always had a
full cup of tea or the orange drink he favored over coffee. Not to
mention his favorite breakfast waiting for him every morning.

In his ideal world, he'd follow the captain to his next ship.
Which, the more time went by, didn't seem as impossible as he
thought. It wasn't just him, either. No one had transferred off
Interceptor after their last assignment. Almost thirty new people
had come in, but not a single spacer had gone on to another
ship.

Maybe it was a coincidence or the distance of their deployment, but he heard the POs talking, and even they thought it
was strange.

Josh shook his head, wiping his hands on the apron tied

around his neck. He needed to get his head in the game, not worry about hypothetical *what-ifs* that might never happen. After all, they needed to survive their current engagement first.

———

PO Tefiti squeezed his eyes shut, listening for even a trace of the telltale gravitational harmonic that signaled another ship out in the black. With the grav waves racing around at the speed of light, it was hard to know exactly where a ship was without consistent bearing changes showing up first.

With enough gravwake readings, he could pinpoint a ship's exact location and speed, and then, based on light-lag, the computer could formulate where they were. Anything farther out than a million klicks became problematic since ships could adjust course—which was why the torpedoes tracked gravwake on their own and weren't guided by the ship's sensors.

However, the six ships chasing them were spread out over ten thousand cubic kilometers and were all running full throttle, banging away at space-time like they didn't have a care in the galaxy.

They certainly weren't trying to hide their presence, and they were making it easy to determine exactly where they were. What bothered Tefiti was how obvious they were about it. Almost like they wanted *Interceptor* to focus only on them. Which immediately made Tefiti nervous as all hell.

As *Interceptor* approached the deceleration point, he wanted to tell the captain to keep going, just run for it. They could always come back around when the enemy ships departed. Yet that wasn't an option. With their food stores running low, their only options were to make the starlane or surrender. After what the Guild had shown it would do to prisoners, he knew surrendering was no option at all.

Lieutenant (SG) Kimiko Yuki ran through the checklists on her board one more time. PO Hanz read off the latest updates while she plugged each one into her DC list. The last time they went into battle, turret number four had given them problems, and she would be dammed if that happened again.

When the yard repaired *Interceptor*, Yuki had gone through and personally inspected every single piece of the turret, not to mention wiping the computer control software, which she reinstalled from scratch—something she could only do when in drydock, since the computers were all hardwired to prevent tampering while underway.

If there was one piece of hardware aboard ship she was positive about, it was turret number four. Which didn't mean she wasn't going to keep updated on its status. The only other thing she wanted to keep an eye on was the forward gravcoil rings. Those were a secondary concern. Chief Redfern did good work and other than an occasional check, she was sure they were good to go.

"Now hear this," Ensign Hössbacher's voice came over the ship's intercom. "Draining the can in five mikes. Helmets on. Helmets on. Helmets on."

Yuki pointed at her two assistants, who stopped what they were doing and slipped their helmets on. Once they were secure and their suits reported good seal, she put hers on and did the same. Across the ship, the behavior was repeated. Once everyone was sealed in, the information was relayed to her, and she passed it on to Ops.

Jacob knelt next to the conference table in the briefing room. There was no possibility of an engagement before they reached the starlane. The math simply didn't allow it. Which meant he had time to do his prayer properly.

He could see the corner of Jennings' elbow from his position, and her presence comforted him, knowing she was there to keep his moment private.

Bowing his head, he prayed. For his crew, for the ship, and for the Alliance. He would have liked to stay longer, but the urgency wouldn't allow him to have more than a few minutes. When he was done, he struggled to stand, his knees popping as he did so.

"Sir, they're calling you from the bridge," Jennings said on their private comms.

"Thanks, Allison." He switched his channel open. "Go for captain."

"Sir," Ensign Owusu said. "You better get up here, Skipper."

Jacob hustled through the broken hatch and then back to the bridge. With no atmosphere in the ship, there was an eerie silence in his suit. He could hear his breathing and heartbeat, but nothing of the ship's usual sounds of the ship—no hum of electronics, nor the quiet chattering of crew.

"I have the con," he said on the bridge-wide suit comms. "Sitrep?"

Ensign Owusu put the forward radar array on the large screen dominating the bridge's forward bulkhead. A yellow blip marked the anchor and the last known location of the starlane. Not far beyond it, though, a red dot blinked.

"What am I looking at?" Jacob asked.

"We designated it Sierra-One, sir. It looks like a large satellite or a small station. We didn't see it earlier because we were running silent when we exited the starlane," Owusu said.

Jacob waved away the man's defense; it wasn't needed.

"Understood, Owusu. No one's blaming you. Tactical, can you hit it from here?" he asked.

If the light codes were right and it wasn't moving, when they came to a stop at the starlane, the station would be just over a million klicks out.

Fawkes double-checked his computer, running the numbers. "If they can't move, then yes, sir. It's a little far for a solid lock, but I should be able to."

Jacob took his seat, glancing at the readiness board on his MFD. The ship was at a hundred percent and they were either going to enter the starlane in less than half an hour, or they would die.

Personally, he hoped for the former.

CHAPTER THIRTY-FOUR

As Supervisor Fenzac entered the command room wearing his perfectly ironed suit and sporting a groomed beard, Operator Harmon listened to the message one more time.

"Harmon, play the message you received," Fenzac ordered.

Harmon had it keyed up already and hit the button.

"Supervisor Fenzec, this is Director Fargo of Group One. Authentication Zero-Four-Baker-Eleven. You have an Alliance ship heading your way. The moment it comes to a halt, you are to destroy it. That ship cannot leave the system, and we don't need prisoners. Remember, do not fire until its motion relative to you has halted. Do not acknowledge this communication. Maintain radio silence. Message ends."

Fenzec looked at the speaker next to his desk like it was a coiled snake.

"An Alliance ship, here?" he squeaked. "How? The computer would have alerted us to any entry."

Harmon tapped the keys on his console, preparing the station's lone weapon. "I don't know. Maybe they came through the other starlane?" Harmon offered.

Fenzec seemed satisfied with the answer. As long as he didn't have to explain to the supervisor what he'd done wrong, everything would be fine.

"Prepare the railgun," Fenzec said.

Harmon nodded, having already done that. As they had to keep their power source small to avoid emissions, their railgun wasn't the top-of-the-line weapon a ship would have. However, it still fired a one-kilogram slug at five thousand KPS—more than enough to seriously damage, if not destroy, the vessel whose deceleration would bring it to zero at any moment.

It would take two hundred seconds for the weapon to impact at the projected range. They could fire it sooner, but they would risk discovery if they missed. They had to know exactly where the ship was going to be.

"Should we prepare a follow-up round, sir?" Harmon asked.

"That seems a waste of resources. They will never see it coming—we don't need to spend the extra per-diem on ammo that won't make a difference," Fenzec said, smiling at himself for thinking of the bottom line above all else.

————

Interceptor's gravcoil strained as it bled velocity, hitting its own wake as it slowed to a crawl. Where acceleration was a smooth event, with barely any vibration on a functioning ship, deceleration was different. Gravity passed from the bow of the ship, through the coil, and out the stern, causing the whole ship to vibrate slightly and putting a significant strain on the secondary gravcoil and the mechanical components as a whole.

A small part of him wished he could help in some way, other than as a leader. He didn't operate any of the ship's systems or perform physical duties unless things went horribly wrong.

The crew could focus on what they were doing and what they

knew they had to do next, whereas Jacob had nothing to do but worry: about the mission, his ship, and the people aboard her. As if he needed more reasons to stress out. In his mind, he presented an image of the stoic-yet-friendly captain, willing to listen to his crew and give them a fair chance. He knew projecting that image comforted the men and women he served with.

Here he was, the rock. The pillar on which the crew rested. Almost like children, they counted on him to make the right call, to lead them in the right direction. It was his job to make sure the ship was pointed on the right path.

For that privilege, he was given the ultimate responsibility, answering to the fleet, the president, and God for his actions as captain. It was a solemn authority, and he took it seriously. Yet here he was, riding the ship from the captain's chair, able to impact the outcome only with his strategic knowledge and tactical skill.

There was none so lonely as a ship's captain.

A lesser person would turn from such responsibility, back away from having so many lives in his hands. Jacob, though, was made of sterner stuff. His mother had imparted upon him a sense of duty, with how she lived her life, and how she died. She didn't abandon her shipmates when her heavy cruiser was breaking apart and in the end, dying, doing the only truly worthwhile thing a spacer could do: saving her crewmates.

Jacob couldn't be any less than her. Not one ounce less. He would do everything he could for his nation, his navy, his ship, and his crew. If today was to be the day he died, then he would do his mother proud.

As he watched his crew perform their duties, he knew he'd prepared them for this moment. When everything was on the line, and life or death could hinge on seconds. The enemy behind them hadn't slowed, so they were planning on destroying *Interceptor* in a fly-by—which they could easily achieve as she attempted to enter the starlane.

Eight minutes. That was all they had.

"Time to zero?" Jacob asked,

"Ten seconds," Owusu said. "Five... four... three... two... one..."

"Retract the towed array. Coxswain, get us in that lane," he ordered.

"Retracting array," PO Tefiti said.

At the ship's stern, the array spool turned, pulling in the line like a giant fishing pole.

"Aye, sir. Plotting starlane egress," Chief Suresh said.

If they could make it into the starlane, then they could get back to Zuckabar, alert command to the threat, and maybe salvage the situation before the Guild came after the wormhole. Was it dumb luck that the Guild had a secret base next to Zuck? Or something more nefarious? He pushed those thoughts aside. He would have time enough to figure it out when they were safely in the lane.

"Energy spike, zero-five-one mark three-three-four. Sierra-One has fired, sir. Probably a rail gun based on the EM readings," PO Tefiti announced.

"Time to impact?" Jacob asked.

"Based on the energy signature and lag, one-three-five seconds-estimated, sir," Fawkes said.

Jacob looked at Chief Suresh. All he could see through the visor were her dark eyes, but he knew it wasn't enough time for them to fall into the starlane. She shook her head almost imperceptibly, letting him know that he was right.

They were in a race where seconds mattered. Moving would mean death since Suresh would have to start her calculations all over.

"Fawkes!" Jacob shouted. "Plot a reciprocal. Go to rapid-fire on all turrets along that heading."

"Sir?" Carter asked.

"It's a railgun, and they're firing it at extreme range. We're not moving, and we know the heading they're firing from. Fire back!"

Fawkes' eyes went wide as understanding hit him.

"Aye, aye, Skipper!"

Fawkes hunched over his console, hitting buttons and bringing trajectories up, performing the complicated math to use the turrets in a way they weren't strictly intended for.

"Got it," Fawkes said.

The excitement, or perhaps the dread, got to Jacob, and he took a hard step toward Fawkes, clenching his fist.

"Fire!"

Interceptor shook as the four single barreled coilgun turrets went to rapid-fire. The individual rounds of a railgun or coilgun were practically impossible to pick up and track via radar/lidar. However, with *Interceptor's* static position and with their assailant also stationary, there was a small window where the fire could travel.

Interceptor's 20mm rounds flashed through space at ten thousand KPS while the larger railgun round from the station headed for the Navy destroyer at five thousand KPS, giving them a closing speed of fifteen thousand KPS.

In order to cut costs, the Guild used locally mined nickel-iron rounds for their weapons. They were easy to replenish and plentiful for long engagements. Alliance ships were armed with nano-reinforced tungsten penetrators wrapped in a steel sabot. Darts designed to puncture up to thirty millimeters of armored spacecraft or penetrate the bow gravwake of enemy torpedoes.

One of the four 20mm's shredded the railgun's shot, and the other three continued toward Sierra-One. Before the

station's occupants realized their round had failed, three tungsten penetrators blasted through the hull at ten thousand kilometers per second. The first spent itself on the shuttle bay,
smashing the cargo ship parked inside. The second deflected off
the lightly armored hull, only to penetrate down at an angle
and rip through the life support section, killing seven laborers
and vaporizing half the circuitry keeping the station with
fresh air.

Sierra-One was broken and dying, bleeding out its very life,
when the third tungsten arrow hit the secondary fusion battery
pack, releasing the stored energy in a flash of heat. The station
remained intact, but its power and life support were crippled
under the assault.

"Three confirmed impacts, skip," Fawkes said. "I'm reading
a mass of escaping atmosphere and a surge in thermal energy."

Jacob leaned against his chair, thankful the plan worked.
"Return fire?"

"Negative, sir."

Jacob contemplated their next move. In just a few minutes,
the makeshift fleet would be in firing range, and *Interceptor*
would be destroyed.

"Status on pursuit?" he asked.

"No change, sir," Owusu said.

He nodded, not expecting any.

———

Director Fargo ground his teeth together as the reports rolled in.
Outpost One was a write-off, a tight beam distress signal
showed the damage and casualties. Embedded in the signal, the
station's computer reported ninety-nine percent systems loss
and only three percent surviving employees. Fargo wasn't fond
of losing people—unlike almost everyone else in the Guild, he

despised wasting resources, biological or otherwise. He wouldn't mourn them, but their loss represented a significant investment in the system. Combined with the other losses, his operation was less profitable than he would like.

For an outclassed destroyer, the *Interceptor* had cost the Guild *trillions*. Even if some of it was the Guild's own fault following upper management's idiotic self-destruct protocols to avoid their little secret from getting out. It was a shame he would blow that troublesome little ship out of the stars. He hated the loss of resources and they were quite skilled.

"Time until range?" he asked his weapons operator.

"Two minutes, Director. May I remind you, the gaser isn't designed for high-speed engagements. One shot per ship is the most we can expect."

Fargo grinned. "Then don't miss."

———

"Fawkes, anything we can do to make them second guess their vector?" Jacob asked his weapons officer over their private channel.

"Nothing comes to mind, Skipper. We can't hide the fact that we're firing. All they will have to do is change course a few meters, and we'll miss."

Jacob nodded, slumping back some. He knew the answer before he asked. As a good captain, though, it was his responsibility to seek the advice of his officers. Young minds, bright ideas.

Torpedoes wouldn't work, either. Maybe if *Interceptor* hauled ass toward the enemy ships and the closing velocity prevented the hostiles from maneuvering, they could score a few lucky hits.

The Guild, though, didn't need lucky "hits" plural. They

only needed one. The gaser's power couldn't be denied—the glancing blow *Interceptor* had taken before damn near destroyed her. A straight shot would shatter her.

Jacob drummed his fingers for the comforting repetition. No. All he could do was rely on the bravery and skill of his crew.

He stared at the MFD, watching the glowing dots representing the Guild ships. "Owusu, what's your best guess on their top velocity?"

The ensign rapidly punched keys on his console, comparing the readings with something Jacob couldn't see.

"Regardless of their weapons, they're freighters, sir. Three thousand KPS at most. I don't think their structural integrity could take the pounding any more than that."

"Thank you, Owusu."

It was what he had thought. Had the Guild used actual warships converted to look like merchant ships, they would close much faster instead of the other way around. All the data floated around in his head as he stretched for some piece of tactical genius that would buy them the extra four minutes they needed. Nothing came to him. He thumbed the button to contact DCS.

"DCS, XO," Yuki said.

"Kim, any ideas?" he asked.

He didn't need to tell her what for—her stations repeated everything he saw and kept her apprised of the situation.

"Other than we run? Nothing, sir. I know that's not what you were hoping to hear."

"I can't expect you to solve the impossible every day. Maybe just on Tuesdays," he said with false cheer.

"If anyone can beat the record, sir, it's Chief Suresh."

Jacob admired her faith in the crew. She'd come a long way since he took command, and he was proud to have her as his

XO. A flurry of activity at astrogation caught Jacob's attention, and he closed the line to the XO.

Owusu turned to The Pit.

"Chief, try calibrating seven-four-point-six on the lateral grav sensors," Owusu said, breaking the unnatural silence of the bridge.

"Sir?" she said as her fingers danced along, programming in the changes.

"The starlane, Chief. We're looking in the wrong direction! The dark star's gravity is well beyond a normal star. It's why the lane was three hours when the computer said it would be five. If we—"

"Got it," Chief Suresh shouted in an unusual display of exuberance. "Starlane at two-five-four degrees mark zero-seven-five. Range, three-five-two klicks. Holy crap, I'm good."

Jacob listened in stunned disbelief, then leaned forward eagerly. "Set course, execute."

"Helm, seven-five degrees down bubble. Accelerate at three-five gravities," Owusu ordered.

Chief Suresh repeated his orders flawlessly as she adjusted the ship's course, nudging her toward the starlane's looming gravity well at barely faster than harbor speeds. They weren't out of it yet, but his stellar crew had given the rest of the ship a fighting chance.

"Time to full stop?" he asked.

Owusu turned to him. "Three-point-five minutes, sir."

Jacob looked down at the clock on his MFD: ten seconds. Their lives hung in the balance of ten seconds.

"Devi," Jacob said over the private channel. "Don't wait for orders. The second we stop, you initiate starlane fall, understood?"

"Aye, aye, Skipper."

———

Harmon stared in abject disbelief as *Interceptor* began to move.

"Are they running for it?" his second asked.

"If they were going to run, they would have. We're what, twenty-five light-seconds out?" he asked.

"Twenty-three," his astrogator replied.

They could run, but he didn't think they were. The destroyer was three times as fast as his armed merchant ships. She could circle back around and try for the only other starlane in the system. Of course, they almost certainly had no idea where that went or if it would help them.

Trying for the lane back to Zuckabar with him in pursuit was suicide—the math wasn't on their side. Even if it had been a civilian ship specifically designed for finding starlanes, they couldn't beat him.

No, more likely, this was a clumsy attempt at a ruse. If this were a typical engagement, the destroyer would stand a good chance. However, the gravity lasers the Guild used would obliterate the ship with a single hit. All they had to do was close for another sixty seconds, and it would all be over. *If* they somehow managed to survive their first pass, they certainly wouldn't be in a position to enter the starlane.

"Forty-five seconds to firing solution," his weapons operator said.

"Fire as we bear," he ordered.

———

"Full stop," Devi informed the bridge. "Aperture opening."

Feeling helpless, unable to change the outcome, Jacob watched the clock counting down. He had to rely on his crew, to trust them, and he did.

"Entering starlane in three—"

Jacob resisted the urge to close his eyes.

"—*One!*"

She jammed the throttle forward, and for a moment, Jacob's stomach lurched as if he were standing at the top of a cliff, stepping off into the void.

Then they fell.

Interceptor vanished from space at impossible relativistic speeds, amplifying her velocity by a factor of the target system minus the pull of the star they were departing. However, *Interceptor* wasn't alone. Six armed merchants of the Guild fired gravity lasers from their bow the instant they were in range.

The crews of the Guild ships weren't as sharp as a traditional navy; they were motivated more by fear than pride. Three of the ships fired too late, a full half-second after *Interceptor* had already disappeared. Two more fired on time, but their vector was off, and they missed the tiny target of the Hellcat-class destroyer.

However, they only needed one hit.

As *Interceptor* accelerated, the last gaser's leading-edge struck her stern, right behind frame seventy-six. Newtonian forces beyond the ship's designers' comprehension smashed the towed array and both long-range antennas into the hull's interior. Torpedo rooms five and six and the eight spacers and two petty officers manning them were obliterated as if a giant intergalactic hammer had come down on them.

Deck plating caved, dropping thousands of kilos of debris into the boat bay, crushing the Corsair. Unable to cope with the sudden vertical sheering forces, the boat bay doors gave, jettisoning the ruined Corsair, the remains of the torpedo bay, and a screaming Petty Officer Kennedy into the void between systems.

CHAPTER THIRTY-FIVE

J acob shook his head, trying to clear his vision and bring back some semblance of reality. He'd thought they were dead when the ship shook wildly a second after starlane fall.

"Status?" His voice sounded thick like he had a mouth full of peanut butter.

Emergency lights flickered on the bridge in a pattern. *Three-two-three.* Jacob swallowed hard; the arrangement signaled *hull breach.*

"Chief, you with me?" he asked the COB.

Life returned to the bridge as the rest of the crew managed to shake the fog caused by starlane entry and doubled by the weapon's impact.

"With you, Skipper," she said, somewhat dazed sounding. "Checking the course... were still on the lane, thank the stars."

Jacob let out a breath of relief. No one wanted to be stranded between systems. It was almost certain death.

"We're way off course, though," she continued. "I don't know where we will come out or if we'll even make it all the way there."

Traveling through the lanes was like shooting at a long-distance target. Even an infinitesimal percentage of a degree off, and a ship could end up too far from a star to make it back to port or could run right into the gravity well of a planetary mass and end up obliterated.

Jacob prioritized their immediate survival over worrying about tomorrow.

He pushed the comms button. "DCS, Captain speaking."

"DCS here, Skipper," Lieutenant Yuki said.

Relief flooded through him, he would need her before this was all over. "Kim, status?"

A long moment passed before she responded. He almost prompted her again, thinking maybe she hadn't heard him.

"Not good, Skipper. The aft sensors aren't responding. Hanz is running a diagnostic. I'm unbuckling and going to go get a look for myself," Kim said.

"Roger that. Be careful and keep me informed."

"Aye, aye, sir." She cut the line.

Only a few bridge screens had power, and none showed any information. He manually released his harness and stood on shaky legs.

"Any idea what happened? Anyone," he said over the bridge-wide comms.

Tefiti motioned him over. "I think so, sir."

Jacob took three tentative steps, using the grab bars above him for balance and stooped over the petty officer's station.

"The computer registered a gravity event the moment we entered the starlane," Tefiti said, pointing at the dim, flickering monitor.

"Sensors aren't exactly reliable at the moment of acceleration," Jacob said.

"EM sensors aren't, sir, but these are the gravity sensors.

Their readings are predictable. This wasn't that. Something hit us, and if I had to guess, it was another gaser."

"Damn. Chief Suresh," Jacob said, turning to the COB. "You're fired."

"Aye, sir," she replied. "I'll pack my bags and catch the next train."

Her deadpan made Jacob smile. A ripple of chuckles hit the bridge, adding much-needed levity to the moment.

"In all seriousness, damn fine-flying, Chief. I'm fairly certain you set a record that won't be broken anytime soon."

"That and a dollar fifty will buy me a cup of Joe at the next stop," she replied.

"I'll pay for the coffee."

"I'll hold you to it, sir," Suresh said.

Jacob turned slowly, making sure everyone was good to go. It would be easy to miss someone in trouble inside their suits, especially if they couldn't talk.

Satisfied his bridge crew was okay, he sat back down and waited for the reports to come in.

———

Yuki climbed up the ladder from deck four until she pressed against the emergency hatch, cutting off access to the next deck. She flipped open the control panel, scanning the status on the other side. While the ship was devoid of atmosphere, there was a verifiable difference between almost no atmosphere and the perfect vacuum of space. Enough to tell her if there was a hull breach on the other side of the hatch.

When a hull breach occurred, the hatches closest to the affected area went fail-secure, with the hatches directly behind them as a backup. Staggering, the hatch closures created a sort of airlock, allowing both a buffer and a way to rescue any trapped crew without exposing the ship.

Lights turned green, letting her know the other side wasn't open to space.

"Bridge, XO," she said.

"Go ahead, Kim," Commander Grimm answered.

"Sir, I'm on deck four, and it looks like deck three, aft, is sealed off. I can open the hatch without any danger to the ship. Permission to proceed?" she asked.

"Do it. I'm sending the marines your way to help," he said.

"Aye, aye, sir."

Yuki punched in her override code, clicking the confirm button when prompted. The ready light blinked.

"Opening the hatch," she said.

She pushed the button, and the deck around her hands vibrated as the hatch slid open. Emergency lighting lit deck three. She pulled herself up and closed the hatch behind her, and the exterior searchlight on her helmet clicked on automatically, illuminating the sealed double doors leading to the boat bay.

She breathed a sigh of relief; grateful the doors were intact.

"This is the XO," she transmitted on the suit's short-range emergency frequency. "Does anyone copy?"

Yuki moved to the control panel, repeating her status check. This time she was met with a crimson glare.

"Damn," she muttered. "Bridge, XO. Looks like the boat bay is breached. Get those marines here on the double."

While she waited for backup, she went to work opening the doors. There were three people behind the hatch that potentially needed rescuing. If any of them were still alive, she wanted them to stay that way.

"Sickbay, XO. Send a team to the emergency hatch on frame

sixty-five. We're likely to have casualties. No one is responding on comms."

"XO, Lieutenant Krisper. PO Desper and her assistants will be there shortly."

She acknowledged him then went back to the hatch. It was tricky because once it was open, none of the hatches behind her would operate without an override. She had to wait for the marines to arrive, but she couldn't wait for the medical people.

"XO," Jennings said, tapping her on the shoulder.

"Just you?" Kim asked.

"The others are ferrying those who can't walk to sickbay," Jennings said.

"How bad is it?" Yuki asked as she pulled the release lever.

"No fatalities so far. That's about all I know," Jennings said.

Yuki finished the override and hit the button. The port side hatch grinded to a halt in a shower of sparks at the halfway point. The starboard hatch stopped a few seconds later.

"*Kami* save us," Yuki muttered an ancient Shinto saying.

She stepped through the doors, careful to keep one hand against the hull—an unnecessary but irresistible action, considering the state of the boat bay. Or what was left of it. From the port side to the starboard, a gaping hole exposed the ship's stern. No, not a hole, a rent. As if something had peeled open the ship like a tin can and the only thing remaining in the boat bay was the collapsed rubble of the control room.

"Bridge..." she said, unable to finish her sentence.

Jennings finished for her. "Bridge, Jennings. Towed array, both aft torpedo rooms, and the boat bay are gone."

"Say again," Commander Grimm replied. "What do you mean, *gone*?"

"Sir," Yuki finally found her voice. "They are gone, sir. As in not attached to the ship anymore."

Infinite blackness spread out behind them. Red emergency

lights blinked in unison, and their suit lights illuminated the space around them.

"Any survivors?" Grimm asked.

His voice changed to the unemotional tone a commander had to have when assessing possible loss of life. Jennings pointed at the boat bay control room. A solid section of deck plating had collapsed on top of it, smashing it flat like some kind of nightmarish art.

"We're looking, sir. Standby," Yuki said. "Come on."

She waved at Jennings and headed for the remnants of the control room. The stern of the ship was virtually unrecognizable. She had never seen anything like it before. Battle damage from particle weapons left gaping holes filled with jagged metal. Directed energy beams melted armor. Yet these gasers were like a giant ram hitting the ship. She looked down for a moment and spotted the glow of the gravcoil. She spent a long second, thankful that they hadn't hit their only means of interstellar propulsion.

Jennings moved to the closest debris, wrapped her hands around a splintered edge, and heaved. Even through her suit, Yuki saw the marine's muscles strain. The rubble shifted and suddenly, the three-meter bulkhead section was above Jennings's head. She turned and tossed it behind her to crash soundlessly onto the deck.

Yuki blinked several times, trying to process what she saw. A black circle of blood, all the water boiled away in the vacuum. Inside, two forms huddled together, their once stark white uniforms covered in sticky black goo.

PO Baxter lay on top, his arms shielding Chief Boudreaux's head from the debris. A large splinter of nano-reinforced steel had pierced his back like a javelin. The jagged metal shredded his suit violently enough that the nanites weren't able to keep him alive.

"Are they—" she choked off the words.

Jennings knelt next to the bloated, twisted corpse that used to be Baxter. She pushed his leg aside, showing where the metal had pinned him to the chief through her leg and into the deck. The marine placed a hand on Boudreaux, connecting to her suit computer.

"Boudreaux's alive. Her vitals are low, but she's alive," Jennings said.

"See what you can do, Sergeant."

Yuki turned away, calling the bridge as she made her way through the partially open doors to the next sealed hatch on deck three.

"Bridge, XO. I need a medical emergency override on hatch three-seven-zero."

"XO, Operations. Confirm there is no danger to the ship?" Lieutenant West asked.

"No danger. I say again, no danger," she said.

"Override entered," West replied.

A moment later, PO Desper and two of her spacers rushed in through the retreating hatch.

"This way," Kim said.

———

For two hours, Dr. Krisper fought to save Chief Boudreaux's leg, but in the end, he couldn't. The jagged splinter that had ended PO Baxter's life had also severed her femoral artery and blocked the nanites from re-attaching it. The tissue was past rescuing, and he had to focus on saving her life and the lives of other critically injured crew.

"Chief Pierre," he called as he backed away from the operating table. "I can't save her leg. Amputate and seal, please."

"Aye, sir," Chief Pierre said without missing a beat.

Dr. Krisper shook his head in astonishment. How blind he had become to the men and women around him. A doctor required a certain level of emotional detachment to do his job—at least, that's what he was always told. He couldn't operate and make decisions if his emotions got the better of him. However, he'd confused keeping himself objective with not caring.

Krisper had done his absolute best to save her leg, and it pained him to have failed. He would, though, be the one to tell her when she woke up. His HUD showed him a crewman on the verge of hypoxia from a crushed lung, waiting for him outside. After that, a cracked skull, broken ribs, and so on. Boudreaux was far and away the most critically injured, but not the only one.

"Desper, get Spacer Alvarez prepped," he ordered.

He prioritized what he had to do next, and pushed all else to the back of his mind.

———

"You're sure, Chief?" Jacob asked as he knelt next to The Pit.

Chief Suresh nodded, running her hand through the strand of black hair that had fallen from her bun. For now, the crew had their helmets off, but they still wore their ELS suits.

With the damage to the ship and the casualties, there wasn't enough time to stand down between leaving Wonderland and arriving in Zuck. The best he could manage was allow the crew to shower and eat, a few at a time, then return to their Zulu station. Letting them remove their helmets was the most he could allow for them to relax.

"Aye, sir. We're off about a tenth of a degree. We'll come out here." She pointed at a spot on the system almost fifty million klicks from where they had entered.

Fifty million *farther* out.

"If the Guild ships followed us in?" he asked, keeping his voice down to make sure it stayed between them.

She adjusted a dial on the controls, moving the pointer closer to Zuckabar.

"Dammit," he muttered.

After everything they had gone through, a lucky shot was going to sink their chances of getting home and warning Kremlin and the Alliance.

"Skipper," Yuki said from the hatchway.

Her once pristine white ELS suit was marred by grime and blood. She clutched her helmet under her arm while pulling off one glove. Jacob patted Suresh on the shoulder. Yuki motioned him to the conference room. She placed her helmet and glove on the table before sinking into the chair closest to the hatch.

He could tell that she was close to exhaustion. The entire crew was, himself included. The lack of food didn't help—they were all on half calories. Even with Mendez's family stew, they were all feeling the pangs of hunger.

Jacob hit the button next to his seat, activating the comms. "Mess, this is the captain. Can you send up a couple of orange drinks to the conference room?"

"Aye, sir. Be there in five," Spacer first-class Mendez said.

Jacob sat, waiting for his XO to look up. When she did, he studied her expression. Even covered in dust and debris, with smudges on her face and sweat-soaked hair, she looked every bit the executive officer. Jacob admired her unwavering commitment to her duty. She was the first person at any problem, and the last person to hit the rack at night.

Mendez entered a moment later, obviously having hustled to get from the mess to the briefing room. He handed Jacob a disposable cup full of orange flavored stimulant drink they used when coffee wasn't an option—which, for Jacob, was always.

"Thank you, Josh," Jacob said.

"Of course, Skipper," he replied with a sheepish smile.

Once he left and Jacob had taken a long pull of his drink, he looked at Yuki.

"Lay it on me, Kim. How bad is it?"

She rubbed an arm across her face before taking a sip of her drink. He watched as the stimulant did its job, re-energizing her and clearing the tired away from her eyes. It did the same for him, but they could only stave off the prolonged exhaustion for so long before it took its toll.

"Where to start?" she asked, mostly to herself.

She tapped a button on her NavPad, bringing up a holographic projection of the ship. Jacob winced. He didn't need her to tell him the yellow, red, and black highlights were awful.

"How many...?" he asked.

Dwelling on the dead wouldn't make any of the hundred decisions any easier, but it was his duty to know.

"Twelve, so far. The latest report from Dr. Krisper suggests that Chief Boudreaux is going to make it, though."

Twelve... ten percent of his crew in one hit.

"Thank you. Go on," he ordered.

"We lost a lot, sir. Both aft torpedo rooms, main comms, and the towed array are gone. There's no fixing it; they're just gone. Both long-range antennas are out, and until we finish re-routing the computer traffic, we're out on short-range as well. The laser works, though, for what it's worth," she said with a tired grin.

He appreciated her attempt at levity. She was correct; there were things to be thankful for here. Normally, main comms would have had three personnel in it at any given moment, but they had been at battle stations.

"To be honest, Skip," she said, "luck was on our side."

"How do you figure?" he asked through a clenched throat.

He was the one who would have to write the letters to the twelve families, letting them know how their loved ones died.

"The vast majority of the energy hit the towed array spindle. Normally, the spindle would have been retracted into the hull, but we were in a hurry to enter the lane, so it was still exposed. If the gaser had hit the hull I don't think we would be alive to talk about it."

Two lucky hits from an experimental weapon of unknown destructive capability were enough for any ship to survive. There wouldn't be a third.

"What's the status on the gravcoil?" he asked.

"The repairs Chief Redfern carried out in orbit are sticking. Lieutenant Gonzales doesn't see any new problems. Assuming that all holds, we'll have full acceleration—or as close to it as we're able when we come out of the starlane."

Jacob listened as she continued down the lengthy damage report. The vast majority of it was either direct damage on the aft sections from the impact, secondary damage from overloads, or the sudden uncompensated motion of the ship.

"That's about it, Skipper. ETA to Zuckabar is under thirty minutes. We've repaired everything we can repair. We're going to have to come within a million klicks to notify fleet, but that shouldn't be a problem—" she stopped as she saw Jacob's face.

He shook his head. "The hit altered our course, Kim. We're coming out of the starlane fifty million klicks farther away than where we entered. Best guess, four days to dock with Kremlin."

Kim glanced at the open hatch, then leaned closer as if the crew were outside taking notes.

"What about the ship's stores?" she asked quietly.

Jacob tapped his fingers along the table's wooden trim. "I don't think the stores are going to be a problem. Even if the Guild ships immediately throw their engines in reverse, they're going to come out of the starlane ahead of us.

"We don't have the time to go around, and we certainly can't hide from active sensors—not with our ship's ECM capabilities crippled. If we're very lucky, we'll see them before they see us. At least then we can build up some velocity before we have to engage."

Kim's eyes widened as she realized the magnitude of what her captain was saying. They weren't going to live long enough to worry about running out of food.

"You mean to fight them, Jacob?" she asked in a whisper.

He looked at her, pleading with his eyes. "Give me an alternative, and I will jump at it. How can we warn the Alliance, save the station, and make it home in one piece?"

When she didn't answer, he waved a hand. "We have three objectives, but only one priority. We must—and I mean *must*— warn the Alliance about the true nature of the Guild. This goes beyond anything ONI ever imagined. We have to find a way to get the word out no matter what. Even if—" He glanced at the hatch. "Even if we lose the ship."

Kim squared her shoulders, stood up and grabbed her helmet.

"Aye, aye, Skipper. I'm on it," Kim said.

"Good woman." Jacob let out a breath as his loyal XO departed. He'd prayed she would have some insight that would allow them out of the no win scenario they found themselves facing.

Every man and woman who set foot on an Alliance ship understood one basic truth: on any given day, they could be asked to make the ultimate sacrifice.

For the crew of the USS *Interceptor*, that day had come.

CHAPTER THIRTY-SIX

C hief Petty Officer Devi Suresh pushed back in her chair, NavPad cradled in her lap and a cup of coffee in her hand. She only had a few more minutes before she needed to return to the bridge, so she had skipped her shower and food for a cup of coffee and some alone time to analyze the enemy.

Something about the way they maneuvered bothered her. Devi downed the last of the Navy brand coffee before hopping up and tossing the cup in the recycle. She grabbed her helmet and headed for the bridge.

The way the Guild operated reminded her of several merchant skippers she had run across in her time—ones who never really took the time to learn their ship's systems, let alone become proficient with them. On her NavPad, she had the sensor recordings of the three encounters: the first one in Zuck-abar, where the ship caught them by surprise, the second one when they snuck up behind the ship in the atmosphere, and the third one when they damn near destroyed *Interceptor* as she jumped into the starlane.

Twenty-plus years in the Navy and she was stationed in The

Pit for almost all of it. In all her time, she'd spent maybe six months ground-side. Ship handling was her calling. The one time the Navy sent her to the Academy, it was to teach the wet-behind-the-ears cadets how to fly. In her experience, new or poorly trained pilots tended to make the same handful of mistakes, and they were slow to respond, letting the computer do too much for fear of making the wrong move.

Navy brass was always floating the notion of automated control of starships, based on the flawed idea that a computer could outperform a human pilot. A lousy pilot, maybe, but not her. She was absolutely against it, but she was just a coxswain on a tin can. She couldn't control what the higher-ups did, only how she responded.

She didn't have anything against computers, per se. She was certainly no Luddite. Computers ran everything. Distances were unimaginably vast in space, and without a computer, no one could go anywhere. Even her manual control was assisted by the computers. Her opposition was to computers making the decisions.

In tight circumstances, like matching vectors, crossing grav wakes, and docking, nothing substituted for the deft touch of a human at the helm. Sure, a computer could do all the calculations in a heartbeat, but they would never anticipate by feel no matter how advanced they were.

The speaker above her crackled to life as she ascended the final ladder to the O-deck.

"Now, hear this. Exiting starlane in ten minutes," Lieutenant West said.

Starlanes ended whether a ship wanted them to or not. Leaving one would happen regardless of what the helm did. If the coxswain was good at their job, it was a fairly easy and routine affair. If they were inexperienced at it, then the ship was in for a rough ride. Or if some moronic superweapon hit them as they entered.

She motioned for Collins to exit. While the PO unbuckled herself and climbed out of The Pit, Devi secured her helmet. Once the seat was clear, she slid in, buckled up, and gave the Skipper a thumbs up in the mirror.

Jacob returned her thumbs up with his own. The next little while would be telling. They still had no way to warn the Alliance, nor did they know what would happen—other than freighters with powerful weapons were coming. The fact that the Guild had a whole star system right next door made conflict inevitable. Combining all those things with the attack on Gamma-7 and the gasers felt like more than a conflict of interest. Like a larger game was being played.

Maybe the Guild had intended to ignore the Alliance and keep their farming planet to themselves. Or maybe there was some grand conspiracy afoot, but the moment they took—and murdered—Alliance citizens, it became his duty to put an end to it.

However powerful those six freighters were, they couldn't hope to take on the light cruiser and two other destroyers in-system, let alone the built-in defenses of Kremlin Station.

Unless....

Were they planning on destroying Kremlin? But how? It had operated successfully in a hostile system for hundreds of years, and it would take a massive kinetic strike to destroy the kilometers-long station. While powerful, he doubted even the gasers were enough to take out the base before their defense systems engaged and destroyed the attacking ships.

He thumbed the comm switch. "XO, captain."

"XO here, sir," Kim instantly replied.

"The rail delivery arm Gamma-7 used—was it military-grade?" he asked.

"I seriously doubt it. The math to fire an object halfway across the solar system and hit a waiting catcher is pretty basic, so why would they need a military one? They also wouldn't need much power."

Somehow, Gamma-7 was the key to the puzzle. What could the Guild possibly gain from destroying the far-flung mining base and taking the crew hostage? Were they using it to resupply Wonderland?

"Kim, could you..." he was grasping for straws, and he knew it. "Reprogram the arm to shoot at something else? Say a stationary target?"

"Easy, Skipper... but why? The canisters are what, six tons each and move along at a lazy one thousand KPS? You could practically shoot them with a pistol long before they hit anything valuable. Not to mention, without the right codes programmed into the projectile's housing, Kremlin's space defense systems would pick them off a few hundred thousand klicks out."

"Unless you had access to a station with the exact codes and on the right heading," Jacob said as he fumbled for the greater plan.

Yuki sucked in a breath. Her brows furrowed as she did the math.

"Maybe, Skip, but that would still require an enormous fusion reactor to power it. Maybe if you docked *Interceptor* and used her as a genny, maybe—"

In a moment of clarity, Jacob put it all together. The Guild *had* built Wonderland long before, but because of the unique nature of the starlane, it was easy to hide. After all, it was far beyond the normal distance starlanes were detected. Once the wormhole came along, they were perfectly positioned to control yet another source of revenue. Maybe they knew about the wormhole, or maybe they got lucky—it didn't matter. With control of the wormhole, the Guild would quickly become the most powerful entity in the galaxy— if they weren't already. A thought that gave Jacob chills.

If anyone tried to take Zuckabar from them, their armed merchantmen would make short work of any unsuspecting foe, let alone if they put that weapon on an actual warship. The only ship who could stop them was one lone destroyer, sent to investigate a signal that should never have gone out. If any other ship had gone to investigate, they would have taken a few hours longer—more than enough time for the mercenaries to wipe any evidence and make it look like a mining accident.

"Wait one, Kim. I'm looping in Chief Suresh," Jacob said.

A second later, he connected to the chief's comms.

"Yes, sir?" Suresh asked.

"Devi, could you plot the course of the CTV Komodo? Extrapolate it out?" he asked.

"Aye, aye, sir, one second..." her voice faded as she went to work.

"What are you thinking, Skip?" Kim asked.

"I'm thinking the Komodo was bringing that colonial fusion reactor to power the Guild base. If I'm right—"

"I think you are, Skipper," Devi interrupted. "When we boarded Komodo, they were heading in the general direction of the Guild's hidden base."

That was the last piece of the puzzle for him. "They're going to use Gamma-7's codes to launch an attack against Kremlin."

"Pardon me, Skipper," Devi interrupted. "But that's insane. They're basically a large corporation, not a government. They can't really believe this will work, can they?"

"Whatever we think their chances are, they seem to think they can pull it off," Jacob said. "Based on their success so far, they may be on to something."

"That also explains their armed merchant fleet," Kim said.

"If Kremlin was gone, they could move in and handle any ships left over and they would control the system. Nothing short of an all-out invasion would unseat them."

"Begging the exec's pardon, but I don't think our current political overlords have the stomach for that," Devi interjected.

"Despite our COB's colorful description of the civilian leadership of the Navy, I agree with her," Kim said.

Debates of a political nature were well beyond Jacob's pay grade.

"Regardless," he said. "We're past merely warning the Alliance."

He hated where this was going.

"How so?" Kim asked.

"Warning them won't be enough. We're going to have to stop the Guild. Let's assume, and I think it's safe to do so, that they have a backup fusion reactor and will be able to fire on Kremlin and destroy it. Knowing the Guild did it would be great, but it wouldn't change the fact that their armed merchants would still be in-system. They could cruise into point-blank range and take out *Corvus* and her consorts before they even knew what hit them."

Jacob glanced up at the clock, noting they had two minutes until they would know exactly where they were going to end up in the system and where the Guild's ships would emerge.

"Full speed ahead, Skipper. We use our maneuverability, velocity, and superior armament to outfight them. We know what they're about now. Those gasers are extremely powerful, but we can control the terms of the engagement," Kim said.

"Chief?" Jacob asked for his coxswain's opinion.

"I agree with the XO. I've analyzed their flight patterns, and I don't think their crews are well trained. They fly like they're following the manual."

"I concur with you both," he said. "God be with us. Captain out."

He killed the line, leaning back in his chair and closing his eyes for a moment. They had two goals as he saw them. One was to destroy or disable as many Guild ships as possible. Even if they managed to obliterate Kremlin—and Jacob shuddered at the thought of that many lives lost—without their full strength, they could never hope to hold the system.

The second task of warning the Alliance was quite a bit easier. With their communications capability shot, he just needed to figure out how.

He took in a deep breath, letting it steady his nerves. This was one decision he never wanted to make, and yet here he was. There were two million people on Kremlin at any given moment. In a perfect galaxy, his priority would be to save those lives, but he couldn't. As fast as *Interceptor* was, there was no way to stop the armed merchants *and* hunt down and destroy the shooting armature hidden on the far edges of the solar system.

Jacob opened up the bridge-wide comms. "When we return to Zuck, I want to go to full alert. If you see anything that might look like a gravity spike, let me know. We have one shot to take them out, and by God, we're going to do it."

"Ten seconds to exit," Ensign Owusu said.

Jacob watched the crew brace themselves. Coming out of a starlane wasn't nearly as smooth as going in. Whereas the former felt like jumping off of something high, the latter felt like coming to a sudden stop in a fast elevator. Poorly done, the crew could vomit, lose consciousness for a few seconds, or up to an hour.

"Brace, brace, brace," Ensign Hössbacher said over the ship-wide speakers.

The pure blackness of starlane travel wavered for a moment;

in the span of a second, the light of the stars returned. A wave of nausea passed over him, and his stomach threatened to leap into his throat. He swallowed hard, balling his fists and making every attempt to keep bile down.

He managed, but just. Others on the bridge and throughout the ship weren't as lucky.

"Sitrep?" he asked after thirty seconds, giving everyone the time they needed to collect themselves.

"Where are the enemy ships?"

CHAPTER THIRTY-SEVEN

Talmage St. John shifted uncomfortably in the military style chair on the Alexander's observation deck. They had arrived in Zuckabar a few hours before and were on their way to the wormhole. A consort of ships traveled with them.

Alexander was its own battle group. While the massive battleships of the Alliance Navy could dish out immense punishment, they were also vulnerable. Large and easy to hit with volleys of munitions. The eight other warships surrounding her in a sphere created layers of defense. Humorously, Talmage realized he was literally in the safest place in the entire galaxy, despite their current location at Zuckabar—a place which was still as close to lawless as one could get in the Alliance.

"Sir," a yeoman said to the president who was seated several chairs away from Talmage. "USS *Corvus* has signaled us and will meet us at the wormhole in forty-five minutes."

"Thank you, Ensign," President Axwell replied.

Talmage was amazed at how relaxed the president put those around him. The vast majority of men and women he met in politics were self-serving, power-hungry, wannabe oligarchs. Much of Senator Talmage St. John's job was about protecting the constitution and ensuring New Austin received fair treatment. Something that had gotten harder since they annexed the Protectorates, not easier.

While he had won the battle, he had made enemies on both sides of the aisle and had cast his lot in with the president and the pro-Navy faction, which was made up of himself, Admiral Villanueva, and the president. Even the other senators who felt as he did—that a strong navy was the crux of their defense— were waiting for more evidence that it wasn't political suicide to openly support the Navy.

Talmage had long suspected that the supposed "hatred of the Navy" was mostly a creation of Congress and their media allies. Initially, it was a way of deflecting the blame from the Great War. However, it turned into a rallying cry for them to easily seek re-election. That was the one truth he had come to realize in the last few years. A politician in office will always seek to remain in office, no matter what. He just hoped that his pro-Navy faction wasn't too late. If the Alliance's enemies realized how weak they truly were, they would launch an attack.

———

Albatross wondered again what he was doing. He was no warship commander. He wasn't even trained on the Guild's ships, yet here he was, standing on the bridge of the *Leopard*. The stealth ship moved easily from system to system, leaving no trace of its location. As long as they didn't power up their energy weapon or open any external hatches, she was a hole in space.

He was glad that the Caliphate hadn't asked for more. The Guild had only produced the one. They required extensive engineering and time-consuming work, and it just wasn't cost-effective to make an entire fleet out of the material they had on hand. However, one ship that could be used as a first strike vehicle was justifiable.

The counter in the corner of the main screen ticked down, and he glanced over at Kasseem's naval advisor, who sat stone-faced and silent. The man had said very little during the trip, but Albatross didn't mind. The people of the Caliphate bothered him on a fundamental level. He couldn't shake the feeling that the Guild, and he personally, was making a huge mistake.

It was a little late for self-doubt, he decided. They were almost at Alexandria, and before long, many of their problems would be gone. Kasseem assured them that once they punched the Alliance in the nose, they would surrender. When the Alliance saw the power of the Caliphate and the Guild, there would be no more need to fight. With their capital at stake, the Alliance would cede rather than lose tens of millions of people.

The Caliphate analyst, along with his own people's planning and intelligence services, all agreed. The moment the *Leopard* appeared in orbit above Alexandria, the war would be over before it began. No one would foolishly risk the lives of their most populated planet.

At least, that was what Albatross hoped. As they passed through Alexandria's outer system, he had to wonder if he was right. The Alliance had surprised the Guild by discovering their centuries-old computer infiltration. Then surprised them again by seizing control of the terraformers.

What if they didn't surrender?

Albatross shook his head and chuckled aloud. There was no possibility of that. No matter what, they would soon learn the price of clashing with the Terraforming Guild.

CHAPTER THIRTY-EIGHT

Outrider Command appeared in the Zuckabar system as if by teleportation. It wasn't teleportation, of course, only the tail end of a three-hour starlane trip from Omega. The freighters weren't the fastest things in space, but starlane travel was the same speed regardless of whether the ship was a million-ton freighter or an eighty-thousand-ton armed merchantman.

Despite the interference of *Interceptor*, Director Fargo was confident that they would arrive in Zuckabar in time to complete their goals.

Two of his ships immediately headed for the semi operational outpost. They would supervise the installation of their micro fusion reactors. It would take time, but that was okay. He had a ship to kill.

"Sensors, any sign of them?" he asked.

His passive sensor station was manned by a man with light-brown skin and no hair. Fargo couldn't remember the man's name, nor did he care to.

"Nothing yet, sir. We may not be in range to detect their gravwake."

Fargo nodded, opening his log and making a notation for the record. Too many things had gone wrong with their overly complex plan—he wasn't going to allow anything else to sabotage it. He checked communications to see if the hidden satellite network had reported any activity around the starlane. Nothing yet.

"All right then. Comms put me through to all ships," he ordered.

The comms man quickly activated the mic on Director Fargo's chair.

"All Outriders, search formation with ten thousand kilometers between us. Go maximum power on active sensors. The first ship to spot *Interceptor* will receive a bonus. Outrider Command, out," he said.

Once they had dealt with *Interceptor*, they could finish their work and move on.

———

"Here we are, sir," Ensign Owusu said, pointing at the map projected above the conference table.

Every officer aboard *Interceptor* crowded around the conference table with the grinning shark logo.

"And the Guild ships?" Jacob asked.

Owusu manipulated the controls, zooming out on the system until a new dot appeared between *Interceptor* and Zuckabar.

"Approximately here. We only detected them for a moment when they came out of the starlane. We would have lost them again, but they're banging away on their radar and lidar, looking for us. Our passive systems can follow them easily with all the noise they're making. To be honest, sir, coming out early saved us. They are practically right on top of where we would have come out if we hadn't gotten hit."

After an hour of floating motionless in the void, with no immediate threat, Jacob had stood the crew down, letting them resume normal duty while his astrogation section went to work finding the enemy ships.

He'd known the hit *Interceptor* took as they entered the star-lane for Zuckabar would throw them wildly off course. He hadn't guessed that it might work to their advantage.

Someone whistled and he let the slight breach in decorum slide. They were way the hell gone and back—he knew it, and they knew it. Jumping on them for expressing their shock would do no one any favors.

"Five days, best speed, and that's if we head right for Zuckabar?" Kim asked. "Is that right?"

"Aye, ma'am," Ensign Owusu confirmed in an almost reverent whisper.

"Five days?" Dr. Krisper said. "Sir, the crew is already showing signs of malnutrition. Five more days and we're in real trouble."

Jacob nodded, he understood all too well. The only people receiving a full ration were in sickbay. They had plenty of water, but even stretching their food further, five days wasn't possible.

"Ensign Owusu, I thought you said we would be four days out?" Jacob asked.

"Uh, yes, sir. Calculating the exit vector proved to have more variables than I anticipated," Owusu explained.

"You did good, Ensign," Lieutenant Yuki said. "We're operating in unknown territory here."

"Yes, ma'am," Owusu replied, but Jacob could see the disappointment in his eyes.

"And of course," Jacob said. "If we run straight to Zuck, the

Guild will see us coming from a light-year away. We'll end up fighting them on their terms."

He looked to Owusu to answer his implied question.

"Depending on their engagement velocity, anywhere from twelve to twenty-four hours, sir," Owusu said.

"Right about when we run out of food," the Bosun added somberly.

His crew would be hungry, exhausted, and going into a battle against overwhelming odds. It was a Catch-22. In order to have a chance at returning to Zuckabar, they had to take the most direct route possible. But doing so would reveal them to the Guild fleet as soon as they were within range. However, they could spoof their exact course by making changes along the way. The Guild would never be sure exactly where they were going to be. It would take longer though, and longer they didn't have.

A knock on the conference room hatch interrupted his thoughts.

"Sir," Sergeant Jennings said, poking her head in. "Mr. Vesper would like to speak to you. He says it's important."

Jacob motioned for her to allow him in. She disappeared for a moment before guiding Vesper through the hatch to stand where she could reach him if need be. Jacob smiled at how carefully she moved. If Vesper tried anything, he'd be in for a surprise. Not that he thought the ex-Guild employee would. The man was a survivor—he wouldn't throw away his chance to live.

"Hello Captain, I, well... I had an idea that might help you. Your Chief Redfern seemed to think it would work, so..." he shrugged.

Vesper's nerves were obvious to everyone in the room.

"Go ahead," Jacob said.

"I figure you have to warn your government of what the

Guild is doing—" He paused to see if anyone would argue. When they didn't, he continued. "Chief Redfern told me the long-range comms are down? Is that accurate?"

Jacob glanced at Kim to answer the question. He made a mental note to remind the crew not to share the ship's status without checking with the XO. Not that he minded his guests knowing, but he would like to be in the loop.

"That's right, Mr. Vesper," Kim said. "The hit we took entering the starlane totaled our comms section."

"I have an idea how you can warn the Alliance—it requires a torpedo," Vesper said.

Jacob's curiosity got the better of him, and he gestured for Vesper to continue. One torpedo would hardly make the difference in the long run.

"We can modify an emergency beacon from one of your ELS suits. I think they're designed to last twenty-four hours and go significant distances, am I right?"

Lieutenant Enzo Gonzales answered. "Yes, but they don't have the power to last five days."

"If you take out the warhead and put in a fusion battery, it will. It only needs to get within a hundred million klicks," Vesper said.

Gonzales frowned. "It could work, Skipper," he said.

"Thoughts?" Jacob asked the officers around the table.

Fawkes tapped his finger on the table. "Sir, even if we fired it outside of their effective range, they would see it and be able to track it. What would stop them from just—" He made a gun with his hand and pretended to fire. "—blowing it out of space."

"He's got a point, sir," Enzo said. "Even at maximum velocity, they could still pick it off."

Jacob sighed. For a moment, he thought they had a solution to warn Kremlin after all.

"Thank you for trying, Mr. Vesper. We appreciate the help," Jacob said as he motioned for Jennings to remove the man.

"I'm sorry. I thought it would work," Vesper said.

Jennings escorted him out, leaving the room a bit more somber than when he'd come in. Jacob hated the idea of a no-win scenario. They were a fact, however. Sometimes a captain could do everything right and still lose. This was shaping up to be one of those times.

"Sir," Kim said, breaking him out of his thoughts. "If we accelerated the old girl to top speed, *then* fired the torpedo, she would hit—"

She paused to look up as she did the math in her head. "Thirty thousand KPS and change before she ran dry. At ten percent of c, they would never be able to shoot her. If we executed this plan in the next hour, they would likely lose track of it, to begin with—especially if we altered course a few degrees to build separation. They would have to peel ships off to find the torpedo—if they even thought it was important to begin with."

"Ma'am," West interrupted, "If we did that, we would be giving up every tactical advantage we have. There would be no way to hide at that point."

West looked down, not finishing his sentence. He didn't have to. The Guild's super-weapon had hit them twice, and they were lucky to have survived. They wouldn't likely survive a third hit.

"And if they did track it and take it out, we would be giving everything up and still not deliver the warning," Gonzales said.

Jacob decided to call the meeting. They weren't getting anywhere. He'd hoped the torpedo idea would work, but it sounded like it was too small a chance of success.

"Thank you, everyone," Jacob said. "Make sure your sections are ready to go. No matter what we do, the next few days will be difficult on crew and equipment. Don't keep anything from your chief's, either. Everyone on board deserves to know what we're in for and the consequences of failure. We're officers in the United Systems Alliance, and we will succeed. Understood?"

They all agreed—albeit less enthusiastically than he would have liked.

"Dismissed," he said.

As they filed out, he noticed Kim didn't move. She maintained her seat opposite him, looking at her NavPad while the officers left the room.

He let her sit, deciding that if she had something to say, he was happy to wait as she collected her thoughts. To be honest, he realized there was only the tiniest possibility of them succeeding at any one of their objectives. All three? No.

Warn the Alliance. Stop the Guild. Save the station.

Pick two.

Every minute they spent at zero acceleration was another minute longer before they were back. Another minute his crew didn't eat. They had to move and move soon.

"I have an idea, Skipper," Kim said.

"I'm all ears."

"We go flank speed directly for Kremlin as we planned. Nothing fancy. We drive straight down their throats. *If* we fire the message torpedo just outside effective weapons range, they'll think we panicked or misfired. When it doesn't home in on any of their ships' grav wakes, they won't waste resources trying to take it out. Who would?"

"Instead of firing now, we wait? Kind of the opposite of what you proposed. Do you think this has a higher chance of success?" he asked.

"I do, Skipper. We would be closer when we fired. They would be locked on us since we would be heading right for them. Finally, with us firing on them, they won't have time to think about one torpedo flying off into space."

"That still leaves us with the problem of flying straight into the enemy's jaws," he said.

Her grin grew wicked, and he saw a bloodthirsty gleam in her eye.

"Yes, sir, that's the plan. I doubt this would work against a trained enemy, but something the COB said got me thinking. If it doesn't work, we'll know pretty quick, and we can adjust our tactics on the fly, but if it does, then they're in for a hell of a surprise."

"If what works?"

"Sir, practically all our weapons—and they know this—are short-range, except for the MK XII's, which aren't great against small targets. If they think they know what path we'll take, what will they do? Come at an angle and turn to shoot us as we blow past them? Run 'away' from us slowly so we overtake them and they can get behind us and take us out? Or will they take the implied challenge and come right at us, the most direct route?"

Jacob contemplated the situation. There was a strong instinct to face one's enemy head-on. One that had led to the downfall of more than one ship's captain over the millennia.

"If they fall for it, then what?" he asked.

"Well, sir, then we light their collective bean-counting asses up," she said with a savage smile.

Interceptor's 20mm turrets had no maximum range. Once fired, the projectile would go on forever. However, they weren't used at long distances because they were point-and-shoot weapons. Any half-decent skipper would keep his ship moving in a volume of space too big for a dumb fire weapon to hit by anything other than luck.

The only exception was a stern chase—which was why

Navy doctrine frowned on chasing a ship's stern. The only thing that had allowed them victory in Zuckabar was a combination of the pirate's poor ship handling and their dogged pursuit of his stern.

"If you're right, Kim, that will make Sir Isaac Newton the deadliest son-of-bitch in space," he said, returning her grin with one of his own.

"Don't I know it, sir. Even if we miss most of our shots, we can still take out a few of them before they realize their mistake."

He had a lot to think about. "Get to work on the torpedo. I'll decide on this in five minutes and let you know."

"Aye, aye, Skipper." She looked like she wanted to say something else but instead exited the briefing room.

Jacob bowed his head and spent a solid five minutes praying. It was his greatest source of wisdom and comfort, and he needed both at the moment. When he was done, not only did he feel better about the situation, but he had also come to a decision. He cleared his throat and pressed the comms button.

"Bridge, captain. Helm, set a course directly for Kremlin Station, flank speed."

"Aye, sir," Suresh answered. "Kremlin Station, flank speed. Course laid in."

Jacob waited a moment, wondering if he was about to send his crew to their deaths. If he was, did he have any other choice?

"Execute," he said.

———

"Found them!" the astrogator exclaimed with a show of exuberance. "Two-one-seven mark one-eight-zero. It looks like they're accelerating at maximum power."

"Show me," Fargo ordered.

The screen lit up showing that the *Interceptor* was even farther away than he'd imagined. Why light off their drive now and show their location?

"Comms, channel to all ships." He waited until he was connected. "All Outriders, form on my ship and accelerate at maximum speed on the following coordinates. We've located the Alliance ship, and we need to destroy her before she is in range to contact their superiors."

He closed the channel without waiting for a response.

They would enter the attack range in just under twenty-four hours. Once the old destroyer was gone, he could turn around and head for Zuckabar Central and accept the Alliance's surrender of the system.

CHAPTER THIRTY-NINE

Nadia feigned unconsciousness as her mind caught up to where she was—restrained in a chair. Panic sprung within her, and it was only by the sheerest of margins she didn't give in to the fear welling up in her.

She hated being restrained. A deep sense of shame filled her, and even though her training allowed her to pretend to be asleep, she struggled to feign. This wasn't her fault. What happened on the Dagger wasn't her fault.

Nadia pushed down the fear, trying to think clearly through the sudden surge of emotions. She hadn't spent all those months in therapy to fold the moment she got in a rough spot.

Magnetic cuffs locked her wrists to the metal chair beneath her. Gently, as not to alert anyone in the room, she pushed with her right leg, lifting the foot of the chair imperceptibly. Good, she decided. If she needed to, she could use the chair as a weapon.

Next, she opened her eyes to mere slits. Her head hung with her chin pressed against her sternum. From that position, she could see to her left and right. Nothing. She strained her ears, listening for the slightest sound.

After a few moments, she decided no one was in the room with her. They weren't likely to come in while she was unconscious. Giving up the pretense, she raised her head.

The room looked like a standard interrogation room, something she had seen a hundred times. Or, she thought with a smile, it could be the nearest supply closet.

On the wall opposite her, a seam appeared, and a door opened. Pelican walked in with his maddeningly languid gait. He leaned against the wall while taking his time to examine her.

If she hadn't realized the Guild had computers in their head, Nadia might have thought he was trying to make her uncomfortable. As it was, she figured he was researching her.

"Commander Dagher, logistics division, assigned to Kremlin Station for supply? Well, that's a damn lie, isn't it?" he said.

She replied with a blank stare, letting him wonder what she was thinking. "Seems like you're a spy. Navy logistics officers don't walk around in custom-made blackout suits."

Nadia didn't think saying anything would benefit her. The best course would be to use silence as a weapon. Make him uncomfortable to the point where he felt compelled to speak and give something away she could use to stop the Guild.

"Well, Commander, you're too late. I'm afraid you missed your chance to kill me. My mission will succeed despite your best efforts. I doubt you even know who I am," he said with a smile.

Was he baiting her? Trying to get her to talk? She did know he was Guild. She looked away, feigning shame. Well, allowing him to see it more than feigning it.

"The question isn't 'do I know who you are,' but 'do you know who I am?'" she said suddenly.

Pelican quirked an eyebrow—the first sign of caution flickered behind his dark eyes. "It's not important. If you knew why I was here, you wouldn't have come for me in my hotel room. Would you? Time, I'm afraid, isn't on your side."

Nadia wracked her brain, trying to think of something to stall him, something she had seen him do. The museum? An image flashed before her. The buildings opposite the museum were all government. In her mind's eye, she ran through each one until it hit. If she was wrong, it would cost her nothing but her life.

"How will sabotaging Space-Traffic Control help you take the station?" she asked nonchalantly.

While his face didn't betray his emotions, his body stiffened, a slight tell that she could use.

"Interesting. I ran over your device," he pulled her NavPad from his pocket. "There was no mention of this to your commander."

He was lying, she could tell. He may have *tried* to crack her NavPad, but no computer in the known galaxy could. At least not without a month worth of effort.

"Listen, Pelican. We know about you and Albatross. You think you have the upper hand here, but trust me, you don't. Your only play is to surrender. Turn on the Guild, and maybe you can escape this with a house on Ohana instead of a cell at Fort Icarus."

He let out a short laugh. "In less than 24-hours this station will be gone, Zuckabar Central will be ours, and the Guild will be telling the Alliance what to do. Not that you will be alive to see any of it."

Pelican pulled a small nanite injector from a side pocket, the kind hospitals used for emergencies. He approached her, injector out, with a smirk on his face. Nadia suppressed her fear, the memory of what happened to her on Dagger threatened to surface. This time, though, it was different. She wasn't taken by surprise or ambushed on her ship. She was in a position she chose.

"I don't think so," Nadia said.

She balled up her cybernetic fist and yanked with all her enhanced might. Pain lanced through her flesh wrist as the bone broke from the counterforce. Her artificial hand tore free of the magnetic restraints and clocked Pelican in the face as he leaned over to inject her. She pushed off with her legs, falling backward. On her back, she reached down and crushed the restraints holding her ankles.

Pelican stumbled back, hand on his swelling cheek. Once free, Nadia turned to face him with her cybernetic arm held in a defensive posture while cradling her broken one against her chest. While the Guild agent outweighed her by more than fifty kilos, she thought she could take him. If both her arms were working, it was certain, but with one broken, her confidence faltered.

Pelican recovered with a shake of his head, cracked his neck and came straight at her. Nadia stepped back from the first blow. He leaped forward, and she stepped back again. A quick glance over her shoulder told her she was running out of room.

He came in a third time, and she ducked, reaching deep down to her toes; she brought her enhanced arm up in a light-ning-fast blow that struck under his false ribs, shattering all three of them and lifting him twenty centimeters into the air.

Pelican's mouth opened in a silent scream as his collapsed lungs refused to work. Nadia knew from experience he would recover quickly and wasted no time bringing her fist down on his face, hitting him again and again until he stopped moving.

Covered in blood and sweat, she rifled through his clothes until she found her NavPad.

"Dagher to Governor Becket. The Guild is going to sabotage Space-Traffic Control."

CHAPTER FORTY

Leopard floated in orbit above Alexandria like a predator preparing to strike.

Albatross squeezed his hands together, willing the ship's stealth systems not to fail. He glanced over at the controller manning the station and saw all the lights were green. Leopard was undetectable to all means. As long as nothing collided with the hull, or they didn't do something stupid like launch all their weapons at once, they would be undetectable.

"Orbit achieved," the Caliphate navigator said in a hushed whisper as if the enemy could hear them speak.

For the first time in the whole trip, Albatross was ready to celebrate. He had always felt optimistic toward the plan. Yes, it was a little desperate, but the Alliance had backed the Guild into a corner.

"Mr. Albatross, I have to say I had my doubts about this ship, but she is magnificent," Istam said.

Albatross smiled broadly, his pride swelling at the navy man's praise.

"Our scientists are the best in the galaxy, sir. Of course, your skilled handling of the ship was of great asset," Albatross said.

"Why thank you." He turned to the weapons console. "Weapons, designate the capitol as the target," Istam said.

Albatross frowned. "Sir, we're to pick a small target, something out of the way to prove our superiority. Once we have destroyed it, then we can move on to much larger targets—if the Alliance doesn't capitulate."

Clearly, something had gotten lost in translation.

"Yes, I have seen your plan, but I'm afraid we won't be doing that today," Istam said with a dismissive wave.

"Then what are we doing?" Alarm sounded in Albatross' voice.

He realized there were only a handful of Guild people on the ship, and these Caliphates could do whatever they wanted. Why hadn't the Guild anticipated a last-minute change?

"Our people say that once we fire, the ship will be visible, correct?" Istam asked.

Albatross stammered over his response. "Only for a moment. Unless they have a radar station pointed at us, they won't see the ship."

"Then we only get one shot."

Istam barked a few words to his men in their native tongue. Albatross felt the blood draining from his face as he caught sight of the weapons they were loading. All signs of the friendly, father-like Captain were gone, replaced by a cold, calculating killer.

"You're insane. If you fire every weapon at once, they will locate us for sure!" Albatross yelled.

"It won't matter. By then, we will have reduced their capital to a smoldering mass of radioactive waste. Allahu Akbar," he shouted, and his crew responded in kind.

Alarms screamed across the ship as the ordnance bays

opened, breaking stealth. Threat radar immediately pinged them setting off a wailing klaxon.

Albatross leaped up, rushing for the weapons console. The ship was the only one. The Guild couldn't afford to throw it away on a suicide mission. They were supposed to live. *He* was supposed to live. Istam slammed him from behind, picking him up and heaving him bodily over his shoulder to crunch against the deck. Albatross' vision swirled and faded.

Istam walked to the panel and pushed the firing button. The ship shuddered as ten space-to-surface missiles launched.

The Alliance wasn't without defenses, but they were designed to stop orbital threats they saw coming. The missile's flight time of thirty seconds left no time for the computers and personnel on the ground to respond.

Nuclear fire lit up the eastern sky, and millions of people died in their sleep. With her weapons fired, every outpost orbiting Alexandria could see her. There was no hiding. A hundred defensive coilguns fired as one. Albatross died screaming as the *Leopard* exploded.

CHAPTER FORTY-ONE
5 HOURS TO COMBAT

J osh Mendez rushed through his checklist, closing each hatch in the mess, waiting for each seal to go green before moving on to the next. Regardless of what happened next, the crew of the *Interceptor* wouldn't have another meal. He'd served the last of the food the evening before.

He ignored his own growling stomach as he made one final check, flipping all the circuits to "off," essentially shutting power down to the entire section. It wasn't like anyone would be stationed there during combat.

He dogged the hatch to the kitchen then walked through the dining room to the main hatch. With all the chairs and tables collapsed and stored, the room seemed cavernous.

Josh stopped at the passageway, turning to look one more time at the place he'd called home for the last year. Seven days a week, twelve hours a day, he'd slaved away in the kitchen preparing food for the crew.

It was grunt work. When he joined the Navy, he had wanted to do the "real work." Yet there was something noble in food prep, something he hadn't realized until the skipper had come on board. The captain had a way of making everyone feel important. Spacer First Class Josh Mendez included.

He worried he would never have the chance to work in the mess again.

4 HOURS TO COMBAT

Marines were both incredibly important aboard ship and absolutely non-essential at the same time. During space combat, they were subordinate to DCS and sickbay. They could perform basic repairs, rescue trapped crew, and deliver the wounded to sickbay.

Jennings closed the last circuit on the armory, and the Raptor suits sunk down into storage mode. Her NavPad beeped, letting her know their duties were finished and their sections powered down.

It always came down to power. Any section of the ship not immediately involved in combat had the potential to damage the ship from an errant hit. If the Raptor bay was hit when powered, a surge could happen, or even an explosion.

During combat they had time to prepare for, they drained the ship of atmo before engaging, making fire impossible. But... they couldn't always see it coming. It made sense to keep the power offline where it wasn't needed.

"Jennings, Owens. Marine country is shut down. How's the Raptor bay?" he asked.

PFC Owens served as their electronics expert. When they secured the ship for combat, he was in charge.

"Secured," she replied.

With one last look, she hit the red panel, closing the large blast doors and sealing the Raptor bay and the ship's armory. The marines all carried sidearms, and if the crew needed access to weapons to repel borders—well, they had more significant problems at that point. Even in the unlikely event of boarders, the Raptor suits would be of little use.

"Roger that, Sarge," he said, using the nickname he knew she hated. "Head for the aft mag storage and make sure the delivery mechanism checks green."

"On it." She knew he loved making her uncomfortable, not that she would ever show it. The next time they had PT together, though, she would make him sweat for it.

3 HOURS TO COMBAT

Chief Redfern scowled as the probe came back negative. He had his torso stuffed in an access hatch underneath turret number three, so he could run down an electrical anomaly. When Lieutenant Gonzales had them run their status check, turret three came back as drawing too little power. The turret hadn't magically become more efficient—one of its primary or secondary systems had malfunctioned.

He could have sent Beech or one of the other spacers, but there was plenty of grunt work to do in the remaining hours until they engaged the Guild ships. The last thing he wanted to do was hang around engineering, trying to ignore his empty stomach while watching the clock tick down. This gave him something to do, something to focus on.

"Chief, Lieutenant Gonzales. Status?" crackled over the suit comms.

Redfern pressed his lips together and reached as far into the guts of the panel as he could. There was one last optical cable to plug in and... he locked it in place.

"Good to go, sir," he replied.

The lieutenant had a rocky start. Like many officers, he had come onto the small boat with no sense of respect for the ship or the crew. The captain had set the man right.

Redfern had enough time in service that he could pull strings and serve wherever he wanted—something officers never seemed to understand. He liked *Interceptor*, sure, she was old and somewhat obsolete, but she had a sense of history about her that newer ships didn't. For forty years, members of the Alliance Navy had walked her decks, manned her guns, and slept in her racks. For a history buff like Redfern, that wasn't something a shiny new ship could match.

He was forced to crawl backward onto the deck until he could contort himself to get out of the hatch. It was a cinch to seal up the access, and he did so with a pat, holding his hand on the panel for a moment.

"Give 'em hell, girl," he said.

2 HOURS TO COMBAT

Lieutenant Max Krisper went through the motions one more time, making sure he had memorized the locations of everything he would need for surgery. The conditions aboard a small combat vessel could change rapidly: lighting, power, even gravity could fluctuate.

Sickbay's location on a ship wasn't an accident. The gravcoil provided a consistent gravity flow, as did the secondary coils. The push and pull that caused the ship to feel apparent Gs when turning were more intense in the stern than the bow, where sickbay was located.

Knowing the exact location of his supplies would allow him to navigate even in total darkness—it could be the difference between life and death.

"Excuse me, Doctor?" Mining Chief Castigate asked from the hatchway.

"Yes?" he asked distractedly. "Is everything okay?"

"Of course. I just... well... I have able-bodied adults who

want to help. I understand we can't operate the ship, but is there something we can do?"

Max Krisper wasn't old enough to remember the last war. He had the delusion of the young that made him believe warfare on the scale of nations would never come again. He only realized recently that warfare between two ships was no different from the war between nations. At least, not to the people doing the fighting.

"I understand, Mr. Castigate," Max said with a grim smile. "I really do. Tell you what, I'll contact the XO and see what we can do. I'm sure we can use your people in DCS or here. Get me a list of whom you have, and any applicable skills."

"Thank you. Really." Castigate hurried away.

Doctor Krisper admired the miner's work ethic. These were people who spent their lives on the fringes of systems, working like dogs to make a future. Even though many had lost half their family, here they were, willing to work in the most dangerous situation imaginable.

He had no way of knowing how the battle would turn out. He had never experienced one before. The other officers, the ones who had, were upbeat and optimistic, so Max was too. Who knew, maybe Chief Castigate and his miners would make the difference.

1 HOURS TO COMBAT

Kimiko Yuki pulled her ELS over her calves, careful to make sure the irksome material didn't bunch up under her knees and bottom. She could pull the suit on and be fully vacuum-ready in under a minute while holding her breath—it was part of training. However, when she had more time, she liked to make sure it was also comfortable.

Suit on, she grabbed her NavPad and attached it to her hip.

The complex electronic device detected the mating and switched to suit mode, allowing her to access the primary display through her HUD, using the controls inside the suit.

Glancing around the small cabin she shared with Sergeant Jennings, Kim ensured there wasn't anything left out. Even a tiny piece of debris could turn into a deadly projectile in the harsh environment of ship-to-ship combat.

She stopped short, realizing she had left something. Returning to the head, she spotted the silver-framed picture of her mom. She could have it electronically, but there was something about a physical image to hold that a screen couldn't duplicate.

It was an older picture from when she was a kid. Her mom holding her hand outside a Shinto temple. She picked up the picture and held it to her forehead for a moment before storing it in the small drawer that sealed shut.

"DCS," she said. "This is the XO. On my way."

———

Jacob walked the ship, starting with the sealed hatch outside what used to be torpedo rooms five and six. He stopped at them, bowing his head, praying for the men and women who had died manning their post when the gaser hit.

From there, he walked forward until he passed through Computer Node Two. The access hatch to the Long 9 was open for the moment, and he stooped so he could look into it. The compartment was built under the 29-meter-long barrel, making it a little more challenging to man. He could go down a deck and climb up through the magazine storage or lie on his back and shimmy through the hatch he stood at. Destroyers weren't known for their excess of space.

"Skipper," PO Ignatius said, bending his head down to look out the hatch. "Everything okay, sir?"

"As you were, PO. I'm walking the deck, is all."

He was about to leave when he noticed Josh Mendez in the back, prepping a nine-kilo projectile.

"Josh, good job on the stew, young man."

The spacer almost dropped the projectile as he fumbled to acknowledge his captain. "Thank you, sir!"

"Carry on," Jacob said.

From there, he slid down the ladder, checking on the top two torpedo rooms, then down the next ladder to the other two forward torpedo rooms. He loved this little ship and had walked every deck, every hatch, multiple times. He would stop and speak to the crew as they went about their duty stations, assuring them that they would be okay.

"Stick to the training and don't lose hope."

Not one of the crew complained about missed meals. They all had a determined spirit about them, a hunger not just to do their jobs but to avenge their fallen shipmates. His old ship had already taken a beating. The lower forward decks were battered, the stern top decks wrecked. The Guild had come only a few meters away from destroying the bridge. Jacob pushed that thought down deep and buried it in a box.

On autopilot, he returned to his cabin, ready to suit up. Sitting on his rack, he picked up his guitar instead of his suit. Placing the wooden instrument comfortably on his legs, he strummed a few cords while he hummed his mom's favorite song. It filled him with hope. They could do this, it wasn't impossible.

It was time to get to work.

CHAPTER FORTY-TWO

Mr. Vesper stood behind Lieutenant Fawkes, looking on as the emergency beacon torpedo was about to launch. Jacob felt it fitting that the man who gave them the idea should see it executed.

"Time to firing position?" Jacob asked.

Fawkes didn't take his eyes off his panel. "T-minus two-zero seconds... mark."

"Mr. West, have the crew put on their helmets and drain the can."

"Aye, aye, sir, helmets on, air out."

A moment later, Mark West's voice echoed throughout the ship. *"All hands, now hear this. Helmets on. Helmets on. Helmets on. Section leaders report ready to DCS."*

Fawkes flipped up the firing shield on his control panel and held his finger over the button. There were several ways to fire every weapon on board, from computer-controlled to manual bridge control to local control. As the tactical officer, Fawkes decided how each weapon was launched.

A countdown appeared on the main screen, starting from

five. When it hit zero, Lieutenant (JG) Carter Fawkes depressed the button. The ship shook as the four-meter-long modified Mark-XII Torpedo shot out of its tube under the Long 9. Jacob smiled, resisting the urge to laugh at what it would look like from the outside since the tubes were about where the painted shark's nose would be.

At 500 meters, the torpedo's gravcoil kicked in, blasting forward at 700 Gs of acceleration on top of the *Interceptor*'s velocity.

"Torpedo away!" Fawkes said.

A blip of blue light from the torpedo's drive appeared on the main viewer for an instant before vanishing a moment later. Once it was well past the enemy, the modified emergency beacon would broadcast the warning in a relatively narrow cone toward Kremlin Station.

Even if *Interceptor* were destroyed, the Guild wouldn't have total success as long as the torpedo made it.

———

"That's odd," Outrider Command's astrogator said.

"What?" Director Fargo demanded.

"Well, sir, we're still well outside the engagement range of the destroyer, and she fired a torpedo."

Fargo was no naval tactician, but even he knew the maximum range of a torpedo and how to use it effectively. The Guild had provided all ships directors with the necessary training.

"Any chance it will hit us?" Fargo asked.

"That's the thing, sir. It isn't even heading in our direction.

It will blow by us with no chance of acquiring a lock on our gravcoils."

Fargo wondered what his opponent was up to.

"Helm, alter course five degrees starboard. No need to take any chances."

———

"I think they bought it, Skipper," Kim said.

The entire crew had their helmets on, and the atmosphere was drained. Even the miners wore ELS suits fabricated for them. No one on board was without protection.

"Fawkes, Owusu, what do you think?" he asked.

Fawkes pulled up his tactical screen and projected it to Jacob's MFD. It showed the dot of the torpedo speeding away from them and the angle of the approaching ships. They were still eighteen minutes from maximum engagement range.

Fawkes mulled it over for a moment. "I concur, sir. There's no way to hide the torpedo's signature. We expected them to alter course when we fired. They did, then changed back shortly after. Other than that, I see no sign they're going to do any evasive maneuvers until they *think* they're in range of our weapons."

"Owusu?" Jacob asked.

"I agree, sir."

"West?"

"Aye, Skipper," he said.

"Okay then. Tactical, commence firing plan Alpha-One. Comms, ship-wide," Jacob said.

"Aye, sir, Alpha-One," Fawkes acknowledged.

That particular firing pattern was their primary plan. It called for *Interceptor*'s two forward turrets to fire one round at each ship. He would have liked to go rapid-fire on all the turrets, but the risk of the enemy seeing the electromagnetic discharge on passive EM was too high.

"You're on sir," Ensign Hössbacher said.

"All hands, this is the captain speaking. I know the last few weeks have strained our patience, energy, and fortitude. I know you have given me your best. Now I'm asking you to dig deep and give a little more. The Guild thinks we're weak. That we'll roll over and give up at the first sign of conflict. We, more than anyone, have paid for this system with the blood of our brothers and sisters. If the Guild thinks we're an easy target—they think wrong.

"Hellcats are the strongest, toughest, swiftest destroyers of their time. *Interceptor* is the strongest, toughest, swiftest of them all. We will prevail. When this is all over, and we're toasting to our victory on Kremlin Station, the first round's on me. Good luck and Godspeed. Captain out."

With their helmets on and the atmosphere drained, he didn't hear the cheer of the crew, but he imagined it.

"Captain, XO. You're going to go broke buying a hundred drinks," Kim said.

"I'd buy two hundred if it meant we brought everyone back home with us," he said.

"I'll buy the second round. We're with you, Skipper," Kim said.

Jacob smiled, thinking of how far they had come since he first arrived aboard.

"I couldn't ask for a better crew," he said. "Good luck."

"You too, Skipper."

The line clicked dead. DCS had a significant role to play in any battle, and there was a lot of work to do before the fight started.

On the other hand, Jacob could only check and re-check his plan. He activated the MFD and cloned astrogation's station.

Gravwakes spread out from the enemy ships in two cones, forward and aft. This allowed them to "hear" the enemy ships assuming they were in range—which varied depending on the power output of the gravcoil.

Tactical tagged each enemy ship with a name on the screen: Golf-One through to Golf-Four. On his screen, they were simply blinking dots. Tiny, coded notations next to them showed direction, acceleration, and observed velocity.

In reality, the combined velocity of *Interceptor* and the Golfs would give them an engagement window of eight minutes. For the first three minutes and change, *Interceptor* could fire unanswered. After that, the Guild could respond for three minutes. Then, if *Interceptor* were still alive, they could shoot for two more minutes. Assuming—and it was a big assumption—acceleration stayed constant.

Did they think their superior weapons technology gave them that much of an edge? Jacob didn't know, but he did know they were flying right into *Interceptor's* trap.

"Firing in five—" Fawkes announced on the bridge-wide comms.

Four seconds later, turrets one and two fired, sending two rounds at Golf-Four before changing targets and repeating three more times.

———

"Ten minutes until they can start shooting at us, Director."

Fargo nodded, dismissing his executive officer. Something about the situation seemed off to him. Yes, the destroyer had superior range, but that was all. His ships were too small to be optimal torpedo targets, not to mention their counter-fire would be far better than anything the Alliance was prepared for. His ships had directed energy defense capable of shredding incoming torpedoes—another advance they had kept secret from the galaxy at large.

While the barbarians fired projectile weapons at each other, the Guild experimented with energy weapons, perfecting them to the point of absolute beauty. The gaser was their most advanced weapon, and it would soon render the destroyer into a hunk of obliterated metal, especially since *Interceptor* was coming right at them.

"Helm, when we're at maximum engagement range, begin evasive maneuvers," Fargo ordered.

"Yes, Director," he replied.

All the major governments relied entirely too much on their torpedo tech. The Guild had eschewed stand-off weapons for the smaller, more nimble craft like the Outriders armed with one-shot-one-kill weapons.

"Activate all point-defense batteries. They're going to be in for a surprise if they try to use torpedoes," Fargo said with a smirk.

Someone on the bridge chuckled. He decided to let it go and not discipline them—whomever it was.

"Sir?" his executive officer asked.

"Yes?"

"I know it's not my place, but... I feel like something is wrong here. Why come right at us? They have to know they can't survive once we are in range."

Fargo agreed. It did seem odd for them to play chicken with one ship against four. What was their captain hoping to gain?

———

Jacob deliberately let out the breath he held. It would do him no good to pass out from lack of air.

"Bridge, Dr. Krisper," crackled over the comm.

Jacob glanced in surprise at the sudden call. "Go ahead," he replied.

"Skipper, I just thought you would like to know, Chief Boudreaux is going to pull through. I put her in a nanite-induced coma. She, along with the rest of the wounded who couldn't man their posts, are in cold hibernation and loaded into the medical escape pods."

"That's a relief. I appreciate your letting me know, Doctor." It did take some stress off of him.

"Aye, Skipper," the doctor said earnestly.

Jacob looked down at the screen in surprise at the sudden shift in tone. "Thank you, Max. Well done."

"Of course. I mean, yes, sir."

Jacob sat up taller and pushed his shoulders back. He felt that *something* a crew had when they were more than just shipmates—when they were a team.

This time the doctor didn't protest the use of his first name.

"Ten seconds to weapons impact, sir. Still no course change," Fawkes said.

Jacob clenched his fist. Praying this would work.

"Five... four... three... two...."

———

Perhaps his exec's warning amplified his own feeling of unease. Fargo had graduated with honors from his corporate class—he wasn't an idiot. However, he was handicapped by the corporate environment that raised him.

"Communications, send a message, alter course by ten degrees," he said.

He tried to sound decisive as if he were making some grandiose tactical decision. In truth, he was afraid. As the range fell, his lack of experience showed, and fear ran through him like a wildfire.

Unfortunately, his decision came too late.

————

Far ahead of *Interceptor*, traveling through space like a swarm of angry bees, were eight 20mm tungsten penetrators fired from her forward turrets. Each was powerful enough to break through five centimeters of nano-reinforced steel armor.

Armor, the merchant ships known as Outriders didn't have.

The first round hit Outrider Four just as the order to change course went out over the comms. Kinetic energy ripped a trench through the starboard side, gouging a line sixty millimeters wide the length of the ship, exposing every deck in its path to cold hard vacuum. While still reeling from the first hit, the second round struck, drilling a hole right through the central plane. Every compartment penetrated turned into an inferno equal to the depths of hell. Flesh boiled and the ship exploded less than two seconds after the initial impact.

Outrider Three barely had time to comprehend what had happened to her sister ship when *Interceptor*'s second volley hit. The first round struck the bridge, obliterating the compartment and its crew and ripping a hole in the ship. The second shattered the gravcoil, sending them veering wildly off course. With no command crew to correct the variation, the gravcoil went into overload and ripped the ship apart as it surged in two different directions.

By the time the first ship was a cloud of expanding gas, Outrider Two had four whole seconds to react. Had any of the ships altered course even a split second after *Interceptor* fired, they would have escaped annihilation. As it was, Director Fargo lost half of his command.

"Turn," he yelled franticly. "Turn!"

———

"Golf-Three and Four, confirmed hits," PO Tefiti announced.

Jacob wanted to ask if they were disabled or destroyed, but he suppressed the instinct. It wasn't like the PO would withhold the information. Then the screen updated, and two light codes were gone.

"Good hits," Fawkes said. "Radar confirms two Tangos destroyed."

"Well done," Jacob said.

The same trick wouldn't work twice; they would have to wait until the ships were closer to engage normally. He'd like to use the torpedoes, but head-on engagements against small targets weren't ideal. Maybe if they turned to run—his screen plot updated.

"Are they... turning at a right angle?" Fawkes asked.

Jacob couldn't believe it. They had given him the ideal shot —plus extending the contact time, which favored *Interceptor*.

"Carter, concentrate fire on Golf-Two," Jacob ordered.

"Aye, sir. Helm, come one-eight degrees port, up bubble zero-three-zero," Carter ordered.

Chief Suresh immediately adjusted their course, even as she repeated the orders.

"Tubes loaded," Carter said.

"Open the outer doors," Jacob ordered.

"Doors open."

Jacob watched as the range counted down. They wanted to fire when the torpedoes had at least ten seconds of maneuvering time left on their gravcoils before impact. When the range pinged correct, Fawkes gave the order.

"Fire!"

Interceptor shuddered as all four torpedoes launched, one after another, only half a second in between.

———

Fargo gripped the arm of his command chair with white-knuckled ferocity. This was no simulation, this was real. Ships were exploding around him. Hundreds of millions in materials and lives gone—and he was responsible.

"They launched torpedoes," someone said.

Fargo didn't know who, he couldn't see past his own tunnel vision.

"Time to impact, sixty-five seconds!"

It wasn't supposed to go this way. They were going to wipe out *Interceptor* then take the system. How had his plan gone so horribly wrong?

"Director, torpedoes incoming. What do we do?" asked his exec.

Fargo shook his head. All hope wasn't lost. If they destroyed *Interceptor*, he could argue that losing two Outriders was a reasonable price to pay.

"Our point-defense will take them out," he said with every ounce of courage he could muster.

———

"I think they got their head out of their aft section, Skipper," Fawkes said.

"Lay it on me?" Jacob asked.

Fawkes slaved his console to the MFD on Jacob's chair. Passive sensors picked up sporadic energy bursts for a few seconds. One-by-one the torpedoes vanished from the plot.

"Damn," Jacob muttered. Their PDW took out every torpedo he'd fired.

"Second volley?" Fawkes asked.

Jacob shook his head. "No need to send good weapons after bad. Let's wait until—" he checked the plot. "Let them close another six-five thousand klicks and fire four more."

"Aye, aye, sir.

Jacob pulled the screen closer, examining the new trajectory of both the Tangos. They had split, heading in opposite directions. Interceptor was slightly closer to Golf-Two than One by virtue of its direct course. However, looking at the replay of the last few minutes, he noticed that Golf-One had changed course first. He couldn't be sure, but that suggested One was in charge.

"Helm, come starboard zero-two-five, mark zero," he ordered.

"Aye, starboard zero-two-five, mark zero," Suresh repeated as she made the change.

Fawkes glanced over at him. The tactical officer's voice sounded in his ear on the private channel a moment later.

"Sir?"

Fawkes wasn't just the ship's tactical officer. His position made him third in line for command if anything happened. He had a duty to know what was going on, as did Lieutenants Yuki and West. Jacob hit the button on his seat, keying in the command crew.

"I think Golf-One is their commanding officer—his ship turned first. The way they split indicates they're running, not thinking," he said. "In a minute, they'll come to their senses and turn back at us. They may even increase speed if they can."

It made sense to him, and his command crew agreed. He cut the line, focusing on the plot and the situation. Every move gave him insight into his opponent, and those who knew themselves and their enemies could never be defeated.

———

Fargo wondered why they only fired one wave of torpedoes. Outrider's PDWs were terrifying in their efficiency. Seeing the torpedoes destroyed long before they were a danger bolstered his confidence.

He pushed his shoulders back as if the shadow of the man he'd been a moment before was gone. Yes, they could do this. What was he thinking? Running. He panicked, that was all. Panicked and made a bad choice. He needed to make the best of the situation and not compound one bad decision with another.

"Change our course back to the original heading and contact Outrider Two. Tell them to alter course parallel to ours."

———

As he expected, Jacob watched the screen refresh and the directional arrow indicating course change.

"Looks like you were right, COB," Jacob said over the bridge channel. "It's amateur hour over there."

Suresh chuckled in response. "To an outsider, the way the Navy does things might seem backward, but we do have our traditions that work. Passing on knowledge is one of them. I don't think the Guild has a single person who's ever seen actual space or ground combat. They've kept their existence secret, and that secrecy is coming back to bite them in the behind."

"So it would seem," he said. "Time to action?"

Lieutenant Fawkes ran several calculations, considering the enemy ships' erratic maneuvering.

"We're looking at optimal range for all batteries in one-five minutes and a combat window of..." he hit a few more buttons. "Four minutes three-seven seconds on either side."

"Thank you," Jacob said.

He looked back at the screen, thinking of how his opponent had already behaved. Like an ensign on his first tour, afraid of everything, they had gone from holding the cards to reacting and giving up the initiative. *Interceptor* was now setting the terms of the engagement.

Jacob activated the line to the XO.

"Kim, are you seeing this?" he asked.

It was somewhat rhetorical. Of course, she was watching. She appeared on the screen in the bottom right corner.

"Aye, sir."

"What do you make of it?" he asked.

She thought for a moment, scrunching her brows. "I feel like we're either fighting a computer or a first-year cadet. We can take advantage of it, sir."

"What did you have in mind?" he asked.

"Full reverse. It will increase our combat window, which favors us, but it will also make them think we have something up our sleeve."

Jacob glanced at the plot. It could work. The enemy had only reacted up to this point. If he threw *Interceptor* into full reverse, and they followed suit, it would buy them more time. Especially since they had already hit them with one trick.

"Good call, Kim," he said before closing the line. "COB, full reverse three-zero seconds after my mark."

Jacob mashed the emergency button on his chair. "All hands, now hear this: we're going full reverse. Make sure you are locked into your harness in ten seconds. Notify your department head if you can't."

He counted down from ten, then said to the COB, "Devi, mark!"

"Aye, sir. Full reverse in thirty... twenty... fifteen...five... zero."

Holding the stick steady, she pulled the throttle back to neutral and continued past into reverse. The ship instantly shook as its gravwake crashed into it from behind. There was no sound accompanying the low-level vibration running through the ship's keel, just a feeling like sitting on a buzzer. The crew's skin tingled as the ship strained to slow down.

"Director," the astrogator yelled, "They just went full reverse."

Director Fargo swallowed hard at the alarm in the man's voice. The captain of that ship was devious. Did he have another trick up his sleeve? Fargo couldn't have imagined the destruction they had already wrought. How had one destroyer wrecked billions in shipping, let alone their base? Either the Guild's intelligence was woefully inadequate regarding Alliance technology or something else was at play.

"Helm, full reverse. Let's not run blind into another trap. Continue evasive maneuvers," Fargo ordered.

"I don't get it," Fawkes said.

He glanced over at the captain to see if he had any answers. "They're making the worst possible decisions over there."

Commander Grimm pointed at the screen. "The Guild is a for-profit company. Now, I've never worked *for* a civilian organization, but I've worked *with* plenty of Navy contractors. It's all about doing the least amount of work for the most amount of money. Not wholly unlike a lazy spacer," Grimm said with a chuckle.

"So what—they don't send their ship commanders to combat school?" Fawkes asked.

"Why would they? That costs money, and they aren't an institution that, up until this point, engaged in space combat. These ships move through our systems with impunity, hidden like spit-snakes on New Austin. Why spend the money training them how to fight when they never intended to use them that way?"

Fawkes shook his head, finding it hard to wrap his head around sending people into battle with inadequate training.

"Recalculate time to engagement?" Grimm asked.

Fawkes checked his numbers then sent them to Ensign Owusu's station for verification. The astrogator signed off.

"Two-three minutes to maximum range," Fawkes replied.

He watched his commander lean back, looking far more relaxed than Carter felt. How did he do it? The Guild ships only needed to hit *Interceptor* once, and they were done for. Yet the Skipper not only looked calm and ready to go, but he also made the rest of the crew feel confident.

Fawkes knew the man was mortal—he wasn't a god, or omniscient—yet somehow, right then, it sure seemed like he was.

————

Director Fargo frowned. He had been sure he'd made the right decision to slow down and evaluate the situation. Now, having considered it, he felt like he'd been suckered again. The *Interceptor* might not equal his command for raw firepower, but the ship did have a range advantage.

"Dammit," he muttered.

Clenching his fist, he brought it down on the command chair in an uncharacteristic outburst. Unnoticed by him, his bridge crew shifted nervously as they watched their commander lose his cool.

"Helm, full speed ahead. Weapons, the moment we're in range, I want that annoying ship obliterated."

———

Jacob noticed the blips changing velocity just as Ensign Owusu announced it.

"Golf-One and Two are back to their maximum acceleration," Owusu said.

The numbers on Jacob's MFD scrambled for a moment, waiting for the ships to normalize. Once they had, the time to maximum range was clarified. Eight minutes to combat.

"It was good while it lasted," he said to the bridge. "I'd be worried if they never figured it out." His smile and friendly tone eased the tension that had resurfaced on the bridge. "Helm, prepare lateral evasive maneuvers. They have to turn their ship, and as you pointed out, Devi, they aren't exactly the most skilled handlers."

"Aye, sir. Hold on to your lunch—it's going to get fun," she replied.

On acceleration and deceleration maneuvers, the primary and secondary gravcoils warred with each other. However, when the ship piled on the lateral Gs, the coils had a more difficult time compensating for those forces.

"Tactical," he said to Fawkes. "Prepare the turret crews for rapid-fire. We're not going to have long to shoot, and I want to get the most bang for our buck."

"Aye, sir. Rapid-fire on all turrets. Are we going to engage with the Long 9 or the torps?" Fawkes asked.

As close as they were going to be, torpedoes wouldn't work as well as he would like at their angle of attack. Plus, there was always the danger of proximity hits as they exited the tubes.

"Negative on the torpedoes. Have the crews stand down and assume DCS. Keep the Long 9 ready."

"Torpedo rooms, secure weapons, and assume damage control stations," Fawkes said into his comms.

Jacob cracked his knuckles. No matter what, it would all be over soon. He would very much like it to go in their favor.

"Shooting range in five—" Fawkes started the countdown.

When he got to zero, Jacob said, "Rapid-fire, all batteries."

"Aye, aye, sir. Rapid-fire on all batteries."

CHAPTER FORTY-THREE

Each turret had a PO and four ratings for a total of five crew members. The PO fired the guns, two spacers loaded the weapon, and two retrieved the thirty-round boxes from storage and lifted them to the loaders. The system worked well enough to keep the turrets firing steadily until their local magazine storage ran dry, at which point the loader would run to the closest magazine storage and bring back a new pallet of ammo on a grav-sled

Turret number one's Petty Officer was the backup coxswain, PO Collins. Her chair cocked at an angle, allowing her to look into the targeting computer while holding the firing stud. She could see the rest of her turret with a glance, including three of the four spacers under her command.

"Prepare for rapid-fire," she barked. Their suits were all tied together on a local channel. In combat, everything she said, was transmitted.

Collins' job was to take over if the bridge took a hit or the computer malfunctioned. However, for now, all she did was pull the trigger when the light turned crimson.

Then the order came. The ship vibrated as all four turrets

fired at once. The barrel assembly above her jerked back, partially absorbing the recoil from the firing mechanism while jamming another round into place. A second later, she fired again. The turret changed position slightly with each shot, but since they were inside it, the only thing they noticed was how the room rotated around the unmoving hatch on the deck.

———

"They're firing," the weapons officer said.

Fargo winced as the computer showed the volume of fire coming from the destroyer. He knew that they were taking potshots and that his computer could calculate the trajectory of each shot and plot an evasive course to deal with it. Despite that, seeing the rounds stream through space at high velocity, he couldn't help but be afraid.

"Evasive," he said.

His helmsman nodded, not speaking as he pushed the ship through the computer-suggested maneuvers.

"One minute to range," Fargo's gunner said.

Fargo doubted they could hit the ship at max range, but dread built up in him at the thought of closing.

———

"Range?" Jacob asked for confirmation.

"Seven-zero-zero thousand klicks," Owusu said.

On Jacob's MFD, it looked like a video game. Tiny dots streamed out of *Interceptor* at the rate of four every two seconds, each turret shooting where the enemy ships *might* be when they intersected. In another minute, the Guild would be in firing range. He'd hoped for a few lucky hits, but so far, nothing.

"Carter," he said to LT. Fawkes, "If you feel you can hit with the Long 9, fire at will."

"Aye, sir. Fire at will on the Long 9."

With the projectile's velocity of ninety thousand klicks per second, it was the highest velocity weapon they had. One hit could devastate even a large ship. However, it could only fire once every sixty seconds.

———

"Sir, we're in range," weapons told Fargo.

A deadly gleam formed in his eye. Finally.

"Order Golf-Two to fire. We'll hold back and see what happens," Fargo ordered.

———

"Range six-five-zero, sir," Ensign Owusu said.

Jacob nodded. If the Guild's range were six-fifty, they would fire at any moment.

"Chief Suresh, don't stay on any one heading for long," he said.

In a way, the Guild weapon had the same deficiency *Interceptor*'s Long 9 had, though to a lesser degree. A light-speed weapon could hit a target as far away as they were, but it would take two seconds. That would give them a narrow window to maneuver.

"Tefiti, ear to the ground. If they so much as hiccup, call for a course change," Jacob said.

"Aye, aye, sir," Tefiti said.

"Main gun, ready firing," Fawkes said. "Sir, I'm going to try and box in the second ship."

"Do it," Jacob said.

So far, they had concentrated their fire on the ship they believed was the command vessel. Rapidly changing targets could confuse them and allow for a hit. Boxing called for forcing the target on a heading then using the Long 9 to end it.

"Gravity anomaly!" Tefiti shouted.

Chief Suresh didn't hesitate. She jerked the stick over, rolling the ship and pulling "up" as she turned. *Interceptor*'s gravcoil vibrated madly from the maneuver.

Power from the lights went to the coil, dimming the entire ship for a moment while the crew fought to stay upright as the two coils' conflicting gravity affected them.

"They missed, sir," Tefiti said. "I got a solid listen as it went by—it's like a high-pitched whistle."

Chief Suresh rolled the ship back over, and Jacob sighed in relief.

———

"How?" Fargo asked.

He thought *maybe* it would take two shots, but they missed utterly—like the damn ship knew they were going to fire right before they did.

"Okay, close in. We'll fire at three hundred thousand. They won't be able to dodge, no matter what deals they've made with demons," Fargo said.

———

"Carter, commence your firing pattern," Jacob ordered.

"Turrets, firing plan Bravo, execute. Helm, two-five degrees port," Fawkes said.

"Aye, aye, two-five degrees port," Chief Suresh replied.

———

Interceptor's sudden course change caught Golf-One by surprise. Her crew had never actually trained outside of combat simulations—sims programmed by the same people who built the ships and had no more experience in actual naval combat than the crews.

When the coilguns shifted targets, Golf-One's helm sighed in relief he didn't have to sweat the evasive maneuvers anymore and could line up on *Interceptor* for a kill shot with the gaser.

Golf-Two was also caught by surprise. The command crew watched their computer screens dutifully, waiting for instructions on what to do next. When the computer detected the first round heading their direction, it ordered a course change.

The helmsman responded rapidly adjusting course as the computer directed, however, Fawkes had cleverly programmed the fire pattern. The first round sent the ship in one direction. The second round sent the ship "down" relative to the ecliptic. The third shot sent her back in her original direction, and the fourth shot required an even more drastic course change.

By the third course change, Fawkes knew precisely where the ship would be for the fourth course change. He sent those coordinates to Chief Suresh, who made sure the ship pointed in the right direction at the right moment, a solid seven seconds before the Tango would hit the spot he aimed for. As Golf-Two changed course the fourth time, she hung in space relative to *Interceptor* for three seconds.

The complex math couldn't be done by hand—they had to use a computer. It took light just over a second to reach them, so they couldn't wait for the ship to "be" there, then fire, because by the time the round arrived six seconds later, the ship would be gone.

Lights on Carter's console blinked green. "Long 9, fire!"

PO Ignatius pulled the trigger instantly, and nine kilograms of nano-reinforced tungsten blasted out the front of the ship at 90,000 KPS. *Interceptor* shuddered from the recoil.

Golf-Two's computer registered the shot and immediately informed the helm of an emergency course change. Already in the middle of one maneuver, the Guild pilot wasn't watching his screen. When it flashed red, he looked down and gasped in horror.

The Long-9 impacted the side of Golf-Two. The ship killer ripped the freighter in half, the forward portion shooting off like a cork from a champagne bottle, while the stern half detonated in a ball of expanding plasma.

Director Fargo swore as his sister ship disintegrated with all hands.

"Fire the weapon!" he yelled.

The gun crew lined up the shot, charging the gaser to green before smashing the firing stud down. The lights on the ship dimmed as ninety-five percent of all available power transferred to the gravity laser.

Shooting out at the speed of light, the gaser crossed the distance between the ships in one-point-five seconds.

As soon as the Long 9 fired, Suresh pushed her right foot down, swiveling the ship three degrees on her axis.

The gaser had a focal width of six meters. The central point of the gaser missed, but not entirely. One meter of the gaser clipped the port bow, and torpedo room two exploded inward, shards of hull spraying into the central corridor and ricocheting around with deadly force.

As he reached for the next box in the forward ammo locker, Spacer first-class Alvarez lost an arm. He stumbled back, a silent scream on his lips as his ELS suit pumped him full of medical nanites and pain killers. He slumped to the deck, his blood blackening the side of his suit.

A shard of the hull hit frame fifteen, deflecting off the reinforced plating and shot up through deck one and then out through the open hatch in turret one. Spacer second-class Teller died instantly as it passed through his chest and helmet, nearly bisecting his body. The shard continued its journey, shredding PO Collins' right leg before blasting through the turret mechanism and out into space.

Collins screamed until blood and bile filled her throat. Her ears rang from the sound. Her body shook, and she felt herself shutting down. Scrambling, she found the override on her medical suite and held the button down, staving off painkillers.

"DCS, Turret one," she said through gritted teeth.

"Go ahead, Collins," the XO said in her ear.

"Two casualties need medics. Turret offline," she said.

Tears leaked down her face as she managed to give her report before letting go of the override. Painkillers flooded her system, and she let out a relieved sigh before passing out.

———

"Turret one, offline," Mark West said in a perfectly calm voice from ops. "All other turrets are green."

"Keep firing," Jacob said.

The ship had lurched badly, straining the harness of everyone aboard.

"Engines?" he asked.

Lieutenant Gonzales appeared on the screen. "We lost some rigidity, Skipper, but she'll hold."

"Devi, flank speed," Jacob ordered.

"Aye, sir, flank speed."

She jammed the throttle forward.

———

"Fire again," Fargo screamed.

"We need twenty more secon—"

Outrider Command shuddered, alarms screamed, and the bridge hatch slammed shut.

"Multiple impacts—"

Fargo tuned them out, fear rampaging through him. What were they going to do? In twenty seconds, they would all be dead. The Guild had made a massive strategic mistake. Fargo could see it now. A single weapon, no matter how powerful, was no match for a warship with a trained crew.

John Fargo looked in horror at the view screen. *Interceptor's* shark's nose was just visible in their long-range optics, bearing down on them like the predator it represented.

In a moment of lucidity, he realized that he, in fact, did not want to die. Certainly not to protect the idiotic Guild VP who had planned this disaster.

"Comms, signal surrender!" he yelled.

"What?" his XO said. "No. We can't—"

"Surrender," Fargo shouted, standing up and charging over to the comms station.

He hit the open frequency button. "*Interceptor*, this is Director Fargo. We surrender. Please respond, don't shoot. We surrender!"

———

Jacob let out his breath, heaving a huge sigh. Golf-One had thrown her engine into reverse after signaling their surrender. As he had instructed, they didn't alter course one iota. If they did, he wouldn't hesitate to blow them out of space.

It would take a few hours, but once their courses matched, Ensign Hössbacher could use the laser to seize control of their computers. If they failed to comply, they would be destroyed.

After that, it would take a while longer to maneuver close enough to dock, and he would send over the marines to make sure they were surrendering. An engineering team would go with them, securing the ship and slaving her to *Interceptor*'s helm.

"Total damage assessment," he asked Kim as she stared back at him from his MFD.

"It could've been a lot worse, Skipper," she said.

He nodded, preparing for what she was about to say. "How many?"

"Six dead, fifteen wounded," she told him.

Jacob closed his eyes, saying a silent prayer to the Almighty for those they had lost and those they still might lose.

"Kim, go with Jennings. Take no chances. Anyone even looks like they're going to resist— shoot them."

"Aye, aye, sir," she said with a savage grin.

CHAPTER FORTY-FOUR

Interceptor came to a stop next to Kremlin Station. Mooring cables reached out like snakes to connect the ship to the external power plant. Once power was provided by one of the station's many fusion reactors, Lieutenant Gonzales began the official shutdown procedure for *Interceptor*'s outdated MKIII reactor.

After the power cables were attached, hoses were guided out, three in total: one to link *Interceptor*'s atmosphere for replenishment, another to fill her water reserves, and a third to evacuate excess wastewater for recycling.

All of that took less than five minutes. The gangplank extended last, stretching the five meters across the vacuum of space to seal against the emergency airlock. Corpsmen ran across, flooding into *Interceptor* through the mess, gathering the wounded and rushing them back to the station's hospital.

Slowly, over several hours, the remaining crew shut the ship down, converting her to maintenance mode to allow the yard dogs to come aboard and start repairs. One by one, everyone left until only Jacob and Sergeant Jennings remained. It amazed him that she stood by him when no regulation called for it. If he had earned the loyalty of such an outstanding Marine, then he had to be doing something right.

Cold air breezed through the bridge as he circled, touching each station in turn. It didn't take long in the small, cramped compartment. As he exited, he ran his hand along the hull before stepping out of the hatch. When he was out, Jennings keyed the secure hatch button. The blast doors slid shut with a clang.

"Ready to go, sir?"

All his worldly belongings were on the deck next to the lift. A single bag with three uniforms and a few mementos sat next to the reinforced case holding his guitar.

"Yes, I think I am."

"Sir, may I ask the captain a question?" Jennings dutifully marched behind him.

"Of course, Allison, anything," he replied.

"Do you think we're coming back? Or are they going to decommission her?" she asked.

He smiled as he heaved up his bag and shouldered it. Jennings didn't know. None on the crew knew. According to Admiral Villanueva, *Interceptor* was his as long as he was in the Navy. Staying with the ship was the only thing keeping him from a forced separation. He wasn't sure if he was allowed to share that information with anyone.

"It's above my pay grade, Allison. I guess we'll see," he told her. "In the meantime, the first round is on me."

He held his NavPad out to her, and she reciprocated with hers. The two machines beeped as he transferred the necessary funds to pay for the crew's drinks.

"Aye, sir. I'll let the crew know."

He bid her goodbye a few minutes later as she headed for the marine billet. Jacob stood at the aircar pickup, figuring out where to go. Kremlin literally had a hundred different hotels, and he had plenty of money. He wasn't rich, but it was easy to accumulate funds if one spent most of one's time under self-sequester.

He let his mind wander as he relished the ability to take his time. For the last few weeks, he'd felt the need to rush every decision, and every single one was life or death.

"Heya, Spacer, you in town long?" a familiar alto said from behind.

Jacob dropped his bags, turned, and came face to face with Nadia Dagher. Her hair wasn't as long as the last time they were together, and there was a hint of sadness in her soft brown eyes, but her beauty was undeniably breathtaking.

"Nadia, what are you doing here?" he asked, stunned.

"I'm here to see you. I thought that was obvious?"

Jacob came out of his brief daze and moved toward her, taking her offered hands in his.

Standing next to her, he whispered, "I sent you letters."

She licked her lips nervously. "I got them. I'm sorry I didn't respond. I needed time."

He smiled, letting her know it was okay.

"I get it. Really. But why are you here?"

She pulled him even closer. "I'm here to see you... honest."

He didn't say no when she stretched up to kiss him.

———

Station Governor Captain Rod Beckett (ret.) whistled at the hunk of circuitry in front of him. How the Guild had done it, he didn't know, but they had.

"Gravity lasers... with a range of six-hundred-thousand klicks?" he asked to make sure.

"Six hundred and fifty thousand," the station's chief engineer, Tara Keys, corrected him.

"That's not even the best part. Look at these PDW weapons. I went over *Interceptor*'s logs; these things had one hundred percent accuracy at a distance that directed energy weapons this small shouldn't have."

Rod shook his head. Unfortunately, the Guild commander had thoroughly wiped their computer, and their engineer had trashed the gaser subsystems. Knowing it was possible was a step in the right direction, but they wouldn't be recreating their incredible feat of technology any time soon.

However... the PDW system existed externally to the ship. They hadn't had the time to go outside and wreck them. From Commander Grimm's report, it seemed the Guild had standing orders to self-destruct rather than be taken alive—something he was sure Director Fargo had ignored to save his own life.

Not that Rod was complaining. NavCom was sure to send a tug to drag this back to Blackrock for analysis. In the meantime, he would go over her with a fine-tooth comb. If he could learn how they could focus the PDWs, he could work up a design and pitch the yard for upgrades. He stood to make a tidy sum if he could patent the design in time. It wasn't like the Guild had any legal standing to defend the tech they kept hidden from the rest of the galaxy.

Not to mention the lives he could save if the Navy adopted it. Navy coilgun tech worked well, but it had a low hit-rate at long range. This tech would push the initial defensive grid engagement out to three light-seconds. He shook his head in wonder.

Then a cold dose of reality hit him. What else did they have?

EPILOGUE
SEVEN DAYS LATER

The door chirped, announcing a visitor. Jacob raised his head from the pillow, looking around the room. Sleep fogged his vision, along with euphoria. As miserable as he had been after the incident at Pascal, he couldn't be happier now.

Nadia sang to herself while she showered, her alto reverberating through the room they shared—the room they had hardly left in the days since she'd surprised him at the aircar station.

All the attraction they shared when they met was still there, and more. When the inevitable happened, they decided room service was good enough.

The chime interrupted his thoughts, sounding somehow insistent.

"Can you get that handsome? I'm not presentable," Nadia called from the shower.

"Yes, ma'am," he said.

Her rank had surprised him almost as much as her showing up. She'd acted cagey about her assignment on Kremlin, but he'd pieced some of it together. Jacob and the *Interceptor* had prevented the Guild from following through on their attack, but the bombardment happened regardless. Stopping the Guild from disabling the space defense grid had saved lives—maybe the station.

He threw on a robe and opened the door.

"Kim?" he asked, stunned to see his first officer.

"Commander," she said, her voice wavering.

Her eyes were lined with red, and tears streaked her face.

"Jacob. We're off duty... What's wrong?" he asked.

"You don't know?" she asked in a hushed whisper.

"Know what?"

Nadia came out of the bathroom in a matching robe that looked much better on her than it did on him.

"Can I come in?" Kim asked, not surprised to see the two of them together.

"Of course," he said, stepping back and letting her through.

She marched past him to the holographic display, waving it to life.

"News," she said. "Any channel."

A sinking feeling hit his stomach; there were very few instances when the same news was on every channel. He felt Nadia's fingers wrap around his as the image resolved itself.

"Good Lord," Nadia muttered.

She picked up on what they were looking at faster than he did. Then he saw the text scrolling under the image of what he finally realized was a series of massive craters.

Alexandria attacked in a surprise orbital bombardment by unknown forces.

The image changed with the words, showing unimaginable destruction, burning buildings, and dead and dying.

. . .

Targets included Anchorage Bay, the Palisade, and Capitol City.

They were all gone. The station didn't say, but if he had to guess, it looked like nuclear blasts. The casualty numbers showed, and Kim let out a soft sob. Fourteen million and counting, with another two million expected to die within the week.

"Oh God," he muttered. "The people..." Then another thought hit him, a more military-minded thought. "Your admiral?" he asked, looking at Nadia.

"You don't know? How do you not know?" she asked.

"Know what?" he pulled his eyes from the display.

"The president, Fleet Admiral Villanueva, and some members of the Senate are here in-system for the opening of the wormhole," Nadia said. "But Congress, Naval HQ, everyone else..."

The news was seven days old—seven days to travel from Alexandria to Zuckabar. There was no indication who had done it, but he didn't need the media to tell him.

There was only one government evil enough to commit such an atrocity. Nadia looked at him, and they spoke at the same time.

"The Caliphate."

———

Join the Commander and the crew of the Interceptor for the third book in the Grimm's War Trilogy, ONE DECISIVE VICTORY.

THANK YOU FOR READING
WITH GRIMM RESOLVE

We hope you enjoyed it as much as we enjoyed bringing it to you. We just wanted to take a moment to encourage you to review the book. Follow this link: With Grimm Resolve to be directed to the book's Amazon product page to leave your review.

Every review helps further the author's reach and, ultimately, helps them continue writing fantastic books for us all to enjoy.

———

ALSO IN SERIES
AGAINST ALL ODDS
WITH GRIMM RESOLVE
ONE DECISIVE VICTORY

———

You can also join our non-spam mailing list by visiting www.subscribepage.com/AethonReadersGroup and never miss out on future releases. You'll also receive three full books completely Free as our thanks to you.

Facebook | Instagram | Twitter | Website

Want to discuss our books with other readers and even the authors? Join our Discord server today and be a part of the Aethon community.

LOOKING FOR MORE GREAT SCIENCE FICTION AND FANTASY?

In the West, there are worse things to fear than bandits and outlaws. *Demons. Monsters. Witches. James Crowley's sacred duty as a Black Badge is to hunt them down and send them packing, banish them from the mortal realm for good. He didn't choose this life. No. He didn't choose life at all. Shot dead in a gunfight many years ago, now he's stuck in purgatory, serving the whims of the White Throne to avoid falling to hell. Not quite undead, though not alive either, the best he can hope for is to work off his penance and fade away.*

This time, the White Throne has sent him investigate a strange bank robbery in Lonely Hill. An outlaw with the ability to conjure ice has frozen and shattered open the bank vault and is now on a spree, robbing the region for all it's worth. In his quest to track down the ice-wielder and suss out which demon is behind granting a mortal such power, Crowley finds himself face-to-face with hellish beasts, shapeshifters, and, worse ... temptation. But the truth behind the attacks is worse than he ever imagined ... **The Witcher** *meets* **The Dresden Files** *in this weird Western series by the Audible number-one bestselling duo behind* **Dead Acre.**

GET COLD AS HELL NOW AND EXPERIENCE WHAT
PUBLISHER'S WEEKLY CALLED PERFECT FOR FANS OF JIM
BUTCHER AND MIKE CAREY.

Also available on audio, voiced by Red Dead Redemption 2's
Roger Clark (Arthur Morgan)

*They've plundered their way across the galaxy and just
found the score of a lifetime. All they have to do is steal from
the most ruthless crime lord in the galaxy. What could possibly
go wrong? Yan and his band of rogues are intent on
plundering their way to fame and fortune. When they stumble
across the score of a lifetime, they quickly go all in for one last
job. With everything on the line, there's no way they can fail.
At least that's what they're hoping. In the end, they just might
have gotten into something bigger than they ever imagined
possible.*

GET MOST WANTED NOW!

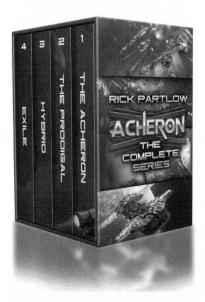

ABOUT THE AUTHOR

Join Jeffery on his mailing list to receive the latest information about his writing. Find his other books on Amazon.com under Jeffery H. Haskell.

https://goo.gl/LJdYDn

Or via his website @ Jefferyhhaskell.com

Made in the USA
Middletown, DE
05 August 2023

36242584R00243